Praise for Gary Gottesfeld
and
BLOOD HARVEST

"Generations of madness peaking in horror. This novel
bends you to its will—chillingly."

James Ellroy
Author of *The Black Dahlia*

"Mr. Gottesfeld, in his second outing, is fully up to
standard."

Gerald Petievich
Author of *To Live and Die in L.A.*

"A page-burner, forcing the spellbound reader to rip
through paragraphs, pages, chapters, at a dizzying
speed . . . If you're a Stephen King fan, you'll love *Blood
Harvest*. . . . Read this book!"

Marcel Montecino
Author of *The Crosskiller*

Also By Gary Gottesfeld
Published by Fawcett Books:

THE VIOLET CLOSET

BLOOD HARVEST

Gary Gottesfeld

FAWCETT GOLD MEDAL • NEW YORK

A Fawcett Gold Medal Book
Published by Ballantine Books
Copyright © 1990 by Gary Gottesfeld

Library of Congress Catalog Card Number: 90-90285

ISBN 0-449-14669-3

Manufactured in the United States of America

First Edition: December 1990

For Nancy and Adam—
The two people who keep me laughing.

Acknowledgments

My deepest appreciation to the following people:

Charles and Stuart Smith—for letting me run free in their terrific winery.

Jay Mortimer, M.D.—for teaching me about psychiatric medicine.

Neal Robb—for keeping me honest about legal matters in the book.

Doctors Gerald and Nadine Levinson—for helping me see the humanity in the abnormal condition.

Ronald Golovan, M.D.—for showing me where the body parts go.

Norman Lightfoot—for taking the time to burrow through old maps.

Steve Franklin—for being Steve Franklin.

PROLOGUE

She said her name was Claudine and that she had turned *fifteen* last month.

Oh dear sweet God, the beauty of this young girl!

That body! Those long, graceful limbs! Her breasts, white and pure like breakfast cream. The aroma of her skin, so damp and pungent.

I sit for hours watching her sleep, her thick, dark curls draped over my pillow. I begin to think that if only this world, angry and cruel with its frivolous wars, could be as blessed as I am tonight!

I look out the window. The night sky is turning to pewter.

It is almost time.

I hear the sound of my toenails scraping against the cool tile as I walk out onto the patio. I lean against the balcony and look out over the hills. The shadows of my beloved vineyards, with their fruit hanging down from them like ripe ovaries, are beginning to take shape in the early light. The vines and I have always been entwined together, as if the same blood flowed through our veins.

How peaceful it is out here.

I wait until I can see the sun rising over the slopes.

It is now time.

Inside, my beautiful Claudine is still asleep, those luscious lips slightly apart. How lovely you are! I hope you are dreaming of me my pretty one.

I sit down beside her on the bed. My fingers stroke her neck, lingering on the pulse under her chin, its melodic throbbing making me hard and wet.

Lovely, lovely Claudine, I'm afraid it is now time.

I reach into the drawer of the night table and take out the nail and mallet I keep next to the scalpel.

3

She awakens for an instant, her pale blue eyes upon my face. The paregoric takes over once again and she slowly closes her lids. She turns away, letting me see the back of her head. You are making it so easy for me, sweetness. The end to a perfect night.

I part her delicate curls. My love, I murmur, as I place the nail lightly on the soft spot where her skull and neck merge, and bang down forcefully with the mallet. It goes in so easily. Her head shudders for a moment, then is still.

I am pleased. I have finally learned to avoid the arteries.

Melancholy follows, like always. Tears run down my face and onto the sheets, mixing with her blood.

I take the scalpel out of the drawer and carry this beautiful girl/child into the vineyards where I lay her gently down on the moist earth.

I then mount her. In minutes it is over, which saddens me. I must learn control! Except if the next one is as beautiful as Claudine, then I don't know how I can.

The scalpel rests on the ground near her lifeless head. I do what is needed.

Her rich blood gushes from her loins like the waters of the Garonne River, then quickly sinks into the porous soil.

I will miss her! I shout to the swollen vineyards around me.

I will miss all of them!

Section forty-three from the journal of Baron Gustave de Montret. Translated by field agent Wilbur Striker on the 3rd of January, 1943.

—WILBUR STRIKER

Inside her modern, spacious loft on Houston Street in New York, Maura McKinney finished reading the section of the worn journal translated by Wilbur Striker forty-seven years ago. A guttural sound erupted from her throat, and her body shuddered from its contents. Over her shoulder the sharp light of the halogen lamp pointed directly at the brittle yellow pages.

The sky outside her window was turning from cobalt blue to ink. It was the last wave of rush hour and the loud city noises climbed up from the street and snaked their way into her room through the open shutters.

Her hands began to tremble as she carefully turned over the next fragile page; beads of sweat ran from her forehead and etched a path down her face. Even though she had read Gustave de

4

Montret's obscene manuscript many times before, it still gripped her in its hypnotic spell.

Eventually she forced her eyes away from the pages and glanced over to the wall clock; it was after eight. She had a dinner appointment with Ray Scollari at eight-fifteen. Regretfully she closed the diary and placed it on the coffee table.

Her head was throbbing, more than usual. She went into the bathroom and took two 100mg tablets of Darvocet and quickly swallowed them down with water. After washing her face, she looked up into the mirror and saw her pallid flesh with her luminous green eyes staring back. She quickly brushed in place the loose strands of her fine hair and put on a new coat of makeup to hide the color of her blanched skin.

She was not looking forward to this night with Scollari. It will be like all those other nights, she thought with disgust. He was always asking her to meet with him at some restaurant, telling her they had to discuss business. *All he really wants to do is get his vile, sweaty body into my bed! He'll try plying me with drinks while he tells me about the sex lives of judges and congressmen. Then he'll try to touch me with those thick fat hands.* She pictured his tan, freckled hand reaching out for her. She trembled at the thought. She felt a hot flash of hate erupt within her body.

After locking the diary in her nightstand, she took the elevator down to the lobby and walked the short distance to the restaurant.

If he touches me one more time with those freckled paws, I'll kill him, she thought. Martin was the only man she ever let touch her.

Only Martin!

Bristling with anger, she turned the corner on Houston Street.

Ray Scollari, the district attorney of Brooklyn, was just finishing off his second Glenlivet on the rocks at the Greene Street Café when he saw Maura enter the half-empty restaurant. He was angry that she had kept him waiting, but as soon as he saw how beautiful she looked, the anger drained from his body and the longing returned. My God, how I want that woman! he thought to himself.

The men standing around the bar, including the waiters and the busboys, all turned their heads to follow the path her body was taking.

She smiled at Ray as she sat down. Her blond hair, the color

5

of an Icelandic sunrise, was pulled tightly in back of her head. "Sorry about the time, Ray. I got caught up studying a brief."

He shrugged and waved his hands, as if to say forget it. Snapping his fingers, he called over the waiter and ordered Maura a glass of chardonnay. "You look edgy. Maybe you should drink something stronger."

She shook her head, no. "Busy day in court. I tried three cases."

He nodded. His loins were hurting from the need of her. "You hungry?" he asked nonchalantly, trying not to show his emotion as he looked into her jade green eyes. Maybe after a few drinks he'd get himself to loosen up enough to tell her how he felt. He picked up the menus from the table and handed her one. "They make the best damn filet mignon in the city."

"Do we need to discuss something, Ray?"

"Excuse me?"

"Why the dinner?"

"Hey, can't two tired lawyers take some time away from those goddamn marble halls?" he said, laughing. He paused to look into her beautiful eyes again, then he said, "Okay, I'll tell you what's happening. I'm throwing my hat into the ring for mayor in the spring."

"Congratulations," she said cautiously.

"I'd like you to be part of it." He reached his freckled hand across the table to touch hers. She quickly moved back in her seat and put her hands safely in her lap.

"In what capacity?" she asked.

"My personal assistant. You can move out of that loft in Soho and into Gracie Mansion with me."

"I like that loft, Ray. Besides, I don't think your wife would appreciate sharing a bathroom with me," she said caustically.

"Think about it," he replied, smiling self-assuredly. "You can get burnt out real easy in this city being a prosecutor for the DA's office." He began to scan his menu.

Ray ordered the steak rare and a bottle of Barolo. Maura ordered a vegetable dish.

Throughout dinner Ray talked about his plans, his eyes never leaving her face. Maura tried listening, but her mind kept going back to the weathered diary. *Who was this translator, Wilbur Striker? No, maybe it's best I don't know.*

She wondered when Ray was going to make his move. Her head was beginning to hurt again. The Darvocets weren't keeping the pain away; nothing she took seemed to keep it away anymore.

Over an espresso and a Sambuca, Ray made his move. "How's your love life, kid?"

"Private, Ray."

"Maybe nonexistent?" he said with a glint of hope in his eyes.

"Maybe." She stared directly back into his tanned face. He always had a tan, she suddenly realized, even in winter. Can't have your next mayor of New York looking pasty and sleazy, she thought. Her head was throbbing now, and she wanted to slip into the bathroom to take another Darvocet.

"I mean what's the story? I've known you for years . . . you're one of my best prosecutors. I've never seen you with a guy. Never even heard about one."

"What's that have to do with my legal skills?"

"Nothing. Just wondering, that's all." His body moved into the table and closer to hers.

She was feeling angry again. Her life was her business and no one else's. The pain in her frontal lobe was now pulsating. Soon that terrible sound of metal scraping against metal would begin echoing in her brain. She shook her head and tried to put it from her mind.

"I care for you a lot," he abruptly said, his lips beginning to quiver. There was a flush to his face from the alcohol.

"It's late, Ray. I think it's time to go." She took her napkin from her lap and put it on the table.

He looked at her sharply. "Did you hear what I said?"

"Yes. I'm not interested in being your mistress, if that's where this conversation is heading," she said sharply. "At least this time you didn't try hiding the real reason you asked me to dinner."

He leaned into the table and grabbed her arm. "I'm willing to leave my wife for you, even during an election year. Doesn't that mean anything?" he whispered passionately.

In spite of the pain spreading in her head, Maura had to laugh.

"You think I'm funny?" he said with an angry, hurt cast on his face.

"Look, Ray, it's been a long day . . ." She tried pulling her arm away, but he held on tight.

His temples were twitching from indignation. Sneering, he said, "I don't like to be laughed at, especially when I'm putting my guts out on the line. What kind of a cunt are you?"

The feelings of contempt and uncontrollable rage ruptured inside her. She twisted her arm that he was holding so that her palm was under his wrist. Then she clamped her fingers around his fleshy white skin and dug deeply into it with her long red fingernails.

Ray gasped in pain. Looking down at his arm, he saw that the nails were at least a half inch into his wrist. Blood spurted out and stained his white shirt. He tried to pull it away, but her grip on him was like a steel vise. The pain was horrible. "Please," he pleaded, looking around. He couldn't afford a scene, not this close to the primaries. Luckily the restaurant was not crowded. Then he turned his head back to her and saw her glacial emerald eyes piercing into him like darts. "Let go . . . please," he whispered. The hatred in her face was frightening.

Suddenly the anger drained from her body. She released Ray and he quickly pulled his wounded arm away from the table.

Scanning the room to make sure no one was watching, he wrapped a napkin around his bloodied wrist. "You're crazy," he hissed at her. After a beat he fixed his tie and jacket with his good hand, then said, "You know, come to think of it, I don't know shit about your life. Who the hell are you anyway? Why am I breaking my balls over some fruitcake like you? Well, maybe it's time I found out who you are. When I do, pray you have a clean slate, kid."

Maura hated that wily smile of his. He usually wore it when he was reducing a witness for the defense into a mass of pummeled jelly. She got up from the table and stormed out of the restaurant, ignoring the stares from the men at the bar.

As she walked down the street, all she could remember was the white hate she felt for Scollari. Suddenly the metal sounds that she feared most began to awaken in her head. Christ, what is happening to me? she thought to herself, frightened. *I could have killed him!*

Maura tried to sleep that night, but what she had done to Scollari wouldn't leave her thoughts. She had always possessed this incredible strength, but she always managed to keep it under control. It was nearly one in the morning and she was far from tired. At least her terrible headache had eased to a distant throbbing.

Trying to get her mind off what happened earlier tonight, she shut her eyes and thought about her dear friend Rena, whom she

8

hadn't seen in years. At last they would be getting together again when she goes to Northern California tomorrow. Next she thought about Uncle Wiggly and how he would throw his arms around her when he saw her. These were good thoughts and Maura smiled at them.

Then that cursed journal of Baron Gustave de Montret entered her head and the smile faded. She had known about that diary ever since she was a child living in Napa. While playing alone in her attic, she came across it hidden away in an old trunk. She had only looked at the first few "sections," but what she read had so disturbed her that she never told her father or anyone else about her discovery. Why had her father kept the diary? She never understood the reason for that. Then last year, while on her annual trip back to her house in the Napa Valley, she rediscovered the journal again in the desk drawer of her father's deserted winery. Perhaps she should have destroyed it then. Instead, she brought it back with her to New York. Now it was too late; she could never destroy it, not after having read the last entry. Something terrible bound her to that evil man, Baron Gustave.

And Maura knew what that something was; the last entry that the baron made in the diary clearly stated it. My God, what if somebody finds it? she suddenly thought.

She quickly sat up, grabbed the diary out of the nightstand, and tore out the final pages. Making her way over to the stove, she turned on the burner and put the pages into the flames. She held them there until they were reduced to ashes, then she threw the remains down the garbage disposal.

She got back into bed. It was late, and she needed to get some sleep because she had to get up early to catch her plane. She would take the diary back with her and return it to the desk in the winery where she found it. Perhaps then she would be able to sleep once more and the noises in her head would go away.

At three in the morning, she awoke to the horrible, scratching noise of metal jingling around in her head once again.

Panicking, she threw the covers off her naked body and sat up. Then the pounding of her heart and the fear set in, like it always did, leaving her gasping for air, needing to breathe.

She felt her way into the bathroom. Her Soho loft was pitch-black; the lights were off and the shutters were closed tight. She grabbed two more Darvocets, a Parnate, and a Xanax from the medicine cabinet, turned on the faucet and put her mouth under it to wash down the pills. Clutching tightly onto the sink, the sweat dripping down her body, she waited for the drugs to kick in.

Please God, please let me breathe! Don't let me black out again!

Closing her eyes, Martin's face began to flash through her mind like a psychedelic light show, and the noise of metal upon metal got louder. She sank down to the tile floor, leaned against the tub, and clasped her head in her hands.

Ten minutes later the medicine took effect. She slowly lifted herself off the floor. Her naked body was soaked and shining with sweat.

She went over to the shutters and opened them, letting the cool night breeze pass over her shape and through her long fine hair that reached to the curve of her back.

The dark streets were deserted, and no one could see her standing there nude. Only the night sky was watching, and that was all right because the night was her friend, and, like Martin, had never passed judgment on her.

Martin . . . he had also seen her standing like this . . . except . . .

Dear Martin. How I loved you!

Maura slammed the shutters closed, along with the memories of him.

Her eyes were hurting. She went into the bathroom and removed her green-tinted contact lenses. As she looked into the mirror, she caught a glimpse of her true-colored eyes: one was blue and the other a deep brown.

Clean slate, Ray? If only you knew! she thought bitterly. *I'm afraid, Gustave de Montret, you and I are destined to be bound together in hell for eternity.*

ONE

Chapter One

"**H**EY, RENA. HOW you doing?"

Dr. Rena Halbrook turned around in the small terminal of Napa airport and looked up into the smiling, beefy face of Sheriff Pinky Swangel. He was leaning against the US Air ticket counter. His big belly was straining the buttons on his shirt to the limit.

"It's been years," she said, surprised. They shook hands.

"Yep. Last time I saw you was right after high school. You were sure a beauty back then. Still are, as a matter of fact." He continued smiling at her as his eyes quickly scanned her body in appreciation. "I wasn't sure if I wanted to become a cop in those days or transport stolen cars to Nevada."

She remembered him as a troublesome youth with a history of problems. "I think this uniform looks a lot better on you than prison blues."

He laughed, showing horsey teeth. "Pay's not as good though. Hear you're a big-time psychiatrist now."

"A psychologist."

"Didn't know there's a difference."

"Pay's not as good."

Pinky laughed again.

"I'm waiting for a friend to pick me up. I guess she's not here yet," Rena said, looking toward the entrance of the terminal. "In fact, you know her. She grew up here. Maura McKinney."

He stopped laughing. "Yes, I know," he said somberly.

She caught his concerned look. "What's the matter?"

Pinky let out a sigh. "There's been a killing."

"Not Maura?" she said, startled.

"No. Someone else. A migrant picker who worked the fields next to Maura's was found murdered in her vineyards. I was

13

hoping she'd be here at the airport waiting for you. That's why I came." His eyes scanned the terminal as he talked.

"In *her* vineyard?" she said alarmed.

He took a deep breath and let it out slowly. "Yep," he muttered finally, nodding his head.

"What happened?" she asked.

Pinky sighed again. "Why don't we have some coffee," he said, pointing to the quick food stand. "Let's give her a couple of minutes. Hopefully she'll show up." His voice was tense. He picked up her suitcase in his fleshy hand, walked over to the counter, and ordered two coffees.

Rena sat down at the formica table. *Why did Pinky hope she'd show up? Was there a reason why she wouldn't?* She could feel Pinky's apprehension, even though he was trying not to show it. His dad used to work in her father's winery as a presser. Pinky would also work there sometimes after school, packing the cartons for delivery. She remembered him as a chunky, oversized boy with a thick neck and blotchy pink skin that always seemed to be peeling around the nose. The kids nicknamed him "Pinky" because of his coloring and the tag stayed with him. Most people had long forgotten his real name. Rena realized that he looked exactly the same now as he did then, except even larger.

Pinky brought the coffees to the table and sat down. He let out a long breath, as if his lungs were too small to supply enough oxygen to such an oversized body. After pouring a large quantity of sugar into his cup, he said, "The body of this Mex, Tomas Sanchez, was discovered a couple of hours ago tied to a grapevine on Maura's property."

She grasped his arm. "Talk to me, Pinky. What's going on?"

"Relax," he said patting her hand. "I'm sure Maura's okay. Some nut killed this Mex . . . slit his throat, then tied him to the branches of a vine. He probably got into a fight with another worker over money or . . . ," he said the next words softly, ". . . maybe a woman. You never know what can set these people off. The dead guy was drunker than hell, I can tell you that. He stunk from tequila. We're questioning all the pickers who worked the vineyards with him. There's always a killing of some kind every year when the field hands get some money and a few drinks in them. This murder was a little stranger than most, that's all."

She watched him stir his coffee. He looked deep in thought

14

and his eyes were red from lack of sleep. "How was it strange?" she asked.

"Well, first of all, he was only wearing his underwear when we found him. Then it's the way he was tied to the vine. It was made to look just like a crucifixion. I've seen Mex's with their throats cut before, but not like this. There was also a lot of blood, more than usual, and there was some kind of puncture wound in the back of his neck. Manuel Ortiz, the man who runs the winery for Miss McKinney, discovered the body."

"And Maura . . . ?" she asked, again picking up on Pinky's uneasiness.

"I don't know," he said, chewing on the plastic coffee stirrer, his eyes glued to the entrance of the terminal. "Manuel told us she had arrived at the house yesterday, a little before sundown."

Rena knew this was true. When Maura phoned her last week, she told her that she would be coming up on Thursday. "Wasn't she at the house?"

He looked down at the table and shook his head.

Something was very wrong, she could feel it. "How did you know she was planning to meet me at the airport?"

"I found her appointment book in her bedroom. Manuel let us in. I took the liberty of going through it and saw your name with the time and flight number of your plane."

She looked at him and saw how distraught he was. "What's going on, Pinky? Come on, tell me," she said, touching his arm.

"I don't know, honestly I don't," he said, forcing a smile.

She could see he was lying. "Don't hand me that. Why did you go through her purse? Something tells me you knew she wasn't going to show up here."

"I was just kind of hoping she would, that's all." Again the long release of air. "Okay, I just didn't want to worry you, not until the facts were in. Her bed wasn't slept in last night, and her rental car was still parked outside her house."

"When was this man murdered?" Her face was white.

Another long intake of air, then, "Early this morning or sometime last night. I'm gonna have to wait for the coroner's report on that." He looked away from her face.

"Did Manuel spend the night at the house?" Rena knew that Manuel and his family stayed at the house and ran Maura's wine business while she worked as an assistant district attorney in New York.

"Uh-huh. Manuel left yesterday, right after she arrived. He

wasn't even supposed to be at the winery this morning. He was on his way to Mexico with his family when he had to turn around because his wife forgot her arthritis medicine.''

"Then she was alone at the house last night?" Rena was beginning to fear for Maura's safety.

"I don't know about last night. She certainly was alone when Manuel left yesterday around sunset.''

Rena rubbed her eyes, then said in a troubled voice, "You think something has happened to her, don't you?''

"No way," he replied, shaking his head, attempting to laugh off her uneasiness.

Rena didn't believe him.

"Give it a couple of minutes, maybe she'll show up here,'' he said, slouching down in the seat. His eyes stayed on the revolving doors and he nervously tapped the chewed stirrer on the table.

They waited a few minutes longer, then decided she wasn't going to show and left.

In the parking lot, he offered to drive her back to her father's summer home in the Alexander Valley.

"Tell you what," she said, getting in the front seat of the Bronco. "If it's all right with you, I'd rather go to Maura's house and see if she came back.''

He thought about it for a minute, saw the concern on her face, then said, "Why not. You two have been friends for a long time.''

"That's right,'' she whispered.

They drove through the lush countryside in silence. Rena was concerned. Both women had known each other since they were ten years old. Maura lived in Napa, and Rena spent her summers here when she was a child. Rena's father, Simon Halbrook, among his other business interests, owned one of the largest wineries in the area.

The last time Rena saw Maura McKinney was when they went to Greece together; that was over thirteen years ago. This was supposed to have been a reunion for both of them.

There was also another reason that Rena came up here today: she needed to take some time off from her affair with Charlie so that she could sort out her emotions.

Charles Halleran was her lover, and recently their relationship was beginning to come apart at the seams. When she first met him, he was an unemployed journalist on a self-collision course. He blamed himself for failing to see his ex-wife's descent into the madness that eventually led to his daughter's murder. Years of self-flagellation followed with too many drunken nights and failed jobs. Redemption came when he met Rena. They fell in love. Wanting to help Charlie get back on his feet, she called a friend, the owner of the *L.A. Tribune*. Charlie was offered a job as a foreign correspondent. Ironically, his immediate success with the newspaper was the major cause of their present problems: they were so busy working at their professions that little time was left for their relationship; the intimacy they once shared was dying from lack of nourishment.

"You know, I listen to your radio show every time I get a chance," Pinky said, trying to break the stillness between them. "Really enjoy it. That psychological advice you give to those callers, it even helps me, although I won't admit it to the guys on the force."

"Thanks, but I'm only supposed to be heard in Los Angeles and the local vicinity. How do you get it?"

"Ol' Suzy here," he said, patting the shortwave radio attached to the dashboard of his car. "Keeps me from going crazy from boredom. Nothing ever happens around her except breaking up an occasional fight, or when a yuppie from the city who's been to too many wine tastings wraps his Mercedes around a pole."

Pinky then began to reminisce about the days when Rena used to spend her summers in Napa; how half the local teenage boys had crushes on her and the other half on Maura.

"Which half did you belong to?" she asked.

Pinky grinned sheepishly. "I'll take that secret with me to my grave."

Rena could see the answer in his face. His eyes lit up every time he mentioned Maura's name. Pinky clenched his jaw and ground his teeth. She knew Maura's disappearance was taking a bigger toll on him than he was letting on.

She began to speculate about Maura being alone in that house while a murder was taking place right outside her door. Pinky said the dead man had been drinking and that he and his companion could have been fighting over a woman. I hope Maura wasn't that woman, Rena thought.

"Remember Martin Bynum?" he asked her.

"Yes, a tragedy," she answered, breaking out of her thoughts.

"No one to this day knows who killed him. A damn waste of a life. He had everything going for him. Looks, brains . . . even had Maura. She wouldn't let any other guy get near her except him." His voice was sad, tinged with bitterness.

Rena remembered clearly. It happened the day of Maura's seventeenth birthday. Her father had thrown a big party for her. Yes, it was a waste of a good life. Martin was always so sensible, so pragmatic—not like most of the kids up here. He had a scholarship to Stanford and wanted to study project management in architecture. He always had a thing for Maura, and she felt the same way about him. In fact, there was never any other man in her life, except Martin. Rena thought about the birthday party and how Martin and Maura tried to sneak out of her house. Everybody there knew where Martin was taking her and what they were going to do. They were going off to the stone winery that belonged to Maura's dad. Later, they went back to his house and unfortunately disturbed a burglar while he was ransacking the upstairs bedroom. He killed Martin with a shotgun blast to the face. Rumors began to spread that it was Maura's father, Peter McKinney, and not a robber who really murdered him. Everyone knew that he hated Martin and that he had forbidden his daughter to see him. It could never be proven because a month after Martin's death, McKinney, while drunk, died in an automobile accident.

Pinky drove through the towns of Yountville and Oakville, then into St. Helena with its trendy restaurants and shops, and up into the mountains.

When they came to Maura McKinney's house, they stopped. It was a white, A-framed structure that was freshly painted. In the vineyards located next to the house, yellow police tape was wrapped around the vines, cordoning off a small section.

As Rena got out of the car, she held her hand up to her head to block out the sun's glare and looked in the direction of the vineyards. She could see police officers cutting the dead man down from the vines.

"They're just now taking the body away? What the hell took them so long?" Pinky said, perturbed.

They watched as they put the remains of the victim into a plastic body bag. Two policeman then put the bag on a gurney and rolled it in their direction, toward the ambulance.

A chill went through Rena.

An older man, holding a medical bag, trailed along beside the gurney, giving orders to the police as they lifted the body into the ambulance. Next to him was a much younger person, thin and lanky, with fine straight hair that fell into his eyes. He walked with his hands on his hips, fingers pointed toward the back, and seemed to be in deep thought. He reminded Rena of an English lord casually strolling through his flower garden on a Sunday afternoon.

Rena turned around and saw Manuel standing next to his truck over by the house. He was in his fifties and wore a denim work shirt and dusty jeans. His heavyset wife was in the front seat, and his two young sons were standing up on the flatbed in the back, craning their necks, trying to get a better look at what was happening in the vineyard.

"The guy with the white hair is Doc Frawley," Pinky said. "I don't know if you ever met him. He has a practice in Calistoga. He's also the acting pathologist whenever an autopsy is needed around here."

When the doctor saw Pinky and Rena, he went over to them. The tall man followed, his hands still on his hips.

"Not a pretty sight," Frawley said to Pinky. He had his suit jacket flung over his arm and he held an old-fashioned, white Panama hat in his hand. His tie hung loosely around his yellowed, frayed collar.

"No worse than some of the traffic accidents I've seen," Pinky replied, wiping the sweat off his brow with his sleeve.

"You look familiar young lady," he said, turning away from Pinky.

"I'm Dr. Rena Halbrook. My father owns Clarmont Winery."

"Oh, yeah, the big one in the Alexander Valley. Your dad . . . what's his name?"

"Simon Halbrook."

"That's it. I once took pieces of shredded glass out of his hand when a bottle of champagne he was trying to uncork exploded. I did it without a local anesthesia and he never once flinched."

"That's Dad," she said, nodding. She looked up at the tall man and saw that he was staring at her.

"Name's Walter Parsons," he said. "I just bought the practice up in Geyserville. Dr. Frawley is showing me the territory."

"Have you seen Maura McKinney yet?" Pinky asked Frawley.

"Not yet," he said shaking his head. He also had a worried look on his face.

"I'm going back to the office and get an APB out on her. Something's not right," Pinky said, wiping the sweat off his thick

19

neck with a handkerchief. "Want me to drive you back?" he asked Rena.

"It's out of your way. I'll get a ride, don't worry. Just concentrate on finding Maura," she said.

"I'll keep in touch, Rena. Good seeing you again. Don't fret about Maura. We'll find her," Pinky said, as he got into his truck and drove off.

She turned toward the older man. "Do you know Maura McKinney, Doctor?"

"Certainly," he said. "I brought her into this world. In fact, she was born right in that house." He pointed to the white A-frame. "She was a month premature. Her father called me and told me to get over here fast, that she was starting to come out. By the time I got here, her mother was dilated ten centimeters and the crown was showing. There was no time to get her to a hospital." He paused for a second, thinking, then said, "If only she could have reached full term maybe Clair would have had a chance." His voice trailed off and his eyes became glazed, as if he were remembering something far back.

Rena knew that Clair was Maura's mother.

"Well . . . that's another story," he said, his mind returning to the present. "Anyway, I've got to go with the body and do the autopsy. I don't know why I even bother. Any fool can see how he was killed. Guarantee you we'll find a gallon of alcohol in his blood. You coming back with me?" he said to Parsons.

"Absolutely, Doctor."

"Good." The old man put his hat on and walked slowly to the waiting ambulance.

"Are you a good friend of Miss McKinney?" the young doctor asked. He had a Bostonian accent.

"Yes," Rena said, sighing. "A very good friend." From the corner of her eye Rena would see Manuel watching her.

"Look, maybe something unusual will turn up at the autopsy. Do you want us to call you in case we find anything?"

Rena understood what he meant by "something unusual." They'll check to see if the dead man recently had sex, and if all the blood in the area was just his. "Please call me," she said. She took a pen and a notepad from her purse and gave him the number where she would be staying.

He took the piece of paper and put it in his jacket. "I'll call you," he said. He turned and walked toward the ambulance.

Rena then went over to Manuel. It had been years since she

last saw him, and he looked older and paunchier. He began working for the McKinneys when he was a young man fresh from the Sonora countryside—first for Maura's father then for Maura. He started out as a grape picker in their vineyards and eventually became the foreman. When Maura's father died and she inherited the winery, she asked Manuel to stay on to care for the vineyards. Maura wanted to live in New York and had no interest in making pinot noirs and cabernets. She closed down the stone winery and had Manuel grow grapes to sell to other wineries. The profit she netted helped supplement her living expenses in New York.

"Remember me, Manuel?" Rena said.

"Of course I remember you. You are Señorita Maura's good friend." He warmly shook hands with her.

His wife, Elvera, got out of the truck, went over to Rena, and hugged her. "It has been so long!" she said in a thick Mexican accent.

"Too long," Rena said, looking at how white her hair had gotten. Elvera used to make wonderful tamales and would give her a bag filled with them to take back to her father's estate. She would have to sneak them into her room because Elaine Halbrook, her mother, would never allow that kind of "peasant" food in the house.

Rena turned to Manuel and saw the fear in his eyes.

"Please, Señorita Halbrook," he whispered. "I must talk with you alone. I am very worried."

"Have you talked to the police?"

"No police!" he said, frantically shaking his head. "Please, no police."

She glanced toward the police who were still in the vineyards, then back at him. "What is it?" she asked him, hearing the urgency in his voice.

"Come with me, señorita," Manuel said to her.

Before she could react, he was behind the house and walking quickly toward the field in the opposite direction of the vineyards. His children and wife stayed by the truck.

She could barely keep up with him. Rena was dressed in high heels and a skirt, and the thick, spiny bushes were shredding her nylons and scratching her legs. Then they were in the woods, the lush greenery on top of the trees almost screening out the sunlight. They continued into the forest for more than two hundred yards until they reached a small hot spring partially hidden by a clump of bushes. The water looked fresh and clean.

"Over here, Señorita Halbrook," Manual said, bending down next to the water. He was separating the grass with his fingers.

Rena knelt next to him and saw what he was looking at. Blood. A small thin trail of it zigzagging for about five yards then stopping abruptly.

"What about this, Manuel?"

"This is the place that Maura always comes to when she stays at the house. She bathes in this pond. She's been doing that ever since she was a little girl. The water is salty and hot, and she says it is good for her skin."

Rena never knew about the spring and found it strange that Maura had never told her about it when they were children.

"Manuel, the blood is probably that of a small animal, most likely a bird—killed and eaten by a cat or a coyote. Next to my home, I find trails of blood like this all the time, and I live in a big city," she said.

Manuel stared at the blood for a long time. She could almost feel his mind racing. Then he looked at her and said softly, "I don't think so, señorita." He pulled up the bottom right cuff of his jeans and took out something from inside his scuffed cowboy boot. It was covered in a red bandanna. Carefully he opened part of it up, revealing the bone handle of a hunting knife.

Manuel said, "I picked it up by the pond when I first came looking for her earlier today after I found the man in the vineyard. I give her this knife many years ago to take with her when she comes here to bathe. She always stays alone in the house and you never know what kind of *locos* would come around if they knew that." He grabbed the hilt and slid the knife out of the bandanna. The blade was crusted over with fresh blood.

"I don't think this is the blood of a bird, Señorita Rena," he said, holding the copper-colored blade up for her to see. "Do you?"

Chapter Two

"You should have shown this to the police," Rena said angrily.

"I don't think so," Manuel said pensively as he slowly shook his head. He wrapped the bandanna carefully around the knife and stuck it back in his boot.

She grabbed his arm. "Listen to me. It may be Maura's blood that's on that knife."

"Or maybe it is not."

She understood his meaning and thought about the man murdered in the vineyard across the way. Scanning the area, she saw horseflies swarming around the bloody section of grass. The blood is fresh or the flies would not be here, she thought. "Whose blood is on the knife, Manuel? Do you know?"

He turned his eyes from her, not answering.

"The worker who was killed from the winery next door?" Frustrated by his stubbornness, she slapped hard at a horsefly that was busily circling her dark, damp hair.

He shrugged.

"You think Maura may have slit his throat? Why?" she asked skeptically.

"It is her knife," he said, touching the place in his boot where the blade was. Deep lines were etched in his leathery Aztec skin. "Perhaps she was protecting herself. That's what it was to be used for. Maybe that man knew about the spring and was waiting for her. She swims here without a suit and she is a *belleza*, Señorita Rena."

"I know she's very beautiful, Manuel," Rena said patiently. "Why would she carry him all the way back to the field and tie him to a vine, making it look like a crucifixion? If she *was* attacked and had killed the man in self-defense, she would have called the police, we both know that." Besides, she thought,

23

Maura couldn't possibly have had the strength to carry him all the way back to the vineyard. Even if she tried dragging him that distance, the bloody trail should have continued to the winery and not have stopped so abruptly after a few feet. "I am going to call the police, Manuel," she said firmly. "They should know about the knife. The blood on it could be Maura's." She turned around and walked back to the house. Rena was enraged that he had hidden the knife from them. In his mind he was protecting Maura, but what he had really done was waste precious time in finding out what happened to her. What did the killer do with Maura after murdering the man and hanging him on the vine? Did he also kill her, or is she still alive and in his hands? The alternatives were not too encouraging, she realized grimly.

As she neared the house, she saw the police and a forensics expert studying the area around the vine where the victim was tied. She thought about telling them about the bloody knife; instead she opted to talk to Pinky Swangel.

She picked up the phone in the living room and called the sheriff's department. When they told her Pinky was still in transit, she demanded to be patched through. Several seconds of static, then she heard his voice.

"You stay right where you are," he said, after she told him about the knife and the bloody section of grass. "I'll be there in ten minutes."

Outside an engine was starting up, then the squeal of tires. Rena glanced out the window. Manuel's truck was racing down the dirt road with his two sons bouncing in the back, holding on for life.

"Oh, Christ! He's leaving."

"That's okay," Pinky said calmly. "I'm on the Santa Rosa end of the mountain. That's where he's heading to meet up with the rest of his family. I'll be waiting for him."

After he hung up, Rena called for a cab to pick her up.

While waiting, she looked around the living room and wondered what had happened here last night. Was that Maura's blood on the knife and on the grass by the spring? "Please, let it not be!" she anxiously said to herself.

None of this made sense. A couple of hours ago she had gotten off a plane eagerly looking forward to spending the weekend with her childhood friend. Suddenly a man is found dead in her fields and she's missing, perhaps also murdered.

Rena looked around the room. It had been a long time since

she'd been inside this house. She could almost hear the walls echoing with her and Maura's youthful laughter as they skipped from room to room.

The furniture was the same as she remembered, except more run-down. Now that Manuel and his family lived here, the house had taken on a Mexican flavor, with colorful wall hangings and old sepia photographs of Latinos in sombreros. Rena went up the stairs and walked into Maura's old bedroom.

Pinky was right: It was obvious that Maura had not slept here last night; she hadn't even unpacked yet. Her suitcase was on the bed with most of her belongings still in it.

Draped over the chair, next to the desk, was an expensive skirt, a silk shirt, bra, and panties. *Probably what she wore on the plane.* Manuel said she doesn't wear a bathing suit when she goes to the spring. Did the murdered man and the killer come upon her while she swam naked? *God, I hope not!*

On the desk, Rena saw Maura's black date book, the one that Pinky had told her about. She picked it up and flipped through it. Maura's familiar handwriting was all over the pages. It seemed like almost every hour of her workdays were filled with appointments. She was a busy woman, Rena thought. When she came to today's date, she saw, MEET RENA AT AIRPORT. It was written in large caps across the page and underlined. Two days before that, printed in bold, red letters, was a dinner appointment with Ray Scollari. Rena remembered Maura mentioning that Ray was her boss and that she wasn't too fond of him.

Rena turned the page. The only thing written on it was, "Uncle Wiggly at 2:00 P.M." That would be tomorrow.

Who was *Uncle Wiggly*? As far as she knew, Maura had no living relatives. Was Uncle Wiggly a nickname for a person that lived in Napa, or was someone coming here to meet her?

The rest of the weekend in Maura's calendar was blank. Rena flipped through earlier dates. The thing she noticed was that her days may have been busy, but there was nothing filled in for her nights. Didn't she go out to dinner or to plays and movies with friends? What about dates with men? In fact, other than Martin Bynum, Maura had never mentioned any other man in her life. Whenever Rena brought up that subject during their infrequent phone conversations Maura would immediately talk about something else.

She put the date book back on the table, then picked up Maura's cosmetic bag. Inside, there was the usual: eyeliner, blush, lipstick, nail polish. She pushed them aside, looked deeper into the bag, and found a large, unlabeled vial filled with different colored pills. Rena unscrewed the cap and emptied the contents on the bed. As a psychologist, she was very familiar with them: Parnate, Xanax, and Darvocet. She knew the first one was an antidepressant, and that Darvocet was normally prescribed for pain, such as migraines. Xanax was mainly used for tension and panic disorders. She was surprised. Was Maura suffering from depression or from some form of psychotic disorder? Why didn't she ever tell her? Perhaps she didn't want anyone to know.

After putting the tablets back into the vial, she looked for Maura's purse. It wasn't in the bedroom.

She went over to the window, pulled open the lace curtain, and looked out. The sky was clear and it was unseasonably warm. She could almost smell the thick aroma of grapes ripening on the vines.

We've known each other since we were ten years old, except we haven't seen each other since Greece. Phone calls on birthdays were exchanged and an occasional letter, but that's not the same thing as being together. People change. What is she like now? She was beginning to realize that there were many things about Maura that she didn't know anything about.

As children, they only saw each other during the summer months because Rena went to a private school back East. Their friendship had more to do with a natural deep affection they felt for each other than the amount of time they had actually spent together.

Staring out at the vineyards, Rena thought back to that afternoon over twenty years ago when they first met.

It was hot, and the migrant workers were laboring to pick the grapes before they rotted in the sun. Rena wanted to help, but her father's vintner, with his French accent, told her to stay out of the way.

She walked to the top of the hill and sat down on the grass. With her knees crossed and her face cupped in her hands, she watched them work. From this height, they reminded her of busy insects scurrying about. As the grapes were being crushed and de-stemmed, she could see the workers pouring quantities of sulphur dioxide into the vat. How it must burn their eyes, she thought. She could even smell the pungent gas way up here. "Ugh. Stinky poo," she said out loud, holding her nose.

"It's a necessary evil," someone said, directly behind her.

Rena turned around and looked up into the most beautiful, silken face she had ever seen. The girl was about the same age as she was, and her emerald eyes seemed to glow with intelligence. Her golden mane, as fine as angel hair draped over a Christmas tree, was braided and ran down the length of her back. Look at that skin! Rena thought; it was so pale that you could almost see through it. The girl wore a flowered dress that was threadbare, and she was shoeless.

She plopped down next to Rena, crossed her legs like her, and said, "Sulfur dioxide serves many purposes in wine making. It kills those invisible, ugly things called microorganisms, it stops the enzymes in grapes from browning, and it also stops the bad effect that air can have on wine."

"I know that," Rena said defensively.

"No you don't. You don't know anything about wine. I can tell," the girl said confidently. "You're rich and your father built this huge winery only last year. This is his first vintage."

Rena took offense to that. "So what? My father knows everything there is to know about wine. He's an expert. If you've ever read any of the magazines you'd know that."

The girl laughed. "Your daddy might know how to swiggle it around in his mouth, but he doesn't know anything about growing grapes. You have to live on the land and work it with your own hands—that's what my father says. Your daddy lives in the city and hires some joker from France to do the work for him. The soil and the weather are different there than it is here."

Rena was furious. "How come your father knows so much, huh?"

"Because we have a winery. He makes the best cabernet in the entire valley. If you read the magazines, you'd know that."

"Then what are you doing here? This is my property," Rena shouted back, standing up.

The girl sighed, then said with a poised voice, "My daddy's down there working in your father's winery. Our vineyards are too small to be the only source of income. He hires himself out every year to other wineries after he finishes harvesting his own fields."

Rena gloated. "Then your father can't know that much can he?"

The sparkling, perceptive eyes of the girl filled with hurt, and Rena felt a pang of remorse for what she had said. Rena turned away and ran down the hill toward the big winery, leaving the pretty girl with the blond hair sitting by herself on the grass. When she reached the bottom, she turned around to see if she was still there. She was. The sun was directly in back of the girl's head, giving the illusion that her golden hair was on fire. Rena also swore that the sun in the background acted like an X-ray machine, and that she could see the blood vessels and facial bones through her opaque skin. The glare made her eyes burn. She turned away and ran into her father's winery.

That evening, the maid came to Rena's room and said she had a phone call.

"Hi, my name's Maura McKinney," the voice said on the other end of the line.

Rena knew who she was by her authoritative voice. "I'm Rena Halbrook." She didn't understand why but she was glad that she called.

"I know who you are. Made any friends up here yet?"

Rena shrugged. "Maybe. Why?"

"Well, I haven't made many friends, either, and I've lived here all my life. You don't seem dumb like the other kids from around here. Think maybe we could try to be friends?"

Rena shrugged again. "Maybe," she answered cautiously.

"Good. We could have a trial run. Maybe we'll do better than we did this morning."

"What are the guys like up here?" Rena asked sheepishly.

"Mostly farmers with dirty ears. I hate dirty ears on boys, don't you? Except there's this one boy named Martin. Hands off that one, okay?"

"Sure," she said shrugging.

"Want to come over for lunch tomorrow? Maybe we could have a picnic or something. You need to have a car to get over here, though. Can you get a ride?"

"Of course. My daddy's rich, remember?" There was silence on the line, and again Rena regretted what she said. "Is your mom going to be there?"

"Nope."

"Does she work in the wineries, also?"

"Nope. She's dead," Maura said curtly. She gave Rena the address. "Do you have pictures of your family and friends with you up here?"

"Yes," Rena said, surprised.

"Bring them with you. See you tomorrow, okay?"

28

The next day Simon Halbrook's foreman dropped Rena off at Maura's house. She had brought along her Monopoly set and a photograph album.

Maura greeted her at the door with a warm smile. She had shoes on this time, and her dress, though made of a cheap cotton cloth, was brand-new. Rena knew she wore it to impress her.

Inside the house, Rena could see a dark-skinned, thick-bodied woman peeking uneasily out at her from the kitchen. She wore a scarf over her head, and she had a black mole coated with fuzzy hairs on her upper lip. When Rena smiled at her, she looked away and quickly moved out of view, back into the dark recess of the room.

"Who's that?" she curiously asked.

"Her name is Semra. She's my father's housekeeper. Don't waste your smiles on her. She's one mean Turk and she doesn't speak any English." It was obvious that Maura didn't like her. "Daddy promises that when I'm older he'll send her back to Turkey. That day can't be soon enough for me."

They made a picnic of tuna fish sandwiches, Oreo cookies, and Pepsis, and ate under an oak tree near the vineyard. Then they stretched out on the grass, letting the sun warm their faces and chattered away about boys, school, and books. Maura was so bright and animated, and exuded such spirit that Rena was completely drawn to her. Two hours later, after a long discourse on how teaching *Silas Marner* in school can turn anyone off from reading novels, Maura suddenly changed the subject, turned to her, and eagerly asked to see Rena's photograph album.

She painstakingly went through every picture asking many questions about who all these people were in Rena's life. Rena was thrilled that this girl, her new friend, genuinely cared.

"You're sure this isn't boring you?" Rena asked her, wondering if she was talking too much about herself.

"No, no. I love hearing about other people's lives. I can actually put myself in these pictures if I try hard," she responded. "Tell me more. Who's this? She's beautiful." Maura pointed to a black-and-white print of a young woman who looked very rich. She was wearing an evening dress and had a cigarette holder and a martini glass in one hand.

"My mother," Rena said with a trace of sadness.

Maura picked up on it. She furrowed her brow and asked, "Don't you get along with her?"

"We're just different, that's all."

29

"At least you have a mother," Maura said sighing. "I wish I had one."

"What happened to her?" Rena asked. "She must have been beautiful like you."

"She died when I was born," Maura said, biting down on her lip.

Rena sat up on the grass. "Do you have a picture of her? I'd love to see what she looked like."

Maura shrugged and turned the page of the album. "No. My father doesn't believe in keeping photographs around the house."

"Aren't you curious?"

"Of course," she said. "Wait, I'll be right back."

Maura stood up and went into her house. A minute later she came back with a sketch pad and pieces of charcoal. "Let me show you what I consider to be *my* album," she said, excited. She turned the cover of the spiral-bound pad over to the first illustration. It was a delicately painted watercolor of a beautiful woman with blond hair and pale green eyes. The lips were the same as Maura's. Rena knew that it was a drawing of her mother.

"Did you do this?" Rena asked in awe.

"Yes. It's my mother."

"How do you know what she looked like if you don't have any photographs of her?"

"I don't. I just imagined her looking like this."

"Does your father think there's a likeness?"

Maura looked away from her. "He hasn't seen it," she said coldly.

"Why not?"

"Because this is what I want her to look like, and I don't want him to tell me I'm wrong, that she didn't look like this at all," she uttered. Changing the subject once again, she blurted out, "I want to draw you, is that okay?"

"You really can do that, huh?" Rena asked, impressed.

"Sure." She turned over the pages in the pad, showing Rena drawings of her father. Then she came to several illustrations of a thin, beautiful boy with long curly hair. All the drawings were precise, with great care given to muscular detail and skeletal structure.

"Gosh, you're good," Rena said.

"Thanks." She told Rena to sit next to the tree.

"Hey, who's the cute boy in those drawings?" Rena inquired, giggling.

Maura blushed. "That's Martin, the one I told you about."

"The hands-off one, right?"

"Right." Staring at Rena then down at the pad, her fingers holding the charcoal busily moved across the paper.

"He's a dream."

"Isn't he though?" Maura said proudly.

They both started to giggle.

Hours passed by quickly. They were so involved with what the other was saying that time had no meaning. It was as if a cocoon had been spun around both of them, and everybody and everything ceased to exist.

At five o'clock, their magnetic contact was shattered by the front door slamming shut.

"It's Daddy," Maura said, startled. She quickly closed her drawing pad and hid it under the blanket.

Peter McKinney walked out on the back porch and looked around. He was a tall man with a stooped back that was formed from years of working in the vineyards. His sleeves were rolled up, exposing muscular arms covered with grape stains and rice hulls. When he saw Rena and his daughter sitting under the tree, his face darkened to a scowl.

"Who are you?" he snapped at her in an Irish brogue.

"Her name's Rena, Daddy. Her father owns the winery you work in." She stood up and moved in front of Rena, almost as if to protect her.

"Ah, so that's who you are." His voice softened slightly. "What time are you supposed to be home, young lady?" His eyes, black as oil, peered into her.

Rena stood up and shrugged. "Soon, I guess." Glancing quickly at Maura, she could see her friend's body trembling with fear.

"Can she stay for dinner, Daddy? Please," Maura pleaded.

At first he looked Rena up and down, then he said, "Let her call home. If it's okay with her parents, she can stay."

Rena called and talked with her parents' housekeeper, Anna. She said it was all right. Thankfully her mother was away vacationing someplace in Europe. She would never approve of her having dinner with such poor people, especially if she knew Maura's father worked for them in their winery.

While washing their hands at the sink before sitting down at the table, Maura whispered to Rena, "Don't mention Martin to my father or that I have his pictures."

31

Rena turned to her, saw the beseeching look on Maura's face, and nodded.

During dinner, Maura and Rena talked nonstop. Peter McKinney didn't say anything. He just sat there slowly sipping a glass of whiskey and listened to them. His elbows were up on the table and his chin rested on top of his hands. There was a gleam in his eyes. Rena could tell, even through his frowning stare, that he was proud of his daughter.

After dessert of banana cream pie, Mr. McKinney drove Rena home. Most of the time in the car was spent in silence. Rena wracked her brain trying to think of something to say to him, wishing that Maura had come with them.

After twenty minutes of listening to nothing but the steady hum of the car's engine, she blurted out the first thing that came into her mind. "I'm sorry that your wife died, Mr. McKinney." As soon as she said it, she wished she hadn't; she could see the sorrow in his face from the headlights of the passing cars.

Several minutes of more silence, then he said softly, "It was a long time ago. Did Maura tell you how she died?"

"Uh-huh."

"She died while giving birth to her. Her heart just gave out. There was no way to save her."

"I'm sorry," Rena whispered.

"The Lord giveth and the Lord taketh away, isn't that right?" McKinney said sarcastically. "He took away a beautiful wife and gave me a beautiful daughter in return. At least I'm grateful for that," he said, not bothering to hide the mockery in his voice.

Rena saw the bitterness in his face and could smell the strong odor of alcohol on his breath. She wondered if he was angry at Maura because he lost his wife during childbirth. Maybe what he really wanted was a son. Whatever the reason, Rena didn't think it was fair. She was sorry that his wife died, but Maura was a wonderful, special person and Mr. McKinney should be able to see that.

He pulled into the driveway of the big house. As Rena got out of the car, he gently grabbed her shoulder, and said softly, "She likes you a lot, you know. She doesn't like many people, but she likes you. Be good to her and don't hurt her. She may come on strong and cocksure of herself, but under that fine skin lies a soul that's very fragile."

She looked at him and saw pain in his eyes. Taken back by it, she said, "I like her, too, Mr. McKinney, and I would never hurt her."

As if an agreement had been reached between them, McKinney nodded, then drove away.

The two girls were together almost every day that summer. The only exception was when Maura wanted to be alone with Martin. Sometimes Rena would feel jealous about Martin taking her friend away from her, but there was little she could do about it. When Maura was with Martin, nothing else seemed to exist.

Rena and Maura would often go to a deserted area in the Napa mountains, and Maura would draw her.

Once, when they were alone in the woods, Maura asked Rena to take off her clothes so she could sketch her like Michelangelo first sketched the model who was his David. At first Rena refused, saying that she was ashamed of her skinny, sticklike body. Besides, if anyone found out, she would just die.

"Don't be a goose," Maura grimaced. "You're going to have a beautiful body when you get older. I promise no one's going to see these drawings except you and me."

Eventually Rena relented. She was embarrassed at first, but after a while it felt natural lying naked in the grass.

"Have you ever drawn Martin in the buff?" Rena asked her during one of their sessions in the woods.

"Uh-huh, lots of times," Maura responded. She was sketching Rena, who was posing like a naked forest nymph sitting on a boulder.

Rena giggled, stamping her foot on the ground. "You didn't!"

"Yes, I did. Now stay still."

She went back to posing. "Where are the drawings?"

"In my room hidden away. If my father sees them, I'm dead."

"Has Martin ever seen you naked?"

A hint of a smile broke on her lips. "Yes," Maura said eventually. "Sometimes we go swimming together in this secret place I know."

"You have!" she gasped, starting to giggle again. "Did you guys ever touch?"

"Sure, but that's all. One day, when we're older, we'll do the other thing."

"How come Martin never comes to your house?"

A shadow crossed Maura's face. "My father doesn't like me being with him."

"Why?"

33

"He's overprotective with me, that's why," she quickly responded. "I wish he was born in this country instead of Ireland. Your father at least leaves you alone."

"Yes, too much," Rena said quietly.

"You're lucky. I wish I was lucky." There was anger in her voice.

When Rena was getting ready to go back to Los Angeles at the end of the summer, Maura gave her the nude drawings of herself. She folded them up and put them in the bottom of her suitcase.

Rena then got into the limousine with Anna, the housekeeper, and began to cry.

"What is it, child?" the woman said in her West Indies accent, putting her thin, black arm around Rena's shoulder.

"I'm going to miss her very much, Anna. We became so close over the summer."

The frail old woman patted her shoulder and said, "You're young, child. You two will have a lot of summers of good playin' ahead of you."

Anna was right, Rena thought as she continued to stare out the window. They did have many years of good playing together.

Rena heard the taxi honking outside.

Yes, she did mention the hidden spring to me, Rena suddenly remembered. *That's the place she and Martin must have gone swimming.* She took another look around Maura's bedroom then went downstairs. There was no reason to wait to hear from Pinky. She knew he'd call after he caught up with Manuel.

The Alexander Valley was beautiful this time of year; even though the weather was warm, it was still fall, and the leaves were beginning to turn colors.

Rena thought about what Peter McKinney had asked of her that first night when she met him: *Be good to her and don't hurt her.* She had kept that promise to him; she had never done anything to hurt Maura.

It had been years since she last saw Maura, but when they spoke on the phone last week, it was as if no time had passed at all. That cocoon they once shared between them was just as fresh as the day it was first spun so many years ago in Maura's backyard. The nude drawings of herself were framed and hanging in her house in Brentwood.

After those childhood summer days up in the wine country,

their lives began to take different turns. Rena went to college up in Stanford, received her Ph.D. from USC, and had gone on to become a successful psychologist. She now had her own radio talk show and had written two bestselling books. In between there was a marriage, a divorce, and Cathy, her ten-year-old daughter.

Maura received a full scholarship from Columbia in New York. After graduating with a B.A. in Greco-Roman history, she decided to become an attorney and went on to NYU Law School. She had no interest in producing quality wines like her father. As far as she was concerned, the doors to Peter McKinney's big stone winery, where the cabernets, merlots, and pinot noirs spent years aging in oak casks, were to be closed and padlocked forever.

New York agreed with Maura; it massaged her soul and fed her intellect. She stayed on.

Rena remembered a letter she had received from her a couple of years ago: *New York, even among the garbage and the despair, contains life. Wonderful life! Here, I can be myself. I can be alone without feeling alone. If I had to go back to live in that valley again with its stink of fermented grapes, I think I would die.*

There was anger and bitterness in that letter. Rena believed it had to do with Martin's death; the memories of him were too strong for her to stay on in Napa. What did Maura do in New York when she wasn't working? Who were her friends? Rena wondered. *There were so many missing parts to her life.*

In the distance Rena could see her father's house perched on top of the hill like a sentinel keeping watch over the entire valley. It was an original seventeenth-century château that was disassembled in Saint-Emilion, France, then shipped over to this country and reconstructed, stone by stone, by Simon. The winery and his many acres of vineyards stretched as far as the eye could see.

Even though Simon bought the best machinery and vines and imported Europe's finest vintners, the wines produced on this land were never more than average in quality.

Rena thought about what Maura had said to her the first time they met: *you have to live on the land and work it with your own hands before you can produce great wines.*

As she turned onto the road leading to the gravel driveway, she asked herself how many people she had met in her lifetime who were capable of spinning cocoons? The answer so far was just one. A decision had been reached in her head: She was going to do everything in her power to find out what happened to Maura.

Chapter Three

RENA USED HER key to let herself in the house.

She put her suitcase down on the oak-plank floor in the foyer. Sounds could be heard coming from the dining room. Passing through the huge living room filled with antique furniture and priceless paintings, she went into the dining room and found two servants setting the giant mahogany table for a dinner party. Overhead, a crystal chandelier that once belonged to the Vienna Opera House hung suspended from the twenty-foot ceiling.

Who was having a party? She wondered if some of her father's friends were staying here for the weekend.

From a distance she could hear a faint rattling noise coming from the bottling plant next to the winery. Looking out of the huge window, she saw the field-workers picking clusters of chardonnay grapes off the vines and tossing them into large vats that were slowly being dragged through the furrows by tractors.

The odor of sulphur dioxide permeated the air, reminding her of the day when she first met Maura.

From the corner of her eye, she saw Simon's helicopter sitting on the pad at the side of the house. She had no idea that he was in Napa. He was supposed to be in Switzerland on business.

Rena went upstairs to her bedroom. Taking off her skirt and high heels, she quickly changed into jeans, sneakers, and a T-shirt. She washed up and brushed her hair, then went downstairs to the den to make a phone call.

She had a strong desire to talk to Charlie, for no other reason than just to hear his voice. They had argued again last night about how they don't spend enough time together, and he had left without staying the night. She picked up the phone, dialed a few digits, then hung up. No, she couldn't risk another confrontation with him, not when her emotions were too caught up with Maura's disappearance. Instead, she left the house and walked down the path leading to the winery. It was harvesting time and the sound of the pressers and bottling machines were deafening.

She went past the huge stainless-steel tanks that were used for fermentation and into the modern wine factory. Inside, teams of workers were standing next to a conveyor belt taping up the cartons of wine that passed by them. Others were stacking up the cases, getting them ready for dispatch.

The computer room, with its vast array of terminals and electronic gear, was visible at the other end. There, data bases were used to predict the effects of weather and to monitor irrigation, temperature, and fermentation.

Inside the barrel room, Rena found Simon. He was talking to a good-looking, well-built man with silvery hair and a deep tan. They were standing next to rows of fifty-gallon oak barrels that were aging cabernets. Simon took out the stopper from one of the casks and poured a small amount of red wine into a glass. He then held it up to the light. The grim look on his face suggested that his award-winning cabernet would have to wait another year.

Rena went over to him. "Hello, Dad," she said loudly, trying to talk over the roar of the machines.

Simon turned around. He was a massive man with a mane of white hair. A smile broke out on his face, and his eyes became alive. "My God. What are you doing here?" he shouted.

"I was going to ask you the same thing. Weren't you supposed to be in Switzerland?" she yelled.

He leaned over and hollered in her ear. "I was. I got bored with clocks that told the same time and green mountains with little tips of snow on them. It's a lot more fun being up here during the harvesting. Why didn't you let me know you were coming?"

She then told him about her planned weekend with Maura and the events that followed.

"I heard about the murder, but I didn't know it happened at Maura's place." His face took on a grim look and the gullied wrinkles on his forehead got deeper. He had remembered Maura as a child and had liked her. Putting his large hand on Rena's shoulder, he said, "I hope there's a logical explanation to where she is. Give it a few hours. Let's see what happens."

Forcing a smile, she nodded.

"How is my granddaughter?" he asked with a hint of sorrow in his voice.

"Cathy's fine, Dad," Rena said gently. Her daughter did not get along with Simon, and she knew it bothered him. She blamed him for her father's death. As hard as he tried, Cathy's love was the one thing he could not buy back again. He never gave up, hoping that one day she'd change.

Simon held the wine up to the light again. "As for this garbage . . ." Disgusted, he tossed the contents of the glass onto the wet floor. Turning to the man next to him, he said, "I'm sorry. I should have introduced you two sooner. Harrison Monroe, this is my daughter, Rena."

The man with the silver hair grinned at her, his tanned face making his teeth seem remarkably white. They shook hands. His long fingers felt warm and smooth in her hand, and his green eyes danced over her face, making her feel slightly light-headed. "I'm sorry about your friend," he said sincerely. "I heard about the murder from my men in the field. That's all they're talking about."

"Let's go into my office, both of you," Simon barked over the noise. "I'm going deaf out here."

The office was away from the machinery and soundproofed.

Simon closed the door, then went around his oak desk and opened up a temperature-controlled cabinet. Taking out a bottle of white wine, he said to Rena, "This isn't *my* wine, not yet anyway. Hopefully in the next couple of years it *will* be. Harrison," he said, putting his hand on the man's back, "is my new vintner. He made this wine for the people who bought the old Pelham vineyard up on Spring Mountain Road a couple of years ago. This man," pointing his thumb toward Harrison, "goes to work for them, and in one year produces this quality. He's a damn genius! He won more awards for some of my competitors than I care to think about."

Ah, another genius! At least he seems different than the others, Rena thought. Each year Simon would hire a new vintner, hoping that this time he found the prodigy that would produce for him an award-winning cabernet and chardonnay.

"Not only is he expensive," Simon continued, "but his ideas for revamping the winery will end up costing me a fortune. Look at this." He took out blueprints from a large, cylindrical case and opened them up on his desk. "I'm going to be buying up all this acreage so we can add more vineyards. What my other vintners have done in the past was to over-crop—pruning back the vines so they could yield more grapes. The problem with that was it also diluted the quality."

It had been a long time since Rena had seen her father this excited. "Is that what you did for the people who bought the Pelham property?" she asked Harrison.

"No. Actually it belongs to only one person now. The husband died a little over a year ago and left his widow the property. Her winery is very small and most of her profits were literally evaporating from the air-conditioning inside. Temperatures need to be kept at fifty-eight degrees if the wines are to ferment properly. Bigger wineries can absorb that kind of loss. Small ones can't. What I did was to dig an underground cave on her property where the wines are naturally kept at the right temperature."

"I told you he was brilliant," Simon said beaming.

"It was no big deal," he said with some shyness. "People have been using caves to store wines in for thousands of years. I threw out high technology and went back to nature, that's all."

"What's the name of the woman who owns the winery?" Rena asked.

"Monica van der Slyck."

"Like in van der Slyck chocolates?" Rena said, amazed, folding her arms and leaning against the desk.

"That was her husband's company. In fact, the murdered field hand worked in her vineyard," Monroe replied.

"Then her property is the one adjacent to the McKinney's?" Rena said.

Monroe nodded, his eyes never leaving her face.

Rena looked away.

"I'm throwing a dinner party tonight. Harrison and Mrs. van der Slyck will be there. Hopefully, you'll come," Simon said. "I've told her all about you." There was a coloring in Simon's voice, and his face became animated when he mentioned her name.

Was there something going on between them? Rena wondered. "Let me see how I feel, Dad."

"Of course," he said, understanding her concern for her friend.

A woman's voice came over the intercom. "Miss Halbrook, you have a call on line two."

Rena took the call in the outer office.

"Yes?" she said.

"Hi, this is Walter Parsons."

The preppy doctor from this morning. "Yes, Doctor."

"You asked me to call if I found anything out of the ordinary during the autopsy."

"Did you?" She could feel her heart racing.

"Yes. Are you busy?"

"No."

"Good. Why don't you come over to the hospital. You're going to have to see this to believe it. It's about a ten-minute drive from where you are now. Officer Swangel will meet us here later."

Rena wrote down the address.

She went back into Simon's office and told them she was leaving. Both men were huddled over the desk looking at the plans.

"Hopefully, I'll see you tonight. I'd like you to meet Monica," Simon said.

"It would be nice if you could come," Harrison said, looking up from the blueprints.

"Perhaps. Let's see if they find Maura first, okay?"

Harrison shook her hand again, and again she could feel the heat coming from his flesh.

Walter Parsons met Rena at the admittance section of the hospital. He had on OR greens and rubber gloves that were cloaked in something wet, sticky, and red.

"What's the matter?" he asked, seeing Rena's face draining color.

"I have a thing about blood."

"I thought you were a doctor." He looked bewildered.

She smiled. "I'm the kind that puts bandages on *psychological* wounds."

"Ahh," he said, smacking his head as it dawned on him. He began to laugh. "You still want to come inside?"

"Absolutely."

"I hope you have a strong stomach."

"We'll soon find out, won't we. Where's Doctor Frawley? I thought he was conducting the autopsy."

"He did. Dr. Frawley found exactly what he was looking for— a drunk with his throat slashed and a puncture wound in the back of his head." There was sarcasm in his voice. He grabbed a rubber apron from the closet and gave it to her.

"You obviously don't agree with Dr. Frawley's conclusion," Rena said, tying the apron around her waist.

"I don't mean to disagree with a colleague, especially someone with his vast experience. But if you've done a thousand autopsies like he has, and everyone's the same, you're not going to look very hard at one thousand and one."

"What are we going to look at that's so different?"

"Ah, wait and see," he said, excited.

He opened the door and they went inside.

The remains of Tomas Sanchez lay on a metal table. The Mexican was small but muscular. His organs—lungs, heart, kidneys, and spleen—were hanging in a scale above the body.

Parsons saw that Rena was turning white. "Are you going to be all right?"

Rena took a deep breath, smelling the odor of formaldehyde and ammonia in the room. "Just tell me what you want me to look at, and please do it as quickly as possible."

"The police are doing a run on the fingerprints. I doubt if they'll find anything. He's obviously a migrant worker, probably an illegal who slipped across the border. The valley is filled with them during the harvesting season."

"He may be a migrant worker, but he's not an illegal," Rena said, starting to gag. She took a tissue from the box on the table and held it up to her face. "Look at the tattooed heart on the right side of his chest. That's the marking of a particular L.A. street gang. That gang doesn't accept illegals. I'm familiar with their symbols because I once had a job as a liaison between gang members and the police when I was doing graduate work. Also, see the tattoo of a teardrop next to his eye? It's a macho sign meaning he's done prison time."

"I'm impressed," he said, with respect in his voice. He pushed back the victim's head exposing his neck. He pointed to the area of the main artery. "See this slice on the neck? This was made with a sharp instrument, approximately two inches wide. Probably a knife."

The knife Manuel had taken from his boot flashed through Rena's mind. It also was about two inches wide and also appeared to be very sharp. "What else did you want me to see?" she asked.

Parsons turned the dead man, Tomas, over on his stomach. He put his finger next to the hole on the top area of the neck. "This is the puncture wound . . . goes right through to the spinal

41

column. A different instrument was used here. More like a large triangular nail or spike.''

Rena fought down whatever was trying to force its way up from her stomach.

"This is the most bizarre thing of all." He turned the body on its back again then took a Papermate pen from his shirt pocket and moved Tomas's penis over to the side with it. "Notice anything unusual?"

"Please, no questions, just comment. I'm about thirty seconds away from passing out."

"Gotcha," he said. "There are no testicles in the scrotum. See?"

Rena's face was already the color of ashes and her forehead was damp, but she looked. She saw a splattering of dried blood on his thighs.

"See these two slits on the right and left side of the scrotum?" He pointed to them with the felt tip of his pen. "They're very fresh . . . probably made right after he was killed."

Rena stared at him. "Wait a minute. Are you saying the killer removed his testicles?"

"Yes. Someone made those slits with an exceptionally sharp cutting tool, most likely a scalpel. There's a lot of tissue damage inside the scrotum."

"I think I need to get out of this room," Rena said. She was beginning to feel nauseous.

Parsons took her by the arm and helped her out the door.

In the hallway, Rena leaned against the wall and took deep breaths until she felt her color returning. *If someone would castrate a man like that then what might he have done to Maura?*

"I'm not an expert pathologist, but I'd say he was already dead before his testicles were taken out. I also don't believe he was killed by the slit on his throat. That puncture wound in the back of the neck was the one that did it." He put three quarters into the soda machine. A Sprite rolled out. He opened the lid and handed it to her. "Drink this, you'll feel better."

"Thanks," she said, taking the can from him. She took two deep swallows.

"One other thing." He put more change into the slot. "There were several strands of blond hairs under Sanchez's fingernails. Now, that doesn't mean anything," he said, seeing the concern on Rena's face. "I've bagged them up in case they need to be tested." A diet Coke came out of the machine.

42

Down the hallway they saw Pinky Swangel coming toward them. He was holding a Ziploc plastic bag in his hand, and he looked grim.

"Did you find Manuel?" she asked him.

"Yeah. The son of a bitch sees my car blocking the road and flings the knife into the bushes. When I tried cuffing him, his damn kids jumped all over me, and his wife nearly bit off my hand."

"Where is Manuel?" Rena said.

"In jail for obstructing justice. I should have thrown his whole damn family in there with him. What the hell was he trying to hide by keeping the knife?" He held up the Ziploc bag containing pieces of bloody grass. "I'm taking this to the lab in Geyserville. I need a blood-type from the dead guy," he said to Parsons. "If it doesn't match up with the blood on this grass, then we've got a real problem on our hands."

"Like maybe it's Maura McKinney's blood?" Parsons asked.

"Maybe. Jesus, I don't want to think about that," Pinky said, shaking his head.

Parsons then told him about his discovery during the autopsy, including the blond hairs underneath the victim's fingernails, and Rena's feeling that the dead man was an ex-con.

"Shit!" Pinky said, removing his hat and wiping his brow with his sleeve. "What kind of nut case do we have here?"

"You're also going to need Maura's blood-type if it doesn't turn out to be the dead man's," Rena said to him. Her voice was shaky.

"Oh Lord!" A worried look came over Pinky's face as it dawned on him what she meant. "How do I get that? She lives in New York."

"Dr. Frawley may be able to help you," she said, tossing the soda can into the trash bin. "He delivered her."

"Do you know which hospital?"

"No hospital," she said. "Maura was born at home, but she grew up here. She must have had a family doctor. Maybe it was even Frawley. Hopefully whoever it was still keeps old records. Did you do a fingerprint verification on the dead man?"

"It's being run now. If he did time like you think, then we'll find out." He turned to Parsons. "You really think he was killed by that wound in the back of the neck?"

"Yup. With a half-inch triangular spike that penetrated the area between the first and second vertebra," he said, pointing to

43

the spot on the back of his own neck. "No one could live after that."

"Christ, maybe I'd better hold Manuel for murder." He nervously put his hands on his gun belt.

"Why?" Rena asked.

"He had the damn knife and was trying to hide it."

"Yes, but he's the one who showed me the knife and the bloody patch of ground in the first place. Why would he do that if he murdered the man?" she asked skeptically.

"I don't know," he sighed. Pinky looked troubled. Finally, he said, "What kind of crazy bastard would rip out a man's . . ." He couldn't finish the sentence.

Now it was Rena's turn to look distressed. "Obviously a very sick person," she answered in a restrained voice.

"I never thought of Manuel as being sick," Pinky said.

"I don't think he is," Rena responded.

Filled with exhaustion, she left the hospital and drove back to the château. The only way she could keep her eyes open in the Range Rover was to think about the appalling things the killer did to that man in the vineyard. What disturbed her most was the knowledge that the act of castration was usually carried out by women in some societies as a form of revenge. *Did a woman murder him?* Then she thought about the trail of blood leading from the spring. *Was the man killed there?* Most women could not carry a man from the spring all the way to the vineyard. However, it could be done if the woman was in a maniacal state. She remembered studying the Malaysian Amoks, a tribe that would work themselves into such a murderous frenzy that eventually one person would have the strength of ten people. Rena suddenly recalled the antidepressant medication that she found in Maura's bag. *Why was she taking them?* A cold feeling gripped her stomach. Could Manuel's fear about Maura killing the migrant worker be right? She shook her head, trying to clear from it such a horrendous idea, but the notion stubbornly clung to the back of her mind.

She saw the château coming up. Right now all Rena wanted was to get some sleep.

Then the same thought that she had when she was in Maura's house popped into her head again: *I haven't seen Maura in years. People change.*

Chapter Four

"**Z**IP UP YOUR sweater. The winds are picking up," Charlie said, popping another peanut into his mouth.

Charlie Halleran and Cathy, Rena's ten-year-old daughter, were sitting on a railing in the L.A. Zoo watching a female Japanese snow monkey picking small, black insects out of her infant's fur. The winds were beginning to blow hard, sending Styrofoam cups and candy wrappers soaring past the animal cages.

Cathy zipped up her sweater and put her hand in the pocket of Charlie's old leather aviator's jacket for warmth. "Don't you hate to see such beautiful animals locked away like that?" she said, taking a peanut from his bag with her other hand.

"Cruel, huh?"

"Yeah." He put his arm round her shoulder and she snuggled into his body. Charlie had become a substitute father to her after her real one was killed. "Think you and Mom are ever going to get married?" she asked.

"We're just good friends right now, Cathy."

"Bullshit. You sleep together. Good friends don't do that."

"You're not supposed to know about that kind of stuff," he said, grinning.

"Yeah? Well, I *do* know about that kind of stuff. If you're doing it with her, you might as well marry her."

"You need more than doing it to make a marriage work. Besides, we don't have time in our lives for that."

"You guys fight a lot, don't you?" She looked up at him from under his arm.

"We don't fight, we discuss."

"God, how grown-up of both of you," she groaned. "I heard you both *discussing* two nights ago when you thought I was asleep. What was that all about?"

"You hear everything, don't you? No wonder your ears are so big," he said, giving her a playful squeeze.

"I bet you think your relationship is not going to work because we're listed in *Forbes* as the seventeenth wealthiest family in America. Sometimes men can't handle that. It affects their masculinity," she said seriously.

Charlie laughed. "You should have bought this month's issue. You guys moved up a notch to number sixteen when that steel honcho from Pittsburgh jumped out of his own skyscraper last week." He finished the bag of peanuts and slam dunked it into the wastebasket. "Nope, money isn't the problem. Finding time to be together is."

"When are you leaving for Paris?" she asked, with a trace of sadness.

"In a couple of days."

"For how long?"

"About a month." He could sense her hurt.

"Mom know?"

"Yes, she knows." He tried to keep the disappointment out of his voice. "I had hoped your mom and I could have spent this weekend together. That's what *that* discussion you heard was all about."

"Oh, and she opted to go to Napa to meet her friend, instead, huh?"

"Yeah, something like that," he said, sighing. There were always "something like that's" coming between us, Charlie thought to himself. Too many. He spent half his time as a reporter traveling all over the world. When he did manage to get back to Los Angeles, his time with Rena was limited because she was usually swamped with prior commitments.

Charlie looked over to the cages. Three teenage boys, wearing leather jackets and gang-colored bandannas around their legs, strutted toward the snow monkeys. One of them began hooting like an ape, jumping up and down, scratching his sides. The other two laughed and scraped beer cans along the bars.

The mother ape, bearing her fangs, hugged her infant to her breast and began screeching loudly.

"Assholes!" Cathy shouted at them, ready to jump off the railing.

Charlie held her back, smiling. "*Macaca fuscata*, otherwise known as snow monkeys, are from the old-world family of apes. If someone gives them shit, they give it right back."

The snow monkey grabbed a mound of feces from the straw-covered floor and flung it through the bars, hitting the three boys. Yelling obscenities, they put their arms over their heads for protection. The monkey continued throwing while jumping up and down and screeching until the boys raced down the pathway and into the tunnel for cover.

"I guess you literally meant it when you said they give shit right back," Cathy said, laughing.

"Yep."

"Gosh, you know a lot about a lot of things, don't you, Charlie?"

He got down from the railing and helped her off. She was getting more and more attached to him. Part of him liked the feeling. He hadn't allowed another child to get this close to him since his own daughter was killed. But what happens if he and Rena stop seeing each other? There was that possibility. How would it affect Cathy?

They ate dinner at a dim sum restaurant in Brentwood, then Charlie drove her home. Anna, Simon Halbrook's housekeeper, was staying at the house and looking after Cathy while Rena was away.

For the next hour, Charlie walked along San Vicente Boulevard, peering into the windows of the overpriced art galleries and clothing stores, thinking about Rena. Cathy was perceptive; she could detect things weren't right between them. He realized he was reaching a turning point in his relationship with Rena. At this moment he just wasn't sure which way he wanted it to turn.

Charlie lived in a duplex off of Sycamore in the old section of Los Angeles, a far cry from Rena's big white house nestled safely away in the Brentwood hills. The apartment had three rooms: a bedroom; a 1950s kitchen with a formica table and chairs; and a living room, which contained a flowered sofa that he bought from the previous tenant and an old Emerson TV with coat hangers taped to the rabbit ears for reception. One side of the living room wall was covered with books, the other three sides with mementos he collected from around the world while working as a reporter. Next to the stereo was a black-and-white photo of himself with Fidel Castro. Grinning, they had their arms around each other, with big Havana cigars protruding from their mouths.

Charlie took a Coors from the refrigerator, went into the living room, and turned on his computer. He punched up UPI on his news service and browsed the headlines. Hopefully if something

47

more interesting popped up, he might be able to talk his editor out of sending him to Paris to cover the OPEC meeting. After just coming back from spending six weeks with the Hezbollah militia in Lebanon, listening to oil barons talking about the price of a barrel of crude would be as exciting as watching wallpaper peel.

Same old shit, Charlie thought, as he watched the international headlines pass before his eyes on the screen: famine, wars, earthquakes.

He then punched in the national news. Again, the same thing, just different names and faces. When he came upon the murder of a seventeen-year-old girl, he stopped scrolling and scanned the article. It was a brief, one-column piece that told about the partially decomposed body that was discovered outside of Peconic on the north fork of Long Island. The part that caught his attention was what the murderer had done to the girl. *The sick bastard had sliced open her lower abdominal area and torn out her ovaries!*

Charlie sighed and turned off the computer. He closed his eyes and sipped his beer. A picture of an elegant snow monkey with its beautiful white coat of fur standing freely on the ridge of a Japanese ice-capped mountain appeared in his head. Darwin had it ass-backward, he thought. *Nothing as glorious as that could have evolved into man.*

Chapter Five

RENA FOUND HERSELF walking up the steps leading to the door of Maura's house. The sun had just set, and the light had darkened to the color of battleship gray. In the sky, black clouds hung low and ominous. The air was cold and the winds lashed out at her, slapping angrily against her face.

Why am I here? she thought to herself. Everything seemed

larger than it should be—the steps, the chairs on the porch, the door.

Her nerves tingled, warning her that there was something forbidden here and that she should leave. She wanted to run, but she couldn't. Some invisible, intangible thing was drawing her up those stairs.

The screen door opened on its own, beckoning her to enter.

Once inside, she found herself alone in the living room. It was dark here, and shapeless shadows darted in and out of corners of the room. Suddenly she heard noises coming from the second floor. Frightened, she slowly made her way over to the bottom of the staircase. Her heart was pounding. She turned the switch to the hall light, but it failed to go on.

Rena knew she should leave. She knew she should run as fast as she could to get away from here. Again she sensed that bodiless force pushing her onward. Something inside her needed to know what was up those stairs. As she climbed the steps the sounds became louder. She froze; the noises, she suddenly realized, were tiny footsteps scurrying across the floor in one of the rooms above. When she came to the top of the landing, she saw a harsh light creeping out from the seams of the closed door that led to Maura's room. Her body was shaking with fear.

Run! Run!

Again she couldn't. Once more that unseen power was drawing her onward. Slowly she pushed the door open. The light coming from the room was blinding. She cupped her hands over her eyes in order to see.

Over by the mirror she saw Maura. Except something was wrong. The girl in the room, with skin as white as milk, was the Maura she knew when she was ten years old. The young Maura was pacing the floor, naked, holding the bloody, bone-handled knife in her hand. Her blond hair on her head was in flames, and her pubic hair, the color of golden threads, glowed from the reflection off the glaring light bulb. She turned and looked at Rena and a menacing smile broke across her mouth.

Rena caught her own reflection in the mirror behind Maura. *My God! I'm also ten years old!* She looked at her hands and feet; they were those of a child. Shaking with fear, she looked up at Maura.

Maura stretched out her hands to her, revealing long red fingernails. She beckoned Rena to come closer. Rena wanted to turn around and run down those stairs, but that invisible thing was now pulling her toward her friend. Then she saw Maura's eyes through the flames that encircled her hair; they were different colors: one was blue, the other brown. Again she tried to get away but that force that kept her here was now blocking her path, refusing to let her escape. The unseen presence began to become concrete and was taking on the shape of a hand. It's fingers started to dig deeply into her shoulder.

Maura started coming toward Rena, her feet making soft sounds on the hardwood floor. She was gripping the bloody knife tightly by the hilt. Closer she came . . . closer. Rena could feel the heat from the flames engulfing Maura's hair. The smile on Maura's pale lips widened, and then she opened her mouth exposing sharp, bloodstained teeth.

Frozen with terror, all Rena could do was scream as the fingers on her shoulder pulled at her. Gasping for breath, Rena opened her eyes and looked up. The hand that was gripping her shoulder was Simon's. For a second she didn't know where she was. Looking around she saw that she was lying in her bed in the château and that it was night.

"I thought it best to wake you. You've been sleeping for hours," Simon said, turning on the light by the nightstand. He sat down on the bed next to Rena and once again put his hand on her shoulder. "Are you all right? It looked like you were having a bad dream."

Rena sat up, brushed the sleep from her eyes, and looked at Simon. He was wearing a tuxedo. "Yes, I'm fine," she said. Downstairs, she could hear the clinking of glasses and laughter.

"I'd like you to come down and meet my guests," Simon said to her.

Simon's dinner party. My God, I had completely forgotten about it! she thought to herself. She was so exhausted that when she got back from the autopsy she went directly up to her room and fell into a dead sleep. Rena had only meant to take a short nap. Looking at Simon, she said, "I'm really not up for it tonight. I hope you don't mind."

A sad expression came over his face. "I can't tell you what to do anymore. It's just that it would make me happy if you would join us."

She saw the pleading in his eyes, and she was touched. "It's this van der Slyck woman, isn't it?" Rena asked, smiling.

Simon looked away and nodded his head slowly. "I would very much like you to meet her," he said softly.

Rena knew this wasn't easy for him. There had been other women in Simon's life since her mother died, but this sounded serious. "Okay," she said after a beat. "Give me about ten minutes to wash up. I must warn you that I didn't bring any evening wear."

Simon stood up, his face glowing. "Hell, come on down the way you are!" Then after a moment, he said sincerely, "Thank you." He left, closing the door.

He's in love, she realized. *Simon the Great is in love!* Rena almost laughed at that thought as she stepped out of her jeans. She took a quick shower, then put on a silk blouse with padded shoulders and a skirt that matched.

As she brushed her hair in front of the mirror, she began to think about her dream. It bothered her. Obviously the terrifying child she found in the upstairs bedroom was not Maura, but her own hidden fears that took the physical shape of Maura. *What am I frightened of? The truth about the murder? Why? Does part of me actually believe that she's capable of committing such a gruesome deed?*

But why the different colors of her eyes? Of course, now I remember! she almost blurted out. When they vacationed together in Greece, Rena once opened the bathroom door in their hotel room not knowing that Maura was inside. She saw her standing in front of the mirror with a towel wrapped around her body and putting in her contact lenses. Hearing Rena enter, she turned around and quickly covered her face with her hands. Rena excused herself and closed the door. It was only a brief second that she saw her, but she swore when Maura turned to her that her eyes were two different colors. Rena dismissed it at the time as the Aegean sunlight playing tricks with her own eyes as it filtered through the glass window.

Rena pulled the brush through her hair one last time, touched up her makeup, then went downstairs.

When she came into the dining room, Simon stood up from the table and proudly introduced her to the guests. The men all wore tuxedos and the women had on evening gowns. Rena smiled to herself thinking about how out of place she must look.

She was given a seat at the table directly across from Monica van der Slyck. After meeting her, Rena understood her father's infatuation. Monica was a slim, impeccably dressed, aristocratic woman, somewhere between forty-five and sixty years old. Her true age, Rena believed, was buried somewhere beneath a couple of face-lifts and a carefully applied makeup job.

Next to Mrs. van der Slyck, sat her son, Otto. He was an elfish man in his mid-twenties with a jaunty air about him. He showed little interest in the dinner conversation, except when the discussion briefly turned to what some of the guests considered to be the best resorts and restaurants in the world. He then looked up from the wine he was lazily swirling around in his glass and focused his bulging, froglike eyes on the speaker. Breaking into a garish smile, he shook his head and interjected his own opinion. He spoke with an upper-crust, New England accent laced with a wine-heavy tongue. "I absolutely disagree," he said. "Nice was the place to vacation a few years back. The city is now overflowing with the typing-pool crowd from West Germany and England. The second they hit the pebble beaches, they remove their tops and lie in the sun for eight hours straight, getting third degree burns on their tender little titties. I suggest you try Sardinia if you want to see some tanned, gorgeous people."

The guests looked at each other, then down at their plates with embarrassed coughs. Mrs. van der Slyck glared at her son. Otto stared back at her with his watery blue eyes, blinked them innocently at her several times, smirked, then returned to his wineglass.

Rena looked over at Simon and saw the rage in his eyes. She knew how he detested boorish men like Otto. *Yes, it had to be love or he would never allow someone like him in his house.*

The other dinner guests included Mr. Yamaguchi, a businessman who was quietly buying up wineries in the United States for his Japanese conglomerate; Mrs. Yamaguchi, his shy, nontalkative wife; Edmond Farnsworth, a multimillionaire who had retired from his microchip company in the Silicon Valley after suffering a severe heart attack and now dabbled in making exclusive, expensive wines; and Blythe, his younger, attractive wife of one year.

Harrison Monroe sat next to Rena. His shaggy, silver hair hung down over his collar. He turned and smiled at her, then went back to the table conversation. Even though he was not touching her, she could feel the heat emanating from his leg under the table. It was not an unpleasant sensation, but it made her uncomfortable.

Farnsworth, who was in his mid-sixties, had his liver-spotted hand around his wife's chair and was telling everyone about how

52

he and Blythe met. The entire room seemed bent on hearing this because Blythe was a strikingly beautiful woman who was almost twenty-five years younger than Farnsworth.

"Here I am in intensive care . . . my chest all bandaged from the bypass and tubes sticking out from every cavity in my body. The only thing I'm looking at are the peaks and lows of the lines on the heart monitor. As long as the lines are moving up and down, I know I'm still alive. Every breath I'm taking I think is my last. Then suddenly I look up and I see this gorgeous woman from the lobby flower shop setting this plant down on my dresser." He turned his glowing eyes in Blythe's direction. "The second she smiles at me, pow!—I know I'm in love."

Everyone at the table nodded their heads and laughed.

Blythe blushed, and Farnsworth gave her shoulder a squeeze. "I suddenly think to myself, 'What are you doing? You have all the money you're ever going to need. You practically killed yourself making it. Now go out and enjoy life!' That's exactly what I did! Blythe and I were married three months later. I always wanted to live up here and own a winery, so I bought one." He turned to his wife with gleaming eyes, and she looked away, smiling. "She gets embarrassed when I talk about how happy I am," he said to the guests.. "And what about you, Simon? When is enough, enough? Ever think about selling out and retiring a billionaire?"

"You and I are a different breed, Edmond," Simon said, pointing his salad fork at him. "The only thing that keeps the arteries in my heart unclogged is knowing that there's a new deal to be made just around the corner. As for companionship, well . . . who knows."

Rena caught the quick eye contact between Simon and Monica.

During the main course of grilled salmon, the conversation turned to the grizzly death of the Mexican worker and the mysterious disappearance of Maura McKinney. All heads turned toward Rena. By this time they knew she had come to Napa to spend time with her childhood friend.

"A very strange affair," Farnsworth said, pouring a glass of a Puligny-Montrachet for Blythe and himself.

"I heard the woman's father was a good wine maker," Blythe said, looking interested.

"One of the best," Simon said. "He used to work for me when he needed money. But he was hard to get along with . . .

53

always wanting to make wines *his* way. He was a private man . . . mostly kept to himself.''

"I certainly hope nothing happened to the girl,'' Mrs. van der Slyck said in her Dutch accent, while looking sympathetically at Rena.

"Unless, of course, *she's* the one that killed him,'' Otto said, casually.

"Otto, please!'' Mrs. van der Slyck said, scowling at her son.

"Yes, please, Otto!'' Rena said coldly. She was outraged that this lout with froglike eyes would dare make such an insensitive statement about Maura. Then she felt Simon's hand on hers, squeezing it. The squeeze was saying, "Let it be, for my sake.'' Rena, lips trembling with anger, sat back in her chair.

After a pause, Monica turned to the guests and said, "The man who was murdered in her fields worked for us.''

"Where did he come from?'' Rena asked suddenly.

"Excuse me?'' Monica replied.

"Did you hire him?''

"Er . . . no.'' She looked confused and turned toward Otto. "My son does the hiring.''

Rena moved her hands away from the table so the servant could take her salad plate, then said to Otto, "Where did *you* find him?''

Otto shrugged in a casual manner, but he looked uncomfortable. He quickly filled up his glass again with wine. "I don't remember. He may have been recommended or he came to the vineyards asking for work. What difference does it make?'' he asked defensively.

Rena believed Otto *did* know how Tomas Sanchez was hired. Why was he being evasive? Perhaps it was not the right time to pursue it, but she said, "Tomas Sanchez was born in the United States and was from the barrio of Los Angeles. Very few migrant workers come from there—the reason being there are no fields to pick in a big city. There's also a good chance he spent time in prison.''

Monica turned and glared at Otto. He looked down into his glass, his face the color of wax.

After a minute, Monica tore her eyes away from her son and said, "Maura McKinney is our neighbor. Her property is adjacent to ours. I remember she was here last year, also around this time. She seemed to be very much of a loner. In the entire time she spent here, I saw her only once. I must say, though, she's an

54

exceptionally attractive woman. She went out mostly at night. Even though I didn't see her, I could hear the sound of her footsteps on the gravel road as she passed by our house. I also thought that to be rather odd. I made a point of watching for her, but she was so evasive.''

Again Rena felt annoyed. Maura was a person who cherished her privacy, yet Monica and her son seemed bent on destroying it with their nosiness.

"Maybe she had a boyfriend. It's been known to happen, mommy dear," Otto interrupted. Slinking back in his chair and running his finger around the rim of the wineglass, he said, "I spent the summer in Italy last year and returned to Napa in September. That's when Maura was here. I never saw her, but some nights I could hear her walking down the mountain about one in the morning and returning around four or five. Yes, I'd say a lover would be the safe bet," he said with a knowing smile. He finished his wine and poured himself another.

"Only out at night, eh? Ah, maybe she's a vampire," Mr. Yamaguchi said, grinning, in very broken English.

Mrs. Yamaguchi laughed, cupping her hand over her mouth.

"I'm sure they'll find her," Rena said, forcing the acid back down in her throat. She wanted to get away from this conversation. These people had no right discussing Maura over their fish fillets and good wine as if they were on a first-name basis with her.

Mr. Yamaguchi changed the subject and talked about this year's harvest. The dinner guests leaned forward, trying to hear what he was saying through his thick accent.

How strange, Rena thought. These rich vineyard owners listening to a man who doesn't know the first thing about making wine. The foreign conglomerate he worked for was buying up more and more vineyards and adding them to its already large stable of cars, stereos, and televisions. *You have to work the land with your own hands to produce great wine,* Maura had told her so long ago. *I'm afraid those days are over my good friend,* Rena said to herself with a deep sorrow for something that was lost and might never be regained.

After dinner, everyone adjourned to the living room. The guests sat back in the Louis XIV sofas and were poured cognac by Simon's valet.

Needing air, Rena walked out on the veranda. The cool breeze was a refreshing change from the stuffy conversation inside. She looked up into the night sky, appreciating the thousands of stars pricking the blackness. Los Angeles's neon signs and skyscraper lights had long ago destroyed this wondrous sight for its inhabitants.

"Beautiful night. What do you think?" Harrison Monroe said from behind.

She turned around. He was walking toward her holding a brandy snifter in his hand. His face, she thought, was exceptionally handsome in the moonlight.

"I think you're right. It *is* a beautiful night." Again, she saw those green eyes skipping over her face and body. He leaned on the railing next to her, his arm touching hers.

"You seemed a little bit defensive when Maura McKinney was mentioned," he said.

She moved her arm away. "She's a good friend. I'm sure bantering her name about makes for great dinner conversation, but people who don't know her shouldn't form conclusions about her life or what happened yesterday in her winery."

"Ah, you mean Otto. He's a good kid—just thinks he's Prince Charles—or Princess Diana—I'm not sure which."

Rena laughed.

"You have a nice laugh. Your father tells me you're involved with someone."

"Yes, I am," she said, beginning to feel uneasy with where this chat was heading. Simon was not fond of Charlie. He once told her that Charlie represented man at his "failed best." She believed the real reason he disliked him was because Charlie could see through her father's deepest defenses and that made him conquerable. The one thing Simon hated was being on an equal basis with another human being.

"Why isn't he up here with you?" Harrison asked.

"We have different priorities this weekend." She rubbed her arms trying to wipe away the evening chill.

"Would you like my jacket?" He put the snifter on the railing and started to take it off.

"I'll be fine, thank you," she said, moving slightly away from him.

Harrison slid the jacket back over his shoulders. "Wrong timing, huh?"

"Something like that. Were you always a vintner?" she asked, changing the subject.

"No. In the beginning it was just a hobby for me. My father

had a small vineyard in his backyard. He pressed and made his own wine, and I learned the basics from him. I studied enology at UC Davis, but I became a mineralogist instead. Less work and more money in it. I worked in mines all over the world—but mostly in the Mediterranean countries . . . Turkey, Greece, Yugoslavia. After a while, it got a bit tiresome. I wanted roots, a place to call my own, so I went back to my first love, wine making.''

"You must feel very content."

"I am. I'm good at what I do. It's like being a doctor. I take sick wineries and make them well again."

"Anyone have a light?" Blythe asked, stepping through the open French doors onto the veranda. She was holding a cigarette.

"Absolutely," Harrison said, laughing. He took a gold lighter from his jacket. Blythe cupped her hands over the lighter, resting her fingers on top of his to keep the wind from putting out the flame. Her hand touched his for several seconds longer than necessary, then she slowly slid her fingers down and moved away.

Rena noticed.

Blythe took a long, hard drag from the cigarette, then closed her handsome hazel eyes and let the smoke out slowly. "Ahh, you don't know how good that feels," she said, smiling. "It's a filthy habit, I know, and someday I swear I'm going to give it up. But right now . . . goddamn, but it tastes good!" She laughed.

"I bet," Rena said. There was a lot of inflection in Blythe's voice; it made her seem animated like Bette Davis and Joan Crawford. Yet at the same time there was also a hardness there. No, indifference might be a better word, Rena thought. To be vibrant and detached all at once—a contradictory combination. It was almost as if she were performing rather than genuinely feeling. Rena scanned her face. Up close, now, she could see that Blythe was older than she originally thought: crow's-feet lined her eyes and wrinkles surrounded her mouth. Her brilliant eyes sparkled with energy, but like her voice, there was an undefinable darkness there.

"Oh, I hope you don't mind me joining you. It's just that I can't smoke when Edmond is in the room. His heart and all, you understand," she said vivaciously.

"I do understand," Rena said.

"Well, I don't think I'm being totally honest about the real reason I joined you." She blushed. "You both are close to my age. Don't get me wrong . . . I love Edmond with all my soul!

It's just that sometimes I miss having someone to talk to who also doesn't remember what life was like before television. Not that I'm a young chicken . . .''

Rena laughed. "You don't have to explain. It's a very natural feeling." She guessed her age to be around forty.

Blythe brushed back her chestnut-colored hair, looked over her shoulder to the guests sitting inside the living room, pouted, then leaned over to Rena and Harrison and whispered, "I bet everyone in that room is questioning my motive for marrying Edmond."

"Not necessarily," Rena said.

"Oh sure they are. It's okay. I understand. Hell, I'd probably be doing the same thing if I was them. What's someone like me, a girl that sold flowers for a living, doing with a man his age? I know that's what they're thinking. I see it in their eyes and hear it in their voices whenever they talk to me. They're thinking it's got to be the money. What they don't know is that I made Edmond sign a prenuptial agreement. If he dies before me, most of his money goes to his kids and to charity. I don't know how much longer he's got, but while he's alive I never want him thinking, even for a second, that I married him for anything but himself." There was concern in her voice.

"Love has nothing to do with age," Rena said warmly. "Ask all of Picasso's surviving ex-wives."

Blythe and Harrison laughed.

"You both seem nice," Blythe said. Turning those beautiful, hazel eyes to Rena, she said, "Do you get up here very often?"

"At least a couple of times a year."

"Good. I hope we see each other again. I have to leave tomorrow for Palm Springs. We have a house there. Ugh! The only thing worse than the heat in the Springs is the boredom. There's no way you'll be back here next week, huh?"

Rena sensed her eagerness. "I doubt it, but you never know."

"Hell, Los Angeles isn't that far. Maybe we could meet, have lunch and do some shopping," Blythe said anxiously.

Why do so many women with time on their hands love to shop? Rena wondered. It would probably make a good study. "I don't know about the shopping part but lunch sounds great."

A servant came out on the patio and told Rena Sheriff Swangel was on the phone.

She excused herself, leaving Blythe and Harrison alone on the porch, and went into the study to take the call.

"Have you found Maura?" Rena immediately asked him.

She could hear him sucking in a long stream of air on the other end, then he said, "No, but we got the fingerprint reports back." He sounded somber.

From the corner of her eye she could see her father's guests sitting in the living room. "Yes?" she said.

"Most of the prints on the knife were smudged or belonged to Manuel. The lab identified a right thumb print belonging to Maura."

"No others?"

"None."

"What about the blood?" Rena was tense.

"The blood on the grass and the blood on the knife were the same type as the victim's."

"I see," Rena said softly.

"As I said before, I think we got a real problem on our hands. We can't find anything that says there was a third party involved." He now made loud wheezing sounds blowing air out of his mouth.

"What about *his* fingerprints?"

"His name was Tomas Sanchez, and you were right about him spending time in jail. In fact, he'd been in and out of jail most of his life—gang-related robberies, drugs, attempted murder. He did heavy time in Soledad for the rape of two women."

"Rape?" Something was beginning to stir in her mind. Manuel may have been right when he said that someone could have come across her when she was swimming naked. "The lagoon where she swam was far from the main road. How did he know where to find it?" she asked.

"He worked at the van der Slyck winery right next to Maura's property. Maybe Sanchez was taking a shortcut to get back."

"Okay, and maybe he came upon Maura swimming in the spring. She's a beautiful woman and rape wasn't alien to this man."

"Yep, and using the knife on him certainly would be considered justifiable homicide, except for the fact that Doctor Parsons says it was a pointed instrument driven through the back of the neck that killed him, not the knife wound. Why would she do something like that?" He seemed disturbed.

"We don't know that she did anything yet," she said. She began thinking about the blond hairs found under Sanchez's fingernails.

"Something just isn't right! I mean this guy was stabbed, spiked in the neck, de-balled, then tied up to a grapevine like he was Jesus Christ himself. If Maura did it—and God help me but I'm beginning to think it looks more and more like it—then would somebody tell me how she managed to move the body all that distance? Unless, of course, she had help.'' He let out a sorrowful, deep breath.

"Meaning Manuel?" she said skeptically.

"Who else? He's been more true to her than a pet dog. He could have shown you the knife and bloodstains thinking you'd be equally as loyal.''

Rena didn't answer. Pinky may be slow, but he was not dumb. There was a lot of truth in what he said. Manuel was frightened and didn't want the police to know about the knife. It was also only a matter of time before forensics would go into Maura's room and find the medications that were used to control mental disorders. Yes, things were beginning to point to Maura.

Pinky said, "Maybe she killed him in self-defense with the knife, *then* went crazy. I don't know, but if she's out there then I'm sure as hell going to find her. I have my men stationed on every road leading out of the valley, also at the bus depot and airport. The New York Police have been alerted, just in case she eludes us and makes it back home.''

"I can't understand why she didn't take her own car and clothes," Rena said.

"Who knows. As I said, maybe she was crazy, and crazy people don't think straight. You'd know more about that stuff than me. The reason she didn't take her car could be because another person—and that person could very well be Manuel—drove her somewhere and is hiding her out.''

Or that person could be Uncle Wiggly, she thought to herself, remembering the name from Maura's appointment book. "Do you know who Uncle Wiggly is?'' she asked him.

"No. I also saw that name in her book. I have a couple of men putting that same question to the people in the valley who knew her. Anyway, I'd better be getting back to work,'' Pinky said.

She felt tired and cold after she hung up the phone, and wished to hell Charlie was here right now to wrap his arms around her and keep her warm.

She started to walk back to the party, then changed her mind. Laughing at bad jokes and making small conversation was something she found totally unappealing while Maura was out there somewhere needing help. Suddenly a heavy tiredness overtook her. Turning back around, she slowly made her way upstairs and went to bed.

Chapter Six

RENA FLEW BACK to Los Angeles early the next day and picked up her Jaguar at the parking lot across the street from the airport.

As she drove home through the lazy Sunday traffic, she felt an urge to see Charlie. We should talk . . . too many loose ends between us, she reasoned. She picked up her cellular phone, punched in some numbers, then put it back on the cradle. *No, let's do this in person.*

Instead of continuing on the 405 North, she turned east on the Santa Monica Freeway and headed toward Hollywood.

Would he be there? she thought. *Damn, I hope so!*

She pulled into his driveway, jumped out of the car, and knocked on his door. There was no answer. Her shoulders sagged in disappointment.

Then she saw him. He was down the block playing touch football with several of the Hasidic kids who lived in the neighborhood. Charlie had the football and was zigzagging down the middle of the street, trying to dodge the hands of the laughing boys who wore skullcaps, ear curls, and tzi tzis. He had on his faded Brooklyn College T-shirt and an old ripped pair of 501 Levi's that he had promised Rena he would throw away.

When he saw her, he broke out into a grin and stopped running. The boys jumped all over him, and he held up his hands in mock surrender. Tossing them the ball, he jogged over to her.

A thrill went through her entire body. All the things she planned to talk to him about suddenly became small and inconsequential. Instead, she threw her arms around his neck and kissed him hard on the mouth.

"Damn it, Charlie! I missed you!" she said breathlessly.

He grabbed her around the waist, lifting her several inches off the ground, and edged his way toward the apartment. The Hasidic boys watched with mouths open in frozen amazement as Charlie carted her inside and closed the door.

She wrapped her legs around his hips, kissing his face, feeling the roughness of his beard stubble against her cheek. He carried her through the living room and into the bedroom, letting out a scream along the way as he banged his shinbone on the edge of the coffee table. While still embracing, they fell onto the bed. He moved his hands over her breasts and thighs. Her skin began to tingle with hunger. Then he started to unbutton her blouse.

It was always like this between us, she thought, as she watched Charlie pull off his T-shirt. *Fight and fuck . . . fight and fuck.* She needed something more from him now. "Charlie, we have to talk," she whispered, trying to fight off the desire for him.

"We are talking," he said, unzipping her pants.

"I don't mean this way. I mean we have to verbally talk."

"I aim to use my mouth, trust me on that," he said, eyeing the triangle of dark hair showing through her silk panties. He started to take off his tattered jeans.

She giggled. "Goddamn you, Charlie! At least give those jeans a decent burial. You promised me that one."

"Hell, they'd just dig themselves out of the ground and follow me back home again," he said, getting on top of her and sliding his naked body over hers.

She moaned, feeling his hardness on her stomach as his tongue traced a slow path along her inner ear. "Oh, goddamn you, Charlie!" she murmured in resignation, throwing her arms around his broad back and locking her legs tightly around his calves.

Fight and fuck. Jesus Christ!

She awoke to the quivering sensation of Charlie's fingers making slow, smooth circles on her back. He was propped up on the pillows, smiling contentedly as he looked down at her. The room was filled with strong shadows from the late afternoon light.

She dug her face into his chest and held onto him. She could feel the roughness of the scar tissue on his body caused from a Claymore mine that exploded next to him during a tour of duty in Vietnam. "What time is it?" she said.

"Why? Do you have to go home?"

"No." She held him even tighter.

"What's going on?" He gently ran his fingers through her hair.

"You really know me, don't you?"

"Yep. You don't normally make love with that kind of appetite unless something's bothering you. I guess having your way with my body eases you over the hump," he said, grinning.

"You got it. When I was a junior in high school, I was stood up on Saturday night by this cute guy. I thought my world had come to an end, and then I discovered Häagen-Dazs. A pint of chocolate during one sitting cured me of that creep. I guess what I'm trying to say is that having sex with you and eating Häagen-Dazs are my shields to the realities of this world."

"At least I'm up there with good company." He stroked her cheek.

She snuggled closer into his body and told him about Maura and everything that happened during the past two days. When she finished, she looked up at him. He seemed to be in deep thought, his eyes focused somewhere within himself.

After a minute, he said slowly, "Tell me again about the part where the guy's balls were torn out."

"I never said they were torn out, Charlie. I said they were removed."

"I know you didn't say it," he said, getting out of bed. "Someone else did."

He walked into the next room and disappeared around the corner. Suddenly the amber glow of his computer screen lit up the living room.

"What are you doing?" she said, peering into the room and seeing Charlie sitting naked in front of his computer. She had the blanket wrapped around her body.

"Looking for yesterday's news," he said, tapping into UPI. Ten minutes later he found what he wanted: the small article about Mary Stevenson, the seventeen-year-old girl who was murdered in Peconic, Long Island. He printed it out and handed it to Rena.

She glanced at the page, flinching when she came to the part about the girl's ovaries. "Is there a reason why you're showing this to me?" There was a hardness to her voice.

"You said the Mexican was found in a winery in the vineyards, right?"

"So?"

"Are you familiar with Long Island?"

63

"No."

"Peconic is one of the major wine-producing areas on the island. Bit of a coincidence, huh?"

"A coincidence about what?" She was beginning to get angry.

"It just seems a little strange that two people were murdered in the same way, that's all."

"That's moronic!" she said, holding the article out to Charlie. "They were not murdered in the same way! This says she may have been strangled."

"It also says that some butcher performed an ovariectomy on her," he said.

"The man in California died from a spike driven through his neck. It says nothing about that here!"

"Yes, I know." Charlie took the article from her and looked at it again. "What do they mean by 'she *may* have been strangled.' Wouldn't you think they'd know? It's ambiguous."

"Shit, Charlie! You've got the sagacity of a pea!" She went back into the bedroom and started to get dressed.

Following her in, he said, "What are you doing?" It had been a long time since he'd seen her this irate.

"Getting the hell out of here!" She quickly zipped up her pants and put on her blouse, not bothering with the bra.

"Rena . . ."

She turned to face him, pointing a finger at his chest. "How dare you make some idiotic connection between what happened in California to what happened on Long Island! I was telling you my feelings about Maura . . . a good friend of mine who could be in trouble, or, who knows—dead! You didn't even hear me, you were so goddamn busy putting her in two places at the same time!"

"I never said that . . ."

"Knock off the shit, Charlie! You were implying it!"

He held up his hands for forgiveness. "You're right, it *was* stupid of me."

"Sometimes I think your brains are in your pants, Charlie!" She pushed past him, heading toward the front door.

His cheeks reddened. "Well . . . my pecker never bothered you before. Of course, it was always used at *your* convenience!"

She opened the door and turned to him, her eyes flaming with anger. "You're right . . . at *my* convenience! Try not to get it

64

caught in a zipper, Charlie. Brain cells can't be replaced!'' She slammed the door as she left.

He let out a long sigh. No, he had never seen her this peppery. Standing naked, staring at the door, he began to feel helpless and foolish. Why the hell hadn't he thought before he said anything? Maura was her lifelong friend. He should have known how upset she was about her disappearance.

He sat down beside his desk. Putting his hands behind his head, he leaned back in the chair and began thinking about the dead girl in Peconic. The part in the article about how she actually died was much too vague. How was she found in the vineyards? Lying on the ground? Buried? Was she clothed? Naked? Rena said the Mexican up in Napa was tied to a grapevine, his arms spread out like a crucifixion. Was she also discovered that way? As a professional newspaperman, he knew that when copy was written this vapory, the police weren't giving out much information. ''There's usually just one reason for that,'' he muttered to himself, reaching for the phone. He dialed Lieutenant Bobby Genero's home number in Queens, New York.

One of Genero's five children answered the phone. He never could remember which name belonged to which child, so he just said, ''Hi, kid, this is your Uncle Charlie. Is your dad at home?''

The patter of small feet on linoleum fading away, then Genero's thick leather shoes coming toward the phone.

''Yeah?'' Genero said gruffly.

''Lieutenant Genero, my oldest and dearest bud! How the hell are you?'' Charlie said.

''Who the fuck is this?''

''I'll give you a hint.'' Charlie did an a cappella version of *Sh-boom*. By the time he got to ''. . . ya-tata, ya-tata,'' he could hear Genero groaning on the other end of the line.

''Jesus Christ! Charlie fuckin' Halleran! What's it been . . . two years?''

''Something like that.''

''We used to sing *Sh-boom* together on the corner of New Utrecht High School when we were kids,'' Genero said, laughing.

''Right.'' Charlie laughed, too.

''So what the fuck you want, Charlie? You ain't callin' me on a Sunday night to serenade me with the Crew Cuts greatest hits.'' His voice was crusty again.

Charlie stopped laughing. Genero could be either an asshole

or a pussycat, depending on his mood. "I hear some young girl got her reproductive organs cut out in your part of town."

"You talkin' about the murder on Long Island?"

"Yeah."

"What about it? It ain't my turf. I'm in charge of the sixteenth, remember? My precinct's in the Bronx—not in some high-class community on Long Island."

"What do you know about the murder?"

"Who gives a fuck! They're killing themselves off by the shit-load in the South Bronx. You think I care about what happens in Yuppieville? Why are you so interested?"

"Because something similar happened up in Northern California. Maybe there's a connection."

"Then get a Long Island newspaper and read up on it."

"I read up on it. The reports are a little ambiguous, which usually means the police are holding back."

"We're nice guys, Charlie. We don't do things like that."

"Come on, Genero. Withholding information from the public cuts down on copycat murders. It also helps you guys quickly sift through the nuts who confess to everything."

"*Oowee!* I got a winner on my hands!" Genero was laughing again.

A good sign, Charlie thought. "Maybe this guy's killed before like this. Maybe he's serial! It would put a clot in the well-oiled machinery of the police department if the public *and* the politicians knew too much at this point in the investigation, right?"

"Okay, *stupido*, you got me interested. How did the guy die in California?"

"With a pointed instrument that was driven through the neck. Possibly a nail." Charlie then mentioned that they were both killed in areas with vineyards and wineries.

"Let me see what I can do. I'll get back to you. Great fuckin' timin' . . . right in the middle of the Knicks first home game this year on TV!"

They hung up.

It was dark out now, and Charlie turned on his desk light. He continued to sit there, naked, with his feet propped up on the desk, thinking about Rena. Had he blown it with her this time? Maybe. Well, nothing was forever and there were no constants in this world—he knew that.

Charlie then went into the kitchen and made himself a salami sandwich. He took it into the living room, along with another beer, and turned on his TV set to the Sunday sports roundup. After adjusting the picture by moving around the coat hanger taped to the rabbit ears, he plopped down on the couch, put his feet up on the coffee table, and waited for the phone to ring.

If he was lucky, maybe Rena would phone him when she got home, but he wasn't counting on it. *Damn, was she pissed!* Usually she always had control of her emotions. Whatever bone he touched in her tonight, had to have been deep.

NBC sports was showing the hardest hits in football this week. Running backs and wide receivers were spiraling in the air, bodies coming down hard on the Astro turf, bones snapping, men lying on the ground unconscious in twisted positions. Charlie turned off the TV. What happened to just showing the scores? he thought. He lay his head back on the couch and sipped his beer.

We need to talk, Charlie. That's what she wanted from him. Why couldn't he have given that to her? Instead, like all the other times, when she wanted closeness, he substituted sex. *So much safer that way.*

They argued a lot. He claimed their problems stemmed from their lack of time together. Now he saw that the "time thing" was nothing more than a smoke screen—an excuse for not wanting to see what was really wrong between them. Maybe the reason Rena had gotten so angry tonight was because she had finally seen the writing on the wall, too.

He thought about his ex-wife, Rosie. He had talked to her about everything . . . he had listened to *her* talk about everything. They were close. And what had he gotten for it? She almost destroyed his life: went crazy one night and killed their daughter with a butcher's knife. It took twenty years to put back the pieces of his shattered self. His ego, he knew without any illusions, was only held together now by spit and willpower. If he gave himself completely over to Rena and she left him, he'd fall apart again, and this time he didn't think he could make the trip back from hell.

Sex was a sure, solid buffer against hurt.

The picture of his dead daughter, Jaimie, came into his mind. She was at her dance recital, and he was in the audience watching her. Wearing a tutu, and with her hands spread above her head, she was spinning on her toes to the music of the *Nutcracker Suite*.

How old was she then? Four?

Oh, God!

Charlie finished the beer and put the bottle on the coffee table. Yup, he thought. Closeness can sure be the pits. *Not this time . . . not ever again.*

Genero dialed the Peconic police department. From the living room, he could hear the Knicks game on TV. The crowd at Madison Square Garden was screaming. Ewing must be tearing the 76ers up, he thought, pissed that he didn't get to see the play. *I owe you for that one, Charlie!*

The desk sergeant at the Peconic station got on the line, and Genero told him who he was. When he asked to talk to the officer in charge of Mary Stevenson's investigation, the desk sergeant said that he wouldn't be in until tomorrow. Then Genero tried to flush out some information from him on the way the girl died. The sergeant at first was evasive, then when Genero started to push a little, got testy. Lieutenant Robert Genero knew a runaround when he heard one.

"Can you at least tell me where the body is now?" Genero asked, as nice as could be.

"At the Hoffman Funeral Home on Fourth Street. She's going to be buried tomorrow."

Genero hung up, then debated with himself whether or not he should watch the rest of the game or take a drive up to Peconic. Then he remembered a sweet little cocktail waitress he used to have some fun with that worked the night shift at the Howard Johnson's in Cutchogue. It was only a ten-minute drive from the mortuary.

A smile crossed his lips as he remembered a wild night with her several months ago. A guy's got to have some fun every once in a while, he thought to himself, as he got out a pair of brown slacks and the new sweater with the cable stitching that his wife bought on sale at Macy's. He splashed a handful of Canoe on his face and carefully combed his thick, black, wavy hair. Stepping back, Genero looked at himself in the full-length mirror on the closet door. *Not bad for a guy who's just turned forty-two. A little thick around the waist, but other than that . . .*

On the way out the door he popped his head into the living room to tell his wife that he was going out . . . police business . . . don't wait up.

She nodded without looking up from the scarf she was knitting. His two younger boys, the six- and the ten-year-old, were in front of the TV watching the game and didn't notice him leave.

Christ, but she's getting dumpy, he thought, as he started the car. He remembered Francesca Marie as a beautiful woman, with white breasts as hard as Italian marble. And what a cute ass she had! All his friends on the block, including Charlie, used to tell him what a winner he got. That was before she had five kids. Well . . . what did he expect from her? She raised them with no outside help, never complained, and was good to him; always had his dinner ready no matter what time he got home. He loved her, Genero at least knew that. He wasn't going anywhere, but that didn't mean he couldn't screw around now and then.

He stopped the car two blocks away from his house and called the Howard Johnson's in Cutchogue from a pay phone outside the A&P. What luck! His cutie was working tonight and told him she would be off at two. That gave him plenty of time to check out the body at the funeral home, then make it to the Howard Johnson's bar and have a few drinks. She'd be wearing that red miniskirt and wiggling her tight little ass for him while she worked the tables. Smiling, Genero hopped in the car and got onto the Long Island Expressway.

Forty minutes later he got off Highway 25 in Peconic. He found Fourth Street with no difficulty and saw Hoffman's funeral parlor on the corner. It was a big white building with a large sign in gothic lettering over the door. There were lights in the foyer; the rest of the place was dark.

Somebody's got to be inside watching the stiffs, he thought as he got out of the car.

He walked over to the oak door and knocked on it with the wooden handle from his Colt Python. The sound penetrated the night like a cannon shot. Within seconds a security guard, no more than twenty years old, opened the door.

Genero showed the pimple-faced young man in the baggy gray uniform his badge. "I want to see the body of Mary Stevenson," he said gruffly, pushing his large torso past him.

"Er . . . look, I don't know about that. Mr. Hoffman didn't tell me that the police were coming. Maybe I should call him first." He was nervous, unsure of himself.

Genero smiled and said quietly. "You do that. Just show me to the room."

"Sure . . . I guess it's okay. The third door on the left."

As Genero walked down the hallway, he could hear the rent-a-cop picking up the phone. He took the wallet with his badge out of his pants pocket and attached it to the front of his belt.

There was no doubt in his mind that the kid would call the Peconic police as soon as he found out from his boss that he wasn't authorized to be here. Hopefully the first thing they'd see when they came storming in the room would be his badge.

He opened up the third door on the left and went inside. The chamber was dark except for two electric candles lit up next to the casket. The coffin was open and the small lights made the shadows dance across the dead girl's face.

"My God, she's beautiful!" Genero whispered to himself. Normally he was hardened toward death, especially after working twenty years in the South Bronx. Occasionally though, one would get through to him, making him wish he had gone into his brother's construction business instead of becoming a cop.

He touched the girl's cold face, looking for marks; there were none. Next, he ran his hand down to the neck, feeling the windpipe. It was not crushed like the newspaper article said. He carefully pulled up her pink chiffon dress. Probably bought for her high school prom and now she's being buried in it, he thought, tisk-tisking. Pushing down her panties, he found the slits sewn up on both sides of her stomach below the belly button. *A cruel way to die, Mary Stevenson.*

Okay, Charlie, let's see if you're right. He lifted the girl's head and ran his index finger slowly down the back of her neck. She was bony, and he could easily feel the spinal column.

Outside, he could hear voices in the foyer. Genero knew the police had arrived. *That was fast. Don't they have anything better to do than to bother an honest cop trying to do his fucking duty?*

"Well, well," he said to himself, as his finger touched the puncture wound. It was deep enough so that Genero had no trouble putting his entire pinkie inside the hole. *Bingo on this one, Charlie!*

The door to the chamber flew open and two uniformed policemen, holding guns, rushed in. They got into the crouch position, the six-inch barrels of their Smith & Wessons pointing at Genero's chest.

"Put your hands on top of your head!" one of them barked at him.

Genero laughed but did as he was told.

The other cop, young, with straight, short black hair and a trimmed mustache, looked down at the body and saw that her dress was pulled up past her waist. Turning red with anger, he cocked his revolver and stuck it next to Genero's ear. "You're one sick, fucking bastard! You get your jollies from doing it with dead people?"

Again Genero laughed. "Do I look like that kind of guy? You boys haven't been telling the truth about Mary Stevenson. At least have the decency to plug up the hole in back of her neck before you bury her."

The ringing of the phone woke Charlie out of a deep sleep. He was still on the couch and still naked. The TV set was on. It was late; he could tell that by the cheaply made commercial that was showing on the tube: a Jewish lawyer wearing a 1970s large lapel sport jacket and a wide tie was talking in Spanish about how little he charges to get amnesty for his clients.

Feeling cold, he went into the bedroom, wrapped himself in a blanket, then picked up the phone.

"You up, scumbag?" the voice on the line said.

"Hey, Genero, what's up?" Charlie asked, clearing the sleep from his voice.

"Well, I'm so glad one of us was sleepin'. I just spent three hours in jail and another hour on the phone with the police commissioner."

Charlie snapped awake. "What did you find?"

"You hit a home run, Charlie, my man! Mary Stevenson has a nice big hole in her neck, approximately one inch down from the back of her head. This whole town's in an uproar over this. She was a nice kid—a high school student from an upper-middle-class family. They found the girl shackled to a vine, like it was J.C. himself."

"That part wasn't in the papers," Charlie said, excited.

"No shit! Like you said, *stupido*, they kept the real way she died and how they found her under wraps so they'd be able to sift through the crazies. It's out now, though . . . especially after I told them that there was a similar death up in Northern California. The FBI was even called in—just in case there's a serial who's jumpin' states."

After they hung up, Charlie laid back on his bed and wondered how he was going to tell Rena. *Shit! Just tell her and let the cards fall!*

He dialed her number, and when he heard her sleep-filled voice, he said, "Before you hang up, just answer me one ques-

71

tion—Was the puncture wound found along the top part of the neck? You never told me that."

He could hear her deep, disturbed sigh on the other end. Then she said, "Yes, between the first and second vertebra. How did you know?"

"The girl from Long Island died by penetration from a sharp instrument that punctured the same area. Her body was then strapped to a grapevine," he said, as gently as he could.

"I see." After several seconds of silence she whispered, "Look, I'm sorry about tonight. I don't usually fly off the handle like that. It's been a hard couple of days."

"I know that."

"I don't think I want to be alone right now. Not after what you just told me. What are you doing, Charlie?" Her voice sounded tired.

"Hanging out."

After a beat, she said, "My house or yours?"

Charlie smiled. The inevitable breakup was being put off, at least for tonight. "Yours," he said. He already had one leg in his jeans.

As he locked the front door and got into his Mustang, he thought to himself, No I don't want the pain from being too close to her, but then again I don't want to be without her either. *Shit, with or without her there's going to be pain in your life. Get used to it, Charlie, my boy.*

He pulled out of his driveway and turned west toward Brentwood.

Chapter Seven

MAURA AWOKE TO a familiar smell, one that she remembered from years ago. *Strong . . . caustic . . . vinegary.* The name of it was on the tip of her tongue but she couldn't think of what it was called.

A vision of her high-school hallway crowded with students rushing to the next class loomed up in her head for a second then receded back again into the dark part of her memory. She didn't know why but that image from her past and the odor that permeated the air were intertwined.

Where am I? she said to herself.

Her eyes tried to focus. She was in a semi-dark room, and the aluminum sky outside streaked through the edges of the paper window shade. There was a constant *rat-ta-tat-tat* sound gently hitting the window. It had to be rain, she thought.

She could sense that she was lying on a soft, lumpy mattress that sagged in the middle. The bedspread with little cotton balls on it covered her body like a shroud.

This is not my bedroom! What is this place? Panic began to rise within her.

She threw off the bedspread and sat up. A wave of dizziness engulfed her, and her mouth felt terribly dry. Her arms were hurting something awful, and when she looked down at them she saw reddish-blue bruises. Was I in a fight? she wondered.

Resting her head on her knees and closing her eyes, she waited until the light-headed feeling went away.

As she put her fingers up to her face, the familiar smell got stronger. She realized that the odor was coming from her hands.

What was I touching?

When she felt better she got up. Steadying herself by holding onto the night table, she walked slowly over to the window. She pulled down the shade to open it and it suddenly sprung up, startling her as it wrapped itself around the wooden dowel with a loud *flap, flap, flap*.

She saw that it *was* raining outside; nothing hard, just a steady drizzle. The windows were dirty, but she could see long stretches of redwoods.

Something was very wrong!

She made her way to the stained pine door, pushed down on the cast-iron handle and threw it open. Rushing outside, she turned full circle hoping to see something familiar. The rain came down on her face and began drenching her body.

"Where am I?" she screamed.

The house was a small, one-room cabin. Who did it belong to? She had never seen it before.

This place was also unknown to her; it was too green and the trees were different than the ones in Napa. These were redwoods—not madrona and oak. Looking out in the distance, she could see patches of sawed off trees dotting the landscape.

She put her face up to the rain hoping that the cool downpour would help defog her brain. The image of her beloved spring hidden away in the hills of Napa appeared in her head. She remembered going to it . . . taking off her robe . . . wading . . . the warm water caressing her burning skin. Then she recalled the knife! Then the blood—lots of it; its salty smell stinging her nostrils!

After that, nothing . . . until now.

Had she blacked out again? *Oh, God! How bad this time?*

She went back into the cabin.

There was a throbbing ache in the back of her head. Did she take the Darvocet with her? Then she saw her purse on top of the varnished pine dresser. Trembling from the cold rain, she turned the purse upside down. Her wallet fell out along with keys to a car and several credit-card receipts from American Express and Visa. Frenzied, she shook the bag hard. There was no Darvocet.

"Christ!" she screamed, banging her fist on the wall. "Make this pain stop!"

Her eyes began to blur from the agony. She wanted to put her head down on a pillow and close her eyes, rest, but she was afraid that if she did she would go back into the darkness again.

No, let the pain stay. Let it keep me awake.

She looked into her wallet. There was some money—perhaps sixty-five dollars—and her credit cards. Then she picked up the car keys. There was an Alamo tag holding both keys together. What was she doing with these? The car she rented in San Francisco was from Hertz.

The credit-card receipts! They might tell her where she'd been. She wiped away the water that was dripping down from her wet hair into her eyes and tried concentrating on the names and addresses printed on the carbon copies. There were five of them:

Alamo Car Rental: Two hundred and sixty-three dollars per week—Fort Bragg, California.

K mart: One hundred and thirty-five dollars and seventy-three cents—Fort Bragg, California.

Café Beaujolais: Twenty-three dollars—Mendocino, California.

Heritage House: One hundred and seventy-five dollars—Mendocino, California.

Thomson Realtors: Sixty-five dollars—Fortuna, California.

The earliest date was from Alamo; that was on the 17th. How did she get to Fort Bragg? That's three hours from Napa! Did she drive all the way? If she did, then what happened to her Hertz rental car?

Thomson Realtors appeared to be the most recent—September 19th. Was it for the rental of this cabin?

How could that be? she thought, confused. She arrived in Napa on the 17th. That was two days ago! Could she have blacked out for two days? She must have; it was *her* signature on the receipts.

Fear overshadowed the pain. Maybe it was even longer than two days; there was no way of telling unless she could find out today's date. She also needed to call Rena and Uncle Wiggly and try to explain to them what happened. They must be terribly worried by now.

Maura looked for a phone in the room. There was none.

Why did I go to Mendocino? Why Fortuna? That's near Eureka.

She grabbed the car keys. Perhaps the rental car was outside.

Going out into the rain again, she followed a pathway leading to the back of the house.

A '90 white Ford station wagon with dark-tinted windows and an Alamo sticker on the bumper was under a carport attached to the cabin.

Why would I rent a large car like that? she wondered.

She opened the driver's door, got in, and unlocked the glove compartment. Pushing the car's manual aside, she picked up the rental agreement and looked at it. Her name was on it.

She got out, went around to the back, and opened the rear door. Other than a spare tire and a jack, nothing. *Wait . . . what's that in the back, tucked away in the shadows?* She reached in and pulled out a folded white sheet with dark stains. As she unrolled it, the spots brightened to the color of dried blood. She could feel hard objects somewhere inside. *A little more unwinding and it would be open. There!* Terror overtook her body like the feel of thousands of hair-legged insects crawling over her flesh, and she backed away. Inside the sheet was a bloodsplattered ball-peen hammer, a six-inch spike, and a sharp, bloodied surgical knife.

She slammed the trunk shut.

Why were these in the car? She knew all about these tools.

Christ, she had read about them enough times in de Montret's journal!

The rain was coming down faster now, and she began to shiver. Holding her arms for warmth, she made her way back into the cabin.

Inside, she quickly took off her drenched flannel nightgown and wrapped her naked body in the bedspread.

Her eyes focused on the nightgown on the floor. She realized that it didn't belong to her. It was made of a cheap flannel fabric that was not her taste.

She went to the closet and opened it. There were several hangers containing inexpensive cotton blouses and skirts. Everything was in her size, and most of the tags were still on them, all marked K mart. There was something else hanging at the end of the closet. When she saw what it was, a swell of fear overtook her and her legs almost gave in. She held onto the door for support and found it hard to breathe. After a few moments she began to feel better, and she looked over to the end of the closet again. What she saw on the hanger was a leather miniskirt with black stockings folded up in its pocket. Yes, she remembered that outfit well. How could she ever forget it?

Maura's eyes moved back to the cheap clothing on the hangers. She was forced to wear garments like these when she was a child. Her father didn't have the money to buy her anything better. She remembered the stiff sizing on the shirts and how they'd cut into her skin whenever she put them on. Why would she buy these now?

There was that smell again.

Looking up, she saw a shelf with a glass jar containing a clear fluid. There were things floating in the liquid. She reached up and brought it down. It was too dark to see clearly so she turned on the lamp next to the dresser.

Yes, now she could see better. There were grayish round things the size of marbles suspended in the solution. The larger ones seemed to have strings attached to them.

She placed the jar on the dresser and unscrewed the cap. The familiar smell came rushing up to meet her.

Formaldehyde!

Now she remembered: her high-school biology lab. She used to immerse her hands inside a jar filled with formaldehyde like this and pull out the dead frogs for dissection.

Suddenly she recoiled in horror. *If formaldehyde was used to*

76

*preserve dead things, then what's floating in this jar? Did the
bloodied scalpel in the car have anything to do with this?*

No, she didn't want to know!

A wave of nausea overtook her, and she put her hands up to
her mouth. The smell was strongest on her hands, and she started
to retch, coughing up phlegm and bile.

My God! she thought. *I must have had my hands in there!
What are they?*

Wiping her mouth with the bedspread, she moved closer to
the jar to get a better look. What she took to be strings on the
oval shapes before now looked like strips of skin. The shapes
were parts of animals. Perhaps glands, she couldn't tell for sure.

No, I don't want to know!

Suddenly a wave of tiredness overtook her. The ache in her
head eased into a distant throbbing. She needed to sleep, but she
was afraid.

I've got to sort this all out or I'll go mad! she said to herself.

Maura collapsed on the mattress. With the bedspread wrapped
around her, she crawled into a fetal position.

*No, mustn't fall asleep. Sleep brings on the darkness and things
happen in the dark.*

Piercing lights of different colors bounced around in her head;
then Martin with his dark, haunting eyes floated through her
mind.

Oh, Martin. Please come back. Please . . .

Wax from seventeen candles quickly melting on pink-and-
white icing . . . white balloons Scotch-taped to pink crepe paper.
Bodies entwined, rhythmically swaying to "Nights in White
Satin" . . . French-kissing in dark corners of the den. Girls hud-
dling near the potato chips, giggling, chattering . . . boys clus-
tering together on the other side of the room, passing around the
Rock 'n' Rye, talking about the '49ers, while at the same time
taking quick, catlike glances at the girls.

A hand reaches out for her. Martin. She takes it and they try
to sneak out. Everyone sees . . . a few even snicker.

Running across the field, past the vineyards, past the red ma-
dronas and the oak trees and the yellow grass. Laughter fills their
lungs.

The old winery up on the hill is made of heavy blocks of stone.
Her heart pounds wildly from fear and craving as Martin opens
the large wooden doors.

No, No! Too dangerous!

He takes her hand. She follows.

Laying on the cold cement floor, looking up she sees the wooden beams crisscrossing, making diamond-shaped patterns on the ceiling. Rice hulls and crushed grape skins stick to her hair. The odor of sweet, pungent wine fermenting in oak barrels . . . the steady hum of motors.

Martin's face now over hers, breathing heavy. Kissing her mouth, her neck. The taste of Rock 'n' Rye and Clorets on his lips . . . the smell of Aqua Velva on his clothing.

Stroking her breasts, her nipples.

Stop, Martin, stop! Not here!

Opening the top part of her dress. Kissing . . . touching . . . sucking. His fingers now on her knee moving upward.

Trying to push his hand away . . . Please, Martin . . . no! He presses on. He loves her, she knows that. He has loved her since they were children. She must trust someone other than Uncle Wiggly and Daddy. She relents.

A gasp of pleasure bursts from her lips, and she throws her arms around his neck.

His hand reaches the top of her underpants and pulls them down. Fingers circling her inner thigh, working their way up to her pubis, then to the silky patch of blond hair.

Her eyes close. Moans of I love you, Martin! I love you! Thank you for loving me, for not caring . . .

Maura tried opening her eyes but they remained closed. She wanted to get up, leave this strange cabin with its stench of formaldehyde, and go home. Her arms and legs felt like heavy steel pipes; they wouldn't move no matter how hard she tried. As she descended into the darkness, she prayed that she would wake up in her Soho loft and discover that this was nothing but a horrible nightmare.

TWO

Chapter Eight

SHARP, WHIPLIKE CRACKS of lightning started around five in the morning, followed by a violent cloudburst. The gutters and spouts on Rena's roof were clogged with leaves from the trees above her house, causing the water to come cascading down on her deck outside her bedroom. It woke her from a restless sleep.

Early for this time of year, she thought, rubbing her eyes. September meant Santa Ana winds and hot weather in L.A., not rain. She was angry at herself for putting off hiring a handyman to clean out the gutters.

Just as well. Charlie has an eight o'clock plane to catch. Better leave early so we don't get caught in traffic. Charlie was lying next to her, sleeping with his head under the covers.

She rolled over to his side of the bed, lifted the blanket off his face, and ran her fingers through his hair. "Hey, get up," she whispered in his ear. "We have to get you to Paris."

"Screw Paris," he groaned, pulling the covers back over his head.

"Come on, Charlie." She put her naked body against his back and rubbed the inside of her leg along his thigh. "Get up."

Charlie peeked one eye out from under the blanket, grinned, and said, "Guess what?"

Rena reached over his stomach, felt him and said, "Hmm . . . so you are."

He turned around and they automatically came together. They made love slowly and silently—partly because her daughter's bedroom was just down the hall, but also because that's the way they liked doing it in the morning, with the heat from their bodies trapped under the thick down comforter.

"It's nice going slow like this, Charlie," she moaned softly. *Different . . . warm . . . wet.*

81

They usually had sex in his apartment, and it was always like a turbulent vortex: ripping clothes off of each other's bodies; scratching . . . clawing . . . biting; sweaty suctional sounds from bellies pounding together and coming apart. Their lovemaking always seemed like it was for the moment, the possibility that this was not going to happen again added a special thrill.

She was attracted to Charlie right from the first. In fact, she had never known any other man except her husband, Terry, that could turn her on like this. These feelings frightened her just as she knew they frightened Charlie. Her biggest fear was that these powerful emotions might rise up like a tidal wave one day and completely devour her. It had happened before when she was married to Terry. The passionate love she felt for that man; then the terrible pain when she found out about the other women; and finally the agony of divorce. It had almost destroyed her. Like Charlie, she also vowed never to let it happen again. Intellectually she knew that these feelings were wrong. Because of the anguish she had known with Terry, she believed that loving a man totally was the ultimate enslavement. Was there such a thing as passion without shackles? She didn't know, but Charlie came the closest of any other man to that experience.

At first she thought it was safe to have an affair with him because they were so different from one another; their life-styles and upbringings were worlds apart. She was reared in luxury that most girls only dreamed about. Charlie grew up differently: he was orphaned at a young age and raised by his strict Catholic aunt in a blue-collar section of Brooklyn. The streets were his home, not country clubs and charity balls.

Rena knew that what they had between them might only be temporary; she realized that there probably would be other lovers. But right now, what they had was good, and she was not ready to toss it away because of her mistrust of intimacy.

They made love for a long time this morning, oblivious to the raging downpour outside.

Two hours later they said good-bye in the Bradley International Terminal at LAX. As she watched the back of his head disappear into the cabin of an *Air France* 747, she bit down on her lower lip trying to force back the tears.

Damn, but I'm going to miss him! she thought.

At least there was one consolation: he was only going to Paris for a month to attend a dreary conference on oil pricing. Normally he'd be going off to some country that few people have ever heard of, reporting about wars and other forms of pestilence. Sometimes he'd come back from these assignments pale and shaken from the things he had seen. When that happened, he usually picked up a half-gallon of J&B on his way back from the airport, locked himself in his apartment, and didn't talk to anyone for a week.

Outside the terminal the rain was still coming down heavy. Rena took La Cienaga Boulevard back into Hollywood in order to avoid the gridlock on the freeways.

Station KROS was a pink art-deco structure erected during the early part of the forties and located on Sunset and Gower. For the last four years Rena worked there three days a week as a radio-talk-show psychologist. During that time she built up a huge following and her program was on the verge of being syndicated throughout the country.

She was early, which was fine with her because she needed to go over today's program. Along with taking calls from her listeners and giving them psychological advice on the air, she would also discuss different ways to cope with the stress of everyday living. Today she wanted to talk about sexual mistreatment of females in the workplace and how to deal with it.

When she got out of the elevator on the fifth floor, one of the secretaries stopped her and told her that three men were waiting to see her in the conference room.

"Did they have an appointment?" Rena asked curiously.

"No. They talked to the station manager."

Interesting, Rena thought. No one was allowed this kind of access during the day of a show. She wondered if it had anything to do with Maura.

She immediately got her answer when she entered the conference room and saw Pinky Swangel's big, toothy grin. Looking uncomfortable, he was seated around the rectangular marble table along with two well-dressed men in suits. One of the men had his hair combed in the style of John F. Kennedy. They stood up as she came in.

"Hi ya, Rena," Pinky said warmly, the smile still pasted on his face.

"Pinky, what are you doing here?" she asked, surprised to see him.

"We need to talk with you, Rena." His tone was pensive and the smile faded.

"You've found Maura," she whispered, expecting the worst.

Pinky shook his head, no.

Rena looked over at the middle-aged man with the Kennedy haircut. He took out a leather folder with his picture and Federal ID inside. He introduced himself as Agent Marvin Grant with the FBI.

The other man, the one with the deep tan, wiry white hair, and gold Rolex on his freckled wrist, grabbed her hand and shook it heartily. He displayed a wide smile. "I'm Ray Scollari, district attorney of Brooklyn."

What's Scollari doing here? she wondered as she put her purse and attaché case down on the chair.

"We won't be very long," Grant said, smiling.

"Coffee, gentlemen?" Rena said, moving over to the Krupps machine on the shelf.

The three men shook their heads. Rena took a mug from the tray and filled it with coffee; she wanted to be as alert as possible. "You're a long way from Brooklyn," she said, turning to Ray.

Smiling, he shook his head. "If one of my people is in trouble, I don't leave them hanging."

His cagey eyes reminded her of a wild ferret. Rena instinctively distrusted him.

"You *are* an intimate friend of Maura McKinney," Grant said.

"I'm a friend. I don't know if you can call it intimate." He wasn't asking, he was making a statement, Rena realized. She sat down on the leather chair directly opposite them and put her cup on the marble table.

Pinky shifted his huge body anxiously around in a chair that was too small for him. Rena knew his uneasiness was due to being around men of Scollari's and Grant's stature.

"We know that she was supposed to meet you in Napa and didn't show. Has she gotten in touch with you since then?" Ray casually inquired.

"No, she hasn't," Rena answered, amazed at the question.

"Do you have any idea where she may be?" Grant asked, leaning forward and resting his elbows on the table.

"No, I don't, Mr. Grant. Can you tell me what this is all about?" she responded firmly.

"You know Sheriff Swangel, so I assume you must have some inkling." He pointed his thumb at Pinky, and Pinky turned a deep shade of red.

"I presume we're talking about the murder of Tomas Sanchez in Napa and, perhaps, the girl on Long Island?"

"That is correct."

"Obviously you feel that Maura's involved in some way or you wouldn't be here," Rena said, taking another sip of the coffee. She was tired and she wished the damn caffeine would kick in.

"We're pretty sure that she *is* involved," Grant said.

"Why is that? Up until a minute ago I was under the illusion that Maura was still considered a possible victim. What evidence do you have that says differently?" Rena could feel the beating of her heart.

Pinky and the agent looked at each other, then at Ray. They all nodded silently as if a silent agreement had been reached among them.

"All right, we'll tell you what we know and perhaps you can help us in return," Grant said.

"How?"

"We need a psychological profile on her."

"I'm sure you have psychiatrists connected with the bureau who do things like that," she said. "Maura also worked closely, as far as I know, with Mr. Scollari for a number of years in the prosecutor's office. He may be able to help you better than I can."

"Our affiliation was on a professional level only," Scollari said, again with that smile and animal stare. "Personal lives were kept separate. As a prosecutor she was excellent. As an individual . . . well . . ." Ray finished the statement with a shrug of his shoulders. "She seemed distant, cold, sometimes displaying a violent temper." He held out his bandaged wrist for everyone to see. "She did this with her nails the night before she left for California. We were having dinner together. I simply asked her to join my campaign committee, that's all. I'm running for mayor in the spring. She automatically assumed I wanted something else from her and went absolutely crazy. Do you believe this? Eight stitches. Caused a terrible scene in the restaurant."

"Did you?" Rena asked.

"Did I what?"

"Did you want something else from her?"

His paternal attitude quickly disappeared and the ferret look came back strong. "That's uncalled for." His tan turned to a red flush.

"I believe I have the right to ask," Rena stated simply.

"Then allow me the right to answer." He leaned toward her.

"The answer is an unequivocal 'no.' I'm a happily married man. All I wanted was her support and hard work in the primaries."

"And when you asked her for those things, she actually became enraged?" she asked skeptically.

"Yes, she became enraged. In fact, that's putting it mildly." His lips were strung tightly across his teeth. "Also, as far as I could tell, I don't believe she liked men very much. I've known her for years and never saw her with a man."

"None as far as you know," she said curtly. "Many professional people prefer to keep their sex lives out of the office." She'd be damned if she was going to discuss Maura's sexual life with someone like him.

Ray sat back in his chair with a smug, knowing look. It bothered her. From the corner of her eyes she saw the anger in Pinky's face directed toward Scollari.

"What we're trying to bring out is that you're not only a close friend of hers but you're also a psychologist. That gives *you* the edge in knowing the internal workings of Maura McKinney better than we do," Grant said, holding his hand up to stop Scollari from saying anything more.

Rena thought for a few seconds, wondering if she would be betraying Maura in any way. *No*, she finally realized. *If Maura did commit these grisly murders, then she's got to be stopped.* "All right, tell me what you know," she said to Grant.

Grant leaned back and said, "On September seventeenth, Tomas Sanchez was murdered in the wine fields belonging to Miss Maura McKinney. A spike, approximately one-half inch in diameter, was driven between the first and second vertebra, severing the spinal cord. On September the fifteenth, Mary Stevenson, a high school senior, was also murdered in the same way and with the same weapon. Like the farm worker, her arms and feet were tied to a vine, giving the appearance of a crucifixion."

"How can you be sure that it was the same weapon? Do you have it in your possession?" she asked.

"No ma'am. It was a three-edged spike with a deep nick on one of the edges. Both victims had the same markings in their wounds with that particular indent. There was also the presence of the same metal filings in the two puncture wounds. Plus, the cuts along the pelvic area of the woman and the deep slits in the scrotum of the male appear to be made with the same sharp instrument.

"Why Maura?" she whispered, not wanting to hear the answer.

Pinky began to fidget in his chair causing it to creak.

Grant continued. "Traces of identical blond hairs were found under the nails of Tomas Sanchez and Mary Stevenson. There were also the same skin fragments discovered under the nails. Obviously the victims put up some sort of struggle. The strands of hair were literally ripped from someone's head which enabled our lab to test for blood particles. The blood grouping found on the hair was B-positive; that makes up ten percent of the population. According to the American Red Cross, which Maura McKinney donated to regularly, she was B-positive. That automatically knocks out ninety percent of the populace as suspects. Hair samples taken from the sheets on her bed in her New York loft were an identical match to the ones found on the victims. We're waiting for the DNA fingerprinting results to get back from Washington. With that, we'll have definitive proof that Maura McKinney is the killer."

"How could she be in different places across the country in that short period? She was a city prosecutor with a heavy schedule." Rena noticed that her voice was quivering.

"It's possible," Grant said gravely. "The murder on Long Island took place before Maura McKinney left for California. The north fork of the island is only an hour-and-a-half drive from the Soho district where she lives in Manhattan."

"What else?" Rena asked. *Jesus Christ! There had to be more.*

"The porter at Santa Rosa's bus station in Northern California remembers a blond woman answering to Maura McKinney's description buying a ticket the night of the 17th to Fort Bragg. Our San Francisco office checked the motels and car-rental companies. An American Express card in her name was used to rent a Ford station wagon in Fort Bragg. She then stayed at a hotel in Mendocino called the Heritage House. She used her Visa card to pay for that."

"It's the same hotel that the movie, *Same Time, Next Year,* was filmed in," Scollari said, smiling.

Who gives a shit! Rena thought, glaring at Scollari.

Grant continued in his staccato voice. "Her credit cards were also used to pay for restaurants in Mendocino. The last thing we have is an American Express receipt from a realtor in Fortuna, California who rented McKinney a cabin. We have samples of her handwriting and signature taken from her office in New York;

it matches perfectly with those on the credit-card receipts. For some reason she's heading north. Why, we don't know, but we have men posted in Eureka and along the Oregon border.''

Rena let out a quiet sigh. Where was Maura going? she wondered. *Why north?* She rubbed her eyes; the first cup of coffee wasn't making it. This was turning into a nightmare. She went over to the Krupps and refilled her mug.

''I think you should tell her what you found out about the female victim,'' Ray said to Grant. Again he had a self-assured look on his face.

''She was a known lesbian and frequented local gay bars on Long Island.''

''Mary Stevenson was only seventeen,'' Rena said. ''How was she allowed into bars?''

''She got in the same way most high school kids get into bars—with a false ID. The girl was tiny—just over five feet, and weighed less than one hundred and fifteen pounds. The bartender at the Pink Monkey, a gay bar in East Hampton, remembers seeing her leaving the place on the night of September the fifteenth with a beautiful woman with long blond hair. He identified Maura McKinney from a photograph I showed him taken off her driver's license.''

Rena looked away from Ray. She didn't want to see his haughty stare.

''Anything else?'' she asked them.

''That's what we have right now,'' Grant said.

''Then I guess it's my turn,'' she said. The large conference room suddenly felt claustrophobic, as if there weren't enough air in the room for all of them.

The three men waited.

''Did you know she may have been on a medication called Parnate?'' she said finally.

''Yes,'' Grant said. ''We found the vial in her room, along with your fingerprints on it.''

Nothing gets past you guys, does it? she thought. ''Then I'm sure you already know that it's an antidepressant.''

Grant nodded. ''Yes, but we can't figure out how she got it. There's never been a prescription given out by any doctor in her name.''

''That's *very* strange,'' Rena said surprised. ''Parnate may not be habit-forming, but the government has laws regulating its dispensation.'' She then told them how long she had known Maura and how they met. "When we were young we spent our summers together. Then we went off to college and started our professional careers on different coasts. We only saw each other again for a short time when we vacationed together in Greece. But," she said, staring at Ray Scollari, "when we were growing up together I never found her to be distant or cold. Private perhaps, but that was her prerogative." That wasn't altogether true, though, she suddenly remembered: in Greece she *was* sullen and withdrawn.

Smiling, Ray shrugged in a way that said, "The facts speak for themselves."

Rena could sense the hate Scollari had for Maura. She was beginning to believe that he actually came to L.A. to bury her, not to help her. She would have to watch what she said in front of him.

"Did she have any lovers or boyfriends?" Ray asked, arching his eyebrows.

"Yes . . . when she was growing up in Napa. I don't know who she saw when she was living in New York."

"Who was her childhood beau?" Grant asked, taking out a pad and pen from his jacket pocket.

"Martin Bynum."

"What happened to him?"

"He's dead. Killed by a burglar in his home when Maura was seventeen."

Pinky coughed.

"Was the killer ever apprehended?" Grant asked.

"No. Her father was the prime suspect at the time."

"Interesting," Ray said, feigning surprise.

"How did it affect her?" Grant said, put off by Scollari's attitude.

"Like it would affect most seventeen-year-olds, I suppose. Perhaps more with her. She was in the house when it happened."

"What part of the house?" Grant asked.

"The bedroom."

"Were they making love at the time?" Ray inquired.

"I suppose. What difference does it make?" she said sharply. "Martin heard a noise in his parent's bedroom. He went to look. A few seconds later there was a shotgun blast. Maura was dozing off in Martin's bed at the time. The sound awoke her and she got up to see what happened. She discovered his body. Yes, I certainly would say it affected her. It would affect anyone who found their lover with his head blown away. They were very close.

Maura had loved Martin since they were children. There was never even the thought of another man in her life." She looked at Ray and saw his mouth twitch with anger. "When he died . . . well . . ." Rena paused, recalling that trying time. "I can only give you a third-person hearsay since I went back to Los Angeles to finish up my last year of high school the day after it happened. I tried writing to her but she wouldn't answer any of my letters. I was told by some of the locals that she stayed mostly alone and hibernated in her house. She would go to school, but that was it. Only four weeks after Martin's death her father died in an automobile accident. He was inebriated. When I returned to Napa the next summer I found out that she had already left for New York. We didn't see each other again until we both graduated from college and met in Greece."

"How'd she do with the men in Greece?" Ray asked.

"I'm afraid I don't understand your question," Rena said curtly. She stood up, leaned against the wall, folded her arms, and glared at Scollari.

"No American girl goes to Greece, especially to the islands to look at ruins," Ray said, smiling.

"Perhaps no girls that *you* would know, Mr. Scollari. Maura happened to like ruins. She was different . . . brilliant . . . inquisitive. She received a degree in Roman-Greco history from Columbia."

"Odd that she would change horses in midstream and get a law degree," Grant said.

"I think multitalented would be a better word than odd. Some people *do* have more than one interest. Da Vinci managed to construct canals and fortifications in his spare time between painting The Last Supper and the Mona Lisa." Rena looked up at the clock. "Gentlemen, I have to be on the air in forty-five minutes. If you like I can write up a psychological profile on her and fax it to you."

The three men, as if on cue, stood up.

"That would be helpful, Miss Halbrook. If we do happen to find her and *if* there's some reason that we may need your help during that time, would you be available?" Grant asked her.

Help in what way? Rena wondered. Then she understood: to talk to Maura into giving up, in case she blockaded herself in a house or had hostages. "Yes, I'll be available if you find Maura," she said with a dry mouth.

"I'm leaving for San Francisco to talk with their police department. Hopefully, we'll find her before someone else turns up dead,'' Scollari said, straightening his tie around his starched collar. The overhead light picked up the reflection off his gold Rolex. "As I said, I don't let my people hang without helping them."

Yeah, right, Mr. Scollari, Rena said to herself, watching him leave the conference room.

"It's been a hell of a week," Pinky said with a heavy breath. He was visibly upset. "You let me know when you're coming back up to Napa, you hear?" He grabbed both of her arms in his paw-like hands and gave them a gentle squeeze. Then he leaned into her and whispered, "That guy Scollari is one hell of an asshole, ain't he?"

Rena smiled at his remark. Pinky had said to her the first day she saw him that he would never tell which one of them he had a crush on as a kid. It had to be Maura. Yes, definitely Maura. He gets red as a beet and sweat breaks out on his brow every time her name is mentioned. "One question, Pinky. Has anyone figured out why the trail of blood stopped so abruptly next to Maura's spring."

"Yeah, we think so. At least the boys from Washington think they do," he said, turning his head in the direction of Grant, who was waiting outside. "Tomas Sanchez was either dragged by someone or crawled by himself those few feet. Then a tarp or something was probably wrapped around him so the murderer wouldn't get soaked with his blood. It looks like he was carried the distance to the vineyards."

"How do you know?"

"Footprints." He put his hand on Rena's shoulder and said somberly, "Sets of shoeless footprints beginning at the area where the blood stopped were deeply cut into the wet soil around the spring. That's where she picked Sanchez up and carried him. The prints belonged to a woman. They were a size seven, the same size as Maura's shoes that we found in her room. Hell, Rena, I'm sorry about all this. You know I'd give anything if it wasn't her." He looked despondent and tired.

"I know that, Pinky. It's still a long distance for a woman or anyone else for that matter to carry someone."

"You saw that idiot, Scollari's wrist, didn't you? She dug her nails all the way into it. He told us he tried breaking her grip but couldn't. He said that he never met a woman as strong as her before." He looked over to Scollari and saw the impatient expression painted on his face as he held the elevator door open waiting for him. "I guess I got to go. I wish these guys would get out of my county so I can go back to scraping upscale drunks off of Highway 128. I'm good at that."

Rena kissed Pinky on the cheek and told him she'd call him.

When they were gone, Rena went into her office and locked the door. So many thoughts and emotions were stirring inside her head. She took a yellow legal pad from her file cabinet and made a list of questions:

1) How badly did Martin's death affect Maura's psyche?
   a: Did the anger over his death transform itself into a psychosis?
   b: If so, why didn't I see it?
2) Why did she drop her art studies? She loved Grecian art almost as much as she did Martin.
3) The murders: bodies draped over vines . . . sexual organs removed. Happened during the harvesting of the grapes. Was there something ceremonial about all this?
   a: If it was ritualism, does it have a base in history?
4) Knowledge of the human anatomy and skill with surgical tools essential in order to perform the castrations. Where did Maura learn this?
5) Both victims were slight of build. Why? Was it because it was easier for a tall woman like Maura to overpower them and move the bodies?
6) Why a lesbian? Was she one herself or did she have a hate for homosexuals . . . or perhaps a gay bar was the easiest place to choose a female victim?

Rena tapped the pencil on the desktop and leaned back in her chair. *Shit, Maura! What happened to you? What kind of cancerous hate had built up inside you for all these years to make you kill like this?* Bits and pieces of memories about Maura in Athens began reassembling themselves in her head.

"Oh my God, that's her!" Rena screamed, when she saw Maura getting off the tram bus that took the passengers from the tarmac into the customs area of the Athens terminal. She jumped up and down, waving frantically, until Maura saw her.

She's changed, she thought, as she watched Maura take out her passport and hand it to the Greek official. There was some-

92

thing older and more pensive about her face than there was before, and the fire that used to burn in her eyes seemed dimmed.

After Maura cleared customs, Rena rushed over to her and threw her arms around her neck. They hugged and giggled.

"You're even prettier than you were five years ago!" Maura said, stepping back and looking at Rena.

"Compared to you I'd be lucky if someone even noticed I was alive," Rena said teasingly. It was hard to believe, but Maura had grown more beautiful.

Arm in arm they walked through the Athens airport, talking over each other's sentences, trying to bridge the five-year gap.

After retrieving Maura's suitcases, they took a cab to their hotel near Omonia Square. Their room overlooked the noisy shopping section of Stadiou Street. When Rena opened the window to let in air, the sounds and smells of Athens came soaring into their room to greet them.

"I love you, Athena!" Rena shouted to the polluted sky, raising her fists in the air.

Maura went over to the window, put her arm around Rena's shoulder, and looked down at the dirty street with vendors hawking their wares. "I don't think this is what Athena had in mind when her subjects built the Acropolis for her as a sanctuary," she said with academic authority.

"What's a little dirt!" Rena said, laughing. "What counts is that we're both twenty-one and finally free from those goddamn scholastic obligations!" She went over to the bed and plopped down. "Three glorious weeks! Just the two of us looking at ruins and sunbathing on Greek islands. What more could we want?"

Maura didn't answer; she continued to stare out at the crowded street below. There was a shadow of sadness around her eyes, and Rena couldn't help but notice it.

If Maura wants to talk about what's bothering her, she will. Don't rush it, Rena thought.

That evening they sat in the open-air theater of Herodes Atticus and listened to the works of Chopin played by the Athens State Orchestra. The night was extraordinarily balmy, and even the full moon managed to break through the thick polluted sky encasing everything it touched in its yellow glow. Rena closed her eyes and leaned her head back on Maura's stomach, letting the music overwhelm her senses. It was a night she didn't want to end.

The next day they woke early. They wanted to get to the National Archaeological Museum before it became jammed with tourists.

Once inside the large museum, Rena somehow got separated from Maura. She had become so entranced in the abundance of early artifacts that when she finally looked up, her friend was not by her side. Rena retraced her steps through the crowded, winding hallways. Eventually she found her in a dimly lit, deserted room on the third floor.

Maura was staring, almost trancelike, at the ancient statues of the fertility gods: Eros, Psyche, Aphrodite, and Priapus. Over in the corner, standing alone, was a primordial bronze statuette showing Zeus with four rows of breasts.

Even though the temperature was soaring outside, Rena felt a chill in this room.

"Maura," Rena said, walking over to her and tapping her on the shoulder.

She didn't respond.

"Maura!" For some unexplained reason Rena wanted to get her friend and leave.

Slowly Maura turned. Her eyes, even though they were directed upon Rena, seemed to be focusing inwardly on something.

Then suddenly she smiled. "Yes, Rena, what is it?" she said gently.

"Where were you?"

"Here," she said happily, turning back to the statues. She held her hand out and touched Priapus, with his grotesque head and large phallus. "I feel as if I belong here—that I've finally come home."

Her face glowed in a mask of serenity. Rena had never seen her look as beautiful and as peaceful as she did now.

"If this is home then don't expect me to be paying you too many visits," she said, shuddering from the cold.

Maura laughed, and for a second that fire from her old self was back in her eyes. "I guess that's what happens to you when you break your ass studying about these characters. You begin to feel that they're part of your family," she said jokingly.

After leaving the museum, they bought cheese, pita bread, and a bottle of retsina and climbed to the top of Mount Lycabettus for a picnic. They ate on a hillside next to the chapel of St. George overlooking the city of Athens. The smog was bearable today, and even the mountains of Peloponnesos to the west could be seen.

Holding her glass of wine, Maura walked over to the terrace of the chapel and looked down over the old and new portions of the city. Again her eyes were drawn inward.

Several minutes went by like this; then she said quietly, "Did you know that the original inhabitants of this country worshiped a woman. She was known as the Great Triple Goddess."

"Triple, like in the Christian Trinity?"

"Yes. It's amazing how important the number three plays in theologies. It's as if all religions branched out from each other. Thousands of years ago in pre-Hellenic times the queen each year would take a lover. Then when the year was up he would be sacrificed and his blood poured over the crops. Her priestesses would then eat his flesh. From this cannibalistic ritual sprang the greatness that was Greece." Again silence . . . then, "At least the queen had a year with her lover before she devoured him." Her voice was melancholic.

Is she blaming herself for Martin's death? Rena wondered. "We never talked about Martin," Rena said softly as she walked over to her.

Maura turned to Rena, her face suddenly becoming hard and angry. "That's one subject we don't talk about, understand?"

Rena drew back. She was about to tell her that it would be better to talk about it, but Maura had already started her descent down the mountain.

"Maura . . ." Rena called after her.

Without stopping, Maura screamed back with tears in her eyes, "If you want to be my friend, never mention him again!"

My God! She is blaming herself, she thought as she watched her rush down the steps.

"You got your wish, Maura," Rena said out loud. Martin was never brought up again.

She looked at the pad and underlined the question about ritualisms. If the murders in the wine fields were ceremonial, then how far back did they go? To ancient Greece? Once again Rena remembered the distant look on Maura's face that day in Athens when she described the blood of the queen's lovers being poured over the crops. Grapes were crops, too, weren't they? Was there a similarity between then and now?

She looked at the first question she wrote down, and a sick

feeling began to develop in the pit of her stomach. She underlined it twice:

1) How badly did Martin's death affect Maura's psyche?

This will have to wait, she thought, pushing away the pad. She had a show to do in a few minutes. *I'm going to have to wing it today.* That's all right; she had done it before.

As she left her office and walked down the hall to the radio booth, she knew that the answers to those questions and more were buried somewhere in the Napa hills and possibly even in primeval Greece.

Chapter Nine

ARNIE BAKER CAREFULLY backed his semi into the space outside of Billy's Diner in Yakima, Washington. He wedged it in-between two larger trucks with inches to spare. Damn, but I'm good! he thought. *Best fuckin' trucker in the Northwest!*

Too bad nobody else appreciated his talent. *You're too small, Arnie,* they'd say, shaking their heads. *No way you could get those redwoods from here to Nebraska. What if your truck jackknifes on a deserted stretch of road? Who's going to move those trees? You? Grow a foot and put on a hundred pounds then come back.* Then they'd laugh and Arnie would get pissed, giving them the finger as he walked out of their offices.

"Fuck 'em all!" he said out loud as he grabbed his leather jacket from the back of the truck and hopped out.

Fortunately it was the harvesting season, and Arnie got a job hauling grapes to a winery in Sonoma from a Yakima vineyard. He'd been doing this for the last five years; at least it paid the rent for a couple of months. Except it wasn't lumber he was transporting, and lumber was the test of a real trucker.

Fuck 'em all!

It was nippy out tonight, and the air had a wet feel to it. *Gonna rain. Always rains up here. Would'a stayed put in Yuma, 'cept the place was crawling with too many goddamn Indians! Hell, at least it never rained there!*

Arnie locked the door of his truck, pulled up the collar of his jacket, and went into the diner.

It was almost empty except for three truckers standing around a girl sitting in a booth at the end of the café. It was one-thirty in the morning, and most of the other drivers were asleep in their trucks outside.

He turned around and tried to see what the girl looked like, but one of the men with a beer belly was hovering over her, blocking his view.

No big deal. Just some fifty-dollar hooker, he thought. They hang out in every truck stop across the country.

Arnie ordered the meat loaf with mashed potatoes and a cup of coffee. As he took his jacket off and put it next to him, he glanced up at the shiny aluminum siding of the shelf directly across the counter and saw in it the reflection of the girl in the booth. Nobody was blocking his view from this angle and he could clearly see her. She was a beauty! Long blond hair . . . tall . . . slim body. *Jesus! What the hell was she doin' in a place like this? She could be makin' big bucks workin' in the city.*

The men were leaning over the booth now, talking to her, laughing. She just shook her head like she was uninterested.

Those guys are probably trying to Jew her down on the price. What assholes! A looker like that don't come along every day! If it was me she was talkin' to, I'd give her whatever she wanted!

His meat loaf came, and he drowned it in ketchup to deaden the flavor. He knew meat loaf in diners meant anything left over from the day before, or even the day before that, and he didn't want to have to taste that *anything*.

While eating, he kept looking up at the aluminum shelf to see what was happening. By this time the men had given up on her and gone back to their own booth. The girl seemed to be staring directly his way now. Was that a smile on her face?

Aw, bullshit! He looked back down at his plate. Nothing like that would be smiling at him. Even his wife, Elke, a two-hundred-pound woman he met when he was stationed in Germany during a four-year hitch in the army, wasn't worried that he'd be fooling around on the road. *"Mein klein mensch,* you're too small for

97

other women to love,'' she'd coo to him while he straddled her lap, sucking on those Teutonic breasts of hers.

Arnie's eyes, as if they had minds of their own, involuntarily went back up to the metal shelf.

She was looking at him!

Jeez! Again he turned away. The food began to feel like gummy oatmeal in his mouth, and he had a hard time getting it to slide down his throat. Shit! She was making him too nervous to eat.

Oh Christ! She's getting up and comin' this way!

As she sauntered closer to him, he could see that she was wearing a tight, black leather miniskirt and a black sweater that stretched firmly across her erect nipples. Her legs were long, and her skin looked smooth and inviting.

Oh, man! Arnie peeked at his reflection in the aluminum shelf. With a shaking hand, he quickly fixed some hairs that had fallen out of place in his wavy pompadour and smoothed down his sideburns that came to the edge of his ears. At least he had worn his new, green-checkered flannel shirt with the sleeves rolled up around his biceps. A black panther with red scratch marks was tattooed on his arm, and she couldn't miss seeing it. Stiffening his biceps, he also hoped she'd notice that he had some muscular definition to his thin arms.

He could smell her cheap perfume, and he knew that she was now standing directly over him. He was getting an erection. Clearing his throat, he turned to her and grinned. She grinned back. Then Arnie's smile froze on his face when he looked up into her eyes—one blue and the other brown. He didn't know why, but a coldness suddenly went through him and his erection started to shrivel. Fighting off the feeling, he removed his jacket from the stool next to him, making room for her to sit down.

The next morning, several miles from the truck stop, Mario Pandini pushed the screen door open and hobbled slowly out of his small house. He dragged his arthritic legs down the wooden steps and made his way to the toolshed across from his small patch of vineyards. He was seventy-five years old, and every year the harvesting took a toll on his twisted body. This would be his last year, because next week he was going to put an ad in the Yakima newspaper saying that his winery was up for sale. The vineyards had been good to him and his wife for the last fifty years, but now they really needed a younger man to run them.

Mario took a small ax from the tool bin and went into his

vineyard. Blight had touched some of the vines, and he needed to shear the bark off before it spread.

Suddenly what he saw several feet in front of him made him get down on his knees and cross himself. *"Jesú Christo!"* he whispered in reverence.

What his old eyes beheld was a man tied to the cross section of a vine. His arms were spread out parallel to the earth, and his head was tilted to one side. He was wearing a loincloth and blood trickled down his legs.

Again Mario crossed himself. It was a miracle, like what happened in Fátima and Lourdes. Now it was happening to him! Tears came to his eyes. The Lord had come to his vineyards!

Then he heard a painful moan coming from deep within the man's throat. Mario, still on his knees, dragged his body nearer to him. The mouth of the *Christo* image was now moving, spitting out blood as he tried to speak. A gurgling sound, like a child blowing bubbles through a straw in a glass of milk came from his parched lips.

Mario crawled even closer, his gnarled body filled with awe.

The figure opened his eyes and looked at Mario. Again he opened his mouth. Little bubbles of blood ran out and dribbled down his chin.

Then Mario noticed that it wasn't a loincloth he was wearing, but white briefs covered in blood. The word *Jockey* was printed on its elastic band. He put his ear up close to the red mouth so he could try and make out what the Christ man was saying. Mario couldn't be sure because he didn't put his hearing aid in this morning, but it sounded like: *"Get . . . me . . . fuckoffahere!"*

Chapter Ten

"**Y**OU'RE DAWDLING TODAY. Why?" Rena asked Cathy, who was sitting halfway slumped over her oatmeal. With her elbow up on the breakfast table and her head resting on her hand, Cathy just shrugged in response. She was lazily twirling her spoon around in the oatmeal, making circular patterns in it. "Life's a bitch," she said finally.

"At times, yes, it definitely can be," Rena said, rolling her eyes as she brought the toast and marmalade over to the table. She sensed it was going to be one of those mornings.

"Do you ever miss Dad?" She stopped playing with the oatmeal and looked up at her mother.

It absolutely was going to be one of those mornings. "Sometimes," she answered. It was partially true. She remembered how deeply she cared for him at one time. *When you're young, love can be so strong and all-consuming.* That kind of passion used to cut deep into her marrow and made her feel so helpless, and yet, at the same time so alive. Part of those feelings she did miss, and she could never evoke them again, not even with Charlie. Except what she had with Charlie right now was better; they were on equal footing with one another. With Terry she always felt victimized, defenseless. That was some shitty way to live, she thought, thinking back.

"You never go to his grave," Cathy said.

"No, I don't." Rena spread the orange marmalade evenly over her toast. "Your father and I had gone our separate ways, both emotionally and physically, long before he died. The only thing we had that formed any link between us was you."

"Do you still have that link?"

Rena looked into Cathy's deep, beautiful green eyes . . . the same beautiful green eyes of her father. "Yes," she said, sighing. "Because when I see you I also see him. Nothing is ever completely lost in this universe." The truth about Terry, the cruelty he inflicted on her and everyone surrounding her, would remain locked away inside Rena. Cathy was never to know about that. Never!

Cathy's eyes moistened. She suddenly broke out into a grin, stood up, and hugged her mother. "I love you, Mom."

Rena returned the hug. "I know, sweetheart."

The phone rang.

"I'll get it," Cathy said, going over to the wall phone next to the refrigerator. "It's for you, Mom," she said, after asking who it was.

"Who is it?"

"Says his name is Grant."

The FBI agent! A nervous ache cut through Rena. She took the phone from Cathy. *Had they found Maura?*

"Yes?" she said, trying to control her voice.

"I asked you yesterday if you would be available in case we needed your help."

His voice was thin, as if he was calling from some distance. "Have you found her?" she asked quietly.

"No, but we're close . . . real close!"

"How can I help you?"

"She hit again. A truck driver was found mutilated up in Yakima, Washington early this morning. This time we got lucky—he's still alive. They're operating on him right now. I have a private Cessna at the Santa Monica airport waiting to fly you up here."

Rena thought about it for a few seconds, then said, "Let me call my replacement for my radio program. I'll be at the airport within an hour."

Rena hung up and phoned Doctor Janis Skinner, asking if she would fill in for her. She was a good psychologist and was well liked by the audience. She then called the station and told them of today's substitution. Rena also tried the number of Cindy, a UCLA college girl who lived down the street from them. She sometimes spent the night with Cathy when Rena was away on short business trips. The girl hadn't left for classes yet and said she would stay with her.

"What's going on, Mom?" Cathy asked, when Rena hung up.

"I won't be home tonight. Cindy will be here when you get back from school."

Cathy's eyes brightened. She liked Cindy. "Where are you going?"

"The state of Washington," she said, rushing upstairs to pack.

"What's in Washington?" Cathy yelled up to her from the bottom of the steps.

"I don't know yet. Finish your breakfast or you'll be late for classes. Before you leave I expect a hug and a kiss," Rena said as she grabbed her overnight bag from the top shelf in her closet.

The phone rang again and Rena answered. It was Blythe Farnsworth.

"Where are you?" Rena asked, surprised by the call.

"In Palm Springs. I'm dying a slow death here. If I see another man walking around in a pink sport jacket and red pants, I'll scream. I thought I'd come to L.A., buy out Rodeo Drive, and stay in town for the night."

"Where's Edmond?"

"Out on the green. Edmond lives to play golf. What are you doing for dinner tonight?"

Rena could hear the despondency in her voice, but she had no time right now to cheer up this lonely woman. She should have seen what Edmond's life was all about before she married him. "I can't tonight. Maybe next week," she said to her.

After she hung up on Blythe, she began to pack her overnight bag. When I find the time, I'll definitely have a talk with her, Rena thought to herself. The woman is bright and pleading for something to do with her life.

Rena took Bundy Drive to the Santa Monica airport and parked her car near the main entrance. It was a small airport with row upon row of private planes.

Rena spotted a younger version of agent Grant waiting for her in the terminal. He also wore his hair in a JFK cut. As she walked over to him, she wondered if J. Edgar Hoover would have approved of his agents trying to emulate Kennedy, his archenemy.

The young agent shook hands with her and took her bag. They then walked out onto the runway and boarded a six-passenger Cessna.

Two hours later they landed at a private airfield outside of Yakima. A Ford van was waiting to take them the short distance to Memorial Hospital in the city.

On the seventh floor of the hospital, Agent Grant stood by the elevator smoking a cigarette with his suit jacket off and his sleeves rolled up. He hadn't slept or showered for two days; dark circles surrounded his eyes, and his usually well-groomed hair was matted and uncombed. The doors opened and Rena and the young agent stepped out. Grant squashed his cigarette in the ashtray and shook hands with her.

"Thanks for coming," he said as they walked to Arnie Baker's room.

"Can he talk?" she asked him.

"Barely. The spike missed the spinal column but nicked his Adam's apple. Claims the woman was a prostitute and made advances toward him. This was around one-thirty in the morning. They agreed on a price, and he followed her to a deserted area of a wine field. He said she took out a blanket and a large bag from the trunk of her car, a white Ford station wagon, and

102

told him to lay down on the blanket. Baker thinks he may have had sexual contact with her before he passed out, he can't be sure. We think he did, too."

"How could you tell?"

Grant stopped at the door where a uniformed policeman stood outside. "Traces of vaginal fluid were present on his organ. There were also traces of skin fragments under his nails. We're going to conduct a DNA fingerprinting test in our Washington lab to see if the fluid matches up with the genetic bands from her hair particles and skin that we found on him and the other victims. If it does, then we have more than enough for a conviction. Damn!" he said, shedding his reserve. "All this happened less than ten hours ago. She's so close I can almost feel her!"

"Ten hours can put her deep inside Canada," Rena said, thinking how close they were to the border.

"We thought about that. The border routes have been sealed off. She can't get out that way."

"You said the same thing about the California/Oregon border," Rena said skeptically.

They went into the room where Arnie Baker lay on a bed with tubes attached to his nose and arm. A thick bandage with a spreading red stain was wrapped around his neck. Two other FBI agents were also inside the hospital room, and a nurse who was monitoring his pulse.

Arnie's eyes were slits that were straining to stay open.

"Mr. Baker, are you awake?" Grant asked, bending down next to him and taking out a small picture from the breast pocket of his shirt.

"Yeah," Arnie mumbled. His voice was low and hoarse.

"I have a photo I'd like you to take a look at." He held up a photograph of Maura that was on her city prosecutor's ID. Arnie forced his eyes open for a second, looked, then nodded.

"That's her . . . the cunt," he groaned in pain, closing his eyes again. "Elke gonna kill me."

"Who's Elke?" Rena asked.

"His wife," Grant whispered.

Rena noticed how small he was as he lay prone in the hospital bed.

"Did she say where she was going after Yakima?" Grant asked.

Arnie opened his mouth, but only a rasping breath came out.

103

His teeth were red with fresh blood from the wound that re-opened again in his throat.

The nurse gave Grant a hostile stare.

Grant lowered his head, hoping to make out what Arnie was saying. "I'm sorry, I can't understand you."

This time Arnie mouthed the word, "Seattle."

"Thank you, Mr. Baker. We'll let you rest now," he said, putting the photo back into his pocket and standing up.

"He's small," Rena said to Grant as they went out into the hallway.

"Like all the rest. I doubt very much that she's going to Seattle. At least we know how she immobilizes her victims. The last thing he remembered, he said, was the feel of a wet rag on his face. When he was brought to the hospital, the medical staff found his blood pressure to be abnormally low, which can be a symptom of certain anesthetics. They conducted tests. Chloroform was found in his system."

"May I see the picture of Maura?" Rena asked.

"Sure." He took it out of his pocket and handed it to her.

It was a typical passport-type photo—a forced trace of a smile with no personality underneath. "It's not a great likeness," Rena said. It was Maura, though, she knew that.

"That, plus the one on her driver's license, are the only photographs we have of her."

Rena nodded, knowing that Maura hated having her picture taken. It was as if she were embarrassed and felt unworthy of being beautiful.

"When was the last time you saw her?" Grant asked, lighting up a Winston.

"Twelve years ago."

"People change in twelve years," he said, taking a deep drag on the cigarette.

"True." She seemed older, as if stress began taking its toll on her, but she still looked beautiful.

"She told Arnold Baker her name was Jasmine Dawn," he said skeptically.

Rena gasped. "Oh, Christ!"

"What's the matter?" he asked.

"Maura was given a Barbie doll when she was a child. She hated the name Barbie, so she renamed it Jasmine Dawn. She also hated those cute little outfits that came with it and she made her own clothes for the doll."

"What kind of clothes?"

"Maura had a bizarre sense of humor. Instead of cute, she went the other way and dressed her up to look like a hooker. She made a black miniskirt for her. Miniskirts were in style then."

Grant didn't say anything for a while, but she could see his mind working. Then he said, "Mr. Baker stated that she wore a tight, black leather miniskirt with a black sweater. He also said that she had two different colored eyes. Do you know anything about that?"

Rena looked at him, stunned. She then told him how she got a brief glimpse of those multicolored eyes when they were in Greece together. "I thought I was imagining it," she said.

"It may just be possible that there's a whole part to this woman that you don't know."

"Very possible," she said, almost in a whisper. Last night she had tried to compose a psychological profile on Maura and found it difficult. There were too many voids about her that needed to be filled, and the long gap between their seeing each other didn't help. She could be outgoing and vivacious one minute and withdrawn and sulky the next. Rena realized something else: as talkative as Maura could be, it was always about things, events, and other people, never about herself. Maura would ask such detailed, intimate questions about Rena's personal life that by the time she answered all of them there would never be enough time to ask her the same questions back. She was so good at tap dancing and weaving spells with her unique persona that Rena used to walk away feeling at one with her, yet at the same time never really knowing her at all.

Rena always had the sensation that Maura was hiding something from the world . . . something deep and forbidden. But what? What could be so terrible? And was it coming out now?

Scattered visions of them playing in Peter McKinney's attic flew by in her memory.

Dust particles floating lazily through filtered sunlit windows . . . a naked light bulb . . . loose plank floors . . . the smell of camphor. Maura going through her mother's clothes that were hanging on the rusty metal rack. She takes a cotton flowered dress with shoulder pads off a wire hanger and pulls it over her head. Rena wears an old, moth-eaten coat with black lambs wool on the lapels and sleeves. An overly large, black veiled hat hangs down over her eyes. She sits on a wooden trunk in the middle of the attic and giggles at Maura, watching her as she puts on faded pink satin high heels and tries to walk. Her little legs quiver when they try supporting themselves in the oversized shoes. Maura finds a tattered makeup case next to the rack. She bends down and takes out a gold lipstick container, opens it up, and covers her mouth with crooked red streaks. Rena grabs the puff and pats her face with tan powder. She coughs. The girls laugh.

Footsteps ascending the stairs.

Peter McKinney enters the dusty, mold-covered attic. The smell of whiskey is strong on his breath. He looks at Maura, and his face turns red with rage. His eyes fill with fury and his mouth opens, exposing strong white teeth with a large gap in the front. A thunderous yell erupts from the depths of his soul and he slaps Maura hard on the face. She reels back from the blow, then defiantly glares at him. Rena freezes with terror.

He looks at Rena. "Get those things off!" he screams at her. She slides out of the coat and it drops to the floor.

"Now get out!" he hisses. His back is bent, and his drunken eyes are bulging and red from the alcohol.

Frightened, Rena races past him and down the steps. As she runs out the door, she hears Peter McKinney scream at Maura, "You witch! You bloody witch! They died because of you!"

So long ago, Rena thought. Peter McKinney apologized to her when he was sober the next day. Maura, her face puffy with red welts from the slap, shrugged her shoulders and didn't want to talk about it when Rena tried bringing up the incident. That was the first and only time Maura had ever taken her to play in the attic.

They died because of you! McKinney had said to Maura. Who were they? Rena always asked herself. She never had the nerve to ask Maura when they were children. *Was he talking about the death of his wife during childbirth? Probably. What a cruel thing to say to a child.*

But McKinney had said *"they."* Who else had died? She wondered.

And why is she calling herself Jasmine Dawn? It was a name she gave to a doll twenty years ago. She was a lonely child then, inventing features for the doll that were directly opposite of herself. It was supposed to have been just a joke, but Rena believed that Jasmine Dawn was a subconscious extension of Maura that she had never allowed to emerge. *The Madonna/whore syn-*

drome. As far as Rena knew, Maura was anything but loose with men. The only man she ever slept with during her years in Napa was Martin Bynum. Had she changed since she moved to New York? Rena didn't think so. Ray Scollari certainly attested to that. Rena knew that deep sexual suppression can cause dual personalities within an individual. Is that what happened to Maura? Was there always a Jasmine Dawn in her psyche waiting to come out? Right now, that was the only answer that made sense.

An agent walked over to them holding a portable telephone. "It's from Napa. They may have found something at the McKinney winery."

Grant took the phone. He listened, and after a few, "Uh-huhs," said he would be right there. Hanging up, he looked at Rena and said, "My men found some papers in the desk drawer of the McKinney winery. They said they're important. Want to come?"

There was a strange, ambiguous look on Grant's face. What kind of papers? she wondered. Yes, she certainly did want to come.

This time, Rena sat in the inside section of the van with Grant and the young agent as they made their way back to the airport. The walls of the van were lined with computer equipment, monitors, and radio gear. On a small table in the middle of the floor was a map of the United States with three bright yellow pins signifying the areas where the murders and mutilations were committed. Looking at it, Rena now also felt that they were close, and like Grant she could almost feel Maura's breath on her neck.

"What kind of papers were found?" she asked Grant.

"It seems to be a journal," he said, still with the same confusion on his face.

"Maura's?"

"No, this one my men say is two hundred years old."

Chapter Eleven

THE DRIVER OF the Ford Fairlane that picked Rena and the two FBI men up at Napa airport wasted no time in getting them to the McKinney winery. He zigzagged in and out of the two jammed lanes on Highway 29, sending BMWs and Volvos scampering out of his way.

They got out of the car on a dirt pathway leading off of Spring Mountain Road and walked up the hill to the old stone winery.

Several police and government cars lined the area. The local sheriff's department and federal agents with plastic containers carefully combed the bushes next to the building looking for foreign objects. Over by the door, a man in a white smock dusted the metal handle and lock for fingerprints.

An unsettling feeling of déjà vu descended upon Rena as she remembered walking this path and entering this winery hundreds of times before with Maura. Pictures of their youth, like splices of film in an editing machine, quickly entered then exited her head.

"Don't touch anything," Grant said to her. "Walk where I walk."

Inside the stone building a gray light filtered through the open door catching thousands of dust particles dancing wildly in mid-air. There was a sour smell about the winery, like the interior of a long-closed crypt that had been broken into. A carpet of dust covered everything, and cobwebs hung from the corners of the cross beams.

The large oak fermenting barrels and the old wooden presser were still where she remembered them.

Nothing had changed, she thought. It was so different from Simon's ultramodern, computer-run winery. With just this basic equipment and his powerful hands, Peter McKinney had produced vintage wines that other expensive wineries could only dream about.

She took a pair of thin rubber surgical gloves from one of the agents and put them on. In McKinney's old office at the other end of the winery a group of technicians stood over the desk shining a light on something. They all wore gloves. When they saw Grant, they moved out of the way to make room for him.

"What do we have here?" Grant asked.

"Appears to be a journal of some kind," one of the lab men replied. "We found it in the bottom desk drawer. It looks like it was recently put in here. There's no dust on it."

Rena noticed the splintered remains of the drawer on the floor. She looked over Grant's shoulder and saw the book. The cover was black with squiggly white lines.

"This can't be two hundred years old," Grant said, annoyed. "It looks like the kind of notebook I used in grade school."

"It contains a translation from a two-hundred-year-old diary, sir," the lab man said. "This man Striker, whoever he is, seems to be the translator. His notes explain that he did this in Nineteen forty-three. From the condition of this notebook I'd say that part's accurate. We'll do further testing on it when we get it back to the lab. It seems like a couple of pages at the end of the book have been torn out."

"Has it been dusted for prints?" Grant asked.

"No, not yet."

"What does this have to do with the vineyard murders?"

The technicians and FBI men looked at each other, then one of them said, "If the contents of this diary are accurate, then a man named Baron Gustave de Montret had been killing people in the vineyards of France over two hundred years ago."

There was a stunned look on Grant's face. "How were they killed?" he asked.

"Perhaps you'd like to read some of it, sir."

Grant saw the excitement in his men's eyes. "Yes, I would," he said. He moved over to the front of the desk and picked up a tweezer to turn the pages.

Rena stood next to him and looked down at the yellowed pages. The script was done with an old-fashioned, ink fountain pen. The penmanship was neat and precise, as if great care had gone into it:

Ah, what unthinkable times we live in!

The rancid breath of those vile peasants are blowing down our necks and these fools think they are immune. Look how they sleep in their slobbering, drunken stupor across my table!

I see that Marquis Barolt, with his head resting in his plate of lamb, has peed in his pants again. And there's Lord Travert snoring like a wild boar in heat. I wonder what happened to his oversized, powdered wig that is all the rage of Paris this year? Ha! Wait, I see it! It's floating like a dead bloated pigeon in the soup caldron.

Is the sight of that wig not an omen of what is to come? Can't these dullards see that Louis will be overthrown! Are they that blind! I dare not think about that now. It is too late to stop the wheels of history. What is done is done.

Now where is Madame Barolt? Oh yes, there she is! The beautiful marquise is passed out by the hearth, with her gown pushed up to her waist and her legs spread apart. Vomit drips down from her mouth and onto my marbled floor. That idiot Baron Lalouch is on top of her, desperately trying to pump his limp rod into her hairy slit. No, my friend, I'm afraid you are too drunk to please anyone, even such a comatose bitch as the marquise.

And Lalouch's wife? Probably upstairs in one of my bedrooms with that pathetic creature, Comte Donatien Alphonse.

I hear a high-pitched giggle coming from behind me and I turn around. It is Donatien Alphonse leaning drunkenly against the door, trying to lift his britches up past his bony knees.

God, how he disgusts me!

His wig hangs down over one eye, exposing his head that is covered with cysts. He also wears too much white powder, and he looks like an aging harlot the way he smears his lips with red paint. The only reason I tolerate Donatien is because he amuses my guests. The dear fellow fancies himself to be a writer but his unpublished works are nothing but filth. His mind has long since eroded from his devotion to absinthe, and he seems to spend his life between prison and the lunatic asylum paying for the vile crimes he has done to women.

The comte is now motioning for me to follow him.

What does the poor fool want? He is so drunk that he cannot get his pants over his wrinkled ass.

I watch in amusement as he struggles toward the cellar. Again he beckons with his hand for me to come.

Why not? Perhaps he will be a diversion. This party has turned into a bore.

I follow him down the damp, stone steps to my precious wine cellar. How does this creature know about it? Has he been prowling through my château again while I've been away? Sometimes he presses me too far!

He pushes open the thick oak door to the cellar. What I see fills me with dread, yet at the same time, makes my stomach ferment with excitement. My stable boy, Yves, is lying on the cement floor bound with hemp and gagged. He is nude. Donatien's semen runs down the boy's buttocks. His eyes are filled with fright, and they implore me to help him.

I look over toward Donatien. He is sitting on a barrel of Graves, his britches still dangling at his knees, and sipping from a bottle of that venal absinthe.

What a monster Donatien is! He looks up at me and grins, unmasking his blackened teeth. He tells me to have my fun with the boy. "Poke him!" he says. "Poke him! The scamp loves it!"

Yes, I know what Yves likes, you cretin! God knows how many times he has flirted with me while he bridled my horse for my morning ride. I have always resisted . . . until now.

His white skin begins to excite me.

It is also the right time of year: the vines are filled with fruit, and I could hear them pleading with me to have him.

I look at Donatien watching what I'll do, and then I turn to the boy with the begging eyes.

Yes! I say to myself. Yes! It is time I shared my secret with someone.

I go over to the bins of aging Pomerol, reach in between the bottles, and withdraw the mallet and spike. Donatien looks at me with surprise.

I laugh. This will be our secret, I say to that drunken lump of decaying flesh.

Then I remove my clothes. I laugh again and move toward Yves. The boy's eyes fill with terror.

Joy! Oh, joy!

I get in back of him and put my knee on his spine to keep him still. His body is shaking and I can hear muffled pleas coming from behind his gag.

Be still, my lad! It will all be over in a second!

Sitting on his back, I part his blond hair, exposing his unwashed neck. I scream at Donatien to watch.

This will be our little secret, scum! I've needed to share this with someone for so long . . . even if it has to be with the likes of you! Tell anyone and they'll think you're more insane than you are now.

I look out the window toward my fields. This is for you, my beautiful vineyards! Let this year's vintage be the best ever! I sing these words with all the rapture in my soul!

Section Sixty-five from the journal of Baron Gustave de Montret. Translated by field agent Wilbur Striker on the 20th of January, 1943.

The guests that de Montret mentioned, except for Comte Donatien Alphonse, were guillotined during Robespierre's Reign of Terror.

Donatien Alphonse, I found out, died in the insane asylum of Charenton in 1814. I also discovered that the Comte had published some books, and that they probably would have been buried underneath the abundance of rich French literature except for the fact that Swinburne and Baudelaire thought he was a writer of some importance. Comte Donatien wrote under the name of the Marquis de Sade.

—Wilbur Striker

"My God!" was all that Grant could utter when he looked up from the book.

Rena had her arms folded across her chest and shuddered. She had the sensation of a cold draft suddenly impregnating the dank air of the winery. These words, so neatly scripted, felt to her like they were dug up from the catacombs of hell.

Grant looked down at the thick notebook for a moment, regained his control, then inquired, "Have you counted the number of victims this person de Montret murdered?"

"Not yet. There seems to be a hell of a lot, though," the lab technician said, his voice still quavering from the find of the manuscript.

"After you dust it for prints I want two Xerox copies made—one for me and one for Miss Halbrook. We'll wait."

As they walked out of the winery, Rena could see a forensic technician bending down and making a mold of a bare footprint embedded in the dust. It was the size and shape of a woman's.

Outside, in the sunlight, Grant lit up a cigarette and began to pace. He seemed uneasy. "None of this makes sense," he said. "Every time we think we have a handle on what's going on, we find out that we haven't even scratched the surface yet."

"We don't know if the journal is real," Rena said, even though she felt otherwise.

"No, but the writing in the notebook is certainly older than Maura McKinney. What's she doing . . . mimicking a two-hundred-year-old killer?"

Rena sighed and sat down on the old wooden bench that butted up against the stone wall of the winery. "Let's see what we have first." She leaned back against the wall and rubbed her eyes. Still more questions, she thought. Did the same type of serial killer actually exist two hundred years ago? Who was Striker? Who did the journal belong to—Maura or her father, Peter McKinney? Then that same old question came up again—Who's Uncle Wiggly? No one knew. Grant and Pinky tried to find out and came up with nothing.

A technician walked out of the winery twenty minutes later with two copies of the notebook. He gave one to Rena and the other one to Grant.

"For some unknown reason, she's in the wine country up north looking for victims. I'm flying back up to Yakima to conduct operations from there. We can get you a plane to L.A."

"No, I think I'll stay at my father's winery and read this. I just need a ride to the Alexander Valley."

Grant asked one of his agents to give Rena a lift. She told Grant she'd get in touch with him if she discovered anything revealing after reading the journal.

As she got in the car, Pinky Swangel drove up and parked next to the other police vehicles. He looked pale and tired. They waved to each other.

Up on a hill overlooking the main road, Rena saw the figure of a man watching everything that was happening at the McKinney winery. She couldn't be sure, because he was standing behind a tree, but it looked like Monica van der Slyck's son, Otto. Rena wondered how many times he had stood there watching the McKinney property, especially when Maura was staying here. That pompous man with his large frog eyes bothered her.

On the drive home, Rena began to scan through the thick stack of Xerox papers. The first entry was dated 1741; the last one in 1793. She sat back and let out a deep breath. Over fifty years of killings, mutilations, and torture were described in these pages.

She realized that she was hungry and that she had better grab something to eat when she got to her father's château. If she started reading now, she knew she would have very little appetite left.

She was let off on the gravel path next to the huge house. It seemed deserted. Her father must have gone back to Los Angeles, and she was grateful for that; she needed to be alone and undisturbed if she was going to sift through this manuscript.

Letting herself in, Rena went upstairs to her bedroom and changed into the jeans and sweater that she had brought in her overnight bag. After freshening up, she went downstairs into the kitchen, brewed a pot of coffee, and checked to see if there was any food in the sub-zero refrigerator. She was in luck; there were fresh cold cuts, yogurt, and salad vegetables. The housekeeper must stock the kitchen daily, because Simon probably never tells her when he's coming, she thought.

She gulped down a ham sandwich and a carton of yogurt, then poured herself a mug of strong coffee to fight off the fatigue she was feeling.

In the den she turned on the lamp, sat down on the couch, and tucked her legs underneath her body as she began to read de Montret's diary. A pad and pencil lay next to her in case she felt it necessary to take notes.

Two hours later, she slowly turned the last page over and put it down with the others on her lap. She looked bloodless and unsettled. Her coffee sat cold and untouched on the desk, and the yellow pad was now filled with several pages of notations.

Glancing quickly outside the window, she saw that night had already fallen. A cold, shivering sensation suddenly shot down her spine causing her body to flinch. She got up and went into the kitchen to refill her cup with hot coffee.

She turned on the lights in every room she entered; there was no way she wanted to be alone in the darkness, not now, not after what she had just read.

Where to start? she thought as she came back into the den with a fresh cup. Rena looked at her notes. Incredible! All told, de Montret had murdered seventy-three people—mostly beggars, peasants, and prostitutes of both sexes.

Seventy-three!

"My God!" she said out loud.

This Striker had divided de Montret's memorandums into sections.

Who was Striker?

Was this journal real or the fantasies of a depraved human being?

Whose fantasies? Maura's? No! Grant says the pages from the diary were too old.

Peter McKinney's? Maybe.

Rena looked at the last section of the diary again, and as she began to reread it, she felt as if something cold and clammy had suctioned itself onto her neck and was slowly inching its way down.

Chapter Twelve

16th of September, 1793

I come every evening to the Grand Theatre to hear Doretta Paolli sing. How beautiful she plays La Contessa d'Almaviva. Her lovely, rich voice fills the auditorium with such delicacy and power! Never once does it flutter and crack like so many of her dreadful soprano counterparts. She even makes this Philistine opera almost tolerable.

It is a degradation that this glorious woman, must be confined to singing the barbaric tunes of that detestable young upstart Mozart! The Marriage of Figaro is even more heinous than Beaumarchais's horrendous version of the play. The only reason it is in vogue right now is because of its rebellious theme. The Committee of Public Safety—may they be damned!—embraces anything that is revolutionary.

Oh, to go back to the tragedies of Racine and Corneille! There was such order and sensibility in their plays. What passes for theater now is blasphemous!

Yet I come every night because of Doretta.

What is happening? The eyes of the audience are moving away from the stage and up to the box seats. How dare they do that during Doretta's aria!

Ah, that's who they see coming in! It's Monsieur Robespierre and several of his murderers! What is he doing here? He should be in Paris guillotining more of Louis' elite. Perhaps there is no one left alive to punish there, and he now must come to the countryside for fresh meat.

A lamentable sorrow suddenly overwhelms me. If there are no more monarchists left in Paris, then now I am truly alone.

He acknowledges me from where he sits. I nod in mock respect. After all, it was he who freed me from prison the night before I was supposed to lose my head. If it were not for his fondness for my Graves Superieures, which he considers to be the best in France, then I would surely long ago have been food for the hungry dogs that roam the Jardin du Luxembourg.

I turn back to lovely Doretta, close my eyes, and let her incomparable voice float softly up to me. It carries me away to when I was young and handsome, when the women and the boys pined for my graceful body as I rode by on my horse. I never touched any of them until it was time, that I swear! My seductive vineyards are a covetous lot and can be vindictive when angered.

When this wretched excuse of an opera is finally over, I applaud like the rest, then work my way past the audience composed of the new Republic's common citizens to Doretta's dressing room. My heart is soaring! She has answered the note that I left for her last week and has consented to come back with me to my château for dinner.

I walk slowly now and with a cane. The Revolution has taken its toll on my health.

When I reach her room, I see Robespierre inside congratulating her. My body seethes with hate! What does this defiler and murderer of old men, women, and children want with this beautiful woman? How can a beast such as he appreciate the wonder of her golden throat?

Look at that verminous man! He is as small as a weasel, and when he talks, he speaks with the voice of a maiden! Yet he is the most powerful man in all France. The people's choice. My God, what a time of madness this is!

Maximilien Robespierre looks away from my lovely Doretta and turns to me. There is a disapproving pout on his white, gaunt face. His face is the mask of death . . . no one, not even his Jacobin friends, will deny that. His eyes are sunken into black pits, and clusters of his flaming red hair, resembling writhing snakes, wind their way down his collar.

Yes, he is death, and I must grovel and kiss his hand if I am to survive.

"Monsieur Robespierre," I say, bowing as low as I have done on many occasions for that headless fool, Louis.

He mildly berates me for being late with my cases of Medoc that I had promised him.

I tut-tut and make several excuses, acting the fop for that creature. From the corner of my eye I can see Doretta watching me with amusement.

He tells me that he is here for a meeting and that he will be going back to Paris tomorrow. Do I have his wine ready?

"Ah, Monsieur Deputy, it is too soon! Much too soon!" I say, bowing once more. "To move wine of this quality and vintage before it has aged properly will surely turn it into vinegar. You will receive the shipment shortly, I promise you."

After he leaves the dressing room, the lovely Doretta bursts into laughter, and so do I. We laugh and hold each other until the tears sting our eyes.

How good it is to be held by a young woman again! Her smooth skin is soft and plump. I have not aged well, and the beautiful ones are harder to come by now.

She leaves with me.

As my carriage takes us through the city, I look out my window to see what effect the revolution has had on the masses. Lice-infected beggars still hold their scurvy hands out to me for a few sous as I drive by. The dead, rotting corpses of the poor still lay in the streets waiting until the city can get around to burying them.

What changes have you made, my dear citizen Robespierre? You have guillotined so many people for what reason? Disease, poverty, death . . . they still abound. Your turn for the blade will come soon, Monsieur Maximilien, that I can promise you!

When we arrive at my château, I explain to Doretta why there is so little furniture. I tell her how those filthy peasants that worked for me ransacked my home while I lay in chains in that maggot-infested, damp prison waiting to die. She shakes her head in disbelief and puts her arms around my waist.

I desire to do the same for she is so beautiful, but I can hear my hungry vineyards warning me against that. Regretfully I push her away and offer her a glass of Pomerol. She refuses because of her voice.

"Take it," I beg her. "After all, I am the greatest vintner in

117

all France. It will be like honey running down your throat, my sweet one.''

She relents and accepts the glass from me.

I wait patiently until the paregoric works its way through her body. It does not take long. She is small, and in minutes she slumps over in the chair.

Tears well up in my eyes. Of all those beautiful souls that have fed my vineyards, Doretta has touched me the deepest. It wasn't my money that made her come here. She liked me for myself alone.

I can hear the winds swirling outside, carrying the voices of the vineyards back to me. Again they warn me about such thoughts.

''Oh, my dear, wondrous woman! You are a rarity! A treasure that will be no more!''

The vineyards are hungry. I can hear them screaming for food. They must be fed.

I hold Doretta's limp head in my arms and sob. Never again to hear that voice!

The winds gust harder through the vineyards, throwing open the doors leading onto the patio. My beloved vines are enraged, and their threatening voices are harsh to my ears.

I have never seen them this angry before. Frightened, I quickly undress and carry Doretta's body outside into the wine field.

The winds are like a tempest now. The branches cut my body, and the leaves of the vines try to engulf me.

''Be still my beautiful ones. You will soon be fed!'' I scream at them.

The winds become even more incensed. The vines are in a frenzy. They can smell the blood.

I look at the pitiful ovaries that hang from their famished bodies. How small and dried-up they are. It has been this way for two harvests because of the drought that has touched this land. The reason Robespierre does not get his Medoc is because my vineyards will no longer produce for me.

''Look what I brought you! Look!'' I say, hoping they will forgive me.

Looking down at Doretta's soft, plump arms, I quickly become aroused. I rip off her dress. Her breasts are so small to my touch. As I begin to mount her in the dark, I realize that something is wrong. I look down and then I understand.

Doretta is a castrato! He is a man! His fruits have been removed from him long ago to achieve that strong voice!

No! No! No!

My ravenous vines try grabbing at me with their leafy arms.

I didn't know, my exquisite ones! I swear to you I didn't know! Forgive me!

They will never forgive me for this. Never! Dear God, I am lost!

Section One Hundred Twenty-five from the journal of the Baron Gustave de Montret. I researched Doretta Paolli and found out that she actually existed and was a man. Doretta Paolli was an alias for a famous contralto, Gaetano Vicci, who toured Europe dressed as a woman during the latter half of the eighteenth century. It appears that there was a great demand for such castrated, male singers during that time. Records show that he disappeared and was never heard from again after an appearance in Mozart's *The Marriage of Figaro* performed at the Grand Theater in Bordeaux, France. There is only one more section to translate from this diary of the damned. It is the most horrible of them all. Then thank God, I will be finished with it forever!

Translated by Wilbur Striker on the 29th of March, 1943.

—WILBUR STRIKER

Rena tossed the manuscript onto the coffee table, almost as if touching it any longer would infect her with its madness. Grant was right she thought: *Every time you think you've scratched the surface, you find something else underneath.*

The baron had a psychopathic makeup. He had illusions that the vines were alive. He even gave them sexual attributes. It was this and not the murders that bothered her the most about de Montret.

She picked up her pad and looked at her notes. The term *ovaries* was used over and over again by de Montret in his description of grapes that hung from the vines. Many times he referred to his vineyards as "the swollen vineyards." Swollen as in pregnant, she thought. *Who impregnated them? Him?* She believed that's what his meaning implied.

In Section Forty-three, the one on his victim Claudine, he used the phrase:

My fingers stroke her neck, lingering on the pulse, its melodic throbbing making me hard and wet.

That confused Rena.

She had divided up his seventy-three victims: forty-seven were males, twenty-six were females.

The vineyards, though, were his real lover. He protected and

119

fed them. He had sex with his dead victims inside the fields as if he were making love to the vineyards themselves. In return the vines demanded everything from him like a spoiled queen. They could be jealous and vengeful if provoked.

All the killings happened in September, just like now. She knew September was also the time when the vineyards were harvested in France. But why then? Again she felt there was something ritualistic, almost sacrificial in all this. It smacked of paganism. She made a mental note to research this avenue.

What was in the last entry of the diary that Striker said was the most horrible of them all? The FBI said someone had torn it out of the notebook.

What happened to Gustave de Montret after 1793? Surely the vineyard didn't kill him.

Did he *really* exist?

Her eyelids were heavy and she needed to sleep. As she walked up the mahogany staircase to her bedroom, she was beginning to feel that Peter McKinney played an important role in all this.

But in what way?

She tried to fall asleep, but it was impossible. Every time she closed her eyes and began drifting into a state of semiconsciousness, she envisioned de Montret's naked body standing over her bed. His gnarly hands with their long, bloodstained fingernails began closing in around her neck. Rena would jump up, startled, gasping for breath.

Eventually she turned on the night-light and rubbed her eyes. Sleep was not going to happen, at least not right now.

How the hell did all this come about, Maura? she wondered.

Rena got out of bed, went over to the window, and opened up the lace curtains. Outside, the blackness seemed endless. Even the crickets and the wind were unusually quiet tonight.

She got back in bed and tried reading Saul Bellow's new novel which she had packed in her suitcase, but her concentration would not go beyond the first paragraph. Images of Maura—hurt, alone, and scared—would creep into her head. Then memories of that bizarre time spent together in Greece once again found their way back into her thoughts. This time, though, her reminiscences were not about Athens, but of a strange incident that occurred on the Island of Paros.

At seven in the morning, Rena and Maura left Athens from the port of Piraeus by ferry. Their first stopover in the Cycladic

120

islands was Paros. They planned to stay there several days sun-bathing and exploring the caves.

The decks of the boat were extremely cramped with students from all over Europe, but both women were too excited to care much about comfort. They had planned this vacation since their first year in college, and now, finally, it was all happening.

Several hours later the ferry left them off on the sun-drenched island in the middle of the Aegean Sea. Women dressed in black stood on the pier crying, "spiti-spiti!" inviting the disembarking tourists to stay at their houses for a few drachmas a night.

Rena and Maura jumped down from the gangplank onto the pier and began searching through a mound of knapsacks and tote bags for their luggage.

"Missy, come here," one of the old women said to them, motioning with her hands.

Rena and Maura grabbed their bags and walked over to her.

"Need room? Mine very nice . . . very clean," she said in a heavy accent. The old woman in black was staring at Maura. She put her hand up to her pale, golden hair and tried to touch it. Maura jerked away.

"Beautiful," the Greek lady said reverently. "Your hair like Aphrodite's."

"How much?" Maura asked.

"For you, seven drachmas a night." Her eyes, clouded with cataracts, remained glued on Maura's face.

"Five," Maura said, holding up five fingers.

"Six," the woman in black quickly responded.

"Hot water?" Maura asked.

The old woman shrugged and held out her hands. "What you need for? The sun on you all day . . . make you very hot. Cold water make you feel very good."

Maura turned to Rena to see what she thought.

Rena groaned and rolled her eyes. "Tell her it's a deal, okay? A bench in Central Park costs more than six drachmas a night."

Maura nodded to the woman.

The old lady grabbed Maura's bag, and said, "Come, Aphrodite."

They followed her off the pier and down the main street of Paros, eventually stopping when they came to a donkey tied to a pole near the harbor. The old lady strapped the bags on the beast. "You want to ride, my goddess?" she said to Maura, paying no attention to Rena.

121

"No thank you," Maura said, shuddering at the thought.

She stared at Maura for a brief moment, again with that expression of amazement on her face, then hit the donkey's hind leg with a stick to make it move. Perhaps it was the cataracts, but the expression on the old woman's face every time she looked at Maura gave Rena the impression that she could almost see right into her soul.

The old woman's house, whitewashed and sparkling in the sun, overlooked the bay of Naoussa.

Their room was small but clean, with a beautiful view of the beaches.

"Let's go swimming," Rena said, digging through her suitcase for her bathing suit.

"Maybe tomorrow. I think I'd just like to rest . . . catch up on some reading." Maura was bending down, putting her things away in the dresser drawer.

"Absolutely not!" Rena said forcefully. "You're coming with me. You can read on the beach."

After a beat, Maura nodded, then quietly said, "All right." She took her black bathing suit from the drawer and went out into the hall bathroom to change.

When she came back to the room, Rena turned and looked at her. "My God," she whispered, open-mouthed. "I am absolutely jealous!" Maura looked stunning standing by the doorway. Her long legs, perfectly proportioned, seemed to take forever to reach the rest of her body, and her skin, except for a few red blotches, was immaculately white, almost translucent. Her breasts stood erect and were straining against the latex material of her bathing suit.

"Are we going or what?" Maura said, embarrassed.

The path leading from the house to the beach was steep. Rena made the descent with little trouble but had to wait for Maura, who was climbing down slowly and clutching her stomach. Her face was etched in pain.

"Are you all right?" Rena asked worriedly.

"I'll be fine," Maura said, holding onto the bushes that protruded from each side of the path. When she touched down on the porous sand, she saw the concern in Rena's face and smiled. "Hey, relax, okay? It's only the female curse. I just get it worse than most, that's all."

They found a deserted spot near the wine-colored sea and set down their blankets. Maura covered her body in a strong sunblock lotion. For the rest of the afternoon they read and napped. Rena occasionally went into the water to cool off, but Maura preferred to remain on the sand, saying that she didn't want to swim.

As the sun lowered itself over the Aegean, casting a brilliant glow in the sky, they reluctantly packed their belongings and made their way back to the house. Rena walked slowly next to Maura, helping her up the hill. Again her face was filled with pain, but she didn't say anything.

That night, Rena put on white shorts and a halter, and Maura wore a lavender sundress that complimented her deep, green eyes.

"How are you feeling? Are you up to going out?" Rena asked Maura as she buckled up her sandals.

Maura was using deep strokes to brush her long hair. "Better. The pain just comes and goes. I took a Midol."

By this time they were starving, and the wonderful smell of food coming from the old woman's kitchen only inflamed their appetites.

"Where you go?" the old woman asked them as Rena and Maura walked past the kitchen to the door leading outside.

"To a taverna for dinner. Can you recommend one?" Maura asked.

"Yes, right here. Sit down," she said, pointing to the table.

Rena began to say, "No, we couldn't . . ."

"Sit! Sit!" the old woman said impatiently, pushing the chairs out from the table.

Just then Rena looked up and saw a beautiful young man, maybe twenty-five years old, with black curly hair and chestnut-colored eyes standing near the doorway. He had on a white cotton, collarless Greek shirt and fisherman boots. He was staring at Maura.

"My son . . . Nikos," the woman said to them.

The man grinned warmly and nodded, his eyes never leaving Rena's friend.

"Plenty food. Stay, please," she implored the women.

They relented and stayed for dinner.

The old woman was an excellent cook. They were served a rich fish stew cooked in wine. When Rena asked what it was, the woman could only answer soupia and oktapodi. Whatever she chose to call it, it was delicious. It wasn't until the next day that Rena found out that she had eaten freshly killed squid and octopus.

They were given a sweet dark wine with their dinner that was made on Paros. It was rough to the taste, and they drank bottled water instead.

All through dinner Nikos remained quiet, but every time he looked up from his plate, his eyes were fixed on Maura.

During a dessert of yogurt mixed with honey, Rena told Nikos and his mother that she and Maura were going to visit the caves of Anti-Paros tomorrow.

Nikos's eyes lit up. "I take you," he said with only a trace of an accent.

Both women looked up, surprised. This was the first time he spoke. They had no idea he knew English.

"My son good with boats. He take you to other island," the mother said, boasting.

The next morning Rena and Maura sailed over to the satellite island of Anti-Paros in Nikos's fishing boat. Once out on the sea and away from his mother, Nikos talked continually, mostly about the beauty of his island and his plans to own several fishing boats. Almost everything he said was directed to Maura.

Rena smiled while watching him do a ritualistic courting dance with her friend. Maura was attentive to him, but remained distant.

When they reached the island, they hired mules to take them to the entrance of the caves. Nikos was the perfect guide: he was witty and articulate and knew the locations of the best-looking stalactites in the caverns.

That evening he took them into the village of Naoussa to his favorite place for dinner. The owner of the crowded taverna welcomed Nikos with a bear hug and gave them a table next to the musicians.

Throughout the night the three of them danced and sang. It had been years since Rena saw Maura this happy.

The black sky had hints of gray in it by the time they made their way back to the old woman's house. They were light-headed from all the Metaxa and ouzo they drank. Nikos and Maura lagged a few steps behind Rena, talking to each other in low tones.

Rena went into the house thinking that they wanted to be alone. As she closed the door, Rena saw Nikos put his hands on Maura's face, lifting it up to kiss.

It was good for her, Rena thought. She had been mourning Martin's death much too long.

She went into her room and began to undress. Suddenly, just as she got under the covers, she heard a piercing scream coming from somewhere outside.

It's Maura! she thought, startled.

She got up and raced out of the house toward the direction of the sound. The old lady was right behind her.

They stopped abruptly when they reached the flower garden with its overhangings of brightly colored bougainvillea. Nikos was laying on the grass. There was a deep gash on his cheek, and blood dripped down his face staining his white shirt. Maura was standing over him holding a steel nail file. Her face, once beautiful, was now distorted with rage.

"I'll kill you!" she screamed, glaring down at him.

Nikos stared up at her, a stunned look on his face.

"Maura!" Rena said, shocked.

"I'll kill you! I'll kill you if you ever touch me again, you bastard!" There was white foam around the corners of her mouth, and saliva ran down her chin. Her face was red, and veins jutted out from her temple.

"Nikos, Nikos!" the old woman shouted, getting on her knees and holding her son's bleeding face in her hands. She turned toward Maura, her eyes fiery. "Why you do this?" she wailed.

The hate that made Maura's body shake only a minute ago began to drain away. Her eyes softened. She looked at Nikos's mother, opened her mouth and tried to speak, but nothing came out.

"Whore!" the old lady screamed at Maura, then spit on the ground. "He good boy! He like you! Why you do this?"

"I . . . I'm sorry . . . I . . ." She shook her head. Tears began to stream down her face.

"You are evil! You are the child of Hermes!"

Maura's head jolted back from the remark.

"You think I don't know, heh! I know! I know!" the woman bellowed. She stood up and pointed a finger at Maura.

Maura put a hand up to her face then ran back into the house.

"I know who you are!" the woman shouted after her.

Again Rena had the feeling that the old woman could see deep into Maura's very being. She went into the house to find her friend.

Maura was in the bedroom throwing her belongings into her

125

bag. Rena did the same; they knew they couldn't stay here any longer.

They found a hotel in the center of town that had a vacancy. It did not have the charm of the old lady's house, but it was the only place available on the island.

As they unpacked, Maura remained sullen, refusing to talk about what happened.

Both women were fatigued from the night, yet they couldn't sleep. They went down to the harbor and found a taverna that had opened early. Sitting down at a table outside, they ordered Turkish coffees and cakes.

The silence between them was deafening as they stirred their thick drinks. Finally Rena couldn't stand it any longer and asked, "Why?"

"Why what!" Maura said, agitated.

"What happened between you two?"

"Nothing!" she snapped.

"Maura, I'm your friend." She reached across the table to touch her hand, but Maura quickly moved hers away.

Her mouth began to tremble, then she said tearfully, "He tried to touch me."

"Where? Here?" Rena said, touching her own breasts.

"No. Here!" Maura hissed, putting her hand below her stomach. Again her eyes filled with anger as she remembered.

"Did he use force on you?"

"What do you mean by force?"

"Did he hold you down against your will? Did you think he was going to rape you?"

Maura shook her head. "No, but that doesn't mean he had the right to try and touch me there!"

"I agree," Rena said. "You seemed to be attracted to him."

"So what?" Maura said, shrugging. "That doesn't mean I have to sleep with him."

"Of course not, but if he wasn't trying to rape you, then don't you think using a nail file on his face was a little excessive?" Rena said, somewhat amazed.

"I'm sorry for what happened, but he had no right to try anything! Now can we please change the subject." There was a finality in her voice. She sipped her coffee, avoiding Rena's inquisitive eyes.

"What did his mother mean when she said you were the child of Hermes?" Rena asked, not wanting to drop it.

Maura didn't answer her.

"Hermes is a Greek god, isn't he?"

"I wouldn't know," she answered stiffly.

"Yes, you do. You have a degree in Greco-Roman history," said Rena.

Maura turned her head away from the table and looked toward the sea.

"Maura, you may hate me for this, but I'm going to say it— Martin's dead! You're young. There are other men. . . ."

"How dare you," Maura said, her face twisting into that ugly rage look again. "You don't know anything about Martin!" She got up and quickly walked down the main street and disappeared into one of the narrow winding lanes of Paros.

Rena sat back, drinking her coffee and watching the sun come up. She'd give Maura some time to calm down, then she'd try to talk to her again.

A couple of hours later, when she returned to her hotel, she found the room empty. Maura and her luggage were gone.

It was the last time they ever saw each other.

The memories of that time in the Aegean so long ago exhausted Rena. Her last thought, just as she fell asleep, was the old lady's caustic remark about the god Hermes. What the hell had she meant by that?

Chapter Thirteen

RENA GOT UP early the next morning. She wanted to make an appointment with Dr. Frawley to discuss Maura. He was the McKinney family physician, and if anyone would have been aware of any abnormal behavior during her developmental years, it would have been him.

She took a quick shower and dressed. As she came downstairs, she could smell fresh coffee brewing.

In the kitchen Harrison Monroe stood by the counter pouring himself a cup of coffee. He was wearing wine-stained pants and knee-length rubber boots. When he heard footsteps coming toward him, he turned around. They both looked surprised to see each other.

"I'm sorry, I didn't know anyone was staying here," he said, smiling sheepishly. "Now at least I know why I found the coffeepot unwashed when I came in this morning. Your father gave me the key when he left and told me to make myself comfortable. I needed a quiet place to do the paperwork and my office wasn't it. The sound of the bottling plant going full blast during harvesting could make anybody crazy."

Rena was glad to see him. She had spent a restless night, waking up constantly from the horrible nightmares caused by de Montret's journal. His smiling, friendly face was a soothing sight.

"Want some?" he asked.

"Black," she said, going over to him.

As he poured her a cup, he said, "You look good in old jeans. I never thought you'd be the type that would wear them . . . at least wear them well."

"What kind of person did you think I was?" She took the cup from Harrison and brought it over to the antique pine table.

"Oh, let's see . . . someone who wears stylish business suits with frilly white blouses during the day . . . and for the nights you have a walk-in closet full of Givenchy gowns—a different one for every social event you ever attended. Maybe even a bulging drawer filled with matching, little striped outfits for the yacht races at Newport. Then . . ."

"Hey, enough!" she groaned, holding her hands up to stop him from going further. She sat down on the chair and dangled her leg over the top of the table. "That's how I really seem to you, huh? Like a pugged-nose, Fifth Avenue debutante?"

His green eyes were grinning at her. "Well . . . maybe a little," he said, holding his thumb and index finger about an inch apart from each other.

"Gee, thanks." She wore a mock frown on her face. Not only was he good-looking, but he was bright and likable. A rare trinity these days in men, she thought.

"What brings you back to the valley?" he asked, leaning against the granite countertop and stretching out his arms. He wore a short-sleeve shirt, and his exposed biceps were tight and defined.

"I left a friend here, remember?"

The smile faded from his face. "Have you heard the news this morning?"

"No, I just got up. Why?"

Harrison glanced at his watch. "The seven-o'clock news is on in a couple of minutes." He turned on the small TV set sitting on the counter.

She did not like the look on Harrison's face. The nervous feeling started to return as she got up off the chair and went over to the television.

Bryant Gumbel and Deborah Norville were doing a promo for their upcoming show, then the hourly local newscast came on.

The anchorman made the murders in the wine fields the featured story. He said that . . . "Strong new evidence now links Maura McKinney, an assistant DA in New York, to the killings." The nickname he used for her was the "Vineyard Butcher."

Rena got out of the chair and moved closer to the TV. She was in shock.

A news conference taped last night from a Seattle hotel appeared on the screen. Federal Agent Grant somberly walked up to the podium holding papers in his hand and read a written statement to the press. Ray Scollari stood next to him.

Grant said that genetic testing has now confirmed that the DNA makeup of the hair samples taken from Maura's bed in New York matched up with the hairs and skin samples found under the fingernails of the victim Arnold Baker. There was no longer any doubt that Maura McKinney had been committing the brutal murders in vineyards across the country. He said that the FBI believed she was hiding out somewhere in the northwestern part of the United States.

That's it then, Rena thought. Any small ray of hope she had that Maura was innocent before this morning now faded.

Grant stepped back from the podium and Scollari took over. He didn't have his suit jacket on, and his sleeves were rolled up, giving him the appearance of having been up all night working. Having met Scollari, Rena had a feeling that it was a well-rehearsed look.

What he said was brief but to the point. Shaking his head in disbelief, he said that after working closely with Maura for so many years, it pained him to find out that she was a killer. He then named several other well-known murderers—sociopaths who lived quiet lives and who were respected by their neighbors—and said that it was impossible to tell them apart from the rest of society. He then promised to do everything that was within his power to help the FBI and other law enforcement agencies apprehend her before she killed again.

My instincts were right about him, she thought. He was probably out to bury her. *The guy's actually using this tragedy as PR for his upcoming election. The Vineyard Butcher! My God, how distasteful!* In fact, she found all titles bestowed on murderers disturbing. *The Hillside Strangler . . . Son of Sam . . . The Night Stalker.* Those names belonged to wrestlers and comic-book characters, not to real-life psychopaths.

"Sorry about your friend," Harrison said, getting up to turn off the TV.

"So am I," Rena said softly. "So am I."

"Why do you think she did it? You've known her all your life," he asked compassionately.

It was a question she'd been asking herself for the last week. She put her hands in her jean pockets, leaned against the table, and said, "There's no simple answer, especially if the crimes are psychopathological in nature."

Harrison let out a small moan and ran his fingers anxiously through his long hair.

"What's the matter?" Rena asked.

He attempted a smile. "Nothing."

She didn't believe him.

He saw her looking at him strangely. "Okay. These damn murders are beginning to cause some problems with the workers. They're afraid to go out alone in the fields. Some of the more superstitious ones say she's a witch and that she's capable of being in different vineyards at the same time."

"That's absurd!" Rena quickly remarked.

"I know that. Many of them are too scared to come to work, and production has fallen off slightly. It's even worse in the smaller wineries where the owners can afford only one or two pickers. If I seem a little edgy, now you know why." He looked at his watch. "Hey, I've got to get going." He grabbed his windbreaker from the back of the chair and put it on. "We're picking the pinot today."

"What?" she said, her mind still on the news report.

"We're picking the grapes for the pinot noir. If you're not doing anything, come on over to the winery."

"I'll be busy most of the day."

"Will you be around for dinner?"

She was flattered. He was a nice man, easy to be with. It was just wrong timing right now. "I can't tonight," she said.

After he left, Rena looked up Frawley's home number and called him. He was already up and said he'd meet her at his office around ten o'clock.

As she brought the cups to the sink, Rena began to think about what would happen to Maura when they caught up with her. Would she be put in jail for life, or would her egghead colleagues at some institution put probes in her head in an attempt to determine why she was different from the rest of society? The vision of Maura strapped on a table with wires protruding from different parts of her body distressed her. The Maura she remembered was a proud, dignified woman who'd rather die than be subjected to that kind of humiliation.

At nine-thirty she took the keys for the Range Rover that were hung in the pantry door and left the house for her appointment with Frawley.

The drive to his office was not far. Rena pulled up in front of Doc Frawley's large Victorian house in the town of Calistoga. He was one of the few doctors left that combined his living quarters with his medical practice.

The last of his kind, she thought as the vision of a modern doctor's office with its rows of impersonal cubicles loomed in her mind. *I bet he even makes house calls.*

Rena walked up the stairs past the shingle that said WINSTON S. FRAWLEY M.D., and opened the door.

The waiting room was directly inside. The couches were aged and frayed, and the magazines in the rack were several years old. Particles of dust covered the table and shelves.

One patient, a woman in her seventies, stooped over, was sitting on the couch next to her metal walker. She nodded and smiled to Rena as she came into the room. Frawley poked his head out from the door of his office. He had on a white shirt, yellowed from age, and wore his tie knotted in a double Windsor.

"Mrs. Briggs, how are you today?" he said to the old woman as he helped her up.

"The same as yesterday and the day before that," she responded, laughing. She grabbed onto her walker with both hands and hobbled into his office.

Frawley looked at Rena and smiled. "I'll be free in a few minutes. We'll talk then." He closed the door.

While waiting alone in the room, Rena could guess what had happened to Frawley's practice: time had passed him by. The younger patients went to the corporation doctors with their insurance forms and cubicles. The older ones who remained loyal to Frawley began to die off, and there were no new replacements.

Twenty minutes later Mrs. Briggs, with the aid of her walker, limped slowly out of his office. Frawley helped her down the steps and onto the sidewalk. He came back and told Rena to come inside.

His office, like the waiting room, was drab green and in need of a new coat of paint. The dirt-streaked glass frame holding his medical degree hung on the wall in back of his desk. To the side, the door to the examining room was open, and Rena could see his medical equipment: a gurney with tufts of cotton protruding from its leather casing, an X-ray machine, a medicine cabinet, an EKG monitor, and a table containing bandages, swabs, and a glass jar filled with wooden throat depressors. The equipment, like everything else about Frawley's practice, was worn and in need of a face-lift.

In the corner of the examining room Rena noticed a much newer machine that contrasted deeply with the rest of the equipment. It looked like an ultrasound with a monitor attached to it. Why would he need that for a general practice? she wondered, somewhat confused.

Frawley sat down in an old, wooden, paint-chipped swivel chair behind his rolltop desk and motioned Rena toward the leather armchair.

"I don't think you're here for a physical, not that I wouldn't mind giving you one," he said, with a twinkle in his eye. "Most of my patients are even older than Mrs. Briggs."

"Actually, Dr. Frawley . . ."

"Call me Winnie, that's what everybody calls me around these parts. It's short for Winston. That's the title the British fondly dubbed Churchill." He took a pipe out of his jacket pocket and filled it with tobacco from a glass canister on his desk.

"Have the police or the FBI contacted you regarding Maura McKinney?" Rena asked him.

"Yes, why?" he said, the gleam suddenly going out of his eyes.

"They seem to have conclusive evidence that she murdered all those people."

"That's what they tell me. Hard to believe, though," he said with concern, puffing on his pipe. "The Maura I knew, and I knew her all her life, could never do a thing like that."

"I *felt* the same way. There are times now when I'm starting to ask myself, 'How well *did* I really know her?' "

"What do you mean?" His eyes hardened with suspicion.

"Look, Doctor, I was her friend. If she's out there, I want to help her. I don't want to see her harmed."

"All I can tell you is the same thing I told the police and the FBI boys. I was her physician from the day she was born up to the time she left for New York. That was many years ago. I know she must have changed somewhat . . . hell, New York could change anybody."

"How was her health as a child?"

"Excellent, aside from the common childhood ailments like measles and the mumps." He put his pipe down on the ashtray, took off his steel-framed glasses, and began to clean them with a handkerchief.

"Was there concern on your part at any time for the condition of her mental well-being?"

Frawley put his glasses back on and slumped into his chair. "Yes," he said. "Right after a boy she used to go with was murdered."

"Martin Bynum."

"That's correct."

Rena leaned forward. "He was killed the day of Maura's seventeenth birthday party. She was the one who supposedly found him."

"Yup, that's certainly true," he said, shaking his head. "I wouldn't wish that discovery on anybody. I was acting coroner then when the police called and asked me to get over to the Bynum house. His parent's bedroom was a mess . . . blood and brains scattered everywhere. The son of a bitch who did it used a twelve-gauge shotgun and aimed it directly at his head. Martin couldn't have been more than a foot away from the barrel of the gun when it went off."

"Was she the one who called the police?"

"No, her father did. According to him, she ran back home and told him what had happened. That night, I received a call from him asking me to come to his house. He said his daughter

133

was acting crazy and that he didn't know what to do about it. I could hear her screaming in the background. When I got there, I found her breaking up the house. Peter was trying to grab hold of her, but she was in such a tumultuous state that she easily broke his hold. At one point she even threw him across the room. I never saw anything like that before. She was calling him all sorts of names, blaming him for Martin's death. Luckily I brought along a sedative. It took 20 milligrams of Valium in order to quiet her down."

"It would have to take an amazing amount of strength to throw a man across a room," she said.

"Yes, I suppose so," he said quickly.

"When did she start coming around?"

Frawley at first didn't answer. He tapped the bowl of his pipe on the wire ashtray, emptying the ashes out of it. "This part I didn't tell the police. I really didn't think it was any of their business—besides, I promised her father I wouldn't tell anyone," he finally said. After another deep pause he continued. "She was put in a private sanitarium up in the state of Washington for several weeks."

"Washington? That's where the FBI thinks she is now."

"Yes, I heard about it over the news. Maura being put away was kept very quiet. Peter McKinney was a proud man and didn't want anybody to know about it. Eventually she came around . . . returned home, and went back to school. Except something was lost in her . . . something subtle. It was as if a flame that once sparkled inside her was no longer there."

"I know exactly what you mean," Rena said, thinking back to the difference in Maura's personality when they vacationed together five years later in Greece. The Maura she spent her summers with as a child was carefree and had a passion for life. The one she saw after Martin's murder was secretive, distant.

"That's all there is to tell I suppose. What else would you like to know?" Frawley asked.

"I doubt if you can help me with this, but something's always bothered me about these mutilations. The castrations seem to be made by someone who seems to be familiar with surgical procedures. The incisions were always done cleanly, as if they were the work of a professional. I don't remember Maura ever being interested in medicine."

"Hell!" He slammed his hand on the desk, then rubbed his cheeks trying to bring life back into his defeated face. Sighing

134

deeply, he said slowly, "You don't have to have four years of medical school to know where the ovaries and the testes are located. You just have to be proficient in the human anatomy, and I doubt if anyone knew the human anatomy better than Maura McKinney."

Rena looked up at Frawley. "Why would she know it better than most people?"

He shook his head from the impact of his own statement. "When Maura was fourteen or fifteen, I don't remember which, I gave her a copy of the book, *Gray's Anatomy*."

"Why?"

"Two reasons. The first one being, as an artist, she was interested in the human anatomy. You've seen her drawings . . . how precisely she sketched the details of her models. You need to know where everything goes in the human body in order to do that."

Rena remembered how literal and clear Maura's sketches were. "And the second reason?"

"Maura had a knack for science . . . especially biological science. She was a whiz at dissecting frogs and guinea pigs for school projects. Sometimes she'd bring her dissections to me to see if she had done them right. She was one of those rare breeds—equally gifted in science as she was in art and law."

Rena nodded in acknowledgment of Maura's attributes.

"Anything else, my dear? I have lots of time. As you can see, nobody's breaking down my door for my medical expertise," he said with a biting edge in his voice. He stood up and walked over to the window and looked out. "This will be my last year practicing medicine," he said quietly. "I have cancer of the pancreas. Whatever time I have left I want to devote to my winery."

"I'm sorry."

He shrugged.

"I didn't know you were interested in wine," she said.

"Hell, everybody around here grows grapes of one kind or another. It's a way of life in this valley."

"Yes, I do have one more question. What happened at Maura's birth?"

"What?" His face turned pale.

Rena noticed. "You once said to me . . . 'if only Maura's mother could have reached full term.' What did you mean by that?"

His color returned as quickly as it had disappeared. "Oh that," he said. "What I meant was, if she had carried Maura for nine months, maybe she would be alive today."

Rena believed when he originally said it he meant more than that, but she wasn't going to push him. "Where are the McKinneys buried?" she asked suddenly.

"Over in the cemetery in Oakville."

She got up.

"Are you going?" he asked. "There's no rush."

"I'm afraid I have to," she said.

Frawley walked her to the door. As he opened it for her, she asked, "Are you an obstetrician?"

"What? No, of course not. I'm a general practitioner. Why?"

"I was just wondering. I saw ultrasound equipment in your examining room. The general purpose for having it is to examine fetuses in pregnant women."

Frawley laughed. "My dear, when you've practiced medicine for as long as I have in a small town you learn to do a little bit of everything."

She thanked Doctor Frawley and left.

As she got into the car and drove back toward the Alexander Valley, she wondered what really frightened Frawley when she brought up Maura's birth.

Then she began thinking about the truck driver, Arnie Baker. Why was he alive? There was no rush for Maura to make the kill; it was late at night, and the Yakima vineyards were located in an unpopulated area. The spike had missed his vertebra by an inch. An inch is a lot when you're talking about a small neck like Arnie's, she thought. Was he left alive on purpose as a macabre kind of joke? If she's caught and put on trial, Arnie Baker's testimony will be the final nail in her coffin. Is that what she wanted?

"Let's see what we can find out about the McKinneys," she said to herself, turning the car around and heading south to Oakville.

She found the cemetery bordered by a Catholic church on the outskirts of the town. Rena crossed the street and went in to see if anybody there would be able to help her locate the McKinney plot.

Inside, an elderly priest who was lighting candles took her back out to the steps of the church and pointed to where the graves were located.

It was a small cemetery with some of the granite stones dating back to the 1800s. Somewhere in the middle of it Rena located the graves.

The first headstone belonged to Maura's father:

> Peter Sean McKinney
> Born November 20, 1921
> Died October 3, 1974

The second one shook Rena up.

> William Tyrone McKinney
> A Loving Brother and Son
> Born September 18, 1957
> Died September 18, 1957

My God! Rena thought. Maura had a twin brother who died the same day they were born! *Why didn't she ever tell me? Why didn't Frawley tell me?* Then she remembered Peter McKinney's words to Maura up in his attic so long ago:

"You bloody witch! They died because of you!"

Now at least she understood who "they" were. McKinney was talking about his wife, Clair, and his son, William Tyrone.

Then Rena looked at the third headstone, and when she read the inscription she gasped in horror.

> Clair de Montret McKinney
> Born April 8, 1925
> Died September 18, 1957

De Montret was Clair McKinney's maiden name.

She had been wrong. The journal of Baron de Montret didn't belong to Peter McKinney as she originally thought. It belonged to Maura's mother.

THREE

THREE

Chapter Fourteen

CHARLIE STARED AT the small red circle painted on the forehead of the pretty Indian reporter. She was sitting two rows in front of him in the balcony of the large conference room. The bright-colored sari she had on clung to her body, exposing her shapely shoulders and dark brown arms.

Stunning, he thought. *In fact, absolutely fucking ravishing!*

He rested his chin on his hands against the small table in front of him and envisioned both of them together in his hotel room. She'd be standing next to the bed, her lustful, almond eyes glowing with desire. He'd saunter over to her. Grabbing hold of the end of her sari, he'd slowly circle her, letting the cloth unravel from her body. The yards of cotton would eventually disappear, revealing nipples that were dark as ebony. She'd then put her arms around him, holding him close, and he'd smell the flower-scented oil in her thick, black hair.

Charlie looked away, but the image of the naked Indian woman wouldn't leave his mind. He glanced around the room and was suddenly reminded that he was surrounded by newspeople from all over the world. *Knock it off, asshole! You're paid to cover the OPEC conference, not to fantasize about the women of third-world countries.*

Except that meant listening to a bunch of greedy bastards holding the world by its throat, trying to squeeze another dime out of it for a barrel of oil.

In the large room of the convention center downstairs the representatives of the oil-rich countries fought among themselves. Nobody seemed to be in control; everybody was screaming at once.

Charlie had long ago removed his earpiece and turned off the machine that translated the Arabic into English.

"Oh, Christ! A month of this shit!" he moaned to himself. There was no way he could listen to this any longer; he'd just have to take his copy from UPI and Reuters, that's all. As long as the Indian woman hung around, he'd have his daydreams to keep him going.

Just as he turned his eyes back to the woman, he felt someone tapping him on the shoulder. It was a young page.

"Monsieur, papers from America have been expressed to you. They're back at your hotel."

"From who?" he asked, hoping it wasn't from his newspaper.

"A Madame Halbrook."

Relieved, Charlie handed him a twenty-franc note, snapped the top back on his lap-top computer, and got up to leave. It had to be important, he thought. As he made his way toward the exit door, he turned and took one last look at the sensuous Indian reporter, then left.

Outside the conference hall, Charlie hailed a taxi. The OPEC meeting was held near the Arc de Triomphe de l'Etoile and the hotel he was staying at was way across town on rue des Ecole. He preferred the university life of the Latin Quarter to that of the solemn hotels on the avenue George where most of the other reporters stayed.

The taxi dropped him off next to his small hotel. It was lunch hour, and the streets and cafés were alive with the students from the Sorbonne.

In the lobby the concierge handed Charlie a thick, heavy envelope.

When he got to his room, he took off his suit and tie and tossed them on the chair. Getting into his faded 501's, he lay down on his bed and tore open the envelope. Inside he found a note from Rena along with de Montret's journal.

Dear Charlie,
I know you're bored as hell by now, so I'm sure you'll be thrilled doing me a couple of favors. First, read the journal I sent you, then see if you can find out if Wilbur Striker and de Montret actually existed. The baron lived in Bordeaux. Clair de Montret is the maiden name of Maura's mother. For some reason Maura is recreating the murders that took place in this 200-year-old diary. One other thing, it seems the last section of the journal was deliberately torn out. Striker thought it to

be important. See what you can learn about that. Will explain more later on.

Ree

P.S. I know the women in Paris have nice white skin but try to stay out of trouble, okay?

Charlie grinned, thinking about the Indian woman. Her skin was anything but white.

He began feeling hungry. Putting on a turtleneck sweater and his aviator's jacket, he left the hotel with the journal under his arm. At the small café on the corner he ordered a cheese sandwich on a *baguette* and a double espresso. Sitting in the back, away from the loud din of the students, he began to read the diary.

By the time he finished the last page, he had consumed another sandwich and two more double espressos. The caffeine flowed through his veins, pumping his heart with excitement. Now *this* was something he could get into! It beat the hell out of writing about oil cartels.

But where do you begin? he thought to himself. *Christ, the diary is almost fifty years old!*

Start with Wilbur Striker. Nobody names their son Wilbur unless the parents have a death wish for him. He's either American, English, or Canadian.

Charlie then looked at the date of the journal.

It was translated in 1943. France was occupied by the Germans then, and the Vichy government was in power.

How did Striker get his hands on the original French version of the journal? *Wait a fucking minute!* After almost every section, he used the term "field agent" before his name!

Yeah! Yeah! Yeah!

He was beginning to have a pretty good idea of what "field agent" meant back then, and the caffeine rush made his heart pound even faster.

He left money on the table and raced back to the hotel to make a phone call, hoping Jonathan Bodine still worked as a liaison officer for the American Embassy in Paris. They had become good friends while serving together in Vietnam, but it had been several years since they last saw each other.

Charlie knew he was in luck when the operator at the embassy said, "He'll be right with you."

143

"How's the liaison business, Bo?" Charlie said when he heard Bodine's low-pitched voice on the line.

"Good, Charlie. Life's been good."

"Hey, that's terrific, I really mean it. Look, I've got to talk to you. It's important."

"What's going on, Charlie?" he asked.

"Over the phone? Are you losing it or something?"

A pause, then, "How about the Café Chagall across from the embassy at six o'clock?"

"How about in twenty minutes. I have a deadline to meet at six."

Another pause, then . . . "That important, huh?"

"Yep."

"See you then, Charlie."

As the taxi pulled up in front of the Café Chagall on avenue Gabriel, Charlie could see Bodine's familiar bald head and walrus mustache through the tinted window. He was standing at the bar, sandwiched between several well-dressed men, drinking a Pernod and water.

Still looks like your typical nonentity pencil pusher, Charlie thought as he paid the driver. *Nobody'd ever suspect ol' Bo of being CIA.*

Charlie had always known who paid Bodine's bills. He had known about Bo's employers ever since they fought alongside each other in Thua Thien Province. One night in a Saigon whorehouse, Bodine had gotten so piss-assed drunk that he told Charlie everything he was doing, including his role in the covert operations in Cambodia. When he finished talking, he then proceeded to throw up all over his *mama san* before passing out cold.

Charlie pushed his way through the crowded section of the bar until he reached Jonathan Bodine. "That stuff will rot your brain, Bo," he said, slapping him on the back.

"You're talking about absinthe. *I'm* drinking Pernod. Get your alcohol straight, Charlie, if you plan on getting shit-faced with me."

They laughed and threw their arms warmly around each other.

"Long time, no see. Looks like you grew a few inches," Bodine said, pinching Charlie's stomach.

"Those are love handles, chum," Charlie replied. He got the bartender's attention and ordered a Remy in a snifter.

They talked about old times and relived war stories over two more rounds of drinks. When the place began to empty out, they drifted over to a table at the end of the café and sat down.

"So, what are you into now?" Charlie asked.

"Now? Not a hell of a lot. Times are tough since *perestroika*. Before everybody became chummy with each other, I would sit at some café, exactly like this one, and some frightened-looking attaché from an eastern bloc country would come over and sit next to me. He'd order a cup of coffee, and his hands would be shaking so bad that he'd spill the shit all over himself. Then he'd give me some papers that he probably found in a wastepaper basket at his embassy, and I'd hand him some money under the table. Real secretive cloak-and-dagger bullshit! The whole fucking café would be watching us and laughing. So, that's what I was into, Charlie." The smile left his face and he got serious. "Now what are *we* into?"

Charlie held up two fingers to the bartender and pointed to their empty glasses, then he turned to Bodine and said, "What do you know about your organization during the Nazi occupation of France?"

"What are you talking about? My company was first formed after the war."

"But your predecessor was around."

"You mean the OSS?"

"Uh-huh."

"Now those motherfuckers knew how to conduct covert operations!" Bodine said, his speech beginning to slur from the liquor. "Alan Ladd parachuting into France in the middle of the night and meeting babes like Geraldine Fitzgerald. Ever see that movie? That's what I thought it was all about when I was a kid. If someone ever told me I'd be spending my life taking not-so-secret documents from Don Knotts look-alikes in cafés, I'd have joined up with Abbie Hoffman in the sixties. At least *he* got laid."

"What were the Alan Ladd guys called when they were on operations in enemy territory?"

"Huh?"

"Were they called field agents?"

"Yeah. Real original, right? We're known for our creative knack with words."

The waiter came with their drinks.

Bodine toasted Charlie by touching glasses then gulped down half his drink. "So, what's this all about, Charlie? You planning on writing a novel about my company? Now that's *really* original! Only one out of every two books are written about us." He wiped the glistening drops of Pernod with his thumb off his walrus mustache.

"How do I find out what happened to one of those field agents?" Charlie asked, sipping his Remy slowly.

"Are you serious? I highly doubt if the OSS kept great records back then. They were just a bunch of regular G.I.s with a little more on the ball than most who could speak another language. They were given a few weeks of training, then dumped out of an airplane over one of the occupied countries. Not many made it back."

"Yeah, that's what I thought," Charlie said, resigned.

"Give me a name. I'll see if any of the old cronies back at the office remember him from their OSS days."

"Wilbur Striker."

Bodine didn't say anything for a few seconds; he just stared at Charlie in amazement. Suddenly he broke into hysterical laughter and slapped his hand down hard on the table. "No, no, no . . . say it ain't so!" He continued laughing and shaking his head until his face turned a deep red.

"Hey, Bo, let me in on the joke, okay?"

"Wilbur Harrison Striker was head of operations in the Paris office until his retirement fifteen years ago," he said, between guffaws. "The fucker's legendary!" Bodine wiped the tears of laughter from his eyes with the back of his hand. "The son of a bitch made everybody's life miserable when he was in charge, but he was good at his job, you had to give him that."

"Shit! And I thought I was looking for a needle in a haystack!" Charlie said.

"Nope, what you were looking for *was* the haystack!"

"Is he still living?"

"Barely. He's got emphysema. Never goes anywhere without his oxygen mask. He owns a flat in the sixteenth *arrondissement*. *Très* posh! A full-time German male nurse lives with him."

"Do you think he'll talk to me?"

"Nope. That ornery bastard wouldn't even talk to the President of the United States when he tried to hang the Medal of Honor around his neck." Bo then stood up and began to button up his wrinkled London Fog raincoat. "Well, it's been fun, but I gotta go and make my country safe for democracy."

"You okay?" Charlie asked, seeing the condition he was in.

"Shit, yeah!" Bodine said, swaying. "It's the only way I can

146

make it through the day." He was having trouble putting the last button through the hole. Charlie stood up and helped him.

"I need Striker's home number. I doubt very much if he's listed," Charlie said, smoothing down Bodine's collar.

Bodine had a smile around the corners of his mouth, and there was an amused, almost playful look in his bloodshot eyes. "I'll tell you what, Charlie, you stand near the phone at the bar and I'll call you with it when I get back to my office. If you tell anybody you got it from me, I'll cut your heart out, got it?"

"I got it."

"If you get that bastard to talk to you, dinner's on me," he said as he stumbled toward the door.

"Hey, Bo," Charlie shouted across the café.

Bodine turned around.

"Thanks."

"Don't thank me yet. If you don't get to talk to him, it's dinner at Maxim's on you, asshole." He smoothed back his thick mustache and staggered out of the café.

Charlie went over to the bar, put his foot up on the brass rail, ordered a double espresso, and waited.

Two minutes later the phone rang. The bartender picked it up. After a beat he handed the receiver to Charlie. *"Pour vous, monsieur."*

Charlie took the phone from him and within seconds had Striker's home number scribbled on the back of a box of matches.

And now for the hard part, he thought.

He gave the bartender twenty francs for the use of the phone, then he called Striker's number.

After several rings, a man's voice answered in French with a German accent.

Charlie asked in English to talk with Wilbur Striker.

"I am sorry but he cannot talk to anyone right now. He is eating his dinner," the German-accented voice said firmly.

Charlie could hear Striker somewhere in the room on the other end breathing heavily into a respirator. "Tell him it's his old friend from Bordeaux calling, Baron Gustave de Montret."

"One moment, *Herr* baron."

The sound of muffled words could faintly be heard coming from the man on the phone, then a gravelly voice responding to him. After what seemed like minutes, he began to talk to Charlie again.

"What is your real name, please?"

"Charles Halleran. I'm a reporter, but this has nothing to do with my job. It's personal."

More clouded voices on the other end, then the man said to him, "Do you know where the Place des Vosges is?"

"Of course. Near where the Bastille used to be."

"At six-thirty this evening go to the Place des Vosges and stand directly in the center of it next to the fountains. If you are one meter off in either direction you will meet no one. Is that understood?"

"Understood," Charlie said.

The line went dead at the other end.

What the hell have you gotten me into, Rena my love? he wondered, as he walked out of the café.

Chapter Fifteen

B Y SIX-FIFTEEN CHARLIE had found the exact center of the Place des Vosges. He found it by counting his steps as he walked lengthwise from one end of the large rectangular parade ground to the other end. Dividing that in half, he then did the same thing for the width. He felt like a damn idiot; late shoppers and people going home from work would stop and shake their heads in amusement, watching him goose-stepping across the field.

Striker was smart, he thought to himself. The Place des Vosges offered no protection, and he was standing right in the center of it. Charlie waited there not daring to move for another half hour.

Autumn had finally come to Paris; it was damp and cold, and the streets glistened from the wetness. He zipped up his leather jacket, pulled up his fur collar, and stuck his hands into his pockets for warmth. It didn't help much; the Parisian dampness seeped down into his bones and made his teeth chatter.

It was getting dark out now, and the square was beginning

to empty out. In the distance he could see headlights of cars whisking by on Rue St. Antoine but none of them stopped.

Where the hell was Striker? He'd better show! I'm going to be up all night as it is trying to make the deadline for my paper. He knew that he was out there somewhere, watching him freeze; Charlie sensed that as deeply as he could feel the cold.

He looked at his watch. *Five minutes more, that's all I'm giving the son of a bitch!* He swayed from foot to foot, trying to keep warm. Suddenly he saw the headlights of a van go on that was parked on the Boulevard Beaumarchais. It pulled out and slowly moved in his direction. When it was a couple of hundred feet away, the van stopped.

I should have been looking for a van all along. Striker's an invalid, and a van would be his best way of getting around.

The driver, a tall stocky fellow with blond bangs, got out of the vehicle, went around to the side, and slid the door open. Inside, on a platform, a frail little man was sitting in an electric wheelchair. He was covered with a blanket. The driver pressed a button, and the steel platform descended to the curb. The little man who Charlie knew had to be Striker motored his chair toward him. He stopped a few feet away.

Charlie couldn't see Striker because he was well hidden in the shadows behind the floodlights. A gurgling sound, like a diver breathing underwater, came from his direction.

"Mr. Striker, I presume," Charlie said.

At first there was no reply, then Striker said, "Get over to the light where I can see you." His voice sounded like there were pebbles rattling around in the back of his throat.

Charlie did what he was told and walked over to the floodlight.

"What is it you want?" Striker asked abruptly.

"To find out if de Montret actually existed."

"Why?"

"His diary was discovered back in the States by the FBI. It had your name in it."

Charlie heard Striker say under the loud sputter of his breathing, "Damn that McKinney!"

He was stunned that he knew McKinney's name. As he began to walk toward the wheelchair, Striker growled, "Stay where you are!"

Charlie froze from the sharpness of the old man's voice.

"I'll tell you when to move!" he crackled.

The flame from a gold lighter appeared in Striker's shaky hand.

He brought it up to his face and lit a Gitane that he held between his paper-thin lips.

For one brief second Charlie could see Striker's face in the glow of the flame. Two plastic tubes protruded from his nostrils and ran down the side of the chair and into a small oxygen tank attached to the armrest. There were traces of a goatee on his chin, and he wore a Basque cap on his head that hung down over his ears. Thick veins, like blue rivers and their tributaries, ran through his thin, bony hands. Then the flame went out and there was darkness again.

Charlie knew better than to go by looks; disease may have ravished Striker's body but his mind was intact.

"Why are you interested in de Montret?" the old man demanded to know.

"Because the same kinds of murders that the baron committed two hundred years ago are now occurring in wine fields across the United States," Charlie answered.

There was no response from Striker. The only way Charlie knew that he was still there was from the sound of his mechanical breathing and the red glow of his cigarette. Then he heard Striker whisper those words again, "Damn you, McKinney!"

"The person accused of the killings is Maura McKinney, the daughter of Peter McKinney," Charlie said, hoping that it would provoke a response from Striker.

It did. Striker began coughing. The hacking sound came from deep within his chest. Then Charlie could hear him spitting up thick wads of phlegm. He wondered how much longer he was given to live. Obviously the threat of imminent death didn't bother Striker, since he still smoked.

Charlie looked over to the van. The big man with the bangs was standing next to the open side door staring coldly at him. I bet that's his German nurse, Charlie thought.

"I didn't know about the murders," Striker said, when the coughing spell subsided.

"It was in all the papers. I even saw an article about it this morning in the *International Herald Tribune*."

"I no longer read the papers," Striker said contemptuously.

"It was on all the TV stations."

"I *never* watch television."

"How did you know Peter McKinney?"

"Why is it important to you?" Striker asked distrustfully.

"Someone I know happens to be a very close friend of

150

McKinney's daughter. That someone asked me to find out if the de Montret journals were real or just the product of a sick mind. I promised to do this for her," Charlie said sincerely.

"You're also a newspaperman," Striker snapped.

"I'm in Paris to cover the OPEC conference, that's all. Nothing you say to me tonight will ever get into print."

"If it does I'll kill you," he said ominously.

Charlie nodded. He believed Striker would do just that.

"You want to know how I met McKinney? All right, I'll tell you. We met during the war. I was in the OSS and he was in British intelligence," Striker said wearily. "He was one of only a handful of IRA combatants that was willing to bury his grievances with the Brits in order to fight the Germans. His French was impeccable, even better than mine. Before the war he spent time in France working in the wineries. We trained together in Wales learning how to be good little spies. Before World War II spying wasn't exactly a revered occupation."

Charlie could tell beneath the sarcasm that Striker and McKinney must have been good friends.

"Our mission was to monitor German troop movements in Bordeaux. On a wet night—similar to this one—we parachuted into France. Several people from the Resistance were waiting for us on the ground holding up lanterns to help pinpoint our landing. One of them was a beautiful young girl named Clair de Montret." Striker sighed deeply, then cleared his throat as if to regain his poise.

Even though Charlie's teeth were now chattering uncontrollably, he picked up the change in Striker's voice when he mentioned Clair. Was this old coot in love with her? he wondered.

"McKinney broke his ankle on the jump. The men carried him to Clair's father's château . . . the Château de Montret. Have you ever heard of it?"

Charlie shook his head. "Not until the diary."

"Of course not. What would you know about great wines," he snickered. "If you owned a bottle with the Château de Montret label, it meant that you possessed the finest Bordeaux wine in all of France. The de Montret family had been producing great wines for hundreds of years."

"I'm a connoisseur of beers," Charlie mumbled.

Striker continued. "It was an old château . . . big . . . lots of character. I only found out later how much character it *really* possessed," he said with a chill in his voice. "Peter McKinney stayed hidden in Clair de Montret's attic until his foot healed. I worked as a French laborer in the winery—picking grapes . . . bottling . . . doing a little bit of everything. In-between, I gathered intelligence for the Allies."

"Is that when Clair fell in love with McKinney?" Charlie couldn't see Striker, but he could feel his eyes penetrate him when he asked that.

"Yes, she fell in love with him," he said sharply. "*They* fell in love with each other." Again Striker let out a sigh, and it sounded like a death rattle. "She was the one who took care of him, stayed with him twenty-four hours a day, wiped his brow when he was delirious with fever. His foot, you see, became infected with gangrene. He would have died if it weren't for her perseverance in keeping him alive."

The dampness in the air had now turned into a fine mist, and Charlie was soaking wet; water ran down his face and into his eyes. "Do you think we could maybe find a drier place to talk?" He was so cold he was stuttering.

"Too wet for you?" Striker asked with some amusement.

Out of the darkness came Striker's skeletal hand holding a silver flask.

"What's that?" Charlie asked.

"Cognac. Take it. I wouldn't want it on my conscience that you caught pneumonia and died because of me."

Charlie grabbed it from him and took two large swallows. It was good cognac and it went down smoothly. Within seconds his body began to feel almost warm again.

Then Striker asked cheerfully, "Hungry, Mr. Halleran?"

His tone caught Charlie by surprise. "Yeah, sure." *Anything to get out of this cold.*

"Hans!" he screamed to the man still standing by the van. The richness of his voice did not sound at all like that of a dying man.

Hans, wearing a black leather trench coat, ambled over to them.

"Our guest is hungry, Hans. Let's feed him," Striker said vigorously, clapping and rubbing his hands together. He turned the power of the motorized wheelchair back on and made his way toward the van.

Smiling at Charlie with cold, dead eyes, Hans motioned for him to follow.

After the electric platform had lifted Striker into the van, Hans said to Charlie in a thick German accent, "Get in, please." He grabbed Charlie's arm in a strong, viselike grip and hoisted him up.

The van was custom-built for Striker. It was dark inside except for a small light next to the table. Hans hopped in and strapped Striker's chair to the wall and locked the wheels. He then picked up the old man in his arms and gently eased him into a plush chair by the table.

"Sit, please," Hans ordered Charlie.

Charlie sat down on the other side of him.

Hans opened the small refrigerator over by the wall; took out cheese, bread, and hard salami, and placed them on the table.

Charlie's mouth began to water; until now he hadn't realized how hungry he was.

Hans also grabbed a St. Pauli beer, took the cap off, and gave it to Charlie. He then got into the driver's seat, turned on the engine, and drove away.

Charlie dug into the food. It was only after the second piece of cheese that he noticed Striker wasn't eating. He looked at him quizzically.

"Please, my friend . . . eat," Striker said laughing. There was still that tinge of sarcasm. "The only thing my stomach can digest nowadays has to have the consistency of watered-down gruel. I prefer my cognac to that."

"When did Clair and Peter McKinney get married?" Charlie asked with a mouthful of salami.

"Ah, yes . . . Peter and Clair. They married in Bordeaux, in the old church of Saint-Seurin. A lovely wedding. I was best man. Unfortunately it was a mistake. I warned Peter that he needed to keep a low profile, that he couldn't afford to stand out and be noticed by the Nazis. But Clair's father, old de Montret, wouldn't hear of it. It was his daughter's wedding, and he wanted her to be married in Saint-Seurin. All the de Montrets have been married there since the early sixteen hundreds." Striker paused a second, then said caustically, "Well . . . all except one." Again he paused to think. After a while, he continued. "The Nazis eventually wanted to know who McKinney was. After all, he had to be someone important to be able to marry the richest and prettiest woman in Bordeaux. Then what I feared the most began to happen. Inquiries were made about him from the Vichy government. When they looked over Peter's documents, they discovered that he was using the name and papers of a man who'd been dead for over fifty years. They came for him in the middle of the night. He was arrested along with Clair and old de Montret. I hid in the cellar and watched from a small window as they took him away. There was nothing I could do. If one of us was killed or captured we were taught to go on with whatever job we were doing and not to look back. Two days later McKinney escaped with the help of the Resistance. It was too late, however, to help de Montret and Clair. The Germans had already executed him the night before, and Clair had been sent to a labor camp in Belgium. McKinney came to get me. He said that we had to leave, that the Germans were coming to pillage de Montret's château and then blow it up.''

''Why do that?'' Charlie asked.

''As a lesson to the people of Bordeaux. If you help the Allies, not only will you be killed, but your belongings taken and your house destroyed. Most of the time it worked. The French, you see, place a higher regard on property than lives,'' he muttered ungraciously.

''What about the journal?''

''I'm getting to that. We could hear the Germans coming. They were only a short distance down the road. I grabbed McKinney's arm to get him to run but he brushed me away and rushed up the stairs of the château. He came down carrying a frayed, leather-bound journal. He was like a man possessed. He said, 'I have to destroy it! Nobody must ever find it! I promised Clair!' He wanted to light a fire and burn it right then and there but it was too late. The Germans were almost upon us. This time I grabbed him by the waist and flung him out the door. We ran and hid in the woods above Montret's château. We watched as the Germans moved in. They took everything that wasn't nailed down. Then they planted explosives and blew up that beautiful estate. . . . Nothing was left standing. We raced through the woods most of the night trying to get to the sea. A fishing trawler was waiting there to pick us up. Not far back, we could hear the soldiers' dogs begin to bark; they discovered our scent. The Germans found us and started shooting. We made it to the sea, but not before I was hit in the stomach by a bullet. As I lay in the sand I could see McKinney deciding about what to do with the journal. He then put it in his backpack. From then on everything was vague. McKinney carried me into the water toward a waiting raft. I remember begging him to leave me, but he wouldn't hear of it. He said that he had already lost two people that were dear to him. I blacked out. When I came around again I found myself lying in a berth on the ship. Peter was sitting next to me reading from those old parchments. I had never seen him looking so distraught, not even when he found out that Clair had been taken out of France by the Nazis. I asked him what was in them, but all he did was shake his head. He took the diary and left the cabin. Then I also became a man possessed: I had to know what was in that diary. What was so important about it that would make McKinney risk his life at the château, refusing to leave without the manuscript? I had to know! Somehow I managed to get my wounded body off the cot and followed him down the passageway. He went into the boiler room. From the crack in the door, I watched him fling the book into the furnace. Just then the alarm sounded, warning the crew that enemy ships were close by. He ran out of the furnace room and back to his quarters. I hid behind the steps until he was out of sight. Then I went into the room, grabbed a shovel, and quickly took out the remains of the book. It was badly charred but most of it was still readable. I took it back with me and hid it under my cot. The next day we arrived in the English Channel, and Peter was rafted over to Brighton to undergo debriefing. I was taken further down the channel to Bournemouth where I spent two months recuperating from my wound. I spent most of my time in the hospital translating that horrible journal into English!''

Striker took out another Gitane and lit it with his gold lighter. As he deeply inhaled the thick smoke, the sound coming from his diseased lungs reminded Charlie of the motor from his tropical fish tank that he kept in his bedroom as a kid.

"Open up the cabinet in back of you," he commanded Charlie.

Charlie turned around and opened up the oak cabinet. It was filled with an array of liqueurs and brandies.

"Take out the dusty bottle. It's one-hundred-year-old cognac. What the hell am I keeping it for!" he grumbled. "I'll be dead in six months, and I don't want my last thoughts to be of regret that I left this beautiful cognac behind to be pillaged by Hans."

Charlie stood up and handed it to him. Striker popped the cork with his frail fingers.

"You're too used to drinking American piss that passes itself off as beer, Halleran. You need crystal for this kind of stuff. Get them out of the cabinet, for Christ sakes!"

Turning around again, Charlie took two Baccarat snifters from the cabinet and placed them on the table. Striker handed him back the bottle so he could pour.

They sipped their cognacs in silence for a while, letting the alcohol warm their bones. Then Charlie asked, "Is the journal real?"

"Yes, it's real, all right. I had it carbon-dated after the war was over. It was written two hundred years ago, that's for sure."

"How did Peter McKinney get the journal into his possession again?"

"I brought it to him, that's how. I heard that he found Clair in a relocation camp after the war. He owned some property in Northern California that was willed to his family by some great-grand uncle or something. He decided to take Clair there and start a new life. The great château of her father was destroyed along with his wine fields, and there was nothing left for them in France or Ireland. Fourteen years later I came to San Francisco on business and I went to Napa to find them. I took the journal with me." There was a pause, then he said slowly, "I didn't know Clair had died in childbirth. I was stunned. Maura was two years old at that time. She was the most beautiful child I had ever seen. My God was she ever! McKinney and I went and sat out on his porch overlooking his vineyards and talked about the war. But I really wasn't listening; I was too busy staring at his daughter playing by herself near the steps. With that long blond hair, she was an exact replica of Clair."

It was dark, but Charlie could see the old man's eyes beginning to water.

"I gave McKinney the parchments and my translation of the diary. He turned pale when he saw them. He took them from me, but he didn't want to talk about it. When I insisted, he became enraged at first, then gave in. I asked him how he originally came upon it. He said that Clair had told him about its existence when they were first married, but not of its contents. For almost two hundred years the de Montret family had been secretly handing down the journal to their children. She said that if anything ever happened to her or her father that he had to destroy it. No one, she said, was ever to know what was in it. That's why Peter was so adamant about retrieving the diary before escaping from the château that night. He now knew I was cognizant of everything in the journal, and he made me promise that I would not tell anyone about it. I agreed, and until now I had kept that promise. That day in his vineyard was the last time we ever saw each other.''

The cognac was doing the job; Charlie was still wet but he no longer felt it. He poured himself another glass. ''Did you investigate the baron? It couldn't have been that difficult for you, being the head of the CIA in France and all that.''

''Certainly I investigated the baron,'' he snapped. ''I even visited his damn grave! According to the records he was seventy-two years old when he died.''

''How did he die?''

''According to the records?''

''Yes.''

''From old age.''

''Did you believe that?''

''Hell, no! What I believed more was the folklore that ran rampant in the flatlands of Bordeaux about the baron.''

''Like what?''

''That it was the souls of the men and women he murdered in the vineyards that rose up from their graves and killed him. They say he was held down by the rotting corpses of his victims and a stake made of vines from his vineyard was driven through his heart.''

''Shades of Bela Lugosi,'' Charlie said.

''All folklore is based on actuality. Let's just say he was killed. I had his crypt opened with the permission of the French government.''

Charlie's eyes brightened.

''Interesting. All the de Montrets had their crypts right next to each other . . . all except Gustave de Montret. His was hastily put together with limestone and kept away from the rest.''

''You opened the casket?''

''Yes. Oh, he was murdered all right. I had his bones shipped to Paris for testing. He was stabbed numerous times, and almost every bone was broken from repeated blows to the body.''

''Who did it?''

''Probably the townspeople. They discovered what he had been doing all those years. The thing is no de Montret was allowed back on the land for almost fifty years after Gustave had died.''

Charlie put his glass back on the table; he was feeling the effects of the cognac. ''I didn't know the baron had a family. He never mentioned them in his journal.''

''He had a brother who owned a winery in the Côte d'Or

157

region of Burgundy. It was the baron's grandnephews who eventually took over the vineyards again in Bordeaux.''

Charlie brushed at his eyes, trying to clear his head. ''The baron was a psychopath. That's not an inherited trait. Why would someone in his family two hundred years later be committing the same type of crimes?''

''I am not a psychiatrist, Mr. Halleran. I'm just a retired employer of assassins.''

Charlie leaned in closer to the old man. ''Do you remember the sections in the journal?''

''Mr. Halleran. I remember *every* section written in that vile diary,'' Striker said coldly.

''What happened in the last entry?''

Striker's eyes hardened. ''I thought you read the diary.''

''The last section was torn from your notebook.''

Striker closed his eyes and smiled. ''Ahhh, then you don't know?''

''Know what?'' Charlie asked, confused.

''I misunderstood you. I thought you said you had read the *entire* translation.'' His eyes played across Charlie's face.

''You wrote that it was the most horrible of all the sections. What was in it?''

Again Striker smiled. ''I thought you knew. That's why this conversation between us has gone this far. Now I *would* be betraying Peter and Clair if we continued this discussion. What was in that last section of the journal has no bearing on Maura or these murders.''

''What was in it? That's all I'm asking.'' Charlie could feel the blood rushing through his temples.

''We'll never know, will we?'' Striker said. ''Now, Mr. Halleran, I'm beginning to feel tired. As much as I've enjoyed your company, I'm afraid our time together is up.''

Shit! Charlie thought. *We were so goddamn close!* ''Look, I promise you nothing we discuss will be in tomorrow's papers if that's what you're worried about.''

''I believe you, Charlie.'' There was an elfish look in the old man's small face. ''Hans, let Mr. Halleran out.''

Hans pulled the van over and stopped the motor. He got out and pushed open the side door. The mist outside had now turned into a full downpour.

''Good night, Charlie,'' Striker said, smiling.

Charlie didn't want to leave, but when he looked at Hans's

thick body and cold, snakelike eyes he knew he didn't have much choice. "Good night, Striker," Charlie replied, sighing. He jumped out of the van and into the darkness. The hard rain hit him in the face, almost blinding him, but he could tell that he was surrounded by woods. "Hey, this isn't Paris!" Charlie yelled, turning toward the van.

The side door slammed shut. A few seconds later Hans stuck his head out of the driver's window and said, laughing, "It's down the road on your left, *Herr* Halleran. You can't miss it." Chuckling even louder, he tossed him the cognac flask, rolled up the window, and sped off into the night.

Fighting the rain, Charlie walked several feet down the dark, deserted road until he came to a sign. His heart sank when he read it.

PARIS - 15 KILOMETERS

Striker made sure this won't make the morning papers, Charlie thought to himself. By the time he reached Paris, morning would have already come and gone.

Pulling the fur collar over his head, he took a long swallow from the flask and began the endless walk back to his hotel. He didn't want to think about how angry his editor would be tomorrow when he found nothing on his fax machine about the proceedings at the OPEC conference.

"You sure as hell owe me for this one, Ree!" he said out loud, as the rain came down harder.

Chapter Sixteen

HARRIET CROWE SAT alone at the corner table of *Pandora's Box* and sipped a Kir through two thin red straws. She preferred this table over the others because the spotlight directly above her head was burned out, leaving the area in darkness.

There wasn't much light in the crowded bar to begin with; mainly just a few tracks, with red and blue gels covering the bulbs for atmosphere. *Pandora's* wasn't the kind of place that liked calling attention to itself by being too well lit. It was a lesbian bar, and lesbian bars were not plentiful nor welcome in Boise.

She sipped her drink slowly, keeping her eyes glued to the wet cocktail napkin on the table. *Why didn't I color my hair before going out tonight?* she angrily berated herself. There were streaks of gray in it, and she suddenly felt very old compared to the other women here.

Harriet tried to avoid eye contact with the customers. Occasionally she would glance over to the small, darkened dance floor at the back of the bar. She could make out the figures of several couples with their arms locked around their partners' hips as they slowly swayed to the beat of an Anita Baker song. Over near the jukebox, two young women were leaning against the wall. They were whispering, giggling, stroking each other. Bottles of Coors dangled from their hands.

Harriet looked away. Her stomach was beginning to tie itself into knots. What if someone noticed her in this place? *My God, I was a fool for coming here!* Boise was a small city, and she held a prominent position on the school board. If it ever leaked out that she was gay or there was even a hint of scandal in that direction, she would never be reelected to that post again.

Finish your drink and leave! she thought, disgusted with herself. She turned her sad, puffy face away from the crowd so no one would recognize her.

The last time she had been to one of these places was right after she finally acknowledged to herself that she was gay. That was many years ago. Then she met Martha, and they had lived together in a monogamous relationship for the past twenty-three years. She was everything to Harriet: a friend, a companion, and a lover. Six months ago Martha had discovered a malignant tumor under her right armpit while in the shower. Three weeks later she was dead. There was not much time for good-byes, not even time to go over old photograph albums and relive youthful memories together. A relationship that took twenty-three years to build was smashed to pieces in three weeks.

The pain of Martha's death was strong, but the pain of loneliness was even stronger. She came here tonight because she needed to go out, to be with people, to be with her own kind. Regretfully she realized that the type of people who went to

Pandora's Box had nothing in common with her, even if their sexual preferences were the same. *What would I talk to them about? They're just here for immediate physical gratification. Would they know who George Sand was? . . . or Gertrude Stein? I doubt it! My God, this was a terrible mistake!*

Harriet looked around the room for the waitress. She wanted to pay her check and leave. Then the front door opened and she saw a tall woman with long blond hair and wearing a black mini-skirt enter Pandora's. The blonde sauntered up to the bar, ordered a drink, then turned to face the room. She brazenly leaned against the counter, resting her elbows on the mahogany top while scrutinizing the tables. The bartender handed her a scotch and water and she drank half of it down in one gulp.

Yes, she was definitely looking for action, Harriet believed. She was beautiful but not her type. Her hair looked greasy, and she probably needed a bath. *Never in a million years!* Much too common. In fact, none of them here had anything to do with her. The only person she was capable of loving, she unfortunately concluded, was buried deep beneath the ground.

She glanced over to the woman again. *There was something strange about her . . . what was it?* She certainly wasn't anyone she knew. Good God, she wouldn't associate with anyone like that!

As if the blonde could read her mind, she turned in Harriet's direction and smirked.

A shudder went through Harriet's petite, middle-aged body. The blonde appeared to be smiling, but it was actually a sneer. Her mouth slit open into a mock grin, revealing lipstick-stained teeth. Then her tongue slithered out of her mouth like a large Moray eel and made a full wet circle around her lips. *Was she ridiculing me?* Harriet wondered, shaken.

Harriet looked away. This woman was evil, she could feel it in her belly. She was frightened; her legs felt weak, as if they no longer contained bones in them for support. She also had this strong urge to urinate. *What do I do?* she thought.

Just pay the bill and walk out!

The blonde was still leering at her. Harriet quickly took ten dollars out of her purse and dropped it on the table for the Kir and the tip. She didn't want to stay around for the waitress to bring the tab. In her rush to stand up, she dropped her purse. Coins, credit cards, Lifesavers, and Kleenex toppled out and scattered everywhere over the floor. A hot wave of fear engulfed her. As she bent down to pick up her belongings, two slender hands with long, deep red fingernails came into her field of vision. The hands began to help collect her things. Harriet looked up and saw two eyes grinning at her; one blue, the other brown. Her mouth dropped open from dread. She had never seen anything like that before in her life. A weak, "Thank you," was all she could manage from her dry mouth.

The blonde didn't say anything, but the smirk remained.

Harriet peered into those unearthly eyes. The pupils seemed dilated, giving the illusion of madness.

She quickly stood up and walked past her toward the front door. Harriet knew the blonde was watching her leave. She could feel those strange eyes, like hot coals, burning into her back.

Standing alone in the deserted, dark parking lot, another surge of fear shot through her. Once again she felt the need to urinate and several drops seeped out before she was able to stop it. She just wanted to get away from here as quickly as possible. If only she had stayed home tonight!

She began running toward her car while fumbling through her purse for her keys. *Now where were those damn things! Ah, there they are!* Harriet got in, locked all the doors, and started the engine.

Never again will I come here! Never! Martha, I love you. I was just so lonely. Please forgive me.

On the way home, she looked in the rearview mirror every other second, fearing that she was being followed. All she could see was the black night broken up by an occasional street lamp. She began to relax a little. Her thighs were wet and cold from her pee, but at least she was safe.

This is nonsense! she thought ten minutes later as she entered Caldwell. *That woman was just probably on something, that's all. She wasn't out to hurt me. I'm just not cut out for these crazy types. But the colors of those eyes . . . how could that be? My God, but she was bizarre. At least I learned my lesson, Martha. Never, never will I do this again.*

She thought about the strange woman. Suddenly the fear returned, larger than before. Holding one hand on the steering wheel, she groped for her purse on the seat next to her and stuck her hand inside. Her fingers scurried around, frantically searching for her wallet. It wasn't there!

"Oh no!" she moaned. It was probably still on the floor back in the bar.

She pulled over to the side of the road and stopped the car. Should she go back? Then she remembered the blond woman and her legs started to shake.

No, she could not go back. I'll call them when I get home, she thought. *Hopefully, they won't recognize my name on my credit cards and license.* At least there was nothing inside the wallet containing her work address.

But her license did contain her *home* address!

Then another thought struck her. What if that woman had it! *Never again, Martha!*

When she reached her house in the outskirts of Caldwell, she drove into the garage and quickly closed the automatic door. It was mostly country around here, and her nearest neighbor was a good three hundred yards away. She and Martha bought this property because they liked the seclusion.

She stopped the motor, closed her eyes, leaned back in the seat, and took a deep breath. She stayed that way for a few minutes, continuing to breathe, letting the oxygen filter out the fears.

Beginning to feel her natural self again, she got out of the car and entered her house through the door in the garage. She double bolted the latch from the inside, turned on the light, then climbed the stairs leading up to the kitchen.

The house was dark but all the doors were locked. When they first bought the house, they argued about the need for security locks. Martha liked the idea that they were living in an area where no one locked doors and ridiculed Harriet about her fears. "You're just afraid of your own shadow," she used to say, laughing. Harriet won out. The locks were installed, and tonight she was grateful for that.

She turned the light on in the kitchen. After she fed Pumpkin, she'd call the bar about her wallet. *Now where was Pumpkin?* Normally Pumpkin, a fourteen-year-old, overfed Pekingese, would rush over with a shrill bark to greet her.

"Pumpkin. Where are you sweetheart?" she cooed loudly as she took off her sweater and hung it neatly over the chair by the kitchen table. Usually Pumpkin would give off a couple of high-pitched yelps, waddle over to her, stretch, then lick the tips of Harriet's shoes. This time, however, she didn't come to her. In fact, there wasn't even a sound.

Harriet went into the dark living room. "Pumpkin pie, are you in Mommy's bedroom?"

Again silence.

The first thing that crossed Harriet's mind was Pumpkin's heart condition. She was old, with bad breath and rotted teeth, and the veterinarian didn't give her much longer to live. Worried, she quickly walked over to the steps leading to the bedrooms upstairs. She listened for noises coming from up in one of the rooms. Nothing, just the *whooshing* sound of the wind blowing against the curtains through her bedroom window.

Harriet turned on the light switch for the upstairs landing. It didn't go on. The bulb must have burned out, she thought. She went up the steps and into the darkness.

"Pumpkin, Mommy wants you. Are you all right?" she whispered nervously. Harriet hated dark places. She groped her way over to the master bedroom, stuck her hands inside, and felt for the wall light. When she found the switch, she turned it on.

Nothing.

Harriet was now terrified. Two different light fixtures burning out at the same time was impossible. *What's going on?*

There was a full moon tonight and its glow shrouded the bedroom in a bluish hue. The wind was blowing so hard outside that it made her Chantilly lace curtains over the window stand straight out.

Why was the window open?

That's when Harriet noticed the jagged edges of the broken glass and splintered wood in the frame.

My God! Somebody's broken in!

Her foot touched something soft on the floor. She looked down. It was dark but there was enough moonlight infiltrating the room to see the twisted figure of Pumpkin lying at the foot of the bed. The Pekingese's neck was broken, and the head was twisted completely around to the back of its own body. Its lifeless eyes were staring straight up into Harriet's frozen, horrified face.

In the next second there was the sound of padded footsteps on the carpet behind her. Someone was in the room.

Harriet didn't want to turn around to see who it was. She already knew. Her bladder gave out and her urine rushed freely down her thick thighs.

Forgive me, Martha!

Chapter Seventeen

S HE LAY IN a fetal position on the grass and watched a large scarab beetle slowly maneuver its body around the weeds and pebbles next to her foot. When it touched her leg, it paused and extended its antennae. Sensing that the black nylon stocking wasn't dangerous, the beetle decided to climb over her calf rather than trek around it.

She watched through slit eyes, entranced, as the insect scampered down the other side of her limb, fell on its back, rolled over again with some difficulty, then scurried under a mound of wet leaves.

The shrieks of crows overhead made the auditory nerves in her ears tingle. She looked up at the dawn sky. *There they were . . . circling above . . . looking for food.*

Food. Oh, God, food! Her hunger was so strong that just the thought of eating caused the saliva to flow in her mouth.

It was cold, and she shivered every time a gust of wind blew up her black leather miniskirt. She rubbed her arms to generate some warmth, but her hands were too numb to do any good.

Once again she heard the piercing clamor of the crows. It was hurting her head. She watched them make one more swooping dive searching for something to eat, then they moved on to another location.

Her head was throbbing fiercely now, and over the pain was that awful sound of metal sliding against metal once more.

She put her thighs up to her forehead and clamped her arms around her knees, squeezing tight, hoping to push away the hurt. Her eyes began to tear from the agony. Within minutes the ache started to fade and she was able to see again. She unlocked her head from her knees and sat up on the grass.

Her body felt dehydrated, and her arms were stiff and aching. There was also a sharp pain in the area of her groin.

The smell of pinecones . . . the sound of distant traffic. She was in a park. *Which one?*

Why am I here?

She looked around. There was a green, wooden bench nearby, and next to that was a jogging path. The grass all around her was covered with pinecones. *What park is this?* It didn't look familiar at all.

A jogger, decked out in black-and-red Spandex, ran by her prone body. For a brief moment she thought she could see a look of distaste come over his face when he glanced her way, then he turned his eyes back to the path, and kept running.

Why was he looking at me like that? she wondered.

It was too cold to sit here any longer. She had to move. As she stood up, she saw a tote bag and her leather purse beneath the bench. She walked unsteadily over to them, bent down, and opened up the purse. Putting her hand inside, she pulled out a bloodstained ball-peen hammer. Why is this in here? she wondered. Then she remembered the spike and hammer she found in the station wagon, and she moaned with fright. She threw it back in the bag and took out whatever else was inside: credit cards, more receipts, Alamo rental car keys for the white station wagon, and the same sixty-five dollars from the last time she looked. The credit card receipts were from a motel and restaurants in Boise, Idaho. She then unzipped the tote. The K mart clothes that were in the closet of the cabin were now inside the bag.

What were these doing here? Where the hell am I?

Maura knew that she must have blacked out again. How long this time? *A day? A week?* Boise! Christ, she needed help! This couldn't go on. *Have to get to a phone . . . call Uncle Wiggly.*

The metal sounds became louder. *Please, dear God, don't let me black out again!*

She put the tote over her shoulder, grabbed the purse, and began following the path, hoping that it would lead out of the park.

The sky was turning a lighter gray now, and there were more joggers on the path. She tried to stop one, to ask where she was, but he gave her that same strange look as the other runner and kept on going.

The trail was long, meandering its way around a soccer field and a duck pond. Her feet hurt from the open-toe pumps, and there was that fierce shooting pain again in the upper part of her groin. Eventually she saw a gated fence with a parking lot on the other side. She continued on the path until it entered onto a main thoroughfare. Her body felt weightless; if a strong wind came along, she believed it could easily lift her up and carry her through the city.

There was a trash can on the corner. She went over to it and searched through the garbage until she found a rumpled-up sports section from a newspaper. Her fingers tore at the pages as she tried to unfold it. Hopefully there would be some mention of the date and the name of the town or city she was in. Then she saw it on the top right-hand corner of the page and she gasped:

BOISE, IDAHO September 20, 1990

This time she had blacked out for three days! *Boise! How did I get here?*

Across from the park was an aluminum trailer-type diner that seemed open. *Maybe they have a phone . . . need to call Uncle Wiggly.* She crossed the street and went inside.

There were several men, mostly laborers wearing jeans and work boots, sitting at the counter and eating breakfast. Their faces were lined and their hands callused from a life of hard work. They turned and stared at her when she walked in. Ignoring their looks, she went over to the counter to talk to the man behind it. Her stomach began to churn from the rich, warm odor of scrambled eggs, bacon, pancakes, and coffee.

The high pitch of sirens could be heard coming from somewhere far away. They got louder and louder, causing the customers in the diner to put down their forks and look out the window. Several police cars sped past the restaurant, heading out toward the direction of Caldwell. The men at the counter looked concerned; it was unusual to see half the police force of Boise going out on the same call. One of the men said he heard that someone was murdered in the vineyards outside of Caldwell. They all agreed that whatever happened had to have been bad.

After that discussion ended, the owner—a short guy with a two-day-beard growth on his face—went over to the end of the counter and looked this strange woman up and down. With a sneer on his face, he put his hairy fists on the Formica top, leaned in, and said, "Need a menu, sister?"

"No," she replied, confused by his attitude. She looked over at the other customers; they were sneaking glances her way while chewing their food. "First I need a phone."

Without taking his eyes off her, he pointed with his thumb to the back of the diner.

"Thank you. I also want scrambled eggs and bacon."

"You got any money?" he asked.

"Of course. Why?"

"You want to show it to me?" Those hairy hands now went up to his hips.

"I don't believe this!" she said indignantly. She opened up her purse, took out a fistful of fives and tens, and held them up to his face. "That enough?"

He shrugged and nodded. "The phone's over near the toilet. It's got a sink in there in case you want to clean up. You must have had a hell of a night, sweetheart," he said, smirking.

Some of the men at the counter snickered.

Oh, Christ, I must look a mess! she thought, now understanding why everyone stared at her strangely.

The clanking of metal came and went in her head. She needed to get to a phone!

She found it right where the counterman told her it was, next to a half-opened door with a sign on it marked "Bathroom." There were some coins at the bottom of her purse. She grabbed a handful and dropped them into the slots. *Please be there, Uncle Wiggly.*

After several rings, someone picked up. "Thank God you're there! It's me, Maura." Tears streamed down her face. "What's happening to me? . . . No, I don't know what's going on. Please help me! . . . I'm sorry, I can't seem to control myself. . . . I know. . . . Boise, Idaho . . . No, I don't know how I got here. . . . I've been blacking out. I need medicine. I don't have any with me. . . . Who's looking for me? . . . The FBI? . . . Why? . . . What murders? . . . Oh, God! . . . Dear, sweet God! . . . I couldn't have!" she screamed.

Then she thought about the bloodied hammer that she was carrying inside her purse. Then about the red stains on the spike and scalpel she found in the trunk of the station wagon. Then she remembered the jar of formaldehyde with those gray things floating in it. Her eyes clamped shut and she squeezed down hard on the receiver; the realization of what she did began to formulate in her mind. *But why?*

"I don't know what to do!" she cried. "I'm in a diner, somewhere across from a park. . . . How could I have done such a thing? . . . I'm going to call the police. . . . Why not? . . . All right, I'll wait until I see you. . . . The airport? . . . I have some money and credit cards. . . . Why can't I use them? . . . Yes, you're right, I'm just not thinking clearly. . . . Can you transfer cash to me?'' She brushed the strands of greasy blond hair from her face. ''Hold on, let me find the number.'' She looked at the pay phone. ''555-0525 . . . No, I can't read the area code, it's rubbed off. Get it from the operator. . . . Yes, I'll be here waiting for your call.''

She hung up and rested her head against the wall. Her legs were trembling from fear as well as from hunger. *How could I have killed all those people? Am I that insane?* Yet when Uncle Wiggly told her the way those people were murdered, it didn't seem strange at all. It was right from Gustave de Montret's diary. *Why have I done these horrible things? Oh, Jesus, I knew I was just like that man!*

Why was she copying the actions of that monster? She remembered, after reading the diary, how cursed she felt. Was that it . . . a curse? If so, then she was grateful that she was the last of the de Montret bloodline.

Please call me back, Uncle Wiggly!

The area near her groin was pulsating. She went into the bathroom. The phone was right next to it, and when Uncle Wiggly called back she would be able to get to it without any trouble. She took the hammer out of her bag, dropped it in the wastebasket, and covered it over with paper towels she took from the rack on the wall.

The mirror above the sink was coated with grime, but she was able to make out sections of her face. She recoiled in horror: her lips, cheeks, and teeth were smeared with bright red lipstick, and her hair was coated with grease and hung down in strings. Dirt and pieces of grass covered her face and clothes. She was pale and gaunt. Then she saw her eyes: they were sunken deep into her skull, and the skin on her face stretched tightly over her cheekbones.

Oh no! She suddenly realized that she didn't have her green contacts in. No wonder people had been looking at her strangely. What had she done with them? She would have to find sunglasses. No one was supposed to see her like this!

My God, what is happening to me?

She turned the tap on above the sink. The hot spigot refused to move and she had to wash with cold water. It was hard removing the lipstick from her face, but with rigorous scrubbing it

169

began to come off. She then took out a skirt and a sweater from the tote and quickly removed the leather miniskirt and black top she was wearing.

That's when she saw her arms. There were scrapes, scratches, and hematomas running down along her biceps and forearms.

She then noticed a drop of blood on her underwear. Taking them off, she searched for the source of the bleeding. She found a deep cut on the inside, upper part of her groin. It was swollen and red. *How did that happen?* It looked infected. After washing the wound, she changed into the skirt and sweater.

She suddenly heard loud police sirens somewhere outside. Her heart beat fast as she rushed over to the small window next to the urinal and looked out.

Across the street, two police cars had stopped next to the white station wagon with tinted windows that was parked near the curb. Four policemen rushed out, drew their guns, and surrounded the car. Using handkerchiefs on the door handles, they opened them up, and looked in. Then one of them went around in back and opened the rear door.

Sweat ran down her face as she watched them take out the bloodied sheet containing the spike and scalpel. Next, they removed the jar with those gray things suspended in the formaldehyde.

She turned away from the window, her face iced in terror.

Do they know that I'm across the street in the diner? Oh, please, no!

A knock on the bathroom door, then a voice saying, "Hey, cookie, your breakfast's getting cold."

"I'll be right out," she managed to gasp.

The footsteps from outside the bathroom faded back into the diner.

Why hasn't Uncle Wiggly called back?

She couldn't afford to wait any longer for him. She had to get away now, before they came after her. Uncle Wiggly was right: she needed to get back to Napa and see him before giving herself up. Her body was strung out and her nerves were on edge. Soon the anxiety attacks were going to start up. She needed her medicine. Why hadn't she taken the pills with her? Grabbing her purse and tote, she stuck her head out of the bathroom and looked down both ends of the small hallway. To the left was a back door. That was her only choice. Hopefully it was unlocked. She tried the handle. The metal door opened easily. The street on this side of the diner was empty. Across from it was a vacant lot, and after that an alley that divided two apartment houses.

As she walked down the steps and into the street, she could hear the phone ringing.

Was that him calling? It was too late to go back. She would have to wait until she could get to another phone to talk with him.

She crossed the street, and when she came to the vacant lot, she quickened her pace. She desperately wanted to see if anyone was behind her, but she knew she couldn't chance stopping. Then she came to the alley with its brick walls. About a hundred yards away was a Main Street. She prayed that Boise had cabs or a transportation system of some kind. What she needed to do now was to gain as much distance from the Ford station wagon and the police as possible.

With any luck she'd make it to the other side of the city, find a gas station with a pay phone, and call Uncle Wiggly back. He always knew what to do.

And Rena . . . yes, she had to call Rena. She's the one other person in her life that cared about her.

She came out of the alley and onto the street. A bus, just a couple of blocks away, was heading in her direction. It didn't matter so much where it was going as long as it was away from here. She walked over to the bus stop and waited for it alongside several other passengers.

She gave the driver the correct amount for the fare when she got in and walked toward the back, ignoring the now-familiar stares of the other passengers. *Yes, Rena would help me,* she thought, sitting down. *Somehow I've got to get to her before I black out again!*

Chapter Eighteen

RENA WAS SHAVING her legs in the shower when she heard the phone ringing. *Eight in the morning. Who the hell is calling me at this hour?*

She got out of the stall, wrapped a towel around her body, and went into the bedroom to answer the phone.

"Hello?" she said, taking a tissue from the top of the dresser drawer and wiping away a drop of blood on her leg from where the blade nicked her. The line on the other end sounded scratchy, as if it were coming from a long distance.

"Bonjour, mon petite," Charlie said. Then he sneezed.

"Charlie? Where *are* you?" She was happy to hear his voice.

"In Paris and I'm soaked to the bone." He sneezed again. "I met Mister Wilbur Striker. Hell of a guy. I'm thinking about putting him on my list as a future drinking buddy."

"He's real?" she asked breathlessly.

"Unfortunately, yes."

She picked up on his sarcasm. "Are you all right?"

"Wet and tired. Did a lot of walking through the French countryside last night. Got lots of fresh air."

"What about de Montret?" Her tone was serious.

"He, unfortunately, was also real. He made Ted Bundy look like Peter Pan."

"What happened to him?"

"Striker thinks he was murdered by the good citizens of France." He then told her how Striker and Peter McKinney were in the OSS together back in World War II.

"Did he remember what was in the last section of the journal?" she asked.

"He wouldn't tell me, but by his reaction I'd say he remembers all right. He claimed that it had nothing to do with Maura or the murders that are happening now. I think the guy's full of shit.

172

He's protecting the memory of Clair McKinney. That bloodless, old bastard had the hots for her. I have to go and dry off,'' Charlie said. Then he added, ''You were one of Maura's best friends. If she's still alive, she may not have anyone else to turn to but you. Be careful, okay?''

That idea had already crossed her mind. ''Okay,'' she whispered.

He said he'd see her in a few weeks then hung up.

At least the diary and Striker are now confirmed! she thought. The cut opened on her leg again, and she stuck a piece of tissue on the wound.

Yes, Charlie's right, I am one of Maura's best friends. Yet she must have made other friends while living in New York. And what about lovers? There was never any mention of them in her letters and phone conversations. Why hadn't any of her friends surfaced since she became implicated in the murders? Is it possible that she had lived in seclusion all these years? *Christ, what a prison that would be!* To reside in a city of so many people and remain alone, an outsider. She had questioned Maura on several occasions about her social life. She was always evasive, only saying that her spare time was filled with theater, museums, and charity events.

Never people . . . just events.

Again Rena was reminded of Uncle Wiggly. *Did he really exist or was he the invention of an unstable mind?*

She went downstairs to the kitchen, grabbed a mug from the shelf, and poured herself a cup of coffee. The phone rang again. She walked into the den to pick it up. It was Agent Grant.

''Another one,'' he said somberly.

''Oh, God! Where?''

''Boise, Idaho.''

''Boise! How did she get that far without being detected?''

''We're not sure,'' Grant said. ''Did you know that there were vineyards in Idaho?''

''There are vineyards all over this goddamn country, Marvin,'' Rena said impatiently. ''Who was the victim?''

Grant sighed. ''A member of their school board. Probably a lesbian.'' He told her what he pieced together about Harriet Crowe after talking with her friends and neighbors. ''She was seen leaving a gay bar an hour before she was murdered. Maura McKinney was also identified as being there at the same time. The bartender said that Maura left the bar right after the woman

173

did. The body was discovered two hours ago tied to a grapevine like the others. There was something different about this one, though."

"Like what?" Rena asked uneasily. She could hear the bleakness in his voice.

He talked quietly. "Semen was found in the victim's vagina. She apparently had sex with a male close to the time she was murdered."

"That's strange," Rena uttered, surprised.

"I agree. Nobody who knew Harriet Crowe had ever seen her with a man before," Grant stated.

"With the little you told me about her I would say that it couldn't be a possibility. She sounded like a conservative lesbian who rarely came out of the closet to confront her *own* sexuality with women let alone have a fling with a man."

"The semen was sent to our Washington lab. Perhaps Maura now has a male accomplice."

"Or perhaps this is a copycat murder."

"It doesn't look that way. Blond hair fibers were found in Harriet's bedroom. It isn't confirmed yet, but I'm sure they'll match the others."

Rena shook her head, confused. "This doesn't make any sense. Unless of course you're right and she now has an accomplice."

"Do you think she may have a split personality?"

"She's sure showing traces of it. It's very rare, though, for someone who suffers from a dual personality disorder to commit murder without knowing about it. Jekyll and Hydes don't usually exist outside of literature," she said.

"One other thing," Grant said, his voice becoming excited. "The police found the car she was driving. Her fingerprints were all over it. The spike and scalpel that were used in the murders were in the back, along with what we believe to be a jar containing the ovaries and testes of the victims. While they were searching the car, it turns out that she was just a couple of hundred feet away, across the street in a diner. The hammer, coated with blood, was found in a wastebasket in the bathroom there."

"Do you have any idea where she is now?" Rena asked tensely.

"Somewhere in Boise, and Boise is a small city. There's no way out."

"What was her physical condition like?"

"Not terrific. Witnesses say she looked sleazy, unclean, wore too much makeup. That doesn't seem to be the sophisticated woman you know."

"No, it's not. It sounds like there's a great deal of mental deterioration going on."

After a pause, he said, "We believe there's a chance she may try and contact you."

"You're not the first one to mention that to me today. I'll let you know if she does." Rena had a feeling that Grant had already put a tap on her phone in case Maura called. She quickly told Grant what she had learned about Gustave de Montret from Charlie and who Wilbur Striker was.

Will they find Maura? Rena wondered as she hung up. Maura was street smart and clever; her success as a prosecuting attorney attested to that. If Maura was suffering from severe paranoia, then she was quite capable of eluding the police; paranoids can be more inventive than the ordinary person.

She went over to her desk, picked up de Montret's journal, and flipped through the pages. Why was Maura reenacting the horrendous deeds of this madman? What was the link that bound them together after two centuries?

Rena skimmed through the diary one more time. When she finished, she came to the same conclusion: there was a strong sense of sacrificial ritualism in the murders. Perhaps that's where she should start looking. *But how do I begin?*

The way the bodies were placed: draped across the vines like crucifixions. Christianity, even in its early stages, didn't condone human sacrifices. No, that part was pagan. Polytheism, however, didn't simply stop when Christianity evolved. They actually began to overlap one another, taking on the other's attributes.

The killings that happened two hundred years ago and now seemed to revolve around the making of wine. Rena knew the strong connotation wine had in religious rites, some of them going as far back as the dawn of human history. Maybe the person she really needed to speak to was an enologist.

She left the château and walked over to the winery. Perhaps Harrison Monroe was somewhere inside and not out in the fields. The foreman in the purification area, where the wine was fine-filtered before bottling, told her that Harrison was in the laboratory checking the density of the sugar and alcohol content of this year's cabernet.

She crossed the packing plant past the barrel room. The lab

was in the corner of the winery, away from the hub of activity. She opened the door and found Harrison holding a glass hydrometer up to the light and talking to a chemist in a white frock. He had a pleased look on his face. When he saw Rena, his eyes brightened.

"Well, hello. I think your father may get that gold medal yet in about four years," he said, flicking his finger at the red liquid in the glass tube.

"Am I disturbing you?" she asked.

"You? Never." He grinned at her, exposing those white teeth.

"I need a good historian who knows enology."

Harrison shook his head and smiled. "I'm afraid I'm not your man. Viticulture is my forte. Wine history was my worst subject at UC Davis."

"Do you know of anyone who's knowledgeable in that?" she asked, folding her arms to her chest.

"Yep," he groaned, leaning against the lab table. "Dr. Seymour Tomain . . . pronounced the same as in Ptomaine poisoning. He's an enology professor at UC Davis. He's also one of the most formidable wine critics in the country. Many a fine vintner has bitten the dust from a stroke of his word processor."

"How did you make out?"

"I passed. The old fart loves my wine. Of course, you're only as good as your last vintage with that guy. Do you want me to call him for you?"

"Would you?"

He took out his address book from his pocket, went over to the wall phone, and began dialing. "To think I'm about to hear this man's voice again. I don't know if I can stand it," he mumbled. "Now you definitely owe me dinner," he said, turning to her.

"You're on," she said.

Three minutes later he hung up the phone and smiled. "We've just been invited for lunch with the honorable Dr. Tomain."

"We?"

"Yes . . . we. After lunch, if we're lucky, we'll be back just in time for dinner. Any particular restaurant you like in town?"

Rena smiled at the man's charm. "As you say, I owe you, so you pick it."

They took the Range Rover and drove east on Highway 128 to the campus of UC Davis. The drive through the fall-colored hills was exhilarating, and Harrison's conversation was uplifting and witty, but Rena was only half listening to him; her mind kept wondering about the semen found in the dead body of Harriet Crowe.

Chapter Nineteen

"NICE OF YOU to come back to your roots, Harrison," Professor Tomain said with a Bostonian accent as he squinted at him from behind thick, wiry eyebrows. He was sitting in an overstuffed armchair that was covered with doilies in his oak-paneled living room and sipping a glass of Lillet. A wrinkled, blue summer suit hung loosely over his portly frame and a paisley bow tie was tightly hooked around his thick neck.

"It's always wonderful to see you again, Professor," Harrison said, unable to hide the sarcasm behind his smile. He sat on the couch next to Rena across from Tomain; they were holding glasses of cold Calistoga water with lemon wedges.

"Please excuse the derision in Mr. Monroe's voice," Tomain said to Rena. "My young friend may be able to bring the world to its knees with his brilliant pinot noirs, but he was the worst student of enological history that I ever had the displeasure of teaching. I flunked this boy twenty years ago, and he's never forgiven me. Isn't that right, Harrison?"

"Not true at all. I forgive you every time you give my wines a favorable review, Seymour. It *is* all right to call you Seymour after twenty years, I hope?"

"Absolutely! At least until I sample your next vintage. If it's dreadful you can always fall back on your first love, mineralogy, and destroy the Earth even further by burrowing more tunnels into it. Tell me Harrison, after your prior colleagues have stripped our planet of all its resources, what will *they* fall back on? Perhaps they'll all become great vintners like you. I wonder if I should teach my students mole digging as a prerequisite for learning wine making."

Harrison groaned, shuffled his frame uneasily on the couch, and grimaced at Rena. It was obvious that this was not the first time that Tomain had blown verbal sparks in his path.

Smiling, Tomain then swiveled his heavy body in Rena's direction. "Now my dear, your name is . . . ?"

"Rena Halbrook. I'm a psychologist."

"Yes. Harrison says you wish to talk to me about these vineyard murders."

"Yes," she said, leaning forward. "I may be off base in trying to understand the reasoning behind them—especially when we're dealing with a serial killer—but there seems to be something ceremonial about these murders, something that has to do with the vineyards themselves. Do you know of any ancient sacrificial rites that were similar in nature?"

Tomain had a pleased look on his face. Excited, he said, "Absolutely! In fact, I phoned the FBI in San Francisco to offer them my expertise, but they didn't seem very interested." Then he frowned and looked at Harrison. "Ancient history is the floor plan of our existence, yet they had absolutely no interest in it—similar to you as I recall, my dear fellow."

Harrison moaned and leaned his arm around the back of the goose-down couch. He whispered in Rena's ear, "You now owe me more than dinner."

"Well, I may not be the FBI but I would like to hear about what you have to say," Rena said, ignoring Harrison's sarcasm.

"The key lies in the ancient Greek feast of Oschophoria," Tomain said, beaming.

"What's that?" Rena asked.

"It took place on the eighth day of Pyanepsion."

"Oh, speak English, Seymour," Harrison said impatiently.

"Of course, forgive me. We don't know how far back in ancient times this feast actually began. We do know that the ceremony occurred at the end of October, after the harvesting of the wine grapes. There were many feasts geared around the god, Dionysus, but the Oschophoria is the one that came to my mind when I read about the murders."

"I'm sorry, it's been many years since I studied ancient Greece. Which god was Dionysus?" Rena inquired.

"The primordial god of fertility . . . the god who first made wine. The festivities in his honor were quite interesting . . . very orgiastic. They included the tearing apart of a live animal, then devouring its flesh, and drinking its blood. There's evidence that the ceremony goes back to the early days of Greece, hundreds of years before Socrates and the great Athenian dramatists. It began with a procession from the Athenian temple of Dionysus to Phalera many miles away. Two small boys dressed in girls' clothing led this caravan.''

"Why this form of transvestism?" Rena asked.

"There were many Bacchic ceremonies during that period where men wore women's clothing. No one knows why exactly. We can only speculate. Personally, I think it was a symbolic gesture for the unisexual regeneration of the Earth. These two transvestite boys in the feast of Oschophoria would carry in their hands a phallic vine stock covered with fruit. This is the interesting part: the Greek word for vine stock is oschophories. The word for scrotum, like the feast itself, is oschophoria. To the Greeks, it probably meant the same thing."

Rena's body began to tingle.

"Why name a feast after the word scrotum?" he asked, as if reading Rena's mind.

"Do you have a theory?"

"Yes, but that's all it is—just a theory. It can never be proven. It is well documented that fruits, some of them encased in cakes resembling phallic symbols, were taken to Athene Skiros at Phalera during the feast of Oschophoria. But what is meant by fruit?— apples? . . . oranges? . . . grapes? I don't think so. As I said, these ceremonies were very orgiastic in temperament. There were sacrifices—most likely human. The fruits, I believe, were also human in origin."

Rena shuddered. "Such as ovaries and testes?"

Professor Tomain nodded. "Human life derives from the scrotum of man, or to the Greeks—the oschophoria. Unisexual Earth also produces life, most importantly the vineyards. In ancient days, I believe human fruit was fed to these vineyards to stimulate the fertility of the soil.

Rena suddenly remembered the story Maura told her in Athens so many years ago. How the queen would kill her lovers and pour their blood over the crops. Wasn't the feast of Oschophoria just another version of this?

Tomain continued talking. "A more symbolic, modern form of this ritual is still going on today. Farmers in many parts of the world go into the fields with their wives and fornicate hoping to produce a good harvest."

179

"And how are the murders being committed in the vineyards today related to this ancient feast?" she asked.

"It's a bastardized form of the original Oschophoria, distorted over the centuries. A few rare instances of this primordial ritual popped up from time to time in enological history. As far as I know it's been at least two centuries since the last sacrifices were performed in vineyards.

"I see," she said, nodding. "Do you remember the name of the winery that last practiced the Oschophoria?"

"No, but I could look it up," he said. "It happened in Bordeaux."

"Is the name Baron Gustave de Montret familiar to you?"

"My God! That's the wine maker who I'm talking about! They say he may have killed hundreds of people! How did you know about him?" Tomain looked at her with an astonished expression.

"Actually, the death toll was set at seventy-three. That was the last time this rite was practiced as far as you know?"

"Yes, I'm quite sure of it. You're an amazing young lady. I didn't think anyone except a few historians like myself knew what the baron did."

No, I'm not amazing at all, Rena thought to herself. The FBI had purposely kept the discovery of the journal out of the media or everyone would have known about the baron. Tomain's theory, she felt, was making sense: rituals usually change their forms over the years to coincide with the present society. "Do you see any Christian influence in these murders?"

"Of course! Why couldn't I have had you as a student instead of Harrison! The celebration of the Oschophoria was probably kept alive through the ages by small cults. When Christianity came into being, changes were made in its rituals to incorporate certain aspects of this new religion."

"Like placing the sacrificial bodies over the vines to give the appearance of crucifixions?" she asked.

"Yes, including the use of the spike: nails were driven through Christ's hands and feet, and eventually He died. Here, the nail is used in back of the head to kill the victim."

Professor Tomain's housekeeper came into the den and announced that lunch was ready.

"Thank God," Harrison muttered to Rena. As they got up to go into the dining room, he whispered in her ear, "He's as boring as he was twenty years ago."

Rena smiled at Harrison's remark, but she didn't think Professor Tomain was boring at all. If anything, he had cleared up much of the fog covering de Montret. She at least understood why the baron had murdered all those people; he did it to fertilize his vineyards. His madness went back to the beginnings of history. That still didn't answer why Maura was following in the shadow of her ancestor; her friend had no deep love for vineyards. Her motives, equally as psychotic as de Montret's, had to have been for another reason.

After a lunch of warm duck salad and a bottle of Pommard Rugiens, they adjourned to Tomain's study for coffee. The walls and shelves were filled with pictures and artifacts of ancient Greece.

Rena was just about to pour coffee into her cup from the silver urn on the table when she noticed a small statue on the mantel of the fireplace. It was a man with four rows of breasts. She put the pot down and walked over to it. There was something about it that seemed familiar.

"Zeus," the professor said. "It's a replica of a bronze statuette that was dug up at Labranda in Caria."

"Yes, I know," Rena said, suddenly remembering where she saw it. "The original is in the Archaeological Museum in Athens."

"My, God, but I like this woman, Harrison," Tomain said, getting up and going over to her. "The breasts on Zeus are a symbol of fertility." He carefully reached up and took down an old vase next to the statue. "Look at this."

Rena took her glasses from her purse, put them on, and peered down at the artifact that Tomain had placed on his desk. There was a drawing on the vase depicting a bearded male figure dressed in women's clothes and mounting a female wearing a false beard.

"This shows a ceremony conducted from one of the feasts of Dionysus. The intersexual disguise of the figures represents the Earth's asexuality—it wasn't man nor woman."

Rena was in deep thought on the drive back to the Alexander Valley. Professor Tomain had cleared up many things, but the reasoning behind Maura committing the murders was still murky.

What the old Greek woman had said to Maura on the island of Paros suddenly cropped up in her mind: *"You are the child of Hermes!"* The image of the old woman's face, with the moonlight reflecting off her cataracts, was as clear in her head as the afternoon sunlight. What had she meant by those words? Maura never gave her an answer. She wished she had remembered to ask Tomain about that.

"You are the child of Hermes!"

What kind of child did Hermes sire? she wondered.

Then Harrison began to talk about new techniques in wine making. Rena broke from her thoughts and turned to listen. The words of the woman began to disappear from her mind and filtered down into the deep recesses of her memory.

Chapter Twenty

SHE TOOK THE bottle of brown tint off the supermarket shelf and put it in the cart alongside the tube of Neosporin, rubber gloves, a bottle of extra-strength Excedrin, a pair of scissors, toothpaste, toothbrush, makeup, a box of Johnson & Johnson gauze, hairbrush, tape, bandages, peanut butter, bread, pears, oranges, a quart of milk, and a container of plastic knives.

The pain between her legs was excruciating; hot sparks shot through her groin every time she moved. Walking slowly down the aisle so her limp wouldn't be too noticeable, she stopped when she came to the row filled with hygienic merchandise. She reached up and grabbed a cannister of liquid soap, shampoo, and a package of sponges. In the sundries section, she took a pair of large-framed, dark-tinted sunglasses off the swivel rack, ripped off the label, and put them on. Now at least no one would be able to see her eyes.

Her legs felt weak from hunger, and her heart was pounding from the series of panic attacks that had come over her since this morning. These attacks, when not treated with medication, were horrible: bodies of the shoppers in the supermarket were distorting and constantly changing shapes; boxes on the shelves had the bright colors of a Disney cartoon; faces took on an evil glow;

paranoid eyes, peering at her like mice, were set deeply into purple sockets. *It's not real, it's just my perception,* her inner self kept saying. She would give anything right now for her prescriptions of Xanax and Parnate. Taking those drugs daily was the only thing that kept her from going over the edge. Right now there was none, and she had better cope with that fact or go stark mad. At least the severe headaches had not come back. Trying to fight off the panic, she gripped the shopping cart handle until her knuckles turned white and seemed as if they were going to break through her skin. She made her way to the checkout stand.

The girl behind the counter, in Maura's nightmare perception, had hair as red as a Raggedy Ann doll; her gums were black and her snow-white skin was pitted with hairy moles. Maura squeezed her eyes shut trying to erase the image. *It's not real, it's just a panic attack!* She opened her eyes. The girl's skin had turned scarlet and the moles now took the shape of volcanoes erupting with puss.

As she reached inside her purse for money, she prayed the clerk was too busy putting her purchases into the brown paper bag to notice how badly her hands were shaking.

Once outside, she crossed the street and painfully limped her way to the small Gulf station on the corner. The burning sensation in her groin was so intense now that she had to stop and clutch onto the lamppost in order to avoid passing out. There was a hint of frost in the air, but her face was coated with a haze of sweat. The entrance to the bathroom located at the side of the station was only a few steps away. Slowly she dragged her leg forward, inching herself to the door. *What had happened to cause this pain?* Before she went inside, she quickly looked around to see if anyone was watching her. She was in luck; there were no cars fueling up at the pumps, and the attendant was inside the garage taking apart the carburetor of a pickup truck.

She went into the bathroom. Stooping down, she wedged the corner of her purse between the door and the jamb, preventing anyone from coming in.

So hungry! she thought, turning the bag over on the dirty tile floor. She couldn't remember the last time she had eaten solid food. Her hands were trembling so badly that she could hardly open up the jar of peanut butter. She tore off the wrapping on the bread, quickly gulped down a slice, then made a sandwich using the plastic knife. The protein raced through her body, giving her some needed strength.

After eating a second sandwich and drinking down half the quart of milk, she ripped apart the skin from two oranges and ate them. When she was finished, she went over to the sink, lifted up her skirt, and looked at the wound around her genitals. Somehow she must have cut herself there. The redness around the area was tender and appeared to be spreading. *Is this color real or is it also in my mind?* No, it was real all right. It was warm to the touch, and she knew that meant it was infected. She washed the wound with soap, covered it with the Neosporin antibiotic, then taped a three-inch-square piece of gauze over it. Maura hoped she had caught the infection in time.

She took off her clothes, soaped one of the sponges, and bathed her entire body. It was good to be clean, but the bathroom was cold and she began to shiver. Her head felt hot, and she downed three Excedrins; she couldn't afford to get sick . . . *not now*!

She looked at her gaunt face in the broken mirror over the basin and knew what she had to do next. Removing the kerchief, she undid her hair, letting the long blond strands fall down her back. Her face was changing shapes in the mirror and her heart was racing as if she were on the downward track of a roller coaster. She grabbed the edge of the sink, clamped her eyes closed, and waited until the feeling eased up. When it did, she picked up the scissor off the floor, grabbed hold of her hair, and began cutting. She chopped away from the neck down. There was no time to think about style.

When it was done, she put on the rubber gloves and applied the brown tint. Her hair was so light that she had to go over it twice before it would darken.

Then came the makeup, a beige base to cover up her pale skin.

She opened the tote and took out a black wool skirt, a checkered, long-sleeved blouse, and a white cardigan sweater. After she dressed, she pushed back the sides of her hair with barrettes and put on the sunglasses.

Looking at herself in the mirror, she saw the image of a tall, drab woman. I could be the wife of a farmer or a steelworker, she thought.

Scooping up as much of the hair as she could from the floor, she tossed it in the toilet, flushing it several times so that it wouldn't back up. She then took out her credit cards and the receipts from her purse, ripped them up it into small pieces, and also flung them into the bowl. *There will be no proof of who I am in case I'm stopped.*

She left the bathroom and walked over to the phone booth near the gas pumps. The pain in her groin was like blinding lights shooting through her legs.

Again she called Uncle Wiggly. There was no answer. *Oh Jesus! No! Please don't do this to me. I need you!*

Maura called information in Los Angeles for Rena's number. The operator told her that it was a private listing. "Hell!" she screamed, slamming down the receiver. The gas attendant poked his head out from under the hood of the pickup truck in the garage and looked quizzically at her.

Don't make a scene! she said to herself. She was feeling light-headed, and the metal scraping was beginning to echo through her skull again. Clenching her fists and resting her head against the black phone casing, she began to realize there was no way she could make it without medicine. The attacks were deepening now, and soon she would get crazy like she did after Martin died. Except now the spells were worse, and Uncle Wiggly said she was killing people.

Then she looked up and saw it. On the other side of the street next to the fruit stand was a sign that read "Pharmacy." *Do I take that chance?* She didn't have any choice, not anymore.

She limped across the street and looked inside the window of the drugstore. It was small and dimly lit, with the sundries up front and the pharmacy in the back. There didn't seem to be any customers in the store.

Maura went inside and walked over to the back. A small man in his mid-sixties, bald, with a wire-thin mustache and wearing a white pharmacist's frock looked up from behind the counter. He was counting out yellow-colored pills and putting them into a vial. "Can I help you?" he asked, wearing a smile that made his mustache stretch across his face.

Maura knew how slim her chances were, but she had no choice. "I need three prescriptions filled. The problem is I left them at home in New York." Her voice was weak and hoarse and she wondered if she had used her vocal chords in the last several days.

The pharmacist looked at her suspiciously. There was a sickly yellow cast to her face that could be seen under the makeup, and she was sweating profusely. "What kind of prescriptions?"

Maura took a deep breath to fight off the panic. The old man's face was changing colors, and his mustache looked like a centi-pede slowly squirming its way across his mouth. "Parnate,

Xanax, and Darvocet." She forced a laugh. "I'm so dumb. I can't believe I left them behind."

"You know I can't release those kinds of drugs without an authorization." His eyes warily scanned her face.

Maura cleared her throat to get the rust out of it. "Then can you call my doctor?"

The man picked up the phone. "New York you said? That's long distance."

"Yes, I know. I'll pay for the call," she replied. "I'm afraid I don't have his number with me."

He grunted and his eyes locked on hers as he dialed information. "What's your doctor's name?"

This is insane! There was no doctor in New York. Her hands balled up into fists. She needed that medicine and she wasn't going to let this little man stop her. The craziness was coming over her again, real strong this time, and she wanted to scream, tear up the place like she did to her house the night Martin died. Maybe it was too late for the medicine to calm her down, but she needed to find out. There was no way anyone was going to put her away in a hospital again like they did when she was seventeen. *Never again!* Suddenly Maura realized there was an alternative to that happening. Yes, she needed the medications, but there was something else she also needed.

"I asked you the name of your doctor," he said distrustfully.

Maura slowly walked around the counter and stood towering over the small pharmacist. He looked up into her face and what he saw made him lower the phone. His eyes filled with terror.

She grabbed a pair of sharp cuticle scissors off the counter. Maura knew the strength she possessed and what she could do with it when provoked. Reaching out and taking the little pharmacist by the collar with one hand, she dug the steel point of the scissors into his Adam's apple with the other. The skin easily ripped apart. Blood spurted out and flowed like a river down his neck.

Chapter Twenty-one

HARRISON WANTED TO stop at a friend's winery on the way back from Doctor Tomain's house, but Rena begged off, saying she had too many things to do. Instead, they agreed to meet for dinner at Mustards Grill at eight-thirty tonight. He dropped Rena off at the château and told her he'd see her then.

When she went inside the house, there was a message on the answering machine to call agent Marvin Grant as soon as possible. He had phoned only a few minutes ago. *Had they found Maura this time?*

Rena went into the den and dialed the number. It was the FBI office in Boise, Idaho. After Rena identified herself to an FBI operative, Grant got on the phone. "She's one hell of a smart lady," he said flippantly.

"Maura?"

"Yes. She robbed a pharmacy less than two hours ago."

"Did she hurt anyone?" There was dread in her voice.

"Yeah, the owner. Except he's more shook up than hurt. She cut his throat with a cuticle cutter—just a flesh wound. Luckily the blade on the scissor was only an inch long. She took him into a storeroom in the back and tied him up. After the pharmacist freed himself, he called the police. The robbery report was sent to our office because the sheriff's department in Boise knew we were looking for a woman around the same age as the suspect. Seems our lady of the vineyards totally changed her appearance. We would never have considered this woman to be Maura from the pharmacist's description. What tipped us off was the kind of drugs she stole. Vials filled with Parnate, Xanax, erythromycin tablets, and another one with Darvocet. There were also sleeping pills called Placidyls scattered over the floor. He thinks she may have grabbed some of those, too. The pharmacist said she was incredibly strong. She actually picked him up off the ground and carried him into the back. A little unusual for a woman."

"I've seen frail, undernourished, paranoid schizophrenics in mental wards toss two-hundred-pound security guards around like they were helium balloons. She must have needed those medications desperately to take a chance like that." Rena wondered if Maura literally carried the Mexican, Tomas Sanchez, from the hidden spring to the vineyards. That would explain why the trail of blood abruptly stopped.

"He said she was acting strange. Holding her head and mumbling something about metal scraping sounds coming from inside her."

This bothered Rena. She then said somberly, "Schizophrenics often hear voices and sounds in their heads. It has to do with a chemical imbalance." Strange, she thought. *If Maura was schizophrenic, then why take those kinds of drugs?* They were used more for the control of depression and panic disorders. There also were no records showing any prescriptions for these drugs written out in her name. Where was she getting them from and who was telling her to take them? "Did she steal anything else?" she asked Grant.

"Yes. She also took a couple of hundred dollars from the cash register and the pharmacist's car that was parked in the back—a blue Chevy Impala. She has a two-hour jump. All roads leading out of Boise are blocked, and the highway patrol have been authorized to pull over all cars that even come close to resembling Impalas. It shouldn't be long before we have her."

"So you've said before," she said with some skepticism. After she hung up on Grant, she called Cathy and told her she would be coming back to L.A. in a couple of days and that she missed her.

While walking upstairs to change for her dinner date with Harrison, she began to be bothered about the Placidyls that the pharmacist also believed were taken. Those were heavy sleeping pills. The thought of suicide entered her mind. She hoped Maura wasn't contemplating that. And why erythromycin? Was she ill?

They're underestimating her, Rena thought to herself as she got undressed to take a quick shower. *She's a hell of a lot sharper than they're giving her credit for.* Rena thought back to a breezy Monday morning in the Napa Valley when they were sixteen years old.

* * *

Peter McKinney phoned Rena at the château asking if she would stay with Maura while he went down to the Orange County State Fair where his cabernet was in contention for a gold medal. He said that Maura was supposed to go with him, but she had suddenly come down with the flu. Rena quickly agreed, and Peter came to the house to pick her up.

"She looks terrible," he said with apprehension in his voice as Rena got into his car. "She's burning up and she can't keep anything down. I hate to leave her like this, but she's insisting that I go. She won't let Semra near her. I wanted to call Dr. Frawley, but the fool girl nearly bit my head off when I mentioned it. She said she'd be fine without him and that you'd watch over her. If her fever gets any higher, don't pay her any mind. You call him at once, is that clear?" His voice was hard and threatening.

"Yes," she said anxiously.

When McKinney pulled up to the house, Rena rushed upstairs to her friend's bedroom. She found Maura lying under the covers, her long, golden hair spread out over most of the pillow. Rena was jolted by the way she looked: her face was a ghostly white and crusted vomit clung to her lips. The sockets around her eyes were dark, turning her face into a deathlike mask. She was shivering, and beads of sweat were draped over her mouth and forehead.

Rena sat down on the bed beside her and reached for her hand. It felt rubbery and clammy. "Maura, maybe you should see a doctor," Rena said, concerned.

"No," she uttered defiantly in a hoarse voice. "No doctor. I'll be fine." She looked up and saw Peter standing over her. "Go to the fair, Dad. It's just a bug. Don't worry." She managed a weak smile.

He shook his head and sighed at his daughter's stubbornness. "You call Frawley if the fever goes up," he said to Rena, pointing his finger at her.

She quickly nodded.

He said firmly to Maura, "If you can't go to the bathroom by yourself, you get Semra to help you. Is that understood?"

"You know I will," she murmured.

He turned to leave. When he reached the door, he looked back again and said, "You're an obstinate girl, Maura. I don't like leaving you like this."

"Please, Dad," she moaned.

He shook his head one last time then went downstairs.

Semra walked into the room and glared at Rena.

"What is it you want?" Maura said harshly to her. "Get out!"

Semra's fuzzy upper lip curled in hate; then she moved her short, squat body out of the room.

Maura squeezed Rena's hand. "Stand by the window and see if he's really leaving. Sometimes he likes to fake me out."

"Your father?"

"Yes."

Bewildered, Rena looked down at her.

"Do it for God's sake!" Maura whispered impatiently.

Rena went over to the window and looked out. Through the lace curtains she could see McKinney getting into his car. He started the engine and drove away. Turning to Maura, she said, "He's gone."

"Good!" Maura groaned loudly. She pushed the covers off her body and weakly sat up. "I'm afraid I'm going to be sick again." She held her stomach and slowly started to make her way over to the bathroom. "Jesus, is this painful!"

"Do you have to throw up?" Rena asked anxiously.

"No, this time I have the shits. It's been coming out of me from both ends." She leaned against the wall for a second until the dizziness passed then went into the bathroom.

"Let me help you," Rena said, going over to her.

"No," Maura quickly snapped. "I'll be fine." Closing the door to the bathroom, she said to Rena, "Go down to the fridge and get me the full half gallon of milk."

"Why?"

"Do it, please!" she groaned demandingly through the other side of the door.

Totally confused, Rena went downstairs. When Semra saw her coming into the kitchen, she scowled and went into her bedroom, slamming the door. Rena found the container of milk and brought it back up again.

A few minutes later Maura emerged from the bathroom. She made her way over to the bed, then sat down on the floor, and leaned her back against the nightstand. Shivering profusely, she huddled her knees close to her chin and grabbed the carton from Rena. She clawed at the top, tearing it open, then ravenously drank from it. The milk slid down her chin and nightgown, forming small puddles on the carpet. Rena stared at her in wonderment. When Maura had finished half the carton, she looked up

190

at Rena and burped. Then she started laughing. Holding her mouth, she said in between giggles, "Damn! What I don't do for love!"

"What the hell is going on, Maura?" Rena demanded. "Aren't you sick?"

"Sicker than I've ever been in my whole goddamn life!" She reached into the drawer of the nightstand and took out several packs of Tums. After ripping one of them apart, she popped several tablets into her mouth. "Calcium," she said. "I need calcium." She held the carton up to Rena as if she were toasting her then took several more gulps of milk to wash the tablets down.

"What do you need calcium for? The flu?"

"No dummy, as an antidote for oxalic-acid poisoning. Be a pal and look under the bed," she said, pointing to the area with her finger.

Rena bent down and looked under the bed. She pulled out several clusters of reddish-looking stalks that resembled celery. "What's this?"

Holding her stomach in pain, Maura smiled and said, "Rhubarb. Your common, everyday, goddamn garden-variety rhubarb." Again she started to laugh. "Except you can't eat the leaves. They're poisonous. If you do you get sick, just like I did. I have to throw them away before my father finds them."

"You poisoned yourself?" Rena held her hand to her mouth in astonishment.

"Yep." She took a few more gulps of milk. Some color was returning to her face, and she didn't seem to be shivering as much. "Don't worry. I'll be fine in a while. I just have to get a lot of calcium into me right now. That's why I'm drinking milk and eating these God awful-tasting Tums. I should have gotten the mint-flavored ones."

"How could you do this? Everybody thought you were deathly sick with the flu!" Rena said furiously.

"As I said, what I don't do for love." She slowly got up and walked over to the window and looked out. Across the road she could see Martin standing next to the wooden doors of the winery waiting for her. Her pupils lit up with fire. Not taking her eyes off him, she said to Rena, "He's expecting me. I planned this for weeks so I wouldn't have to go to that damn fair. My father would kill Martin if he knew I was still seeing him." Maura went over to the closet and removed a sleeveless pink dress. She

191

turned to Rena. "I have to take a shower first to get this sickening smell off of me."

"You're crazy!" Rena screamed, as Maura, holding the dress, dragged her feeble body into the bathroom. "What's the name of that poison called again?"

"Oxalic acid?"

"Can it be fatal?"

"Sure," Maura said, leaning against the bathroom door.

Rena was horrified. "How much of it do you have to eat before you die?"

Smiling, Maura shrugged, "Hell if I know."

Rena watched in disbelief as Maura calmly turned on the shower then quietly closed the door.

When she exited the bathroom, her hair was already brushed to a silky sheen and she had on a light makeup base that covered the red blotches on her pale skin. The pink dress she was now wearing only accentuated her beauty. She smiled at herself in the mirror, then turned to Rena, and hugged and kissed her. "You're a friend. I love you," she quickly said, then rushed out of the room to meet Martin.

Looking out the window, Rena was amazed as she watched Maura run out of the house toward Martin's open arms. She watched as they kissed passionately and held each other tightly. Only ten minutes ago Maura looked like she was dying, now she seemed more alive than Rena had ever seen her look before. Can love be that powerful? she wondered as she stared at them walking hand-in-hand into the winery.

Rena spent the rest of the afternoon alone in Maura's bedroom reading a book. They were making love in the winery, Rena assumed. She was furious at being used like this. Maura didn't have to trick her into coming over. They were best friends and she would have come anyway. Then she remembered the look on Maura's face when she first saw Martin outside her window and her anger subsided. Rena sighed. Yes, Maura did love him with all her soul. Her father had no right to keep them apart. To poison oneself for love! My God! How many people are there in this world who can feel that deeply?

That happened almost a year to the day before Martin was murdered, Rena thought as she applied the last finishing touches to her makeup. *One hell of a smart lady, Agent Grant? You don't know how smart!*

Chapter Twenty-two

THE TRAILWAYS BUS pulled into the Idaho Falls depot at seven-fifteen on a wet, cold Sunday evening. A handful of passengers got off. Maura was among them.

The winds were blowing hard and sheets of rain were coming down on a slant. Wrapping the cardigan around her body for protection, Maura slowly made her way into the station. It was almost deserted inside except for an old woman with vacant eyes who sat at the end of the long brown wooden bench; she had a shopping bag between her legs. At the other end of the bench, a young marine, fresh out of boot camp, was sleeping with his shaved head propped up against his duffel bag.

Spotting a phone booth near the newsstand, Maura went over to it and dialed Uncle Wiggly's number once again. She let it ring for several minutes before she hung up. *Where is he? What am I supposed to do!*

She was feverish and her body was shaking from the chills. Maura limped into the bathroom to once again examine the wound near her groin. She removed the dressing, which was soaked in green puss. The cut was now badly infected: it was painfully swollen and felt like hot coals to the touch. Obviously the toxin was too far spread in her body for the erythromycin tablets to work. If only she wasn't allergic to penicillin! she thought. There was nothing more she could do now except use aspirins to help keep the fever down. All she could do was just hope that the natural antibodies in her system would kill off the infection by itself. It would be taking too big a chance if she tried to see a doctor in this city. At least she had the Parnate and Xanax to control the attacks. The headaches had been starting up again and the Darvocet helped that. Her biggest fear right now was not knowing what would happen if she blacked out again, or even fell asleep!

Maura quickly undressed, grabbed a striped dress from the tote bag, and put it on. She knew the police would be looking for a woman wearing a black wool skirt and a white sweater as the one who robbed the pharmacy. She then left the bathroom and went over to the ticket booth and picked up a bus schedule.

The smart thing she did was to leave the blue Chevy Impala in Boise. If the police suspected the vineyard murderer and the person who robbed the pharmacy were one and the same, she knew they'd set up roadblocks looking for the car. Taking a bus to someplace as unsuspecting as Idaho Falls gave her a better head start. She hid the car in an unlit area of an underground parking lot several blocks from the Boise bus station. It could be days before it was found.

Her suspicions turned out to be right. As the bus made its way east to Idaho Falls, she looked out the window and saw an unusual amount of highway patrol on Route 20. They seemed to be indiscriminately pulling cars over to the side of the road, especially large blue ones.

Then what's the next move?

She couldn't go back to the Napa Valley. They'd be waiting for her there. As much as she needed to see Uncle Wiggly, it would have to wait.

What about New York? No, she had no friends there.

On the front page of the schedule booklet was a map of the United States with all the routes the bus company took. An idea began to form in her mind. She would take three buses. The first one to Salt Lake City, the next one to Las Vegas, then the last one to Los Angeles.

She would get to Rena. It was her only hope.

Looking at the departure listings, she saw the journey would take at least a day and a half. That meant she would have to spend a lot of time hanging around in bus terminals. *No. Too dangerous! Find a movie theater . . . a diner. Anything but bus terminals. That's where they'll be looking.* The trip could be made in much less time than that, but she couldn't afford to be on one bus for any great length of time.

Maura went over to the ticket booth and bought her first fare to Salt Lake City. It wasn't scheduled to leave for another three hours. Where was she to go in the meantime? She couldn't stay here. Then she saw her reflection in the mirror on the green-painted wall. Her hair was now a mouse-colored brown. It was early, and drugstores were still open. Yes, it was time to change her appearance again. This time she would have black hair.

How easy this is, she thought as she walked out of the terminal. Years as a deputy district attorney taught her that most perpetrators were caught by the police and convicted because there was no real thought behind their criminal act. Her theory had always been that with a little ingenuity most lawbreakers would never be caught. How ironic that she was the one who would test this principle.

Chapter Twenty-three

RENA WALKED INTO the bright, noisy atmosphere of Mustards Grill. She had been especially conscious about the way she dressed tonight. Her blue silk pants and jacket worked well with her slender body; she knew that by the way the male patrons in the restaurant sneaked glances in her direction. It was because of Harrison that she wanted to look good. There was no doubt in her mind that there was a definite attraction between them. At this point, however, she wasn't sure how far she wanted to take it.

She immediately spotted him deep in conversation with Edmond and Blythe Farnsworth at the bar. The couple were sporting healthy, glowing tans. They must have just returned from Palm Springs, she thought.

As Rena walked over to them, Blythe's face lit up. She was wearing white cotton pants and a tight white blouse that exposed the curves of her firm figure. Rena's immediate impression was that the style of clothing would be better suited for an eighteen-year-old.

Blythe slid off the stool and enthusiastically grabbed Rena's hands. "It's so good seeing you again. When Harrison told me he was meeting you tonight, I couldn't believe it! I thought you weren't coming back to Napa for quite a while."

"I changed my mind." She could see rather than sense Blythe's joy. Once again she felt that this woman was playacting. Rena turned to Edmond and shook his hand. The liver spots on the back of his hands were more pronounced because of his tan. His lips were cracked, and he was continuously licking at them. Probably because of the dry weather in the desert resort, she thought to herself. "How was Palm Springs?" she asked.

"Hot but lovely," Edmond replied.

"Boring," Blythe immediately followed up.

The Farnsworths turned and glared at each other for a brief second.

Rena sensed that not all was tranquil between them.

"Blythe and Edmond asked if it would be all right to join us," Harrison said to Rena, shrugging helplessly.

"Of course it's all right," she replied. He seems edgy tonight. Not his usual, relaxed self, she thought.

The maître d' came over and told them that their table was ready. As they followed him through the maze of tables, Rena could see a large percentage of Asian patrons in the restaurant. She was aware that every year more and more wineries were being bought up by the foreign companies. Once this valley was filled with independent vintners like Peter McKinney. They came from Italy, France, and other parts of Europe with little or no money. The one thing they all had in common was that their roots were planted firmly in generations of wine makers. That and the desire to grow grapes in a new land was enough for them.

So much has changed, Rena thought. When she spent her summers here as a child, the visitors were at a minimum and the quaintness was real. Now all the streets of St. Helena, Calistoga, and Yountville were lined with souvenir shops and trendy restaurants. Every day thousands of upscale tourists in their BMWs, drunk from hitting one too many wineries, swerved crookedly down Highway 29 trying to make it to the next tasting room before it closed. The men wore Ralph Lauren sweaters tied around their necks and the women were dressed to the hilt in their Anne Kleins. They'd hold glasses of cabernets up to the light, gently swirling the red liquid around and sniffing it. Closing their eyes, they'd take a small sip and swish the wine from cheek to cheek as if they were gargling mouthwash. If they liked what they tasted, they nodded their approval; if not, they wrinkled up their noses. The wine makers always waited patiently, their eyes filled with amusement. They had learned tolerance because these city people with their peculiar affectations have made them very rich over the years.

Throughout most of the dinner Edmond ignored his wife and leaned over Harrison's chair to talk to him about the wine business. His hands were trembling and there were muscle spasms in his face. She wondered if he was feeling well.

Rena looked over at Harrison. He seemed anxious, deep in thought, and was only half listening to Edmond. Occasionally Harrison would glance over to Rena with a "what can I do" expression. Blythe talked on and on to Rena about Palm Springs and how it's become nothing more than a retirement village— 'God's waiting room,' she caustically referred to it. She was chain-smoking, no longer seeming to care about her husband's heart condition as she did the night of Simon Halbrook's dinner party. Every few minutes she would look at Rena, roll her eyes dramatically in Edmond's and Harrison's direction, and silently mouth the word *boring*.

Things have deteriorated between her and Edmond, Rena believed, and she wondered if the difference in their ages was beginning to take its toll. How old was she? Thirty-eight? Forty-five? She couldn't really tell. Blythe looked good—tall, slim, and tight-skinned. The looks she received from their young waiter confirmed this.

From the corner of her eye, Rena saw Otto van der Slyck enter the restaurant and saunter over to the bar. Like most of the other male customers here tonight, he was wearing a cotton sweater slung over his shoulders and tied around his neck. He sat down on the stool and began talking to the bartender. Whatever Otto said made him laugh. The bartender, still chuckling, then poured a bourbon over crushed ice and handed it to him. Otto took a cigarette out of a gold case, lit it, and slowly exhaled the smoke.

Rena turned back to the table. The busboy was serving coffee. Edmond was still deep in conversation with Harrison, and Blythe was now having eye contact with their waiter across the room. The last time they were together, Blythe told Rena that she had insisted she and Edmond sign a prenuptial agreement. Rena wondered, as she watched Blythe flirt with the waiter, whether she would soon regret that decision.

Glancing back at the bar, she saw Otto staring at her. When he caught her eye, he held his glass up to her in greeting then finished off the rest of the bourbon in it. Rena had been meaning to talk to him and perhaps this was as good a time as any. Other than Harrison, she doubted very much if anyone else at this table would miss her. She excused herself and said she'd be back in a few minutes.

As she walked over to Otto, she noticed the reddish haze in his frog-eyes and realized that this was not the first bar stool he had sat on tonight.

"Greetings and salutations, my sister," he said smiling at her as he handed the bartender his empty glass.

"Excuse me?" she uttered, surprised by his remark.

"Didn't you know?"

"Know what?" Rena slid onto the stool next to him.

"Right now your father and my dear mother are spending an amorous, carnal weekend together in Monterey." He batted his long, white-blond eyelashes at her.

"No I didn't know," Rena said. She was a little disturbed by that. She didn't particularly like Monica van der Slyck, but that was Simon's business and not hers. "They're grown-ups. They can do whatever they want."

"If they marry we *will* be brother and sister you know."

"We'll deal with that monumental event when and if it comes to that," she said with an icy tone. Again Otto fluttered his eyes. The light color and thin hairs of his eyelids reminded Rena of cocoon fibers closing around a caterpillar. A wave of anger rushed through her, and she fought to dispel it.

The bartender brought Otto his bourbon. Rena ordered a Calistoga water.

"I saw you up in the hills near Maura's winery when the FBI was there," she said.

"Did you? I saw you, too. Who was that cute man with the blond hair you were talking to?" he asked playfully.

"What were you doing on the McKinney property?" she asked, ignoring his question.

He was jolted by her directness. Then resuming his frivolous composure, he said, "Contemplating life. Pretending I was Thoreau. Why?"

"I don't think so," she said casually, squeezing the lime into her drink. "I think you were spying. In fact, I think you do that a lot. It's sort of a hobby with you."

The inane smile finally disappeared from his face. His eyes hardened and he said, "Are you trying to insult me?"

"No, just being open. That's what sisters and brothers are

supposed to do. So tell me, why were you hanging around Maura's property?''

''I don't have to answer you,'' he said abruptly. He stood up to move to another stool.

''You *will* have to answer to that cute man with the blond hair if I relay my suspicions to him. He's with the FBI.''

He turned back to her. ''What suspicions?''

She patted his stool. ''Sit down, Otto, and I'll tell you more.''

He slowly sat down.

''At my father's dinner party you mentioned that last year you used to see Maura leave at night and return at five in the morning. Where did she go?''

He let out a deep nervous breath. ''I don't know.''

''Oh, yes you do. You were confident she was going to meet her lover.''

''Was I?''

''Yes. Since your hobby is snooping, I strongly believe you made it a habit of following her.''

''Oooh please!'' he moaned. Taking another cigarette from his case, he tapped the end on the bar top to pack the tobacco down, then lit it. ''I don't need this craziness in my life.'' He looked dramatically up at the ceiling and let out a long stream of smoke.

''Otto, I *will* tell the FBI.'' Then Rena decided to take a gamble. ''Especially about my thoughts on Tomas Sanchez.''

Otto's bulbous eyes widened in fear. He turned his face to Rena. Clearing his throat, he said, ''What the hell are you talking about?''

''You were in charge of hiring the workers in your mother's winery. What possessed you to hire a man like Tomas Sanchez?''

''He was Mexican. Picking fruit is in their blood,'' he said with a smirk.

No, she did not like this man at all. ''I don't think that's the reason, Otto,'' Rena said, trying to control her temper. ''Tomas Sanchez was from the *barrio*. He didn't know a grape from a watermelon. He also spent most of his life in jail. I think that's what probably intrigued you about him.''

Otto gave her a scathing look. She liked the fact that she was getting to him.

''I bet you found him somewhere on the streets of Los Angeles. Maybe even in the *barrio*. You go in for a little rough trade, don't you, Otto?''.

His forehead was now glistening with sweat. She liked that, too.

"His tattoos turn you on, Otto? Maybe to the point where you invited him to spend the summer with you here in Napa? Of course you couldn't tell Mama, so it had to look like he had a job picking grapes."

His temples began to throb with anger, and his face turned red. "You are a bitch, you know that?"

"Sometimes I *can* be, Otto," she said sweetly. "Tomas was a sex offender. I knew about his rape conviction. I bet if I dug deeper, I'd find out that he also liked boys, especially since he spent a good part of his life incarcerated. Did that turn you on, too, Otto? The part about him being a rapist?"

His mouth was now quivering. He looked up at her with pleading eyes, then looked around him. "Let's go to the end of the bar. It's less crowded there," he said with a shaky voice. He stood up and moved over several stools. Rena followed. When he sat down again, he hunched his torso over the counter and held his face in his hands.

Rena turned and saw Harrison looking in her direction. She waved and held up one finger, meaning that she'd be back in a minute. At first Harrison frowned, then he nodded in understanding. Rena turned again to Otto. "I'm bordering on being rude to other people right now so I don't have much time to be subtle." She pushed her drink aside and leaned into the counter so that she was only inches from his face. "Where did Maura go at night?"

Otto let out a sigh, rubbed his face, then said, "To some kind of lagoon or pond that was hidden away by trees and bushes. I only followed her there a few times last year."

"I know about the spring," Rena said. "How did Tomas know about it?"

"What?"

"Tomas wasn't killed in Maura's vineyards. He was killed next to the spring."

He nodded slowly in acknowledgment then finished off his drink.

"You knew? How could you? That was never brought out in the media," she said, shocked.

"Yes, I *know* where he died. *Oh, Gawd*, if my mother finds out about any of this!" His hand was twitching as he brushed it through his hair. He looked at the bartender and once again

200

pointed to his empty glass. In a quivering voice, he said, "Tomas was getting bored. He tolerated me, I suppose because living up here was a hell of a lot better than living in the streets. That's where I first met him—cruising the streets around La Brea and Sunset as a male prostitute over a year ago. I picked him up. I knew he wasn't gay, that he was only in it for the money. The thing that turned me on about him was you never knew when he'd turn violent. That's *my* thing, I guess." There was an excitement in Otto's eyes as he visualized some of the *things* that Tomas had done to him. "Last summer was nice. I took him to Europe. Then he came back to Napa with me. You're right, I pretended he was the help so no one would suspect. He suddenly disappeared in the fall, and I didn't see him again until several months ago when he just showed up at my door in San Francisco. He came back up to Napa to stay with me this summer. A couple of weeks ago, the day before Maura came up, he told me he wanted to leave, that he missed the action in the streets. I didn't want him to go." Again he sighed.

Rena knew he was ready to talk about it. "Go on, Otto," she said gently. She had him open now and there was no reason to close him up again by being harsh with him.

"I found out from Manuel, the man who runs Maura McKinney's winery, that she was expected up here sometime that day. I told Tomas. I knew he liked women better than men. In order to get him to stay, I told him that there was a beautiful blond goddess coming up to Napa and that she always swims naked in this pond. He laughed at me. He said that he already knew about her and where she swam. He said that he had plans for her."

Rena was stunned. "He said that he *already* knew about her? How?"

Otto shrugged. "I don't know. He didn't tell me."

"What kind of plans?"

"What do you think? Don't be naive. The night Maura first arrived up here, Tomas told me he was going out. I asked him where, but he wouldn't tell me. When I tried to press it, he smacked me across the face." Looking embarrassed, Otto touched the place on his cheek where Tomas must have hit him. "I followed him down to the spring on Maura's property and watched him hide behind some bushes. He was waiting for her. He didn't know I was there, about thirty feet away. When it was turning dark, Maura came to the spring. The fog was so thick

201

and the sun was almost down, so it was hard to see." Otto paused to finish off the drink. "I could only make out shadows. I saw her take her robe off and go into the spring."

"Go on," she said to him. Her stomach was beginning to twist inside her because of what was about to come.

"A large fog bank rolled in. I couldn't see anything. In a few minutes I heard her scream. Then I heard Tomas scream. Except his scream was pain where hers was rage. Hers wasn't human. It was like a cornered animal." His eyes were popping from their sockets with fear as he told the story. He paused again.

Rena knew he was contemplating another drink. "Continue," she said softly, swallowing the bile that was coming up in her throat.

He rubbed his eyes, trying to clear the alcohol from them. "There's nothing more to tell. I ran like hell. If you heard that sound coming from her, you would have run, too."

Again Rena turned to her table. Harrison was looking annoyed and Blythe was also glancing her way with a quizzical expression on her face. Rena turned back to Otto. "Quickly, Otto," she said between clenched teeth. "You said Maura may have had a boyfriend. Why do you think that?"

"Because I saw him. When I followed her to the spring last year he would meet her there."

"How do you know he was a boyfriend? Did you see him do anything with her?" Rena felt queasy discussing Maura's sex life with him.

"Yes, I saw." He rolled his large eyes affectedly to the fan on the ceiling, then lit up another cigarette.

"What did you see?"

"Oh my, we are digging tonight, aren't we?" He attempted a smirk but quickly dropped it when he saw the look on Rena's face. "It was always dark when she went to the pond, and she never carried a flashlight. She seemed to know instinctively where she was going at night. This disgusting old man would meet her there. Sometimes he'd be waiting. Other times he'd come after she swam."

"Once again," she said impatiently, "What did you see?"

"Not very much. She'd lie down on the grass and this old creep would touch her all over."

"Was she naked?"

"Yes."

"Was he?"

"No."

"Where did he mostly touch her?"

"My *Gawd*, you are something!" He flipped the ash on the floor from his cigarette. "He touched her all over, mostly by the genital area. I couldn't see much because it was night."

Strange, she thought. *Why would Maura let an old man fondle her? She almost killed that beautiful Greek boy when he just tried kissing her on Paros.*

"Do you know who that man was?"

"No."

"Have you ever seen him before?"

He just shook his head no and held his glass up to the bartender.

"Was there anything unusual about him?" she asked, frustrated.

"Nothing, except . . ."

"Except what?" She leaned in closer.

"He always wore a white hat. The kind you saw Sidney Greenstreet wear in those old Bogart movies."

Rena closed her eyes as it hit home. Dr. Winston Frawley! She had seen him wearing that hat the day they took away the body of Tomas Sanchez in Maura's vineyard. Then something else hit home: Frawley wasn't sexually groping her—he was most likely inspecting her!

But for what? What was wrong with her, and why did he do it under the cover of night?

Chapter Twenty-four

RENA LEFT OTTO at the bar and went back to the table. Harrison seemed irritated by the length of time she was away. She took her jacket from the back of her chair and leaned over him. Touching his arm, she said, "I've got to leave."

He looked up at her and saw something was wrong. "Where are you going?"

"I'll talk to you about it tomorrow," she whispered nervously. She said good night to Edmond and to Blythe, whose face was etched with disappointment, then left the restaurant.

She got into the Range Rover and drove north to Calistoga. *Frawley had to have been examining her!* There couldn't have been anything sexual about their relationship. He was the one who brought Maura into the world. *But why see her at the spring— and only at night?* Frawley had a lot of questions to answer.

What a sick, pathetic man Otto was! He actually was going to set Maura up to be raped by Sanchez at the spring. He said Tomas already knew about her. How? Did he see her swimming naked in the spring last year? No, she didn't think so. Then another thought occurred to Rena—one that made more sense: perhaps someone else had also told Tomas about Maura. But who? Who else other than Otto, Frawley, and Manuel knew that Maura went alone to the spring?

Maura's scream sounded like that of a cornered animal, Otto told her. What did he expect a woman to sound like who was about to be violated? Rena was pulsating with rage. Brother and sister? Not in this millennium! She would deal with Otto in her own good time. Right now she had to see Winnie. He knew more about Maura than he was willing to talk about—she was sure of it.

Then clouds began to part in her head, and she finally saw some sunlight. *Winnie . . . Wiggly.* My God! Maura probably substituted Wiggly for the name Winnie as a child and called him Uncle Wiggly as a term of affection! The nickname "Uncle Wiggly" probably stuck between them throughout the years.

Traffic was light this time of night, and she stepped on the gas. She wanted to get to Calistoga as quickly as possible. Fifteen minutes later she pulled up at the curb directly in front of his house. The area of his home that was the office looked dark but the top floor was lit up. Rena assumed that he used the upstairs as his living quarters.

She got out of the car, walked up to the door, and rang his bell. No one answered. She waited a minute then tried again. This time she listened for his footsteps. There were none. She tried the door and found that it was locked.

He has to be home, she thought. Over to the side she could see the trunk of his car through the crack in the garage.

Rena walked around to the back. The earth was damp, and her high heels dug deeply into the soft ground. She tried the back door, but it was also locked. Then she saw his small winery about a hundred feet down from the house. It was a wooden building no bigger than a large shed. All the windows were closed, however there was a small light on inside. The path was dark, and she had to watch where she was walking in order to avoid the ditches. Rena peered inside, but it was impossible to see anything through the dirt-streaked windows. She pushed down on the door handle, and the lock clicked open.

Except for a dim naked light bulb hanging near the door, the winery was filled with dark shadows. There was also a strong, thick odor of fermenting wine saturating the room. The air was so dense that it was almost impossible to breathe. She felt both sides of the wall next to the door until she came to the light switch. When she turned it on, the room erupted into a strong halo of light that temporarily blinded her. She let her eyes adjust to the brightness for a couple of seconds, then looked around. Over to the left was the destemming machine. Next to it was the metal press. She felt light-headed from the carbon dioxide that the fermenting wine released in the air. *If Frawley was fermenting wine, why did he keep the windows closed? He had to have known how dangerous this was without proper ventilation.*

Then she looked over to the five-thousand-gallon stainless-steel tank in the back of the winery and got her answer.

Frawley's feet were on the top rung of an eight-foot ladder with his head and body slumped over inside the open tank. His arms dangled lifelessly at his side.

Rena was feeling too weak at this point to be shocked. She knew that if she didn't get out of here she'd soon be as dead as Frawley. Her body swayed from side to side as she made her way to the door. Outside in the fresh air she dropped to the ground. Holding her head in her hands, she breathed deeply until the dizziness passed. Then she got up and went over to the back door of Frawley's house. Picking up a rock from the ground, she put it through one of the windowpanes, reached her hand in, and unlocked the door.

Once inside she quickly found the telephone by the kitchen wall and called the police. She told them what had happened.

"The paramedics will be there in five minutes," the voice on the other end said.

Obviously this policeman doesn't know anything about making wine. "It's too late for the paramedics. Send the coroner's wagon," she replied, then hung up. Rena *did* know something about wine making and also knew about some of the dangers. While wine is fermenting in a tank, there's an invisible one-foot layer on the top that's pure carbon dioxide. If someone put their head in that "no man's land," he'd die within seconds. *Frawley must have known that. He was a vintner as well as a doctor.*

Still feeling dizzy, Rena went over to the sink and put a dish towel under the cold faucet. She then sat down at the kitchen table, put the cold compress on her head, and waited for the police to arrive.

Chapter Twenty-five

"JEEZ, WHAT A shitty thing this is," Pinky muttered, shaken up. He was standing next to Rena near the open door of Frawley's winery. They watched solemnly as two firemen wearing oxygen masks stood on ladders and carefully lifted the doctor's body down from the steel tank. When the light came directly over his head, they could see a purplish cast on his face and his swollen tongue protruded halfway out of his mouth. "I know he's been fighting cancer for a long time and his practice was next to nothing, but still . . . ." Pinky didn't finish the sentence. He was taking in deep breaths of air.

"Maybe he was carrying something around with him that just got too heavy," Rena said thoughtfully.

The firemen brought the body out on a stretcher, and Rena and Pinky moved away from the door to let them through. The headlights from the morgue truck at the side of the house captured hundreds of insects fluttering wildly in their glow.

Pinky looked at her with a confused expression. "What could he be carrying?" he said finally. "Doc Frawley's been around forever. He's one of the most up-front guys you ever met."

"I don't know. I'm pretty sure that Frawley is the Uncle Wiggly that Maura planned to see in Napa."

He shot her a quick look. "How do you know?"

Rena then told him about Otto, and also about Frawley going to the spring last year to see Maura.

"You mean to tell me that van der Slyck guy knew that Tomas Sanchez was being murdered and didn't call the police?" Pinky's face was red with anger, and his lips were quivering.

"He also planned to have Sanchez rape her. It didn't work out that way."

"That little faggot shit!" Pinky slammed his hand hard against the door of the winery. The sound was like an explosion ripping through the still night. He then turned and looked out at the road when he heard a car engine.

Dr. Walter Parsons pulled up to the side of the road next to the morgue truck and got out of his sedan. He walked over to the back of the van, pulled the sheet from Frawley's face, and looked at the body. Parsons's fine blond hair dropped down over his eyes, but he didn't bother to push it back as he touched the side of the doctor's neck. His face was bleak.

"He's dead, Doc," Pinky said, walking over to him, still trembling with anger over what Rena had told him.

"Yes, I can see." He emitted a long, steady sigh. "I was just hoping you may have made a mistake when you called me. You think it was suicide?" Parsons's voice was steady when he asked that, but he couldn't hide the glassiness in his eyes. He and the old doctor had become close over the past few months. Frawley had taken him under his wing while he was setting up his new practice in Geyserville.

"Can't be anything else *but* suicide. Frawley's been around too long to know you don't stick your face in a vat of fermenting wine. You've seen him a lot lately. Did he seem depressed?" Pinky asked Parsons.

"Bitter, not depressed," he said grimly as he slapped a mosquito from his face. "But who wouldn't be? Over forty years of practicing medicine and the only things he had to show for it were a handful of unpaid Medicare bills and a diseased pancreas."

Rena walked over to them, rubbing her arms from the night air. "I'd like to see his files," she said to Pinky.

Pinky let out a stream of air and shook his head slowly. "Gee, I don't know, Rena."

"I think Frawley was treating Maura medically for something, and it just may be important. That's why she probably came up here for two weeks out of the year. She always went to the spring at night, and Frawley would meet her there. Otto said he watched him touch her sexually, but it sounded more like Frawley was performing some kind of an examination. Manuel told me there's salt in that water. Maybe she had a skin disease. Also, maybe it was Frawley who was dispensing the drugs to her without a prescription. Perhaps he kept records of those transactions."

"The FBI should be looking at those papers then, Rena."

"Let me find out if there's anything for them to look at."

Pinky kicked a pebble from under his foot, rubbed the back of his neck, and thought about it. "I have to get back to the station and fill out a death report on Frawley. I can leave a man with you, I guess."

"I'll stay with her," Parsons said. "If there's anything technical in his papers I can help."

Pinky looked up, scratched the smooth fat skin under his chin, then finally nodded his head. "Just don't take anything out of there," he said. He walked over to one of the officers, told him to stay at the house while Rena and Parsons looked through Frawley's belongings, then drove back to the station.

Rena and Parsons went inside the house and into Frawley's office. She turned on the lamp. The desk was covered with patients' dusty, medical-history folders that Frawley had never bothered to file away. Parsons began to browse through them. She went over to the oak file cabinet and looked under "M." The only McKinney folders she found were Peter's and Clair's. Maura's wasn't in there.

"What did he do with them?" she wondered out loud. Rena quickly skimmed through the file on Peter McKinney. It said that he died from a car accident. He was pronounced dead at San Francisco General Hospital on October 3, 1974. Then Rena looked over Clair McKinney's folder. Her health was poor the last couple of years of her life. She had undergone a mastectomy on her right breast for cancer a year before she died. Under cause of death Frawley had typed: "internal hemorrhaging due to pregnancy." He then went on to say that the child born to Clair, christened Maura Wilma McKinney, was a seven-pound, eight-ounce healthy baby girl.

Rena put the files back into the cabinet. Strange, Rena thought. There was no mention of William Tyrone McKinney, Maura's twin who had been born dead. *Why not?* Then out of the corner of her eye Rena saw Frawley's medical equipment through the doorway into the other room.

"Nothing in those files?" Parsons asked, dropping a bunch of folders back down on the desk.

Rena didn't answer him. She went into the examining room and stared at the ultrasound machine. It was new and barely used. *Why would Frawley purchase such an expensive machine when he knew he was retiring?*

"Do you have ultrasound equipment in your office?" she asked Parsons.

"No reason to," he said, walking into the room where Rena was. "Gynecologists use that toy." He stopped short when he saw the machine. "What the hell!" he uttered. "What would Winnie want with this?"

"You never saw it before?"

"No, he always kept this door closed when I came here. This machine is for seeing fetuses in their mothers' wombs. But pregnant women in Napa don't go to general practitioners any longer."

Next to the small refrigerator containing drugs, Rena saw another file cabinet. It was made of black metal and had only one drawer. She bent down and tried the handle. It was locked. Parsons took a suture scissor from the instrument drawer and knelt down next to Rena. He stuck the tip of the scissor between the lock and the cabinet and lifted up. The lock snapped and Rena pulled it open. There were several files inside, each one filled with papers and photographs. Some of the folders were torn and yellowed with age. The tab on each one of them had Maura McKinney's name on it and was dated with the year and month. Excitement and fear raced through Rena's body. She grabbed a batch of the files and put them on the gurney in the middle of the room. Parsons snatched up the rest and did the same.

"Start from the earliest one," she said to Parsons.

The date on the oldest folder was 1957, the year Maura was born. Rena opened it up and saw a black-and-white photograph attached by a paper clip to the inside of the folder. It was a close-up of the sexual organs of a newborn baby. An adult male's hand was in the picture holding the penis of the child over to the side. What Rena saw next made her gasp. Under the scrotum was a vagina. Rena turned the picture over. Printed in faded pencil markings were the words: Maura McKinney—three weeks old.

Parsons grabbed the file and scanned Frawley's notes. He then looked at Rena. His breath was heavy and shaky when he said, "This says that Maura has all the telltale signs of true hermaphroditism. That means she has the exterior organs of both male and female. He writes that the penis as well as the vagina appear perfectly normal." Parsons put down the notes and said, "I remember studying hermaphroditism in medical school, but there were so few cases in existence that there wasn't much discussion for it."

"My God!" Rena blurted out. *No wonder Maura couldn't stand being touched by a man. He would find out what she was! The lonely existence she must have led having to hide this from everyone!*

Again Rena was reminded about the words of the old lady in Greece: *"You are evil! You are the child of Hermes!"* Now she finally understood: The child of Hermes *must* have been the god Hermaphrodite. The old woman somehow knew.

Except there were operations that could correct this kind of permutation. Perhaps she had one as a child. *Maybe I'm just jumping to conclusions in order to have a better understanding of Maura.* Let's see, she thought. Her head was spinning.

They took the rest of the folders into Frawley's office and browsed through them. Black-and-white photos turned to color as the dates on the files changed. Some of them were full shots of Maura standing naked and unsmiling against a wall. How beautiful she was then! Rena thought to herself. Her breasts were beginning to flower, and pubic hair was starting to grow. In each picture she could see the penis transforming itself from that of a child's to an adolescent's.

There was no operation!

Rena didn't understand why Maura was never sent to a specialist. Why would Frawley, a general practitioner who obviously knew nothing about this rare abnormality, try to treat her himself?

Rena skimmed some of the other files until she came to the one dated 1974. That was the year when Martin was murdered. She opened the folder. It contained only a few brief notes about Maura's erratic behavior the day of Martin's death. There was also the address of a private mental institution outside of Tacoma, Washington. Riverside Hospital. *That must be where Maura was sent when she had her breakdown.* Frawley's handwriting was on back of the piece of paper. It said that Valium and lithium were recommended by a psychiatrist named Neil Tompson at the hospital. Was that the place she was getting the Parnate and Xanax from? Rena thought. She doubted these drugs were available in 1974. Prescribing lithium and Valium was the standard procedure back then. Rena knew that Xanax is now substituted in many cases for Valium.

"Oh Christ!" Parsons muttered. "Look at this!"

Rena moved her chair closer to his and looked at the folder he was holding. It was the latest one, dated last year at this time. Inside were several black-and-white Polaroid snapshots. She put them under the desk lamp to see them better. The pictures were translucent, almost like X rays, but it was obvious that they were of the interior lower half of a human torso. Except there was something different about them. Something very different!

"These photos were taken right from the pictures on the monitor of the ultrasound machine," Parsons said with a quaver in his voice. "You're looking at the internal workings of someone who's both man *and* woman. I've never seen this before," he said in awe. "Even in medical school I've never seen this! Look here!" He pointed his finger to the white outline of the scrotum. "There's only one testicle, and it's on the right side." He then pointed to the upper left portion of the picture. "This round thing here is an ovary!"

Rena stared at the pictures. She was astonished.

"Here's the uterus and it's attached to the vagina. Over here is the fallopian tube. That means she probably has menstruation cycles. See this?" His finger moved over to a gland above the penis. "It's the seminal vesicle. Only a man has that! This just can't be real! Look at this." He pointed to the outline of a duct under the scrotum. "This tube is known as the vas deferens. That's where semen is stored before it joins the urethra."

"That means Maura is capable of having sex with a man as well as a woman," Rena uttered softly as she thought back to what Grant had said about finding semen in the body of the victim Harriet Crowe. Did Maura kill the woman, then have sex with her just as Gustave de Montret did with his prey?

Parsons picked up a single yellow page from a legal pad that was in the folder. After scanning it for a second, he said, "It looks like Winnie bought the ultrasound machine last year in order to see what's inside Maura. That's when he found out that she had ovarian as well as testicular tissue."

"Half man, half woman. Unbelievable! This form of her-

211

maphroditism is as mythical and rare as the unicorn,'' Rena said. She was shocked. All these years of hiding something like this!

Still looking at the page, Parsons said, ''Winnie believes her condition was probably caused by whole-body chimerism.'' Parsons slouched back in the chair. ''This is fascinating!''

''What's that?'' Rena asked.

''The fusion of embryos. All this happens early on when the egg in the woman first gets fertilized.'' He made one hand into a fist and cupped the other hand. ''Say you're having fraternal twins—one's a boy and the other one's a girl. This is the brother.'' He held up his balled fist. ''This is the sister.'' He showed Rena his cupped hand. Then he put the cupped hand around his fisted one. ''The sister embryo fuses together with the brother, taking on his chromosomes. The chances of this happening have to be one in a billion.''

Rena's mind was racing. She was thinking about Maura's eyes. ''Maura has two different-colored eyes. One is blue and the other brown.''

Parsons became excited. ''That seems right! That medical peculiarity is known as irideal heterochromia. Remember, one half of Maura is actually her brother. Think of it as one of her eyes belonging to him. She has light skin and blond hair, right?''

Rena nodded.

''Then I'm willing to bet her twin would have had brown eyes if he could have been born. Even though he was devoured in the early stages of pregnancy by her embryo, in reality he still exists today in her body. Jesus, this *is* fascinating!''

''What you're saying is that no part of the male twin ever came through the birth canal?''

''He couldn't. He no longer existed. As I said, it happens very early during pregnancy. Think of it almost as cannibalism—one embryo swallowing the other and taking on its characteristics.''

Rena brushed back her hair. Something wasn't making sense. *Why was there a grave site for Maura's twin brother then if there never was a body?* No, it wasn't making sense at all. She went over to the phone and dialed Pinky at the station.

When he answered the phone, she said, ''Pinky, you're going to have to dig up a grave.''

''Whose?'' he asked surprised.

''William Tyrone McKinney.''

''Who's that?''

''Maura's twin brother.''

"I didn't know she had one." He sounded surprised. "Why do you want me to do that?"

"Because he never was. And if he never was, then I'd like to know what the hell *is* buried in that grave."

By the time Rena drove back to the Alexander Valley it was after ten. There was no moon tonight, and the clouds were low and thick. The château up on the hill looked like a black, shapeless form that loomed forebodingly out of the earth. She turned off the alarm system and let herself in. The house was dark and silent, which meant the help had left for the night.

Rena turned on the lights and went into the living room. She walked to the record cabinet, put a Mozart Concerto on the turntable, then poured herself a stiff cognac. She kicked her muddy shoes off, sat on the three-hundred-year-old couch, and put her feet up on the antique table next to it. Her head was spinning from the events of the past few hours.

Winston Frawley's suicide.

Maura—half man, half woman. Jesus Christ!

She rubbed her temples and took a deep sip of the cognac. It burned her throat and stomach, but it helped quiet her mind.

A true hermaphrodite! How phenomenal. There couldn't be more than twenty documented cases like hers in existence today. Except Maura had an attached uterus and fallopian tubes. That was something Rena never heard of before. *My God, she may actually be able to bear children!* Maura is rarer than rare, she thought. She *is* a unicorn!

A wave of sorrow suddenly swept over her. This woman/man had kept it a secret from the world for all these years. She had been Maura's best friend and she never knew—never even had an inkling that she was different from everyone else. Only Dr. Frawley and Peter McKinney knew of her abnormality. No, that's not true! Martin also knew! He had to. Didn't Maura tell her how she and Martin used to go swimming naked in the spring when they were young? There was no doubt in her mind that they had also made love later on when they were older. Rena shivered thinking about how totally and unquestionably Martin accepted her. How *totally* they accepted one another.

Rena's eyes began to water, and she took another sip of cognac. Very few people had loved as completely and with such passion as they had. Martin was her real link to the outside world. With him she could be open; he was the guardian of her secret.

When he died, her access to the world closed, and she withdrew into herself—never allowing anyone to touch her or wanting love again.

Rena sighed. The tears were flowing freely down her face now, and she didn't bother to wipe them away. Were they not the same, she and Maura? She, too, had loved her husband with such passion. When he betrayed her, didn't she also withdraw? And Charlie—when his wife butchered the one thing he loved, his daughter—he surrounded himself with thornbushes, daring anyone to touch him. Rena silently toasted all the broken wings and scarred carcasses of the world, then finished off her drink.

The record ended and she got up to turn it over. Mozart's Concerto 21 in C minor filled the cavernous living room. She poured herself another drink, something she rarely did, and sat back down on the couch. Rena always felt Maura was an enigma. Knowing about her condition now helped fill in so many missing pieces. Rena thought about Maura's preoccupation with ancient Greek art. She remembered the day in Athens when Maura slipped away from her when they were touring the Archaeological Museum. She found her upstairs in a room far from the rest of the crowd, preoccupied by the statues of the fertility gods. She said she felt at home there. Now Rena understood what she had meant: Hermaphrodite was also a Greek god. Maura needed something, even if it was mythology, to make her feel like she belonged, that she wasn't alone in the world. That's why she majored in it in college. But mythology had no place in today's world—a world that Maura subconsciously longed to belong to. Those gods, including Hermaphrodite, were long dead. That's why she abruptly dropped her studies after graduation and went on to law school. At least the law was alive and changing; it dealt with people, not dust-covered myths.

Rena thought about the time Maura had changed into a bathing suit on the island of Paros. *She went in the bathroom to change because I was in the bedroom!* When they trekked down to the beach, Maura walked very slowly, holding her stomach in pain. She said it was her period and that she got it bad every month.

"Oh, shit!" Rena said out loud, suddenly understanding. What Maura probably was doing all that time in the bathroom was taping down her male genitals so that they wouldn't be noticed in the tight bathing suit. The pain must have been terrible, Rena thought. Especially when she had to physically climb down the path leading to the beach. Why the hell hadn't she told her? She would have understood.

"Or would I have understood?" she mumbled out loud. I was so young then, she thought. *So desperately wanting to be accepted by the world myself. Would I have accepted Maura, who was so different?*

Rena continued to sip her drink. Her eyelids were becoming heavy, and she was grateful that sleep would soon be engulfing her.

Peter McKinney's skulking face appeared in her mind. Why had he hidden Maura's extraordinariness from the medical profession? She remembered him as a powerfully built, brooding man. A man whose universe caved in when his wife, Clair, died in childbirth. *Yes, he, too, like the rest of us, had been scarred from love.* He was a proud Irishman who kept to himself. There were moments when he seemed alive and showed warmth when he was around Maura. Mostly, however, he sat on the porch sipping his Bushmill and silently watched her every move. On rare occasions, like the day in the attic when he had too much to drink, an angry outburst would erupt from somewhere deep within him. The next day when he was sober, he'd apologize, then go back to working his fields like nothing ever happened.

So why didn't he get proper medical help for Maura?

Peter McKinney came from a European, male-oriented society; both sexes knew their places in it. To conceive a child, especially a male child, was a cause for great celebration. But to plant his fertile seed in Clair and produce a child that was double-sexed must have been painful for a man like him. His pride would never allow his neighbors to know what his loins created. Frawley knew because he delivered Maura. Perhaps the doctor agreed to treat Maura rather than send her to specialists. Why would he do that? Maybe he felt unappreciated by his colleagues and wanted to take care of Maura as a means of showing them he was their equal. There was no doubt in Rena's mind after meeting him that he was bitter about his failed practice.

Perhaps there was another reason Frawley took care of Maura, she thought as she stretched her tired body out on the couch. Many civilizations, especially male-dominated ones, have been known to slay newborns that were physically deformed. Did Peter McKinney threaten Frawley with that? Rena knew how terrifying McKinney's anger could be. According to Charlie, he was schooled by the IRA in Ireland, then the OSS during the war.

Peter was well-trained and quite capable of murdering someone, perhaps even his own child if need be.

Was that why Frawley killed himself? Maybe he became frightened by McKinney's threats and took on a commitment that was way over his head. He was not a well man. Did he feel responsible for Maura's slide into insanity? Was the guilt of what he did, or rather of what he didn't do, become too much for the old man? By the time McKinney died, Maura's secret had become a way of life for her. Without proper psychological counseling, she would never bring herself to get correct medical treatment. That would mean letting the world into places that only Martin had been allowed to see. Maura, in her own way, had become like Peter McKinney: proud, secretive, and very much alone.

"Ah Maura. My dear, strange friend," Rena muttered as she closed her eyes. "I know you're out there looking for me, aren't you? What the hell will you do when you find me?"

The phone rang sharply, startling her. Pushing the thoughts of Maura from her mind, she picked up the receiver. "Hello?"

"Is Maura a man?" It was Agent Grant. He did not sound happy.

"What?"

"We ran a DNA fingerprint check on the semen found in Harriet Crowe. It contained the same genetic bands as the vaginal fluid discovered on Arnie Baker's penis. The hair samples belonging to your buddy, Maura, also contained the same DNA markings. Is this some kind of a goddamn joke?"

Rena massaged the back of her neck, took a deep breath, then said. "I was going to call you in the morning, but I guess now is as good a time as any. I suggest you sit down for this, Marvin." She told him everything.

When she finally hung up on him, she felt totally exhausted. Within minutes she fell into a sound sleep on the couch in spite of the second movement to Mozart's Concerto blasting away on the phonograph.

Chapter Twenty-six

A T SIX-THIRTY IN the morning Rena was awakened by the scratchy ring of the old French telephone sitting on the end table next to the couch. The lamp was still on and there was a faint, staccato *swoosh* coming from the needle on the turntable that was endlessly circling the edge of the Mozart record. She brushed the sleep from her eyes, stretched the stiffness out of her body, then picked up the phone. "Hello," she said, clearing the fog from her throat.

"You up?" It was Pinky Swangel.

"I am now," Rena said, yawning.

"I haven't been to bed yet." He sounded euphoric. "I've been on the telephone all night with Judge Howell of the municipal court trying to convince him to issue us a court order to open up the grave of William Tyrone McKinney."

Rena bolted up. "How did you do?"

"I got it!" He was like a proud child who had just won a potato-sack race.

Rena was now fully awake. "When are you going to open it?"

"I got three men digging at the grave site right now. Probably have it open in about a half hour."

"Have you called the FBI?"

"Hell, no! This is my baby," he said adamantly.

Rena could almost see the smirk breaking out on Pinky's face thinking that he, a hick cop, was one up on the Feds.

"I talked to Dr. Parsons last night. He told me what you found out about Maura. Is what he said possible?"

She could tell he was upset. It was going to be hard for him to understand what she is, just as it will be for most people when all this is made public. "Yes, it's possible. But she's a rare phenomenon. There's nothing freakish about her. You've known Maura all your life. She's a brilliant and beautiful woman."

"There's got to be a mistake," he said sharply.

"There's no mistake, Pinky. She's just different."

"I just never heard about someone having two sexes before."

"Very few people ever did. Look, I'll see you at the cemetery in about twenty minutes." After hanging up, she went upstairs to the bathroom and washed. There was no time for a shower; she wanted to be at the grave site when the casket was opened. She then changed into a fresh pair of jeans and a sweater and quickly sent a few brush strokes through her hair. Downstairs in the kitchen, she made herself a mug of instant coffee, grabbed her jean jacket from the closet, and took them with her.

Twenty minutes later she drove the Rover through the gates of the old cemetery in Oakville. Pinky was looking over a gaping cavity in the ground watching three of his men standing waist-deep in the hole shoveling out dirt. His cheeks were redder than usual because of the autumn nip in the air. The old priest who headed the parish connected to the cemetery was by his side, talking to him. A light, visible mist flowed from his mouth. His face was as red as Pinky's, except his color seemed to come from anger rather than the cold. Whatever he was saying made Pinky emphatically shake his head no in response.

Rena got out of the four-wheeler. She buttoned up her Levi's jacket to ward off the early-morning dampness, took the mug of coffee from the Rover, and walked over to them.

When Pinky saw Rena he pointed his thumb at the old priest and said to her, "Father Corrolli's telling me that I'm going to rot in hell if I don't stop this digging."

"This is consecrated ground!" he said indignantly. His lips were trembling. "William Tyrone McKinney was given a Christian burial. It's a sacrilege against the church, against God, to do this! You need permission from the archbishop to unearth a Christian body."

Pinky held out blue-colored, legal-sized papers that were folded in half. "This here is a court order, Father, and this gives me the permission." His voice now matched the priest's in volume.

"I'm talking God's law. Church and state are separate in this country! You have no right to be here!" He pointed his thick finger at Pinky's bulging stomach.

Rena put her hand on the priest's shoulder and led him away from the aggravated sheriff. He was a small man, and she had to look down at his bald head when she spoke. "Father, I don't

218

believe this to be a violation of anyone's rights. William Tyrone McKinney did not exist. I don't think that whatever is buried in this grave is Christian, let alone human.''

Stunned, he looked up at her. ''What are you saying?''

''Peter and Clair McKinney *never* had twins. They only had a daughter, and she's very much alive.''

''Very sad. I know about her and what she's been doing,'' he said, shaking his head.

''Were you the parish priest when Clair McKinney died?'' she asked.

''No. Father O'Connell was. He passed away about twelve years ago.''

''He must have kept records of who he buried.''

''Of course. They're in the office.''

''Would you please look at these records and see if Clair McKinney and William Tyrone were buried on the same day.''

''They must have,'' he said. ''They *died* on the same day. Look at the dates on the stones.''

''I'll tell you what. I'll ask Sheriff Swangel to discontinue the digging until after you've had a good look at the records.''

The priest thought about it for a second, then nodded. He turned and walked back to his parish.

''What did you say to him?'' Pinky asked her when she returned to the grave site. He looked exasperated.

''That you'll stop digging if the services and the burials of Clair and William McKinney were held on the same day.'' She took a sip of her coffee.

''You can't do that!''

She patted his chest to calm him down. ''Trust me. They were not buried together. Besides, you don't want your soul to rot in hell like the priest threatened, do you?''

''Shit! I'm half-Baptist, half-Mormon. I'm guaranteed to rot in hell.'' He held up his hand to the other policemen, telling them to stop digging.

Rena sat down on top of an old gravestone, drank her coffee, and waited for the priest to return.

In a few minutes she saw the old man leave the rectory and scurry toward them, his long black gown dragging on the leaf-ridden path. He was holding a tattered ledger under his arm. When he arrived at the grave, he opened up the thick book, wet his thumb, and quickly turned the pages until he came to the one he wanted. ''You're right!'' he said to Rena, thrusting the book in her direction to look at. "William Tyrone McKinney was buried on December twentieth, Nineteen fifty-nine. That's two years *after* the date on the stone. How can that be if he died on the same day as his mother?" With his brow creased in confusion, he turned first to Pinky then back to her.

"There *is* no William McKinney," Rena stated again.

"So you told me before. Then who in Jesus' name is down there?" The priest nervously brushed imaginary hairs away from his bald head.

"Perhaps no one. But as long as there is some form of misrepresentation, then the burial can't be sanctified. Wouldn't you agree?"

He thought about it for a long moment, sighed, and eventually nodded his head in accord. Within seconds the policemen were back digging.

"How could Father O'Connell allow such a thing?" the priest asked, mostly to himself.

They moved out of the way from the projectiles of dirt that were flung out of the grave by the diggers. "Did Peter McKinney and Father O'Connell know each other?" Rena asked him.

"They were supposed to have been very good friends. Both of them came from Dublin. Father O'Connell had a small drinking problem. The story I heard was that McKinney would often come over to the rectory to visit Father O'Connell at night. The two of them supposedly downed many a good bottle of Irish whiskey together over the years."

"Was it possible that Father O'Connell did his good friend and drinking partner a favor by allowing him to plant something in the ground next to his wife?" she asked.

"Possible, but unlikely. If that gravestone is a lie, then it's a sacrilege for it to be on hallowed ground. Father O'Connell knew that."

"Yes, but Peter McKinney was his good friend. What's one little lie among fighters of the Crown. I remember hearing stories about how priests in Ireland would help IRA combatants by hiding weapons in fake graves."

"This isn't Ireland," he said sternly.

Rena was about to say something clever, like how you can take the man out of Ireland but you can't take Ireland out of the man, when she heard one of the shovels down in the grave hit something hard.

"Bingo!" Pinky said.

The priest and Rena went over to the hole and peered in. One of the policemen was down on his knees brushing away the dirt from a two-foot-square pine box. When he tried lifting it, the rotted wood broke away in his hands. The other officer carefully dug around it until the object was completely freed. Slowly both men lifted the box out of the grave and handed it to Pinky and the uniformed officer that was with him. Before they had a chance to put it on the ground, the box crumpled, and something wrapped in a thick woolen shawl dropped out. Pinky bent down to touch the material, and it came apart in his hands.

Rena bent down next to him and painstakingly ripped away at the decayed fabric.

"This sure as hell isn't a body," Pinky said. The dank-smelling pieces of wool clung fast to his hands as he tried brushing them away.

Rena continued to claw through the layers until she felt something damp and leathery. A few more yanks and then she saw it: it was a book held together by three strips of rawhide. The pages were made of thick parchment. A sick feeling came over her as she slowly opened the book. Age and dampness had destroyed some of the pages, but most of them were still legible. Around the edges were burn marks.

"What is it?" Pinky asked.

The words were neatly scripted, as if written with a quill.

"It's not English," Pinky said.

"No," Rena replied. Sweat had broken out around her lips. "It's French. This is the original diary of the Baron Gustave de Montret."

"Who is that?" the priest asked.

Rena said, "A man who has absolutely no business being buried in hallowed ground, Father." She turned the pages over until she came to what she hoped was there: the last segment of the diary. It *was* there! The last entry was dated on the twenty-third of December, Seventeen ninety-three.

With Pinky's permission, Rena took the diary with her to the château so she could translate it. Before she drove back, she suggested that Pinky call the FBI and tell them about the journal. Begrudgingly he agreed.

As she pulled up to the house and got out of the Rover, she could smell the aromatic odor of fermenting wine coming from the oak-and-steel vats in her father's winery. The harvesting had come to an end, and hopefully, so had the killings.

In the kitchen she found a half pot of coffee brewing on the Krupps machine. Harrison must have already been here, she thought. She poured herself a mug and took it along with the journal into the den. Sitting down at the desk, she grabbed a legal-sized yellow pad and a pen from the drawer. Opening the diary slowly so the tattered parchment wouldn't break apart, she turned to the last entry. Thankfully the dampness hadn't affected the legibility of the script. The burns around the edges she suspected were caused when McKinney had tossed the journal into the furnace aboard the English ship after he and Striker were rescued in France.

This was the entry that Wilbur Striker hated most, she remembered. Taking a deep breath, she brought the pad closer to her and began the slow task of translating.

Two hours later she was finished. As she looked up from the pad, she caught a glimpse of herself in the gilded mirror on the wall, and she was shocked at the drained, pallid color of her skin.

You're right Striker, this was the most horrible entry of them all!

23 December, 1793

They are coming for me. I can see them from my bedroom window. They are like hordes of locusts racing across my beautiful vineyards, screaming for my blood, begging to rip my soul out from within me. Let them come, I am ready.

Brutes! Wretched, filthy creatures all of them! They toil all day in their small fields that are no bigger than bread crumbs, then they go back to their hovels to fornicate with their beastly, fat wives so that they can turn out little gargoyle versions of themselves. How pointless they are! To be content to live in such squalor. When they smile, their rotting teeth and disease-infested gums sicken my stomach. When they look at you, it is through dull, ignorant eyes. They stink from sweat and hay and putrid gruel and cheap wine. It is these vile, insignificant cretins who are coming to kill me. Me!

Yet I willingly give myself up to them. I am like Jesus who is to be sacrificed on the cross so that these lowly vermin will feel sanctified. Did our Lord not give his life for those Jewish ogres and forgive them when they tortured his beautiful, slim body?

Oh, my Jesus! You would have made such a wonderful sacri-
fice for my vineyards. My vines would have licked and sucked
and feasted upon your blood and the fruits from within your
loins. They would have thanked you and bowed down to you.
They never would have laughed and stoned you like those Jewish
swine! I can almost hear the joyous laughter of my vineyards as
I write this. They would have loved to have partaken of your
body. Ah, the superb wines your flesh would have made! Only
then can it truly be said that we drink of your blood!

They are coming closer to my château. I hear voices crying
out for my death!

I take my clothes off and wait for them. Let them see me now,
I don't care. My breasts, once supple and soft as goose-feather
pillows, now droop down my hairy chest like half-filled sacks of
onions. My cock, once so hard and wanting, hangs dead and
shriveled between my legs. My cunt used to be wet and full-
flowing like the Seine. Now . . . now it is only a dried-up brook,
a crack in the hard ground, withering away beneath the hot des-
ert sun. My body is dead, so take me now you wretched sots!

Now, on the day of my death, I suddenly begin to think of you,
Papa. I am thinking about the beatings and humiliation you in-
flicted upon me, and my screams as I cried out for you to stop. I
remember how you would laugh and beat me harder the more I
begged. But it was the sting from your words that hurt me more
than your riding crop. You said I was a creature from the pits of
hell, a monstrosity of nature. You wished that I were born dead!
Mother pleaded with you to cease torturing me, but you paid her
no heed. I was a woman, Father, that was my preference. But
you would not hear of it. No! A man was to run your vineyards,
only a man! I became a man for you, Father, because your other
son, René, ran away to Burgundy. He also hated you. I was the
only heir left to run your vineyards. But I could have become
anything, Papa, if I wanted. Anything! For I am the creation of
Aphrodite and Hermes. I am androgynous. I have the soul of
both man and woman!

How you hated, dear Father, when I would ride off across the
fields to Comte Henri Maureau's château. He was your rival. His
wines were so much better than yours, and you despised him for
it. How it thrilled my heart to know that you were watching me.
I would beat my horse, making him go faster toward Henri's
vineyards. He was the only man who ever loved me. So kind and
gentle. He never saw me as a monstrosity. My naked body was

revered by him. Ah, the look of love that came over his face when he touched me all over. How he adored fondling my breasts, my cock! It was he who taught me the secrets of the Oschophoria. I was fifteen when he first let me go on the hunt with him. It was during the harvesting of the Pomerol. We found a trollop in town, and we took her back with us to Henri's stable. I looked on breathlessly as he took her from behind and banged his cock deep into her, pushing her head down into the straw with one hand while holding the spike to her neck with the other. Then I watched in awe as he sliced out her organs and buried them in the vineyards. It was all done so quickly and so rakishly. Henri was an artist, Papa! And his wines—they were so much better than yours because of it.

My life died the day he fought a duel with you and lost. Bastard! Your rapier found his beautiful heart! You murdered him, Father, because you knew he loved me. How you hated that! You could not stand the thought of anyone loving me. Even though you killed him, you could not kill my memory of him and what he taught me. I waited a year after his demise, and then I poisoned you. I doled out the oleander in small doses and made sure you died a slow, painful death. When you finally made the journey to hell, Papa, the vineyards became all mine!

Wait! What is that I smell? It is smoke!

Dear Jesus! Look what those paupers are doing! They are burning my fields. Stop! Stop! Oh, Lord, the shrieks of agony coming from my vines! Their pitiful cries cut deep into my soul. I fall to the floor and cover my ears. Bastards! Bastards! I scream. Take me instead! Take me!

Oh, Papa, I wish you were here to see this day! To watch you cry out in pain as they murder your vineyards. To hear your screams instead of theirs!

Their voices are horrible now! They are begging me to help them. My beautiful ones, please understand. You will only feel pain for a short time, then you will see and know nothing but sweet darkness. Soon I will join you. No longer will I be trapped inside a cursed body that only Henri and the ancient gods can love.

I hear them breaking down my door. Their squirrel-like footsteps will soon make their way down into my wine cellar and then up here to look for me. I must stop writing and hide the journal in a false wall I built in my bedroom. Perhaps it will be found someday, perhaps not. It matters not, my brave, magnificent vineyards. What matters is that we shall soon be together for all eternity!

This last entry was like a cracked mirror into Maura's tortured soul. Now at last Rena understood the hold that de Montret had on her friend. They were genetically linked together—something that science didn't think was possible. She also understood what the baron meant when he wrote that he was both hard and wet at the same time.

She refilled her coffee mug then went over to the giant, arched French window. She sat down on the sill and looked out. The sky was darkening and the pregnant clouds seemed to be ready to unleash a barrage of thunder and rain over the valley.

Yes, part of the bond between Maura and the baron had to do with being double-sexed, she thought. But there was something more, something much deeper, and yet something very universal. It had to do with the fear of being different and the loneliness that follows. There were many similarities between them: both were loved for themselves by one man. When they died, they found themselves alone again. To taste the light of happiness and then to have to go back into the solitary darkness again must have made both of them very bitter.

She and the baron were also forced to hide their true sexual needs. Maura and her ancestor had the unique choice of either becoming a man or a woman. The baron, even though his nature pushed him toward the feminine side, was coerced into taking the role of a man because of his father. Maura was more fortunate than Gustave in the fact that she was allowed to follow her natural instincts and become a woman. However, she was suppressed sexually by Peter McKinney's fears that her true identity would be discovered. That's why he hated Martin so much and forbid Maura to see him.

The deepest comparison, Rena noticed, was the way their fathers treated them. Both men withheld the one thing their children needed desperately: love. Even though Maura was not beaten physically like the baron, she was abused mentally by a cold, sullen, withdrawn man. McKinney blamed Maura for the death of his wife. He also wanted a son. Frawley must have explained chimerism to him; that he almost had a son but the fertilized egg that was to be Maura had destroyed it. A closed-off, simple man like McKinney could never have understood the medical complexity of this theory. All his drunken mind could grasp was that Maura not only murdered his wife but his male heir as well. It became a no-win situation: he drank to stem his anger of her, and the more he drank, the angrier he became. Why did he bury the diary next to his wife's grave? Why didn't he just destroy it? Perhaps his anger had also spread to Clair. It was her genes that were causing all this misery in his life. On one of his drunken binges he probably talked Father O'Connell into burying the diary next to her and then having a gravestone with the date of his imaginary son's death chiseled onto it. It was a way of him washing his hands of the de Montret family.

Yet he kept Wilbur Striker's translation. He could have buried it along with the original but chose not to. As much as he may have wanted to forget Clair and the misery she had brought to him, he still wanted a piece of her next to him. McKinney's soul must have been torn apart with pain.

Then she thought of the baron. He had the madness of the Oschophoria to use as a substitute for love. But what did Maura have? Her art? Her work? Was that enough? Rena doubted it. What real substitution could there possibly be for love?

Yet Maura was not the baron. Their bloodline may have sprung from the same river, but their tributaries flowed in different directions. She was an extremely strong and intelligent woman who was outgoing and happy when Martin was alive. Unlike the baron, her mind was not satiated with hate. De Montret became a part of that ancient, sacrificial feast as a way of revenge against his father and a society that would have condemned his abnormality. He was not unlike the followers of Charles Manson and other weak, misguided souls who belonged to murderous cults in our present-day civilization.

She believed Maura was stronger than that. What she had done in the vineyards went against everything Rena had learned about human nature. Why would Maura suddenly follow in her ancestor's footsteps? What set her off on this murderous, bloody rampage?

Wait a minute! Suddenly Rena stood up and put the coffee mug down on the sill. Maybe her mistake all along with these murders was in looking for the "what" in Maura.

What was that "thing" inside her that made her kill?

No, that's wrong!

Perhaps it's not *what*!

If not what, then . . . ?

Who?

Yes, *who*!

Yes!

The clouds opened and the rains came down hard on the fertile, green valley of Napa.

No, this is crazy! Why would anyone . . . wait, who knew about Maura's affliction? Martin . . . Peter McKinney . . . Frawley. They're all dead. There *had* to be someone else. But why would that someone want to do this to her, and how was he or she doing it?

"Hold on a sec! Yes, there certainly was someone else who knew about her. In fact, more like *several* someone elses!" Rena said out loud. She went over to the phone and dialed the operator. When she picked up, Rena said, "Can you please give me the area code for Tacoma, Washington . . . Thank you." After hanging up, she dialed area code 206, then information. "Operator, I'd like the telephone number of Riverside Hospital in Tacoma, please. Yes, I'll wait."

Chapter Twenty-seven

THE RAIN HAD been coming down heavily for hours now without any sign of letup. The Vegas Strip was flooded. Stalled cars were abandoned in the middle of the boulevard; sewers were backed up and torrents of water overflowed from the gutters and onto the sidewalk, seeping under the doors of the major casinos. Janitors worked feverishly trying to swab up the saturated red carpets. They squeezed their wet mops quietly into metal pails, trying not to disrupt the hitters at the blackjack tables and the robotic old ladies cranking down on the handles of slot machines.

The Las Vegas Free Clinic was located a few blocks off the strip on Eastern Boulevard. Since the city's fathers considered the homeless and the destitute eyesores and refused to let them take up residence in Vegas, the clinic's clientele were comprised mostly of hookers with venereal diseases and UNLV coeds being fitted for diaphragms.

On most afternoons the reception area was "standing room only," and there was at least an hour-and-a-half wait before a doctor could get free to see a patient. Today, because of the raging downpour, there were only two people waiting to receive medical attention: a black hooker and a strung-out, male college student with a long ponytail. The girl wore a pink-colored, curly wig and a tight red miniskirt. She was leafing through a magazine with her feet propped up on the coffee table. A pink wad of Bazooka bubble gum would occasionally balloon from her mouth then splatter across her lips before being sucked back in again. On the couch near the bathroom, the boy with the ponytail was rocking back and forth, silently mouthing the lyrics to an Iron Maiden song. He was coming down from a long weekend of crack.

Most of the staff had been told to go home earlier in the day. Marjorie Porter, a hefty, honey-skinned black woman was the only nurse on duty. She was sitting behind the reception desk reading this week's *People* when the door opened. A woman entered carrying a tote bag and wearing dark glasses. Her skin was as pale as sea salt. She looked weak and stooped over, and she was drenched to the bone. Steadying herself by keeping one hand on the wall, she slowly inched over to the desk.

Marjorie looked up from the article about Cher's new flame and over to the woman with the dark glasses. She'd been a nurse too long not to see that something was wrong with her. "You all right, honey? You need to sit down?" she said, closing the magazine.

Maura opened her mouth to say something but only faint, unintelligible words came out. "Fever . . . cold . . . can't stop shaking." She was shivering uncontrollably. Suddenly her knees buckled and she started to sink to the floor. Lying there with her back propped up against the desk, she could hear hurried, muffled footsteps, then the crinkling sound of Nurse Marjorie's starched white dress as she bent down next to her. From somewhere in the distance Marjorie's voice was yelling, "Dr. Barney, quick! We got a live one here!" Her mind was starting to fade. She shook her head, fighting it. *No, mustn't pass out! Can't! Can't!*

Two sets of strong hands grabbed her under the arms and lifted her up; then the feel of leather as her body was hoisted down on a wheelchair. There was the sensation of the chair moving, the sound of swinging doors opening then closing, the odor of ethyl alcohol, iodine, ammonia. The *swish* of curtains being opened. The hands again, this time lifting her off the chair and onto a soft mattress covered with a stiff, sterile-smelling sheet. The feel of someone removing the cardigan sweater from her body. Fingers on her chest quickly unbuttoning her blouse. Then the sound of her own voice screaming: "No! No!" The hands moved away from her chest.

Again, from a distance, she could hear the nurse saying, "You're sick, honey, and you're wet and cold. I got to get these clothes off of you or you're gonna catch pneumonia, that is if you haven't already."

"I'll do it myself," Maura said, barely audible. Her voice sounded like it was coming from deep underwater. She was still shivering.

"That's fine with me, but I don't think you can."

Maura felt her sunglasses being removed by the nurse. She quickly covered her eyes with her arm.

"The light bothering you?"

"Yes," Maura said.

"You a hype, honey?"

"No."

"Lights bother hypes."

"I'm not a hype." The nurse gave her back the glasses and Maura kept her eyes closed until she could put them back on. It seemed like a fog was coating her vision. The light-headed feeling soon began to subside. When her sight cleared, she saw a nurse and a handsome young doctor staring down at her.

"You still want to change into this gown by yourself?" the doctor asked her. His voice was gentle.

"Yes." Her teeth were knocking loudly against each other.

"You're the shy type, huh?" the nurse said skeptically.

"Yeah," Maura replied.

Before they left, Marjorie closed the circular curtains around the gurney. Fighting off the dizziness, Maura slowly stood up, leaned against the mattress, and took off her soaked clothes. She let the garments drop heavily to the floor.

She didn't want to be here, but she had no choice if she was going to make it to Los Angeles. The two harrowing bus trips, one to Salt Lake City and the other to Vegas, had taken their toll. Her fever was up and aspirins were no longer helping. The infection was sapping the strength from her body. She had to take

229

the chance and get help or she would either find herself in a prison hospital or dead.

Keeping her underwear on, she changed into the dressing gown. A minute later Nurse Marjorie poked her head between the curtains and asked if she was ready. Maura nodded weakly as she sat back down in the chair.

"Let's get you to drier quarters," she said, wheeling Maura toward an empty cubicle. Inside, the nurse helped her up on the cot and put a thermometer in her mouth.

A few minutes later the handsome doctor came in. His hair was long and curly, and he wore a gold stud in his left ear. He smiled at her, then took the thermometer out of her mouth. His smile faded. "A hundred and two. What the hell were you doing out in the rain with a hundred-and-two fever?"

Maura had her story prepared. She had purposely sliced open her arm with a scissor a few hours before coming to the clinic. Weakly, she pulled up the right sleeve of her dressing gown partway. There was a thick piece of gauze on her arm held together by tape. "I cut myself on a rusty can a couple of days ago. I think I'm infected."

The doctor ripped off the tape and examined the wound. It was a semi-deep slice. "It doesn't look infected. In fact, the wound doesn't look two days old," he said suspiciously. "What's the real story? Are you doing drugs?"

"I told you . . ."

"Give me a break on that one. Are you using?"

"Okay, yes." That was her backup in case the first story failed.

"You told the nurse you didn't."

"I lied. Wouldn't you?" she answered, annoyed.

He pushed up the sleeves on both her arms. "Jesus Christ!" he uttered when he saw the scrapes and bruises on her pale skin. "What the hell happened?"

"Nothing!" she said angrily.

"Were you in a fight, or did you do this to yourself?"

She looked away, not answering.

"Okay, be that way," he said, shaking his head. He ran his fingers lightly over the inside of her arms. "Where're the needle marks?" As he was about to move his hands away, Maura grabbed his arm and held it tight. "Hey, you're strong." He tried to release her grip with his other hand, but she held firm.

"Look, even a fucking kid in kindergarten can see that I'm

230

infected," she said vehemently, through clenched teeth. "I need antibiotics!"

The door opened and Nurse Marjorie walked in. When she saw what was happening, she crossed her arms over her big bosom and frowned. "Try not to break his hand, okay? He's the only doctor we got right now."

Maura let go.

"You got a name?" she asked sternly.

Maura didn't answer.

She picked up a clipboard from the table. "Then how about a first name so I don't have to write you down as a Roman numeral."

"Nancy," Maura said.

"Like in Reagan."

"That's right."

"How's Ronnie and the kids?"

"Goddamn it!" Maura screamed, looking up at the ceiling as she grasped the sheets in her fisted hands.

"You a prostitute, honey?" Marjorie asked.

"Sure."

"And a user?"

"They usually go hand-in-hand, right?"

"You also lie like this all the time?"

The doctor peered down at her. "Okay, Nancy, or whatever your name is, are you allergic to penicillin?"

"Yes."

"Erythromycin?"

"No."

The doctor looked into Nurse Marjorie's tired, veteran eyes. "Get an IV ready with 500 milligrams of erythromycin. I also want to do a blood test." The nurse nodded, glanced down at Maura one more time, then walked out. The doctor bent over Maura and tried taking her glasses off, but she moved her head away. "Look, you've got a hundred-and-two fever, you're shivering, and you're sweating like you spent the last five hours in a sauna. Another day without help, and you'll be in an intensive care unit in some hospital fighting for your life. I've *got* to check you out."

Maura took a deep breath then removed her sunglasses. She turned and stared directly into his eyes.

There was a brief register of shock on his face, then his expression became immobile again. "Irideal heterochromia," he said. "I've never seen a case as radical as yours. Most people with that symptom have blue-green eyes."

"Perhaps I should be put into a sideshow at the circus," she said bitterly.

"We certainly share different opinions about that. I think they're quite lovely . . . in fact, even exotic."

His eyes were warm and playful as they looked directly down on her face. With the fever racing through her brain, she felt for a second as if she were back in the Napa Valley again, laughing and running through the hills with Martin. Then the moment passed. She remembered where she was and what she had done. Her expression hardened, and she looked away from him.

"There are rings around your eyes," he said. "When was the last time you slept?"

Sleep! Dear, sweet sleep! To sleep . . . perchance to dream. No, no! Never again! "I don't remember," she finally answered.

Nurse Marjorie came back into the cubicle bringing an IV setup with her. She, too, looked at Maura's eyes for a moment, then she glanced down at her purplish, bruised arms. "They look like a war zone. I guess we won't have no trouble finding a vein. Your skin is like milk-colored glass," she said as she expertly pushed the needle into the blue vein in her hand. When she was sure the IV was flowing properly, she tore off the plastic coating from a syringe and took a sample of her blood from the other arm. After she left with the specimen, the doctor put a stethoscope around his neck and told her to remove the top part of her gown. Hesitant at first, she finally sat up and let the gown fall from her shoulders. Her breasts were firm and smooth like porcelain. She shuddered when she felt the metal part of the stethoscope on her skin.

"Who are you?" he asked.

"No one." She was shivering again.

"Put your top on." When she did, he covered her with a blanket. "Look, I'm not going to call the cops. We don't work that way around here. I think you knew that or you would have gone to the emergency room at University Medical Center."

"I knew that," she said quietly.

"Okay, so tell me who you are."

The fever was now playing tricks in her head, and without thinking she said softly, "Maura . . . Maura Bynum." *Martin's last name.* Why not? He was dead, but my spirit will always be wed to him, she thought, with a smile.

"All right, Maura Bynum it is. I guess it beats Nancy Reagan." He wrote it down on his clipboard. "I'd like to do a full physical on you. I want to see where this infection is coming from."

"No," she said ardently, her hands instinctively going down near the area of her covered groin.

Smiling, he said, "Okay. Let's take it step-by-step first. I'm going to keep you here for a few hours feeding you intravenously. Let's see if the erythromycin helps get your fever down. If not, I'm going to call an ambulance to take you to University Medical."

She nodded. At least this gives me a *few* hours, she thought.

He squeezed her hand reassuringly, then said, "There are more patients waiting for me. I'm the only doctor on call. Get some sleep. I'll come back in a while to see how you are."

How warm his hand was when he touched me. It had been so long since she let a man near her. *Oh, God, Martin, help me please!* She shook her head to get rid of the thoughts. She had to use her energy to find Rena, not on fantasizing about what could have been if she had been born normal. Then she thought about the only alternative left to her now. Death was her only salvation, she knew that. But she didn't want to die alone. Not alone! She had been alone for so much of her life. To die next to someone she loved, with that person holding her as the breath of life slipped from her body. That's all she wanted now. It would be so easy with the Placidyls. Rena would understand, wouldn't she?

The fever was raging through her body.

They would sit on the bed together, talking and giggling, just like they did when they were children. Then, when she began to feel drowsy, she'd lay her head on Rena's lap and hunch up into a fetal position. Rena would gently rock her, whispering soothing words in her ear until her eyes closed and the black nothingness descended over her for eternity.

For eternity!

Maura suddenly opened her eyes. She was beginning to fall asleep. *No, mustn't do that! Sleep brings on the other thing. I begin to kill. Something inside me makes me kill . . . wants me to kill. Christ, what is happening to me!*

Then she remembered the name she had given the doctor. *What a fool I was for doing that!* She hoped he wouldn't put the name and who she really was together. Suddenly she thought about her pills, and she quickly sat up. Had they taken her pills?

Her eyes darted around the small cubicle until she saw her tote hanging from the back of the chair next to her. Pushing the IV stand to the side, she grabbed the bag and tossed everything out on the cot. All the pills were there, including the Placidyls. Thank God! Her strength zapped, she lay back down again and waited for the good doctor to return with another dose of antibiotics.

Five hours later she glanced up at the third plastic bag of erythromycin that she received and saw that it was half-empty. She then looked at the clock on the wall: it was eight-fifteen. The bus to L.A. left at nine o'clock. There was no time to wait until the last one was finished. Maura ripped the needle from her hand and got up off the cot. She felt weak, but she was no longer shivering. That meant the fever had subsided. A good sign. Thankfully Nurse Marjorie, before she went home for the evening, had brought her a turkey sandwich and made her eat it. She quickly dressed in the black skirt and white sweater she wore in Boise then poked her head outside the door. The doctor and the night nurse were busy in another cubicle with a sick patient. She quietly made her way down the hallway to the waiting room. It was now filled with people. A small boy with a desperate, hacking cough was sitting on his mother's lap. His sad, watery eyes watched Maura as she took the nurse's umbrella from beneath her desk, opened the door, and went out into the rainy night.

In a few minutes she was on the strip where cabs were plentiful. She hailed one and told him to take her to the bus terminal.

At nine-fifteen the bus left the bright lights of Vegas behind and headed west toward Route 15. Most of the passengers were senior citizens who had spent the day at the slot machines and were now heading back to their homes in Los Angeles.

Maura sat in the back, away from everybody. Her heart was racing from expectation. Tomorrow she would be with Rena.

The methodical drone of the wheels on the smooth, paved road made her eyelids heavy. Images of her seventeenth birthday jumped around in her head. She was in her father's winery. Martin was also there. They were naked. He was on top of her . . . then inside her. Both of them were writhing on the ground, oblivious to anything but the glorious, slapping sensation their bodies were making as they lay entwined together.

Then they were holding hands, racing through the vineyards back to his house. His parents weren't home. They made love again, this time in his bed. Afterward, she began to nod out to Roberta Flack on Martin's stereo.

There was the moving sensation of Martin's body getting up from the bed. The door to his bedroom opening. Sounds, like footsteps in the hallway. Another door opening. Then the sound of . . . of what? The sound of . . . the sound of metal. Yes. A metal sound. A sliding, metal sound. Metal upon metal. Then . . . then a sound like no other sound. A sound like the deep roar of thunder. A sound so loud and so final that her organs shook inside her body. She opened her eyes and jumped up. Where is Martin? Was there an explosion at the winery? She saw the bedroom door ajar. Getting out of bed, she called for Martin. No answer. Then she was out in the hallway, again calling his name. The door to Martin's parents room was open. She walked in. All the drawers of the bureau were pulled out. Clothes were thrown indiscriminately over the floor. Why were the walls all red? Suddenly she yelled in pain. She had stepped on something sharp. Sitting down on his parents bed, she picked up her leg to look. It was a small fragment of bone embedded in the sole of her foot. When she glanced down, she saw that there were small pieces of bloody bones all over the floor. What were they doing in here? Martin didn't have a dog. Then she heard sounds coming from outside the room—footsteps racing down the stairs . . . the front door opening, then slamming shut . . . footsteps again, this time running down the pebble path outside the house. She got up and hobbled over to the window to look out. As she stood there she could feel something warm and wet on the carpet. Outside, she saw for a brief second the shadowy shape of someone rushing into the forest, then it was gone. Her foot hurt. It was when she reached down to pull the sliver out that she first saw Martin. He was lying in a twisted position on the floor. Much of his face was missing. She knew it was him because he was wearing the leather wristband that she had made for him. Looking down, she realized the warm wetness she felt on her feet was from her standing in his blood. She screamed again, this time not from the pain of the sharp bone, but from the pain of knowing Martin was dead.

The snores of the senior citizens were the only sounds breaking up the steady hum of the bus's motor. There *was* another noise, except this one was in Maura's head: metal scratching against metal. This time, though, it sounded distant, coming from somewhere far off.

Then Maura did something she prayed she wouldn't do before she got to see Rena: she fell into a deep, sound sleep.

Chapter Twenty-eight

SOMETIME DURING THE night the torrential rain had eased to a steady trickle, and by dawn it had finally come to a complete stop. By the time the sun had risen over Boulder Dam, the Nevada desert was steaming hot. Only a few hours ago the strip was like a frenzied river; now the boulevard was dried up, and traffic flowed smoothly, as if nothing happened.

Nurse Marjorie and Dr. Barney sat in the FBI office across from the Sands Hotel staring at a three-foot copy of Maura's unsmiling face pinned to the corkboard. It was a blowup of the photograph that was on her assistant district attorney's license. Next to it was a sketch done by a forensic artist of the woman they saw at the clinic last night. Grant and three other agents stood in back of their chairs. The room was littered with coffee-stained Styrofoam cups, and the rancid smell of nervous, tired men filled the air.

"They're one and the same," Marjorie said, nodding as if there was no doubt in her mind. She turned to look at agent Grant.

"And you, sir?" Grant said, standing behind the doctor.

Barney didn't say anything. He just stared at Maura's picture with tired, sad eyes. Finally he nodded. "That's her," he whispered.

"I wish I had bothered to look at the notice you fellows sent to us about her," Marjorie said. "If I had, then I would have called you while she was still there. We get tons of flyers from police departments all over the country, mostly looking for runaways. After a while we just let them pile up and forget about them. I could see the way she acted last night that she was a little out of it, but I sure didn't know she was that crazy killer."

Grant nodded. He was staring at the drawing. Other than the

similarity between the thin lips and small nose, the two pictures looked like two different people. The photo showed Maura's stark, long blond hair combed straight back in a sophisticated, conservative style. In the artist's sketch, the hair was dark with bangs and cut jaggedly above the neck.

"I don't know if they're the same two women," a tall, lanky agent with a gap between his teeth said, shaking his head doubtfully.

"Well, I *do* know, honey," Nurse Marjorie said caustically. She folded her arms and glared at the Federal agent over her bifocals. "That is definitely her! I know what I saw! The composite you sent to the clinic said she had a brown eye and a blue eye. Tell me, Sherlock, how many people do you know that's got one brown and one blue eye?"

"It's her," the doctor said again. He let out a sigh and rubbed his eyes. "She said her name was Maura Bynum."

Grant could see that the doctor liked her. He said, "Maura is her real first name and Bynum was the name of her dead lover." Then he added, "Did you examine her without her clothes on, Doctor?"

Barney looked at him strangely. "No, it never got to that point. Why?"

Ignoring him, Grant put the same question to Marjorie.

She also answered no.

Dr. Barney stood up. "Look, I've got to get back to the clinic. Is there anything else you need from us?" he asked sullenly.

"I don't think so, Doctor. Thanks for your help."

Barney and Marjorie left.

Grant waited until the door closed before he turned back to his agents. "All right fellows, listen to this," Grant said, clapping his hands together. "A bus driver for Trailways identified this composite drawing as a woman who got into Las Vegas yesterday morning around nine o'clock from Salt Lake City." Grant went over to a large map of the United States that was pinned to the wall. He drew a line with a blue-marking pen from Boise to Salt Lake City, then one from there to Las Vegas. "This is the route she took."

A pot-bellied officer with a five-o'clock shadow covering his face said, "That doesn't make sense. Who does she know in *those* cities?" He leaned against the desk and folded his arms.

"Maybe she doesn't know anyone," Grant responded quietly.

"We could dragnet this town, turn it upside down," the lanky agent said.

Grant didn't reply. He stared a long time at the map. Finally he said, "I think I'm beginning to get a handle on this woman/man, or whatever the hell she is. I think she's been taking these out-of-the-way routes to avoid detection."

"But why settle on Vegas? She'd stick out like a sore thumb here," said the third agent, the youngest one.

"Maybe she hasn't settled here. Maybe this is just one more stopover. According to Dr. Barney, she had an infection of some sorts. It had to have been bad or she wouldn't have taken the chance of going to a clinic." His finger slowly traced Route 40 across the width of the map to the East Coast. "I'd say the next bus she's on goes east or west." Then his finger suddenly made a U-turn, moved back across the country, and stopped in Los Angeles. Tapping that area with his knuckle, he said, "Most likely the West Coast. It would be too dangerous to go east all that way by bus. It's one long haul, and she'd get caught sooner or later."

"Who does she know in L.A.?" the chubby agent asked.

Grant looked at him and smiled for the first time in days. "An old and dear friend." Turning back to the map, he put his finger on Los Angeles and said, "Yep, that's where our lady killer is going. I'd bet anything on it. The question is, once she's there, does she start the slaughter all over again?"

FOUR

Chapter Twenty-nine

THE RENTED WHITE Porsche Carrera that Ray Scollari was driving back to Los Angeles crept along Highway 10 at sixty miles an hour. It was frustrating going this slow. He wanted to go faster, like he did when he first left Desert Hot Springs, but he couldn't chance getting another ticket, not after he was already stopped once for speeding.

The cops in New York are a hell of a lot more human than the ones in this fucking desert, he thought. There at least he could take out his DA's shield and flash it in front of the officer's face. The cop wouldn't dare bother him when he saw that. Out here you could be the fucking mayor of the entire fucking city and these blond robotlike assholes with their well-trimmed mustaches would still nail your butt.

Scollari looked over at the girl sitting next to him. She was wearing a red tube top and tight black shorts that barely covered the cheeks of her ass. He gave her tanned, smooth knee a soft pat, and he suddenly began to get hard. He couldn't help it, he got hard every time he looked at her. She was absolutely beautiful; not swift, just beautiful. He met her at the hotel at the Hot Springs where he went to relax for a few days. She was the masseuse there, specializing in Swedish massages. Her name was Rita, and for three great days she rubbed Scollari down until his heavily oiled body was covered with big red welts. Rita was very impressionable, and Ray impressed her a great deal with stories about being the head of the prosecutor's office in Brooklyn. One morning, while lying prone on the massage table, he casually mentioned to her that he was going to run for mayor of New York. Rita giggled loudly and her eyes opened wide with delight as she kneaded and pulled on his rubbery, thick skin. She absolutely loved being around celebrities, even if she never heard of them before. She showed Ray that she appreciated his notoriety by suddenly pulling the sheet off his body, putting her head between his thighs, and sucking on his surprised, but already hard, penis. It wasn't long before she made him forget whatever business problems he was having back in New York.

In Brooklyn the justice system was bottlenecked, and he had found himself working sixty-hour weeks. That, plus the negative statements the media was saying about him, had whittled his nerves down to the bare bone. Shit! It wasn't his fault that his assistant district attorney turned out to be a crazed serial killer. Four days ago he left his wife and children back home in Queens and took off across country for Hot Springs. He needed to mellow out, get his strength back, or he'd never last that long haul of running for mayor. The good thing about taking this trip was that the city of New York was paying for it without knowing it. He was supposed to have a meeting tomorrow with the police chief of Los Angeles to talk about the illicit flow of drugs between their two cities. Scollari made sure the meeting was well publicized from coast to coast. He needed all the public relations he could get if his mayoral candidacy was to be taken seriously.

Now if only those jerk-off Feds would find McKinney, his life might get back to the way things were before. Christ, what a cunt she'd been to him, he thought. Why the hell had he taken that kind of garbage from her! Just to get laid? *I hope when they find her they blow her the fuck away.* Why waste good money on a trial? Unless she was found insane, it would take years to try her because she crossed state lines to do her killings. *If she was found in my jurisdiction, I'd make sure she wouldn't live to spend one night in jail.* The public would quickly forget, and then he could go on with his life.

Scollari's thoughts were interrupted by Rita's hands trying to unzip his pants. Ray laughed. "Here, darlin', let me help you." Keeping one hand on the wheel, he used his other to fiddle with the zipper until his organ jumped straight out like a jack-in-the-box.

Yes, by God, he *was* hard!

Giggling, Rita pushed her hair back from her face, opened up her big red lips, and plopped her mouth down on his joint.

Whoowie! He stepped on the gas pedal and popped the clutch into fifth. "Fuck L.A. cops!" he screamed at the top of his lungs. Within seconds the Porsche was soaring down Highway 10 doing eighty-five.

At three-thirty in the afternoon, the dust-covered white Porsche pulled over to the curb on Avenue of the Stars in Century City. Rita planted a wet kiss on Scollari's forehead, winked, and got out. Ray drove alone the two blocks to the Century Plaza Hotel. He got out of the car and waved to the bell captain. Within a couple of minutes a bellhop was opening up the trunk of the Porsche and putting Ray's matching black Lark bags on the dolly. Scollari turned and saw Rita walking toward the entrance of the hotel. Without saying anything to him, she licked her lips and slipped quietly up the steps to the hotel lobby. Grinning to himself, Ray stayed behind with the bellhop. It was an arrangement he and Rita had made beforehand. Because of the media, too many people knew he was in town and where he was staying. He couldn't afford anyone finding out that he was here with a woman; his chances of becoming mayor would be all but lost, not to mention the city council becoming suspicious about his expenditures. Plus his wife would nail him to the cross in court. He knew from past experience how to have a few laughs and not get caught. As planned, he and Rita would catch up with each other in the elevator.

The Century Plaza was Scollari's favorite hotel in L.A. He liked the modern curvature of the building and the large lobby that always seemed to be bustling with people. *Hey, if Reagan stayed here when he was president, then it's good enough for a second-generation wop like me,* he constantly told his friends back in New York.

The concierge behind the check-in counter knew him. He immediately gave Ray a key and told him to register later on at his convenience. As he made his way to the elevators, the bell captain and several of the other employees said hello to him. Smiling, he nodded in return. He was obviously well-known at this hotel, and Rita, holding the elevator door open for him, was in awe of his popularity. When he stepped inside the elevator, she first looked to make sure the bellhop wasn't watching, then she leaned over and whispered something in his ear, touching the hairy rim lightly with her tongue. She giggled. Laughing, Ray gave her waist a squeeze as the door started to close. His mind was jumping with all the things he was going to do with her once they were alone in his suite.

She sat on a rust-colored couch at the end of the lobby and watched the elevator doors close on the laughing couple. The black leather miniskirt was now dirty and stained. Her eyes remained fixed on the digital numbers above the door. She watched intently until the numbers stopped changing and the fourteenth floor stayed lit. She quickly stood up, went into an empty, waiting elevator, and also pushed fourteen.

Seconds later, the copper doors opened on the fourteenth floor. Down the hall, in a secluded wing, she could see the bellhop opening the door for Scollari. The girl was standing several rooms away, pretending to fumble with her keys. After the bellhop put the bags in his room, Scollari gave him a ten-dollar bill, patted him on the shoulder, and watched him go down on the service elevator. Giggling, the girl tiptoed over to Ray, grabbed his crotch, and led him inside his room. The door closed.

She went over to the emergency door that was a few feet away from the room, opened it, and went in. Standing by the stairwell, she put her ear to the door and listened.

Wait until I hear the shower, she thought, touching her tote bag and feeling the weight of the steel hammer inside.

Scollari lay on the rumpled, greasy sheets in the bedroom of his hotel suite, his naked body glistening with baby oil. He lay there with his eyes closed and a contented smile plastered on his face. From the bathroom he could hear the sound of the shower running and Rita's voice singing "La Bamba" off-key.

What a killer she was! That bitch could do things with her body that he didn't think possible. Up until today he thought he had done it all: from having sex under the covers with his frigid wife to the Times Square hookers who gave twenty-five-dollar blow jobs in alleys behind the garbage dumpsters. He once had three girls at the same time; even picked up an occasional transvestite when he got real drunk. None of them compared to Rita. She was the best lay he had ever experienced. His whole body ached.

Fucked my goddamn brains out!

She didn't expect anything from him—no money, no jewelry, absolutely nothing. The only thing he had to do was whisper in her ear the names of famous people he knew while he was fucking her. She went crazy every time he did that. Cuomo . . . Quayle . . . those two niggers, Dinkins and Bradley. Today she actually had an orgasm when he muttered Donald Trump. He never met most of them, but she didn't have to know that.

Scollari was in the middle of devising a plan on how he could take Rita back with him to New York when someone knocked on the door. "Yeah, who is it?" he asked.

No answer.

"Who's there?" he said, sitting up.

More knocking.

"Shit!" he muttered, getting out of the bed. He wrapped a towel around his flabby waist, went over to the door, and looked out the peephole. He could see a brown eye staring at him from the other side.

"What do you want?" he grunted.

No answer, just another knock.

Angry, Ray flung open the door.

The last thing he heard in the one split second that remained of his life was Rita starting up another chorus of "La Bamba."

Chapter Thirty

THE OVER-SIZED BLUE van was parked a block away on the other side of the street from Rena's house in Brentwood. Inside the van the air was hot and smelled of partially-eaten McDonald's cheeseburgers and perspiration. Grant and three other officers were cramped together in the small quarters watching Rena's house with powerful binoculars. Four other agents were sitting in an unmarked Ford only twenty feet away from the house. Two TV cable repairmen, also agents, were across the street looking into a small manhole and pretending to fiddle with the thick cable television wires. Up on the roofs of two residential houses across the street, several snipers lying on their stomachs were looking through the telescopic sights of their rifles, the cross hairs aimed directly on Rena's front door and driveway.

In the blue van the agent with the gapped teeth wiped away the sweat from his brow as he took the last bite of his Big Mac. "You sure about this?" he said to Grant. A drop of ketchup clung to his chin.

"Yeah, I'm sure." He looked away from the binoculars and rubbed his tired eyes. "She's got absolutely nowhere else to go."

"A cab's stopping off at the house," the other agent said excitedly.

Grant looked through the binoculars again. He watched the back door of the taxi open and a man holding a frayed leather jacket, wearing jeans and a sweatshirt, get out. The driver also exited, then opened up his trunk and took out a suitcase.

"Who the fuck is that?" said Grant. He saw the agents dressed as TV repairmen looking up from the hole at the man and asking themselves the same question.

The stranger paid the driver, picked up the bag, and made his way to the front door.

Grant quickly glanced up at the rooftops across the street. He could see the rifle barrels aimed at the man. He leaned into the microphone on the console and whispered to the S.W.A.T. team on the roof, "Hold your position. Don't fire." His body was tense. *Who the fuck is he?* He watched the guy ring the doorbell. When no one answered, the stranger reached in his pocket for something, perhaps a key—Grant couldn't be sure—and stuck it in the lock. Suddenly Rena's daughter opened the door from the inside and leaped up on his body, hugging and kissing him. The man swung her around and brought her inside the house.

"Who is he? A boyfriend of the mother or something?" Grant asked once more. He sounded pissed.

"Oh, Christ! I know who he is," the agent with the gap teeth said, shaking his head. "He's a reporter. I met him at a presidential news conference in Washington last year when I was with the secret service. He's supposed to have a reputation for being in the wrong place at the wrong time."

"Well, he still has as far as I'm concerned. He was within a hair's breadth from getting his balls blown away by the S.W.A.T. boys," Grant said annoyed.

"Oh, Charlie," Cathy said exuberantly, still hanging from his neck with her feet dangling off the ground. "What are you doing back from France so soon?"

"I got tired of eating snails," he said, closing the front door with his foot. He was looking out the front window, up at the roof across the street. Holding her around her tiny waist with one hand, he put his bag down on the carpet, then gently disengaged her arms from his neck. He walked over to the edge of the window, leaned his back against the wall, and peeked through the slit of the lace curtains.

"What's wrong, Charlie?" She went over to him.

Without taking his eyes away from the window, he held his arm out, preventing her from coming closer. "Stay away from the window, sweetheart."

"Why, what's the matter?"

He didn't answer her. When he had paid the taxi driver outside, he noticed the sun's glare reflecting off metal coming from the roof across the street. Charlie instantly knew what it was; he had seen that same glint of light coming from the rooftops of Beirut too many times before. A hailstorm of bullets usually followed. When the firing finally stopped, innocent people would be lying dead in the street.

He scanned both sides of the block. There was the blue van and the unmarked car with men inside wearing suits and ties. Feds, he thought. *What the fuck is going on?* "Where's your mom, honey?" he said to Cathy, forcing a smile.

"In Napa. She called early this morning and said that she was staying over because she has to go to Tacoma tomorrow."

"What's in Tacoma?"

Cathy shrugged. "You never know with Mom."

Ain't that the truth, he thought. "Who's staying with you?"

"Cindy. She goes to UCLA. She's upstairs taking a nap."

Fuck! Those scumbags have guns trained on a house with kids! Charlie fought back his outrage, turned to Cathy, and smiled. He put his arm around her shoulders and steered her away from the exposed living room window toward the kitchen. "Let's get Cindy and take her back to her place. I've got a surprise for you."

"What?" she said, excited.

"I'm going to take you up to Napa to see your mom."

A smile spread across her face. "What about school tomorrow?"

"Forget school. You deserve a holiday."

She threw her arms around his waist and hugged him. "Oh, Charlie, you're so *baaad!*"

Chapter Thirty-one

THE SKY WAS a deep scarlet by the time Rena turned off Highway 29 and onto Spring Mountain Road in St. Helena. The muddy shadows from the fading sunlight made the road treacherous, with curves looking more like right angles than arcs. Rena kept the Rover at a steady thirty-mile-an-hour clip. The tires squealed each time she made a sharp turn. She didn't feel afraid; she had used this road hundreds of times in the past, and she was familiar with every bend and turn on it.

Neil Tompson, the psychiatrist at Riverside Hospital in Tacoma, Washington, said he wouldn't be able to meet with her until tomorrow. Instead of waiting around doing nothing until then, she decided to drive up to the McKinney winery and see if there was something she may have overlooked. Someone was behind Maura committing these murders—she was sure of it.

As she passed by the van der Slyck winery that was located next to Maura's property, she saw Pinky's black police Bronco parked off the road in a section of the vineyards. First she thought about continuing straight to Maura's house, but instead pulled over next to the four-wheeled truck and peered in. The Bronco was empty. Suddenly she heard a cry coming from somewhere deep within the wine fields. It sounded like a small animal, perhaps a cat being attacked by a coyote. Then she heard it again.

It was no cat. Even though it was a high-pitched yelp, there was a pleading tone about it. Only humans know how to plead, she thought. Rena got out of the Rover and looked toward the area where she thought she heard the sounds. From out of the darkness at the end of the fields she could make out two human shadows coming toward her. One of the silhouettes was big and wide. He seemed to be pushing a smaller shape who was walking unsteadily in front of him. Every time the big one shoved, the little one would let out a scream as he fell to the ground.

Rena's heart was pounding with terror. Just as she was about to get back into her Rover and take off, the murky figures got caught in a glimmer of fading light coming through the leafy grapevines. They were like a tableau frozen on stage. Rena could now see their faces—Pinky's and Otto's.

Then the figures moved again. Pinky leaned over and grabbed Otto by the back of his hair and lifted him off the ground. Otto screamed once more. Pinky turned the little man around and slapped him hard with the back of his hand. Otto fell to the ground. He tried crawling away, but Pinky put his huge foot on his spine and dug his boot heel into it.

Rena ran down the furrow toward them, ignoring the vines and leaves slapping at her face from both sides. "Stop it!" she screamed.

Pinky looked up and saw her. An expression of surprise registered on his face, and he quickly removed the heel of his boot from Otto's back.

"Help me!" Otto pleaded as he held one hand out to her. His face was covered with blood, dirt, and spit. "He wants to kill me!" His movements resembled a lizard as he started crawling toward her. Pinky slammed his foot down on Otto's calf, and he cried out in agony.

"Where the hell do you think you're going?" Pinky said harshly, looking down at his prey.

"Pinky, you're killing him!" Rena grabbed the jacket sleeve of his uniform and tried to push him off of Otto.

"He resisted arrest," Pinky said, glaring at Rena.

"I wasn't!" Otto cried out. "He came to my house, broke down the door, and dragged me out."

Rena looked away from Pinky and down at the pathetic figure of his captive. Otto was crying now, and the tears were turning red from the blood on his face. Mucus ran from his nose and mixed with the blood. "He doesn't seem to be resisting now," she said, squeezing Pinky's arm. He stared back at her, his face a bright red, and his thick lips trembling. Rena was shocked; she had never seen this gentle giant of a man show so much hate. "What did he do?"

Pinky took a deep, wheezing breath before he answered. He removed his foot from Otto's leg, and said, "You know damn well what he did. You told me about it, remember?" His voice was breaking up, as if he were about to cry.

"What?" she asked.

"What he did to Maura. He's a piece of shit. A fucking animal!" He kicked Otto's thigh hard, and the little man let out a wail.

"Pinky, stop," she said softly, touching his arm.

"Don't Pinky me!" He pushed Rena's hand away. "Maybe she was crazy, maybe she murdered all those people. But this son of a bitch is sicker than she is. To set her up like that. To have some fucking Mex try and rape her. She didn't deserve that." Tears began to run down his face.

"Nobody deserves that," Rena said.

"*She* didn't!" His voice was hard again. "She was a good kid," he mumbled. "Never hurt nobody."

Rena could see he was ready to hit Otto again, and she stepped in between them. "Arrest him, Pinky. Don't kill him."

"There's no proof. Do you think he'll go up in front of an entire courtroom and admit to what he did? Give me a break."

"He confessed to me. I'll be a witness."

He looked down at Otto's bleeding face, then back at Rena. She could feel his thoughts reassembling themselves inside his brain. Calming down, he took the steel cuffs from off his belt and got on his knees next to Otto. He twisted the elfish man's arms behind his back and locked the cuffs tightly around his thin wrists. Standing back up, he grabbed Otto by his belt with one hand and lifted him off the ground. "Wait here," he said to her as he pushed Otto toward his Bronco. He opened the door, picked him up by the belt again, and literally tossed him inside. He closed the door and went back to Rena. "You know it'll never stick," he said. "It won't even get past the arraignment."

"Maybe not, but everybody will know what happened. If there's one thing that Otto can't stand, it's the world and especially his mother finding out about his private life. If he gets off, I don't think he'll ever come back to this part of the country again."

Pinky nodded slowly. "You know, if you hadn't shown up, I think I'd have killed him."

Rena believed him. "It wouldn't have been worth it. I told you once before that you wouldn't look good in prison blues."

"Yeah, you're probably right," he muttered, taking his hat off and running his stubby fingers through his damp, sweaty hair. He put his hat on again then turned and walked back to his truck. Rena watched as he started the engine and drove down the hill with his prisoner toward St. Helena.

"Yes, you probably would have killed him," she whispered to herself. Pinky had never harmed anyone in his life.

As she made her way back to the Rover, she wondered how many other men had fallen in love with Maura over the years and had kept it to themselves, afraid of being rebuffed. It wasn't a hard thing to do, she thought. Maura was brilliant, beautiful, and elusive. When combined, these qualities became an intoxicating elixir to men.

Rena got back into the Rover and drove the quarter-mile up the road to Maura's winery. About two hundred feet from the house, a government-owned brown Ford with a radio antenna on the trunk was parked off the road and hidden between a patch of madrona trees. Feds. Grant must have stationed some of his men to watch the house in case Maura showed up. *Do they really think nobody can see them, even at night?* Maura would have spotted them even before she did.

She parked the Rover near Manuel's truck. The pickup was filled with furniture, a box spring, and a mattress. She got out of her car and rang the buzzer. A few seconds later Elvera, Manuel's wife, opened the door. When she saw Rena, a large smile erupted from her round, weather-beaten face. She put her thick brown arms around Rena's shoulders and gave her a big squeeze. Moving away, she slid her callused hands down Rena's arms and called her affectionately, "Little one." She had called Rena that since she was ten years old. *Leetle one.* "Come in. Come in," she said, moving her huge body away from the door so Rena could find some space to enter.

Inside, several suitcases of all sizes, textures, and colors, totes and plastic garbage bags filled with household objects littered the living-room floor. Pictures of Manuel's family that once hung on the walls were now placed on top of the bags. Confused, Rena turned to Elvera. "Are you moving?"

The smile faded from Elvera's face. "*Sí.* We have to."

"Why do you have to? Don't you want to stay here?"

"Yes. This has been our home for many years." Her frantic eyes began to water. She wiped them with the edge of her apron. "We were told by Señor Kaplow that the house will have to be sold and that one day we will have to leave. It is the law, he said. Manuel has much pride."

"Yes, I know," Rena said.

"Manuel says that if our work over the years means nothing, then we will leave now."

251

Mr. Kaplow was Donald Kaplow, Maura's attorney in Napa. Rena had known him all her life. What law would force Manuel and his family to leave? she wondered. "Where is Manuel?" Rena asked her.

"Over by the winery, de-stemming the grapes from the late harvest."

The late harvest, Rena knew, was the grapes that made up the sweet dessert wines.

"Let me talk to Manuel," she said.

The darkness had set in now, and she carefully made her way across the road. She had come here on a vague feeling that there may have been something here that she and the police had disregarded. After talking to Elvera, that vague feeling was beginning to solidify itself.

There were lights outside the winery. She saw Manuel and his two sons feeding grapes into the crusher-stemmer machine located next to the oak door. The dessert wines were the only grapes that Manuel crushed; the rest were sold in the original clusters. The machine resembled a huge corkscrew several feet long that was encased in an open, horizontal vat. As the grapes were poured into the vat, the screw turned and began to squash the fruit, pushing them into an enclosed cylinder for the removal of the stems.

Manuel looked up from his work and saw her. Like his wife, he also grinned at her, showing his gold front tooth. He bent down and turned off the machine. "Señorita Halbrook," he said.

"Hello, Manuel." She rubbed her hand through the youngest boy's hair. "I need to talk with you."

He saw the seriousness in her face. "Move!" he said to his two boys, pointing to the door. Happy that they could play and not have to do any more work, they raced out of the winery.

"What is the matter, señorita?" he asked, wiping the juice from the grapes off his hands and arms with a towel.

The winery smelled sweet from the sugar content in the grapes. "Why are you moving?"

He shook his head and clicked his tongue, then took the towel and slammed it against the crusher-stemmer. "Laws! Your country has laws that make no sense."

"What laws, Manuel?"

"I work for Señor McKinney since I was a young man. I work long and hard. He promise me that I would always have a job as

252

long as the winery was owned by him or his daughter. Then when he die, Señorita Maura tells me to move into the house, that she was going to live in New York. She tell me that I can live here forever, that she would never sell the winery."

"Did she sell it?" If she did, the deal would have to have transpired before the murders.

"No, señorita. Señor Kaplow say that the winery will have to be sold, even without Señorita Maura's permission."

Something was beginning to stir around in her mind. Perhaps her instinct about coming here was right after all. She looked at her watch. It was after seven. "I want to call Mr. Kaplow."

Manuel nodded. "Good. Maybe he made a mistake, and we could still stay here."

"Perhaps," she said. Rena left the stone winery and went toward the house.

She entered the kitchen from the back door. Elvera was standing over the sink, wrapping plates in newspapers and placing them carefully into a brown cardboard box. There was a sadness etched in her Aztec face, and Rena felt for her. They've been here too many years, and the McKinney winery was their home. Whatever was happening was wrong. She asked permission to use the phone then called information to get Kaplow's home number. Rena figured he would be home by now and not at his office.

Kaplow picked up after several rings. Rena told him who she was and asked if he remembered her. With a mouthful of food, he assured her that he remembered her very well, then inquired about her father's health. After a few more pleasantries, she asked if she could come over and talk with him; that it wouldn't take very long.

"Absolutely," he said. "My wife died about a year ago, and I could use the company."

When Rena left the house and got into the Rover, she could see Manuel standing by the door of the stone winery. "Are you going to see Señor Kaplow?" he yelled at her from across the road.

She stuck her head out of the half-open window and said, "Yes."

"Will you ask him if he made a mistake about selling the winery?"

"Yes, Manuel, I will."

Kaplow lived in Yountville, about a twenty-minute ride from the top of Spring Mountain Road. Her stomach began to rumble as she made her way down the dark winding trail. When had she last eaten? Breakfast this morning. That was it.

She pulled up to Kaplow's house. The back of his Chrysler Le Baron was sticking halfway out of his garage. As she turned the ignition off, Kaplow opened the screen door, walked down from the porch, and met her by her car. He was a tall, thin man with white curly hair. Even though his shirtsleeves were rolled up, he still wore his tie knotted up past the top button of his white-on-white shirt. His suspenders were off his shoulders and dangled from his waist.

He opened the door of her car. "You hungry?" he asked.

Rena looked at his smiling face. He seemed genuinely glad to see her. "Actually," she said, laughing, "I'm starving."

"Good. I have some fried chicken left over that I made. The problem with living alone is that you can't buy a chicken small enough for one person. I wind up throwing half my food away."

There were all the telltale signs inside the kitchen that Kaplow was recently widowed: dishes piled up in the sink, a weeks amount of newspapers stacked next to the door, an overloaded garbage bag, boxes of cereal that were never put back in the pantry.

Kaplow sat her down at the kitchen table and brought the food over to her. Rena ate a breast and a thigh, along with some potato salad and coleslaw. She sipped a glass of chardonnay that Kaplow barrel-fermented himself down in his cellar.

"You seemed anxious on the phone," he said while watching her tear through the meat from the chicken.

"I was. Manuel said you told him that Maura's property would have to be sold. They're packed and ready to go."

"Damn!" he said, bringing his hand down on top of the Formica table. "I didn't mean that they'd have to move out right away. It could be months, maybe even a year or so down the line before they'd have to do that."

"Why does the property have to be sold?" she asked, wiping her hands on the paper napkin.

"There's no regulation in the books that says it has to, but a judge will rule that way. You know anything about the 'Son of Sam' law?"

"No," she said.

"Okay, the 'Son of Sam' law came about after Berkowitz, the

254

crazy bastard who murdered those people in New York City, was convicted. The law basically says you can't make money from the misery and death you inflict upon others. In other words, neither he nor any other murderer can sell their story for a profit. It's a damn good law. Having money and property, that's something else.''

She perked up at the mention of "property." "How?''

"Let's say, conjecturally speaking, that Berkowitz had money or property. If the family of the people he killed wished to bring wrongful death action suits against him, then it's a ninety-nine percent chance that a probate court would uphold the lawsuits. There would be execution proceedings.''

"Which means what?'' she asked.

"That if the murderer owned land, like Maura, it would involuntarily be sold in order to pay the litigants off after the judgment is made.''

Rena stopped eating and pushed the plate away. "Did Maura have a will?''

"Yes. I helped her write it.''

"What if she died? Would the will still be legal?''

"Remember the old adage about wills—'being of sound mind and body.' A will is meaningless unless the person who wrote it is considered sane by the courts at the time he or she made it out. Would you consider someone who committed these murders to be of sound mind?''

Good point, Rena thought. Even if she appeared sane at the time, it could be disputed, because Maura spent time in a mental institution when she was seventeen years old. "What assets did she own other than the winery?'' she asked.

"Actually, other than a few signed lithographs, not much at all. The winery was her most valuable possession.'' The water in the kettle began to boil on the stove, and Kaplow got up to turn it off. He took two cups off the counter, inspected them to see if they were clean, then put two teaspoons of Maxwell's instant coffee into them. Holding the kettle handle with a towel, he poured the water into the cups. "How do you like yours?''

"Black,'' she said, deep in thought. "Who did she leave the winery to?''

He brought the cups over to the table and sat down. "Manuel. He was the one who kept everything going after her father died, and she felt that he was the one who deserved to have it if anything ever happened to her.''

255

Again Rena's mind started to race. "Something *did* happen to her."

"Right. If and when Maura's captured, she'll have to stand trial. If she's found guilty or judged insane, the grieving families of the victims have the right to sue Maura's estate. Since the estate is composed mostly of land and vineyards, then that's what will most likely be sold off."

Yes, the *why* was beginning to come into focus now. "Have any of the families filed lawsuits?"

"A couple. It's a little premature right now because Maura hasn't been convicted yet. Trust me, when she is, more suits will follow."

Then a thought occurred to her. "Have there been any recent offers to buy Maura's property?"

"Several. The McKinney vineyard is a solid piece of real estate. It has good soil and drainage, and the sun hits it just right."

"But it's a small piece of property considering the acreage of other wineries. Peter McKinney, as good as his wines were, could barely make a living from his vineyards."

"True. But nevertheless, there have been several offers."

Rena gulped down her coffee. "Do you remember who made these offers?"

"I'll tell you in a second." He stood up and went into his den, which he used as a home office. A few minutes later he came back holding a thick folder with expanding pockets. He emptied the contents out on the kitchen table. "This is all the work I've done for Maura and her dad." He sorted through stacks of different sizes of paper until he found what he was looking for. "Here it is." Putting his reading glasses on, he said, "Interesting. Two of the offers were from your father."

Rena nodded in understanding. "Peter McKinney had a good piece of property to make his award-winning wines on. Dad wanted to buy it for the wines he'd be able to make."

"Your father's offer was turned down by Peter McKinney and then later on by Maura."

"Who else?"

"A couple of years back a conglomerate out of Germany and one out of Japan made Maura an offer, but she also said no to that."

"Anyone else?"

"One other company. In fact, they made several inquiries about the property within the last year alone."

Rena stiffened. "What's the name of the company?"

"Let's see." Kaplow searched through the file. "Here it is." He pulled out a white piece of 8½ × 11 paper with a fancy letterhead. "Clurman Enterprises. I've never heard of them before. I did a search on them but came up blank."

Rena tensed up. She could sense the *who*'s foul breath on her neck. "Do you know how Peter McKinney originally came by his property?"

"Yes. It was willed to his family by one of his ancestors who settled here about one hundred years ago. The will was then handed down from generation to generation. No one came to this country to claim the property except Peter."

"Who has the original deed to the land?" she asked.

"I don't know if the original still exists. I'm sure the county recorder's office in Santa Rosa has at least a copy of it."

"You've been very illuminating, Mr. Kaplow," she said, standing up.

"The name's Donald. Only my clients who are broke call me Mr. Kaplow. How about another cup of coffee?"

Rena sensed the man's loneliness. She understood what a rough time he was going through: his wife dying after thirty years of marriage. "How about a rain check on that coffee until the next time," she said to him, shaking his hand.

"You got a deal. Are you going home now?"

"Yes," she said, opening the screen door. "I want to be at the county recorder's office first thing in the morning."

"You seemed disturbed when I mentioned Clurman Enterprises. I suppose I couldn't find anything on it because it's still privately owned and hasn't gone public."

"Maybe," Rena said. "Or maybe Clurman Enterprises doesn't really exist." She could see the surprised look on Kaplow's face as she closed the screen door behind her.

The *who* was so close now that she could almost feel the sick bastard tickling her bones and laughing.

Chapter Thirty-two

RUSH HOUR WAS still heavy by the time Charlie and Cathy landed in San Francisco. He rented a car from Budget, and they spent the next two hours crawling through glutted freeways trying to get to the Napa Valley.

Charlie saw the dark shadow of the government van as soon as he left Highway 128 and turned onto the steep gravel road that led up to Simon Halbrook's château. It was parked under a cluster of trees, partially hidden by thick foliage. *These guys are here, too!* That meant they had no idea where the hell Maura was, he thought. *If they have guns trained on the house, I swear I'll kill them!*

He let out a gasp when he turned the curve and saw the medieval building looming up before him.

"You never been here before, huh?" Cathy asked him when she saw the astonished look on his face.

"Uh-huh."

"It was built by a famous duke or something in the sixteenth century. Grandpa likes to own things that once belonged to famous people. I guess that makes him feel like he's important," she said with disdain.

"Immortal would be a better word."

"Like Dracula, huh?"

"Knock it off. He's your grandfather."

"I hate him," she said folding her arms to her breast. "I don't know why you're defending him. He certainly doesn't hide his feelings about you."

Charlie laughed.

"You're the only person he can't buy," she said proudly as she blew a pink bubble out of her mouth with the gum she was chewing.

"He could buy me. He just doesn't think I'm worth making an offer to."

She giggled. "God, Charlie!"

The château was lit up by floodlights. As Charlie parked the rental car near the front door, Cathy let out a groan.

"What's the matter?" he asked.

"Look." She pointed to Simon's helicopter sitting on the circular pad. "He's here. Let's go back to L.A.," she said, tugging at his sleeve.

Charlie sighed; he wasn't too fond of Simon, either. He got out of the car and opened the door on her side. She refused to move. "He's an old man. He loves you," he said.

"Fuck him. My father would still be alive if it wasn't for that old bastard."

Charlie wanted to tell her to watch her language. That's what adults were supposed to tell children. But he didn't. He understood her anger. Terry, Cathy's father, was a scumbag who deserved to die. The truth about how evil he had been was always kept from the girl. The only thing she knew was that her grandfather had hated Terry when he was alive. That and that alone made him the chosen person to vent her rage and hurt on.

"Move it," he said.

"Shit," she whispered under her breath as she got out of the car.

Charlie grabbed her suitcase from the backseat and pushed her toward the door. He rang the antique bronze bell. After a minute, a butler about Simon's age wearing a black suit and tie answered the door and let them in. They followed him into the massive living room filled with Louis XIV furniture. Monets, Cézannes, and Renoirs hung off the antique white walls giving the cavernous room a semblance of color. Simon was on his knees stoking the fire that was blazing in the large stone fireplace. Harrison, with a cognac snifter in his hand, was sitting on a couch going over papers that were spread out before him on the coffee table. Simon heard them enter, and when he turned and saw Charlie he froze.

"Hello, Simon. How's it going? It's been a while," Charlie said, forcing a smile.

Simon's eyes darted from Charlie over to Cathy, and his face softened when he saw her. "I wasn't expecting you," he said with a tremor in his voice.

"Gee, I guess that makes both of us," Cathy said contemptuously while popping her bubble gum.

259

There was pain in the old man's eyes from the sound of his granddaughter's tone; then they hardened again when he looked at Charlie. "Why are you here?" he said, standing up. The poker was still in his hand.

"There are men on rooftops pointing rifles at your daughter's house in L.A. I figured it would be a lot safer for Cathy to be up here with her mom. Where is she?"

"I don't know. The servants told me she's been staying here. I've only just arrived a few minutes ago. Who are these men with guns?" he asked, concerned.

"S.W.A.T. or FBI. There's also a truckload of them just down the road from here."

"Why?"

"Looking for Maura McKinney, I suppose. I didn't ask."

"They have no right to be on my property," Simon said with rage. He dropped the poker on the hearth and stormed over to the door.

"They're here to protect Rena, Simon," Harrison said, standing up and blocking his way.

Charlie saw Harrison for the first time, and his stomach tightened. A primitive instinct deep inside his gut said that something could easily happen between this man and Rena if it hadn't already. He didn't like the feeling and tried to shake it.

Harrison went over to Charlie and held out his hand. "Rena mentioned you. My name is Harrison Monroe." Charlie nodded and shook his hand. "And you're Cathy, right?" he said, smiling.

She answered him by nodding and cracking her gum again.

"You knew these men were here?" Simon said to Harrison.

"Yes. They've been on the perimeters of the property for the last few hours."

"Why the hell haven't you gotten in touch with me about this?" Simon was angry. He did not like being kept in the dark.

Harrison held up his hands to calm him down. "Because you would have demanded that they leave. They're trying to get this maniac. The FBI thinks that she'll try and make contact with Rena."

"Damn it!" Simon took a deep breath to get his control back. "I've been out of the country for the past week."

"What's going on, Charlie?" Cathy asked him, pulling at the pocket of his leather jacket.

He suddenly remembered that the girl knew nothing about

260

this. Putting his arm around her shoulder, he said, "Nothing, baby."

"Come on, Charlie. What's happening. You told me you'd never bullshit me."

Charlie felt like kicking them all for opening their mouths in front of her. "A friend of your mom is in trouble," he said, bending down to her height.

"You weren't talking about a friend. You were talking about a killer," she said, giving him a dirty look. "Is Mom's friend a killer?"

"Yes," Simon quickly said.

Good show, Simon, Charlie thought.

"Where's my mother?" she said frightened, pushing his arms away and backing up. "Where's my mother?"

Charlie put out his hand. "Cathy . . ."

"You've been lying to me, Charlie!" Her eyes were glaring with anger.

"Who's been lying to you?" Rena's voice said coming from the entranceway. She had just come back from seeing Kaplow.

Cathy turned and saw her. "Mom!" She ran to Rena and clutched her around the waist.

Rena put down her travel bag and hugged her tightly. She could feel her daughter's body trembling in her arms. "What are you doing here?" she said, stroking her hair. Then she looked up and saw Charlie, and her eyes opened wide in surprise. "Charlie! Why aren't you . . . ?"

"In Paris? I decided to take a sabbatical." He could see how pale and tired she looked. These murders were beginning to take a toll on her. His body ached to touch her right now, and he wished she'd come over and throw her arms around him right in front of her father and whoever this tanned Adonis was. She didn't. Instead she continued to cradle Cathy.

"Mommy," Cathy said, with tears in her eyes. "Did your friend kill somebody?"

Rena looked at Charlie.

He shrugged and shook his head, as if to say, I didn't tell her.

"I told her," Simon said. "What difference does it make?"

"I thought you might have been killed, too," Cathy said, not letting Rena go.

Rena scowled at Simon. "Your sensitivity amazes me sometimes."

"She's killed again," Harrison quickly added.

261

"What?" she gasped.

"This afternoon. She killed her boss. He was staying at a hotel in Los Angeles."

"Ray Scollari?" Rena was stunned.

"That's the name," Harrison said.

"My God!"

"That's why they're watching the place. If she eludes them in Los Angeles, she could be coming up here next." Looking disturbed, Harrison bent down and picked up the papers on the coffee table. Putting them in a leather attaché case, he said, "I think I'm going to turn in. A big day tomorrow." He shook Charlie's hand again, showed him his white teeth, then glanced nervously over at Rena. She looked away.

Charlie caught the look, and a feeling of hard anger surged through his body. There *was* something between them. He wondered if whatever they had together was consummated yet. Once again, except this time without success, he tried pushing that thought from his mind. He quickly explained why he brought Cathy up to Napa, then he said to her, "Your friend is right. It *is* late. I'd better get going."

"That's ridiculous," Rena said, going over to him. "Stay here tonight. I need to talk to you."

"Another time," he said, looking away from her. He bent down and kissed Cathy on the cheek then went toward the door. He could feel Simon's eyes on him.

Rena followed him out into the night. "Charlie, wait. What's wrong with you?"

"I'm tired," he said, opening the door of his rented Taurus.

She held the door, preventing him from closing it. "Come on. It's me, Charlie, remember?"

He looked at her and saw the concern and caring in her eyes. Suddenly he realized how childish and foolish he was being. What they had together was special, and it would take a lot more than some George Hamilton look-alike to come between them. As if a plug had been pulled, the jealousy ebbed from his body. He threw his arms around her and he kissed her mouth, her face. They held each other for a long time, their bodies pressed firmly against each other. The sounds of the country night—crickets, an occasional frog, the far away bark of a dog—broke up the stillness.

"Why are you back, Charlie?" she finally murmured, still holding onto him.

"I can't stand garlic."

"Did you quit?" she asked, looking up at him.

He pushed her head back down on his chest. "Yep. I wasn't made to be Sam Donaldson. I need to be out in the bush."

"Ducking bullets . . . getting your ass shot off," she said scoldingly.

He stroked her head. "You look tired, kid. How close are these Federal yoyos *really* coming to capturing this woman?"

She moved away from Charlie and sat down in the front seat of the car. He bent down next to her, resting his arm on her lap. "Would you think I was crazy, Charlie, if I told you somebody is doing this to Maura?"

"No. Just in need of a rest, maybe."

"Somebody is doing this to her, Charlie," she said in all seriousness. "It has to do with her property, I'm sure of it." Rena told Charlie to wait, then got up and went back into the house to see if Cathy was all right. She found Cathy on the couch with her hands folded stiffly on her lap. Simon was sitting next to her, his hands also clasped together. Avoiding each other's face, they focused their eyes on the fire that was raging in the hearth. He was awkwardly attempting to have a conversation with her. She would occasionally nod her head at something he said. Both of them reminded Rena of two friends trying to make up after a fight. It was about time. She smiled, then went back outside to talk to Charlie.

He was sitting in the driver's seat of the car smoking a cigarette. She got in on the other side. While looking at the full moon hanging over the château, she told him everything.

He listened. Twenty minutes later he asked, "You've never even suspected that she was a hermaphrodite?"

"No. She hid it so well. She was forced to do that by her father."

"Who took care of Maura when she was a baby? Someone had to have been around to change her diapers. That person would have known what she was."

With her eyes still fixed on the lit moon, she said, "There *was* such a person. When I first met Maura, I saw a woman in her house. Maura told me she was the housekeeper. She was Turkish and spoke no English. When Maura was sixteen, McKinney felt she was old enough to be alone, and he sent her back to Turkey to live. Up until the time Maura went into that private hospital in Washington, the housekeeper was the only other one who would have known about her affliction."

Even though he knew Rena hated his smoking, Charlie lit up another cigarette.

Rena continued. "Here's an emotionally disturbed woman who has hidden her true identity for all these years. Suddenly she goes insane, just like her ancestor, the Baron de Montret. Insanity can be inherited—everybody knows that. It all works so damn well *logically*. The problem is it doesn't work *psycho*logically. De Montret was a lonely, abused child with very little ego, who was molded by his depraved neighbor, the Comte Henri Maureau. He became what the comte wanted in order to gain his approval and love. Maura doesn't fit that profile. Yes, she was abused mentally by her father, but unlike de Montret, she retained her sense of self. Her will was like iron. I doubt even Martin could have changed her."

"According to you, somebody did. Who?"

"I don't know. I don't know if it's even possible." She shook her head.

Charlie took the last puff from the cigarette, then flipped it out the window onto the gravel path. "People go insane and kill other people," he said. "A guy who everybody thinks is the greatest family man on Earth one day goes into the factory where he works and blows twenty people away with a semiautomatic. These things happen."

"Yes. But those are onetime acts, Charlie, that eventually end in suicide or the person being killed by the police."

"What about serial killers?"

"Serial killers are sociopaths. Maura's not."

"You said yourself that she changed drastically after Martin died."

Rena turned to him. "Sociopathic behavior begins during the first years of life, maybe even earlier. When Martin died, Maura was seventeen. She had a breakdown, and her personality was somewhat altered from it, but that was all. The killings in the vineyards are too ritualistic. It would take a psychopath like de Montret to carry out such unspeakable acts. The baron actually believed that the vineyards were alive. That's craziness of the highest order. Maura doesn't belong in that category."

Most of the lights in the chateau went out downstairs. Simon must be taking Cathy to her room. Good, she thought. Perhaps they'll become friends again. Rena knew the depth of Simon's love for his granddaughter. "Someone is doing this to her. How? I don't know yet. And the why . . . I think it has something to do with her land. Maybe I'll know more after I go to the county recorder's office. Will you go with me tomorrow, Charlie?"

Charlie smiled and put his arm around her shoulder. She leaned into him. "Yeah, I'll go with you," he said. "What time is your appointment with this shrink in Tacoma tomorrow?"

"One o'clock."

"Do you also want me to go up there with you?" he asked, pushing the hair out of her face with his hand.

"No. I don't think he'd like it. He didn't sound like the friendly type when I talked to him on the phone. I'll be back late in the afternoon. We could see each other then."

Most of the lights in the upstairs part of the house went out, and in the darkness the night sky suddenly appeared, becoming a sea of stars. For the next half hour they held each other, staring up at the maze of bright white dots, each lost in their own thoughts.

When Rena went back inside the house, Charlie drove to a Holiday Inn in St. Helena. She had asked him again to stay the night, but he told her that he didn't trust Simon. Grinning, he said that he'd probably cut his throat while he was sleeping.

After he checked into the motel, he bought a vial of Excedrin and a bottle of J&B at the liquor store and took it to his room. Ripping off the plastic top on the sanitized drinking glass in the bathroom, he opened up the bottle and poured three fingers of scotch into it. He quickly downed it and poured another. Knocking off a bottle was a tradition he usually reserved for the first night home after covering some bloody war for the *Tribune*. Tonight, though, was special. After listening to Rena's theory about the murders and after agreeing to help her prove it, he felt he deserved to get a bit loaded.

Pouring his third drink, he again wondered who the fuck the good-looking, tanned guy was at Simon's house. He didn't want to ask her. That's her business, he thought, as he lay down on the bed and turned on the ESPN sports channel on TV. He watched twenty minutes of a tractor-pulling contest, then fell asleep.

Chapter Thirty-three

A QUARTER TO seven the next morning Charlie woke up with a scaly taste in his mouth and a vibrating headache. The half-finished bottle of J&B was on the dresser.

He made his way into the bathroom, downed three Excedrins, and called Rena. She picked up on the first ring. "You're up bright and early," he said, opening his tote and taking out his toothpaste and brush. He told her where he was staying, and she said she'd pick him up in a half hour. Charlie then spent the next ten minutes scrubbing his teeth, trying to remove the thick film of scotch that stubbornly clung to it.

He was waiting for her by the front entrance of the motel when she pulled up. The morning was crisp and clear, and Charlie noticed the healthy pink glow on Rena's cheeks. She looks good, he thought to himself. He kissed her on the lips, tasting her lipstick. She snuggled in his arms for a second then stepped on the gas and drove back onto the highway.

They rode silently into the city of Santa Rosa and ate breakfast at a diner across from the county recorder's office. It was scheduled to open at eight-thirty, which was twenty minutes from now. Charlie and Rena ordered another cup of coffee and waited.

"You really quit, huh?" she asked.

"Yep," he said, stirring the cream into his coffee cup until the color was a milk chocolate.

"What will you do?"

"Find another job. There are other papers."

Rena sighed, nodding. *Yes, there were other papers that would be more than happy to send you off to the ends of the world to die, Charlie.* I suppose that's what you really want, isn't it? she thought.

As if reading her mind, he said, "I like what I do."

She smiled, pushing down the sadness that was springing up

inside her. Rena turned to look out the window. A Mazda pulled up in front of the recorder's office and a thin, bald-headed man got out. He went up the steps, stuck a key into the door lock, and opened it. "I think the recorder's office is now open," she said, wiping her mouth with her napkin.

Charlie tossed a few bills on the table and left the diner with Rena. They crossed the street and entered the white-bricked building.

The bald man was behind the counter carefully putting his wash-'n'-wear suit jacket onto a hanger. After brushing some dandruff flakes off his coat with his hand, he hung it up in the closet. When he saw Rena and Charlie, he grabbed a cardigan from the rack, put it on, and went over to them. "Can I help you?" he asked as he adjusted his tortoiseshell glasses around his small ears.

With the cardigan on, the man reminded Charlie of Mr. Rogers. *Welcome to my neighborhood.* "I'd like to see the original deed to the Peter McKinney property on Spring Mountain Road in Napa," Charlie said.

The bald man laughed and shook his head. "What's with that piece of hill? I get more requests about it than anything else."

"Requests from who?" Rena asked, surprised.

"There were some telephone calls about it first. A couple of different people. Nobody would give a name. Then some strange fellow came in a few weeks ago to look at the deed, same as you."

"This strange guy have a name?" Charlie asked.

"Didn't give one and I didn't ask for one."

"What did he look like?"

Mr. Rogers shrugged. "Didn't really pay attention to what he looked like either. I was too busy watching his movements. Real weird. I think he was old, though." He turned to the metal shelves in back of him and took down a black cardboard file box. He moved papers around inside it until he came to an old manila file.

"How was he acting strange?" Rena asked him.

"His eyes were queer; glazed over. He said he wanted to buy the property. I tried explaining to him that I had nothing to do with it, that I just worked here. It was hard to understand him. He was shaking, and he couldn't stand still. And when he walked, he looked like he was drunk. Real unsteady. I bet he must have downed a few before he came here."

267

"What else?" she murmured.

"What else, what?"

"What other unusual things did you notice about this man?"

"Funny that you'd ask that. He looked like he had a bad cold. His nose was all stuffed. Oh, yeah, one other thing."

"What?"

"He was real yellow looking—like the color of a ripe yam. I guess everybody has their own kind of troubles." He handed her the copy of the McKinney deed.

Rena and Charlie took it over to the window to look at it. The deed stated that the original owner of the property was a Liam O'Connor. It was purchased by him in 1880.

"Do you have the original request for the deed by Liam O'Connor?" Rena asked the clerk.

"That goes back a ways. Is it necessary to see it?" The thought of digging through piles of old boxes in the cellar didn't please him.

"It's necessary," she said.

He scratched the top of his bald head and said, "Can you come back tomorrow?"

"It shouldn't take you more than fifteen minutes to find it. If you don't mind, we'll just wait," Charlie said with an edge to his voice.

The man glared at Charlie then went into the back room. Ten minutes later he came out with an old ledger that was two feet long and several inches thick. His cardigan had a coat of dust over it, and there was sweat on his brow. "These are the requests for land in the Sonoma Napa counties in the year eighteen eighty," he said, banging the tome down on the counter.

"That many?" Rena was amazed by its size.

"If you knew your history of California, then you'd know lots of things were happening in those days." He turned the pages until he came to Liam O'Connor's request. "Here it is." The aged paper was encased in plastic.

Rena and Charlie bent over the ledger and looked at the old-fashioned quilled lettering. The Irish immigrant was twenty-five years old when he bought the land from the United States government on January 26, 1880. He came from the city of Waterford. O'Connor put down toolmaker as his occupation. The reason he wanted to purchase the land was to dig for ore. There were words scribbled on the bottom portion of the aged ledger: *Died of spotted fever on March 4, 1880.*

O'Connor had the land less than two months before he died, Charlie thought. "What kind of ore was he looking for?" he asked. "It doesn't say."

The clerk laughed. "What kind of ore do you think it was? What would make so many people purchase land in California around that time?" he said pointing to the thick volume on the counter.

"Gold!" Charlie said, suddenly understanding.

"You got it," the clerk said, wiping the sweat from his face with the sleeve of his sweater.

"Was gold ever discovered in the Napa hills?" Charlie asked.

"Sure," he said. "A large deposit was uncovered in Calistoga in the late eighteen hundreds. The Silverado and Palisades mines. People like Liam O'Connor spent their lives digging in these hills."

"Not Liam O'Connor. He died right after he bought the land."

The man pushed his glasses up on his nose and looked at the ledger. "Oh, yes, I remember. There was a typhus epidemic around that time—killed lots of people in this valley."

They thanked Mr. Rogers and left.

On the drive back to Napa Charlie was silent. Rena could tell that his head was spinning. "You're seeing a story, aren't you, Charlie?"

"Yep." He put his knee up on the dashboard and lit a cigarette. "I wonder if there's gold in them *thar* hills?"

Rena smiled. "The clerk said gold was discovered in Calistoga. That's only ten miles away from Maura's property."

"Liam O'Connor put in his request in Eighteen eighty. There's no record of him finding gold," Charlie said, letting the smoke curl out from his nose and mouth.

"That doesn't mean anything. He could have found the veins but didn't report it right away because he was frightened of poachers. Land stealing at that time was a common practice."

"True," he said. "O'Connor willed the property to his kin in Ireland. Then he died of typhus. He probably didn't even have the time to write to his family or make a new probate stating his find."

Perhaps there *was* gold on McKinney's property, Rena thought. What other reason would someone be interested in it? She glanced over at Charlie. His eyes were alive with excitement. At least *this* story wasn't in some disease-ridden jungle where he could get killed. Her veins were on fire like his. Yes, she could feel it starting to come together.

"You don't have to be at the airport for a couple of more hours. Why don't we take a look and see what's in McKinney's backyard?" he said.

"What do you know about gold, Charlie?" she asked caustically.

"Once when I was covering the Angolan War, I toured a gold mine outside of Johannesburg."

"Once, huh?"

"Once."

"That should make you an expert." Smiling, Rena headed for the McKinney property.

An hour later they had completed surveying the perimeter of the vineyards.

Sitting down on the bench outside the winery, Rena said, "What now, genius. What were you looking for?"

Charlie sat down beside her, stretched his legs outward, and rubbed his sore thigh muscles. "Something that says there's gold here. Igneous rocks maybe. There's always some traces of gold in them. Gold comes from the Earth's core."

Rena turned to him. Her face was staid. "From the Earth's core. Like where molten lava comes from?"

"Yeah. Why?"

She stood up. "I think you'd better come with me, Charlie. There's something in the vineyards that I forgot to show you."

Charlie followed her into the fields. When she came to the spring, she stopped walking and knelt down beside it.

"It's a hot spring, Charlie. Molten lava heats hot springs."

"I know." He squatted down beside her and put his hand in the water. He cupped some in his palm, brought it to his face, and sniffed. "Saline," he said.

Rena suddenly understood why Maura always went wading here. She had sensitive skin, and sometimes red blotches appeared on it. Dr. Parsons told her that blotching is a common malady of chimerism and that it affects many hermaphrodites. The warm, saltwater must have soothed her.

"Hot springs are warmed by geothermal activity," Charlie said. "Underground springs like this one are heated when molten lava escapes from the cracks in the Earth's core and finds its way up to the surface." He grinned and wiped his wet hand on his jeans. "Lava also brings gold up from the core. Usually the first

270

thing that happens after a hot spring is found is to check to see if there's gold in the same vicinity.''

Rena stood up. "I wonder if this one was ever checked."

"I'll bet you anything that Liam O'Connor checked.'' He got up from the ground and wiped the grass and mud from his jeans.

Rena nodded. She no longer had doubts about the *why*. The *who*, however, was still up for grabs.

Chapter Thirty-four

CHARLIE DROVE HER to the airport. Two hours later Rena's small plane let down in Tacoma.

Two days ago when she had called Neil Tompson, the head psychiatrist of Riverside Hospital, he was not about to discuss one of his patients with her over the phone. He would, however, begrudgingly grant her a meeting if she chose to fly up there. Rena told him that she understood and that she respected his concern about client/doctor confidentiality.

She took a cab to Browns Point overlooking the East Passage of the Puget Sound. The mist was so thick that the water was barely visible.

The cab took a left off Route 509 and wound its way up a curved, private road, away from the other residential houses. Two miles of twists and turns and the road ended abruptly at the wrought-iron gates of Riverside Hospital. The grounds were immense, covered by several acres of an emerald green, manicured lawn. In the middle loomed a large, white, Colonial-style building supported by four pillars.

Several patients wearing robes slowly wandered around the grounds. One man was walking in small circles, talking to himself. Sitting on a bench watching them were two black male aides dressed in white uniforms. They looked bored. As Rena made her way toward the house, she passed by the patient walking in circles. He looked familiar. Perhaps an actor, she thought. Yes, he was a cowboy actor who had his own TV series in the early sixties. When Westerns went out of vogue, his career took a downward plunge.

The front door was open, and she walked into a large vestibule. The floor was made of Italian marble squares, and a staircase in the middle of the entrance hall wound its way up past a large chandelier to more rooms on the second floor. Off to the right was an oak-paneled reading room with wall-to-wall books. A woman patient wearing a pink cashmere robe was sitting alone on the couch leafing through a *Vogue* magazine. French doors on the left opened up to an even larger room with a fireplace. If Rena didn't know this was a mental institution, she'd swear it was someone's estate and the patients were really weekend guests.

She had heard about these kinds of hospitals. Only the rich could afford their treatment. Confidentiality was what they were known for, and in return for that the patients, families, or employers paid them huge sums of money. Mental illness was still a stigma in today's society. Movie stars, business heads, and political leaders suffering from stress and depression could lose everything once the public got wind of their sickness. Peter McKinney was far from being a rich man; it must have taken everything he had to pay for the time Maura was here. Rena knew that insurance would not cover even a small percentage of the costs.

Directly over to the right side of the foyer was a door marked PRIVATE in black stenciled letters. Rena knocked. A woman's voice answered, "Come in."

Rena opened the door and walked into Riverside's administration office. Over at the end, two secretaries were seated at metal desks containing computer terminals. The larger, more central desk was taken up by a big-boned, middle-aged woman wearing a nurses outfit. She looked surprised when she saw Rena. "Yes?" she said.

"My name is Rena Halbrook, and I have an appointment with Dr. Tompson."

"Oh yes," she said, slightly annoyed. "He said you were coming." She picked up the phone and dialed Tompson's secretary. After she hung up, she told Rena to go upstairs to the second floor. Dr. Tompson's secretary would be at the top of the stairs waiting for her.

Rena found Tompson's secretary a lot friendlier than the large-bodied nurse downstairs. She was a pretty woman with blond hair, small white teeth, and freckles along the bridge of her nose.

sponse. "You know as well as I that she should have been closely regulated when given that kind of medication."

"Let's just say that I consulted with Dr. Frawley from time to time."

From time to time! "Those were potentially harmful drugs! She should have been personally monitored at least twice a month." *My God, the irresponsibility of this man!* Rena took a deep breath to calm herself down, then asked, "Who else worked here that knew about Maura's affliction?"

"About her being double-sexed? The entire staff and most of the patients, I suppose. This knowledge was to have been restricted just to me, my assistant, and an aide, but the hospital is small, and you know how things get around. I mean, she wasn't exactly your run-of-the-mill convalescent." Tompson picked out the lemon wedge that was floating in his Pellegrino and began sucking on it.

Rena sighed in disappointment. She had hoped the list would be narrower than that. "May I see the patient files during the time she was here?" she asked knowing what his reaction would be.

"Absolutely not!" He walked back over to his desk and put his glass down on it. "Those files are confidential and . . ."

She stood up, her face trembling with anger. "Don't hand me that shit about confidentiality! What you should be more concerned about is responsibility. You've illegally sent one of your patients drugs, and she's been taking them without any supervision. The only man who *knew* about it was a small-town doctor, and now even he's dead."

He looked shocked. "Dr. Frawley is dead? I didn't know . . ."

"No one commits these grisly acts, Doctor, without first showing signs that it was going to happen. You were her doctor. You should have kept closer tabs on her, and not pawned her off on an inexperienced man like Frawley. The only reason this hospital is in existence is to make money, so please don't insult me by using professional words like patient confidentiality. Now will you let me see those records? I'm not interested in the medical treatment she received, even though I'm sure I'd find that fascinating," she said with contempt. "All I want to know is who the patients were during the time she was hospitalized."

"This is highly irregular. I can lose my license if I divulge that information."

The fear was back in his eyes, and she liked that. "I can

promise you that this information will go no further than me at this point in time. If I don't get to see those files, I *will* contact the FDA and explain to them how you dispense drugs and how well you oversee your patients who take them. Then, my friend, I can guarantee you that you *will* lose your license."

Tompson had a bitter smile on his face as he shook his head in disbelief. He pushed the intercom button on his desk and said into it, "Miss Dewhurst, my guest, Dr. Halbrook, is on her way downstairs. Please give her access to our patient files for the year Nineteen seventy-four. Make sure they're *only* for that year." He clicked the machine off, looked at Rena, and said through tight lips, "You're a hard woman, Dr. Halbrook."

"These are hard times, Dr. Tompson," she replied, staring right back into his eyes.

Miss Dewhurst was waiting for Rena at the bottom of the stairs. She was the unfriendly, fleshy woman who was sitting behind the desk in the administrative office when Rena first came in. Without acknowledging Rena, she quickly turned and walked toward her office; the spongy soles of her white hospital shoes squeaked like hungry mice every time her feet touched down on the marbled floor. Rena followed her into the office toward the back room. Dewhurst unlocked the door with a key and went inside. A personal computer was on a desk. Lining the walls were several rows of black metal file cabinets.

Not even bothering to look at Rena, the administrative nurse said, "Would you prefer to see the files on the computer or in the original folders?"

"In the folders," Rena said.

Dewhurst bent down and unlocked a file drawer. "This contains the patients who were here in Nineteen seventy-four. Please refrain from trying to open the other drawers to look at more files. It won't do you any good. They're all locked."

As soon as she left, Rena began looking at the folders. She was in luck; there was a photograph of each patient stapled on the admittance forms. Rena went through them slowly, studying every name and every face. Some of the names she knew because they were famous: one was a well-known opera star; another was the head of a car company in Detroit. She knew him personally because he was a good friend of her father's. The patient list was small, and in a couple of minutes she came upon Maura's file. Her photo was on the front part of the folder. *How sad and alone she looked!* Her eyes were sunken into her cheeks, and they

278

looked lifeless. Perhaps she was drugged. After meeting Tompson, she wouldn't put it past him.

Rena carefully went through the file. Most of it contained things about her that she already knew: fits of violent outbursts followed by total inertia—almost to the point of being comatose. This lasted for a period of a month. She refused to see her father during that time. When he tried seeing her, she would throw fits and would have to be physically restrained. After Peter McKinney was killed in the car accident, she began to come around: her appetite returned, and she started talking in coherent sentences.

Rena scanned the rest of it. Many intricate details of Maura's life, past and present, were written down by Dr. Tompson and his head attendant. Everything was here: Maura's apprehension of the world finding out she was a hermaphrodite; her feelings toward Martin; her yearnings, her hates. Yes, everything was here, even the part about the Barbie doll she renamed Jasmine Dawn. Maura had opened up a great deal to these people.

Except there was nothing in these files that could be of any help. What the hell was she looking for anyway? A name—something that could make sense to all of this.

Just as she was about to close Maura's file, she saw it—a small notation written by her attendant. The skin on top of her skull started to pulsate. It wasn't what the note said that caused this sensation; it was the name scribbled under it. Maura's attendant was Julian Clurman. Like in Clurman Enterprises.

She was right! There was a *who* behind this.

Rena backtracked through the year '74, hoping to find more on this Clurman. The name occasionally appeared in conjunction with other patients, but there was nothing that said who the person was. Nothing in here that gave him a personality . . . a face.

There has to be more than this! she thought.

She turned her head toward the other file cabinets. *If there was more, then it just may be in these other files.* She quickly got up from the desk and went over to them. They were locked. "Shit!" she yelled, kicking at one of the metal compartments.

Miss Dewhurst walked in. She looked at Rena and scowled in disdain. "Dr. Halbrook, you were told not to touch the other files."

"I need to see these other files. Open these drawers up!" Rena said severely, pointing to the cabinets.

Miss Dewhurst's jaw tightened, and she put her hands on her

thick hips. "You promised you wouldn't go near the other files if we let you in here," she responded stubbornly.

"Open up these goddamn drawers immediately!" She was screaming now, but she didn't care.

Dr. Tompson walked in and saw the wild look on Rena's face. After a beat, he said to Miss Dewhurst, "What's going on here?"

Exasperated, the nurse replied, "She wants to see more of the files. I told her . . ."

"Please open the drawers," Rena said forcibly.

"Just what are you looking for?" Tompson asked.

"The truth about the vineyard murders," she stated.

He folded his arms to his chest and glanced at the cabinets. "It's one thing when you want to see files that are sixteen years old, it's another thing when you're asking to see our entire patient list. It would be unethical of me to let you look at any more names, Doctor."

"People are being murdered, *Doctor*!" she quickly stated, her eyes glued to his.

Tompson felt her urgency. He thought about her request for a few seconds, then said, "All right, I suppose there's nothing wrong with that if we keep this quiet."

Nurse Dewhurst, mouth open in disbelief, said, "But Dr. Tompson . . ."

"Do it," he said to her.

"But . . ."

"Do it!"

Dewhurst shook her head and clucked her tongue. She bent down and unlocked the file drawers one by one, then stepped back.

Rena leaned over and quickly opened one of the drawers. Suddenly she turned to Tompson and asked, "Does Julian Clurman still work here as an attendant?"

"Absolutely not!" he answered with contempt.

She heard his tone. "What happened to him?"

"First of all Julian is a *she*. We had to let her go. We found out that she was physically abusing some of the patients."

Rena stared at him, stunned. "A *she*?"

"Yes."

"When was she fired?"

"A year ago. Why?"

Rena didn't answer. She turned back to the files.

"What's the point in this?" Tompson said impatiently, after watching Rena go through almost all of the drawers.

Rena chose not to answer him. There were two more files to look at. So far she found nothing. She opened up the 1989 folder and scanned through the names with her finger. At the bottom of the list her finger stopped. Startled, she looked up at Tompson.

"What is it?" he asked.

"One of the patients who was here last year."

"Who?"

Her breath was heavy. "Edmond Farnsworth."

"Yes. What about him?"

"I know him. He's a friend of my father's. What was wrong with him?"

"A breakdown. He tried to kill himself. It happens frequently to men in high-level, high-pressure jobs."

"He told me that he had a heart attack last year at this time."

Tompson laughed. "Very few people will admit that they tried to take their own life. I'm sure he was just substituting another hospital for this one so he wouldn't feel embarrassed."

True, she thought. While looking through the files, she had come upon several names that she either knew personally or were business acquaintances of her father's. None of them would ever admit to why they were here.

"Edmond called me a few months ago to give me a progress report. He said he was happily married now and that he was in the wine business."

Rena looked down at Edmond's file and saw that his attendant was also Julian Clurman. "What did Julian look like, Doctor?"

He furrowed his brows, thinking. "Oh, reddish hair . . . fifty-five years old . . . tall . . . heavyset. Edmond was one of her last patients at the hospital. In fact, he played an indirect role in her dismissal."

"What happened?"

"She broke his arm. Clurman was alone with him in the room at the time it happened. She claimed he slipped on some wet tile in the bathroom. The surgeon who examined the arm told a different story. He showed us the X rays. You could see where the limb was literally twisted out of the socket until the bone snapped. A fall could not produce that kind of trauma. This made us very suspicious."

"What did Edmond say?"

"He didn't know how it happened. The man was fairly well

sedated at the time. We then checked with some of Clurman's other patients. At first they were too frightened to talk. After assurances were made, they began to lose their fear of her and started telling us about the things she did to them—verbal and physical abuse, prolonged enemas, purposely missing the veins when she gave needles. Sick things! She was promptly discharged.''

''Do you know what happened to her?''

''No, nor do I care.''

Rena glanced up at the clock on the wall. *Shit!* It was already four-twenty. The last plane to San Francisco was at four-thirty. There was no way she could make it in time. She'd have to spend the night in Tacoma. ''May I use your phone, Doctor?''

''Certainly.''

She first dialed the airlines to find out what time the earliest flight left for San Francisco tomorrow, then she called Charlie's motel. He wasn't in. She left a message for him to pick her up at eleven-thirty the next morning.

Hanging up, she thought, The *who* finally has a name. Now how the hell do I find her?

Chapter Thirty-five

MAURA PICKED UP the pay phone located outside an all-night movie theater on the corner of Sixth and Main in Los Angeles. She got the phone number for KROS radio station from the operator and dialed the number.

Near exhaustion, her body racked with fever once again, she vaguely remembered where she'd been for the last day and a half. Most of it was a blur. She remembered wandering the streets and maybe going into an all-night movie theater and falling asleep. She just wasn't sure and that frightened her more than the fever returning.

She hugged her body; the chills had come again.

The sun was setting, causing a brilliant wash of red-and-purple light to bounce off the windows of the seedy, off-white stucco buildings surrounding her. The glare was so strong that it hurt her eyes, and she had to cover them. When the operator picked up, she cleared her throat, then asked for the name of the station's owner. After she was given the name of Bud Masterly, she then asked for the personnel department.

"Personnel," the woman's voice on the other end said.

"Yes, this is Federal Express. I have a delivery for a Miss . . . let me see . . . a Miss Rena Halbrook. The address on the envelope is partially obscured. I can make out that it's somewhere in the Brentwood area from the zip code, but the street and house numbers are illegible."

"I'm afraid I can't give out that information over the phone. Why don't you call the sender for the address?"

"I am. The sender is a Mr. Bud Masterly, and the address of the sender is KROS. I was transferred by someone in your company to get the info from personnel. If there's a problem, I'll be more than happy to return the package. Make up your mind on this, okay? I don't have all day." She sounded impatient.

"No, that won't be necessary. Bud Masterly did you say?"

"That's what I said." She could hear the nervousness in the woman's voice.

After several seconds the woman in personnel got back on the line. "One hundred and three Canyon View Drive."

"Thank you," Maura said, about to hang up.

"Except she isn't there. She's out of town."

Her heart sank. "Do you know where she can be located?"

"Yes. She's staying up in the Napa Valley. Her father owns a winery. Let me get you the address."

Maura hung up. She already knew the address. Banging her fist against the wall in frustration, she took a deep breath to control herself. Now was not the time to lose it. She had to think. Could she chance going up there? She had to. There was no longer any choice.

The clicking of the metal started racing through her head once again. The panic feeling was setting in and so was the headache. *No, there was no longer a choice!* Last night she did the one thing she feared most; she had fallen asleep. Had she killed again? She didn't know. There were just fogged-over images of the last twenty-four hours.

She put more change into the slot of the phone machine and

tried calling Uncle Wiggly. No one answered. *What happened to him?*

She quickly walked outside and flagged down a taxi. Her body was soaked in sweat from the panic attack and fever. "LAX," she said as she got in.

"What airline?" the driver asked. Through the rearview mirror he could see how white and damp her face was. "You okay?"

"Yes," she said, taking out the Xanax and two Darvocets from her bag. "Drop me off at Terminal One." A bus was safer, but she couldn't afford the time it would take to get up there. She had wasted too much time as it was. With luck, she wouldn't be recognized.

She undid the cap on the vial and popped one milligram of Xanax in her mouth along with the Darvocets and swallowed them. In a few minutes the horrible feeling of anxiety would shrink back into the recesses of her psyche and the fear would subside. Until then, she shut her eyes and tightly clutched onto the folds of the backseat as the cab made its way through the rush-hour traffic on the 405 Freeway.

At the Western ticket booth she was told that the plane leaving in a few minutes for San Francisco was sold out but that there were several seats still open on the next flight, which departed an hour later. Maura paid for the ticket in cash. She rode up the escalator and toward a line of people that were making their way past the metal detector. In front of her was a man with his arm around his young daughter's waist. Maura watched as he lovingly squeezed the girl toward him. He was telling her something and she started giggling. He'd say something else and she'd laugh some more.

A wave of sadness descended upon Maura. If only her father had been that loving to her. Then the feeling of hate came over her. It always did when she thought about Peter. She watched the girl with her father make their way toward the departure gate until they were out of sight. Sighing deeply, she hoped she'd be with Rena soon and this horrible nightmare would finally come to an end.

She landed in San Francisco at seven in the evening.

Maura saw the two uniformed officers as soon as she came out of the arrival gate at the airport. They were standing next to the entrance holding a composite drawing of a woman's face and watching the passengers as they disembarked from the plane she was just on. Their eyes were scrutinizing the faces and the builds on the women. Her hand went quickly into the pocket of her sweater and clutched the vial of Placidyls. Looking straight ahead, Maura walked by them. She was shivering from the fever, and she prayed they wouldn't notice.

One of the officers glanced her way then looked down at the drawing. From the corner of her eyes she could see a wisp of suspicion cross his face, then it quickly disappeared, and his eyes went back to scanning the crowd.

She let go of the vial. If the officers had approached her, she would have swallowed the pills. Then she realized they would have gotten her to a hospital and had her stomach pumped before the Placidyls would have done any good. No, the best thing to do if trapped was to end it by attacking them. They would shoot her. There would be a flash of pain, then it would be over. The thought of how good death would feel comforted her as she made her way out of the terminal.

FIVE

Chapter Thirty-six

S AN FRANCISCO WAS wet and cold tonight.

Maura spent most of the time wandering the streets of North Beach and going into all-night Italian coffeehouses to keep warm. Whenever she lingered too long and a proprietor got suspicious, she'd leave and find another espresso joint. Eventually she went into an X-rated movie house open on Broadway. Tired and weak, her mind still fogged over, she climbed the stairs leading up to the empty balcony and fell into a deep sleep in the back row.

She awoke three hours later from the touch of someone's hand on her breast. Maura looked up and saw a grubby, middle-aged man sitting next to her. His fly was open and he was quickly stroking his hard penis while squeezing her breast with dirt-caked fingers. Grunting sounds emanated from his throat, and the stench of his breath was nauseating.

Fuck me, Jack. Fuck me! came from the sound track on the screen.

Just as she pushed his hand away, he ejaculated. He released a deep groan and the milky liquid squirted through his hand and onto her dress.

Oh, hump me! Ooooh, yes, yes!

Maura cringed in horror. The mist over her head lifted. A rage, deeper than she'd ever known before, erupted within her whole body. She clawed at the man's face with her jagged nails. He let out a piercing scream as strips of skin were ripped from his face. Again and again she tore at him. When he instinctively put his hands up to protect himself, she clawed at his head, his arms, his body. Animal sounds were coming from her mouth, and her lips were covered with foam.

Something inside her was telling her to stop, that she was going to kill him if she didn't, but she couldn't stop. This beast had defiled her. Her eyes were glaring with rage. *Only Martin! Only Martin!*

The man stood up and tried to run. His vision blurred by the salty blood that was pouring into his eyes from the head wounds, he stumbled and fell across the seats. He got up, groping blindly in front of him. As Maura tried to grab him by his coat, he fell headfirst over the brass railing of the balcony. He let out a short yelp. A second later there was a thud, then screams from the few customers that were seated in the orchestra.

Maura looked over the railing. The man lay between the aisles, and his feet were dangling in a strange position over a worn velvet seat. There was no movement, but painful moans were coming from his mouth. Several frightened people ran out of the side "Exit" doors. The manager, holding a flashlight, went over to the stilled figure. He looked down at him then looked up, shining the light in Maura's direction. She covered her face with her hands and raced up the aisle until she got to the balcony stairs. An usher was coming up the steps. Maura ran down past him.

Do it to me, Jack. You're so big. Soooo big!

She pushed open the tainted brass railing on the glass door and raced out into the streets. There was an ache in her rib cage, but she wouldn't stop running until she was several blocks away from that theater.

When there was no strength left in her, Maura grabbed onto a lamppost and bent down, fighting desperately to catch her breath. Her throat felt as if it were on fire. When she finally looked up, she saw that dawn, the color of steel wool, was just rising over the city.

Where am I? she thought.

She glanced up at the street sign. Van Ness Avenue. That was good because Van Ness turned into Highway 101 further north. She needed 101 to get to Napa. Then she noticed the wet, sticky substance on her skirt and her stomach churned in disgust. Again that feeling of rage. *Fucking animal! I hope I killed him!* She grabbed a newspaper that swirled by her and frantically wiped the semen from her clothes.

A shudder went through her as she suddenly remembered that she left the tote with her money in the theater. She put her hands in the pockets of her sweater and prayed that the pills were still there. They were. But what was she going to do without money? How could she get to Napa? Maura leaned against the post and shut her eyes. *Please, just let me die!*

She reached for the vial containing the Placidyls. So easy, she thought. Lafayette Park was only a couple of blocks away. Find a deserted spot in the foliage where no one goes. Swallow those flaming red beauties. It will all be over in less than an hour.

Maura took the vial from her pocket and twisted off the child-proof cover. While pouring out a handful of tablets, she suddenly heard a noise and looked up. What she saw over by the street corner brought tears to her eyes: an old pickup truck with wooden sides was parked against the curb. A dark Mexican with a pencil-thin mustache and ripped Levi's was jacking up the front right end while another man with long sideburns was taking out the spare tire from the back. They pulled off the flat and began replacing it with the good one.

Tears stung her eyes as she began walking over to them. When she got closer, she could see a woman in the back of the pickup cradling a baby in her arms. A small girl, about twelve, with blunt Indian features, was also in the back. They stared at her as she came toward them.

Then she could smell the familiar odor coming from the truck, and the tears ran freely down her face. It was the pungent, thick aroma of fermented grapes.

These people were field-workers, and the nose of their truck was pointing toward the north. They were going to the wineries, probably to pick the late harvest.

Take me with you! Oh, please God, take me with you!

Then the little girl smiled at her. Then one of the men holding the lug nuts looked up from the wheelbase and touched his straw hat with his greasy hand in greeting.

Maura smiled back, and she could taste the salt of her own tears in her open mouth.

Chapter Thirty-seven

A T ELEVEN-THIRTY THE next morning Charlie picked Rena up at the Napa airport. When they saw each other, they hugged tightly.

"Want some breakfast?" he asked as he breathed in her familiar smell.

"No," she said, breaking away. "I *would*, however, like to pay a visit to Edmond Farnsworth."

They had talked on the phone last night.

"Let's go," he said.

They drove the short distance to Edmond's office.

The middle-aged secretary at Farnsworth's high-tech winery told Charlie and Rena that Edmond was not in today because of a cold.

"Gee, that's too bad," Rena said.

Charlie looked at Rena. She was tired, but he could tell adrenaline was flowing through her veins.

"Yes. He's been living on decongestants. He could barely swallow, his throat's so sore."

When they got back in the Rover, Charlie touched Rena on the shoulder and said, "Do you know where this guy lives?"

"Somewhere off of Dry Creek Road in Heraldsburg. Simon told me his house would look terrific sliding off a Malibu cliff during a rainstorm."

Ten minutes later they drove up to the white, square monolith on top of a hill. Old Simon was right on about this place, Charlie thought; it was pure Southern-California hip. The trim on the large stucco house was turquoise and peach, the hot colors of *this* year. Bubbled windows, resembling NASA space helmets, bulged out from all sides like cysts.

Rena parked the Rover off to the side of the road. They got out and walked the twenty feet to the house. The sun reflected off the white stucco, hurting Charlie's eyes, and he wished he had brought his sunglasses with him.

When Rena pushed the pearl button of the bronze chime it played the first two bars of "Buttons and Bows." Charlie looked at Rena and smirked.

A black housekeeper, dressed in a cotton uniform with white lace, answered the door. "Is Mr. Farnsworth at home?" Rena asked.

The woman's uncertain eyes quickly darted from Charlie to Rena. "Yes, ma'am. Did you have an appointment?"

"No, but it's important that we talk to him."

A wary look came over her face. "I'm sorry, but Mr. Farnsworth is not feeling very well. He's sleeping."

"Is Mrs. Farnsworth here then?" Rena asked patiently.

"No ma'am. She went to the club for tennis lessons. Can I give them a message?"

Rena took a deep breath, then said, "Would you please tell Mr. Farnsworth that I'm Simon Halbrook's daughter, and that I know all about Riverside Hospital."

"Simon's daughter . . . Riverside Hospital. I'll tell him," she said, closing the door.

"Do you think he'll bite?" Charlie asked her as they made their way back to the car.

"He has no choice," she said.

They drove the rest of the way in silence.

Simon's manservant approached Rena just as she entered the house. "Your father has taken your daughter to Palo Alto with him. He told me to tell you that they'd be back later this evening."

Rena smiled. Perhaps the fracture between them was beginning to knit together.

The servant continued. "Oh yes, a Mr. Farnsworth called for you. He'd like you to phone him as soon as possible." He handed her the telephone number on a slip of paper.

Rena looked nervously at Charlie.

"I guess he bit," he said, winking at her.

They went into the den. She picked up the phone, took a long nervous breath, then dialed.

Farnsworth's sick, raspy voice answered. "Hello?" he said weakly.

"Edmond, this is Rena Halbrook."

There was a long pause on the other end. Finally he said, "I heard you wanted to see me."

He tried sounding jovial, but she could hear the anxiousness in his voice. She cleared her throat trying to hide her own jitters. "I need to talk to you about Riverside Hospital," she said.

"I'd certainly *like* to talk to you about that." He sounded cautious. "Would it be asking too much if you came back here again? We'll have lunch on the patio. It's only a ten-minute drive."

She looked at Charlie. "Yes, it's possible," she said. "I'd like to bring the man who was with me."

"No, I want to talk just with you," he quickly stated.

Again she looked at Charlie. He had his ear to the phone and shook his head, no.

"Yes, I'll meet with you alone," she answered Farnsworth.

Charlie closed his eyes and groaned.

"I'll be at your house in a few minutes," she said.

"Good." Edmond sounded relieved. "I think you can understand my need for privacy."

Rena hung up. Charlie punched the pillow on the feather down couch. "Thanks," he said, pissed.

"I couldn't take the chance, Charlie. Farnsworth won't talk if I go with you. Mental illness is an embarrassment with most people."

He put his hands on her shoulders. "This old man may be more than just an embarrassment. The FBI is one hundred feet down the road sweating their asses off in a two-by-four van. Let me talk to them."

"No," she said moving away from him and toward the door. "I'll be back in an hour."

She was out the door before Charlie could say anything more to try and change her mind. He stood there until he heard the engine of the Rover and then the crunch of gravel as Rena drove down the hill. "Goddamn it!" he screamed, kicking the edge of the antique couch, putting a chip in its mahogany leg. No, he couldn't let her go alone. Not after what she told him about this Clurman creep.

He rushed over to the window and looked outside for another car. There were several rows of automobiles belonging to the employees over in the winery's parking lot. Then he saw the butt of Simon's Mercedes in the garage by the side of the château. He glanced in the direction of the white circular pad; the helicopter was gone. Simon must have used it to take Cathy to Palo Alto, he thought.

Charlie ran into the kitchen and found Simon's manservant. His sleeves were rolled up and he was sitting at the kitchen table polishing the silver. "Do you have the keys to the Mercedes in the garage?" Charlie asked tensely.

Simon Halbrook told the old man this morning not to cater to Charlie if he came back to the house. He was just about to tell the man standing over him that he didn't have the keys when he saw the somber look in Charlie's eyes. Instinctively the servant knew he'd better keep his mouth shut and just give him what he wanted. If he didn't this grim-faced man looked like he would rip the kitchen apart trying to find them. He got up, shuffled quickly over to the pantry, and opened the door. Inside there were several sets of keys on hooks. He took the ones with the Mercedes emblem and quietly dropped them into Charlie's waiting hand.

Without saying thanks, Charlie ran through the marbled hallways and out the front door.

The garage was a large structure, almost as big as an airplane hangar. It housed Simon's priceless car collection, which included a '65 Shelby Cobra, a '52 Cunningham Continental, and a '48 Kurtis. All kept in mint cherry condition, never driven, and worth a bloody fortune.

Charlie walked out of the bright sunlight and into the darkness of the huge carport. He went around to the driver's door of the Mercedes. As he was about to stick the key in the lock, he heard a noise in back of him—the sound of footsteps scraping gently over concrete. He turned around, just in time to see the flat, rusty metal from a spade coming directly toward his face. His instincts, honed in the streets of Brooklyn and 'Nam, made him duck. The shovel crashed into the door window a half-inch from his ear, shattering glass and sending slivers into Charlie's face. The pain felt like tiny razor cuts, and his arm automatically came up to his eyes to protect them. He threw himself to the floor and rolled over until he felt the rubber tire of the Mercedes.

Again the shovel came flying in his direction, this time hitting the rear fender right over his head. Charlie wanted to open his eyes, but he could feel the powdered glass clinging to his lids. He brushed at them trying to clear his face as he rolled over trying to get away from the spade. Then he felt something hard against his body. Reaching out, he touched the polished frame of the Kurtis.

Shit! he was trapped between both cars.

There was no choice; he had to see if he was to survive. The glass clung onto his brow, his lashes, but he opened his eyes anyway. For a split second he saw something red hovering above him, like the color of a cable sweater; then the shovel was coming down at him again. Charlie moved his head to the right, but it was too late. The first thing he felt was the *swish* of air as the flat end came down, then excruciating pain in his right temple. There was a wet, tickling sensation on the side of his face from the blood pouring out of the wound.

Again Charlie tried opening his eyes; except this time he couldn't. For a brief second he smelled his blood intermixing with the odor of oil, grease, and rubber coming from the garage. Then the smell was gone and there was nothing.

Chapter Thirty-eight

RENA RANG EDMOND's doorbell. This time the chimes played "Moon River." In the distance she could see Blythe lobbing tennis balls with a good-looking young man in their private court across from their Olympic-sized swimming pool. Why was she here? She was supposed to be at the club.

The white tennis outfit Blythe was wearing darkened her tan to the color of deep mahogany. Her body was tight and lithesome. Rena watched her serve and hit an ace, then scream with delight. The young man, as tan as she was, wore a McEnroe bandanna around his forehead. He threw up his racquet in mock disbelief and moaned. They both laughed.

Why was she here? Damn! She took a deep breath, trying to calm her nerves. She had hoped to be alone with Edmond.

The door opened. This time it was not the maid who answered, but Edmond Farnsworth himself.

She was shocked by his appearance. He was bent over and his skin and eyeballs were the color of dry mustard. Wiping his red nose with a used, crumbled tissue he held in his liver-spotted hand, he said, "Come in. Come in." He was wearing a white terry bathrobe with his initials on the breast pocket.

She went inside.

He turned around and shuffled unsteadily into the living room. Rena followed behind. "Excuse my appearance," he said. "I caught this damn cold a couple of weeks ago, and I can't seem to shake it."

The living room was painted a pale peach and was sunken two steps. Large, white silk couches covered most of the bleached-oak floors. The abstract paintings, like hazy pastels, hung on the walls and complemented the color of the house. The room reminded Rena of a display window in a trendy furniture store on Robertson Boulevard. There was nothing in here that felt warm and lived-in; nothing about it that said people laughed, ate, and made love here.

"Have a seat," he said, blowing his nose.

Rena sat down on the couch, and Edmond took the matching silk chair. When he crossed his legs, Rena noticed that he wasn't wearing pajama bottoms underneath the robe. His legs were very white, spindly, and freckled.

Rena took a deep breath to stem her nervousness and said, "Edmond . . ."

He waved his hand at her, as if to say let's drop the pretenses. "What about Riverside Hospital?" he said sharply. His lips and jaw were impulsively moving, almost as if he had no control over them.

"You were a patient there for several months in 1989."

Edmond didn't say anything. He just stared at her with yellowed eyes. His cheeks continued to move spasmodically, and he licked his dry, cracked lips.

"You were treated for deep depression."

"You must be mistaken. I had a triple bypass in 1989." His voice was nasal from his stuffed nose.

"I don't think so. Veins would have been taken from your legs and transplanted in your chest for a triple bypass. That would have left deep scars on your legs. I see no scars, Edmond," she said, pointing to his naked calf that was crossed over his leg.

Edmond quickly uncrossed his legs and tucked them back into

his robe. "What is it you want?" There was something resigned about his tone.

"It was you that went to the county recorder's office in Santa Rosa."

"What?" He flinched.

"The clerk there said that a man your age was inquiring about the McKinney property. I'm also looking right now at the physical symptoms he was talking about—shaking; unable to walk straight; yellow, jaundiced skin."

"What the hell are you saying?" He was aggravated.

"You're on some form of chlorpromazine or antidepressant—perhaps both. Aren't you?"

"What?"

"What kind of medication are you taking? Thorazine? What else?"

"I don't see . . . ."

"You're having adverse side effects, and I strongly suggest that you discontinue using them and get yourself some proper help."

"What *are* you talking about?" he said angrily, wiping his nose with the tissue.

"You don't have a cold, Edmond. A stuffy nose and a sore throat are reactions to some tranquilizers and antidepressants. So is jaundice. That's why your skin is so yellow. You have no muscle control in your face, and you can't even walk a straight line. If you don't stop taking these drugs, there's a possibility that you could go into convulsions or a coma. Who prescribed the medications that you're taking? Dr. Tompson at Riverside?"

"No, I . . . ."

"Rena!" a voice said from behind, interrupting Edmond.

She turned around. Standing at the French doors leading in from the tennis court was Blythe. Her white blouse was soaked with perspiration. She was holding the tennis racquet and wiping the sweat from her face with a terry wristband she wore on her arm. She smiled at Rena. Her hazel eyes were animated. "What a lucky break that I decided to have a tennis lesson here rather than the club. Why didn't you let me know that you were coming? I would have canceled it."

Rena stood up and tried to match Blythe's smile but couldn't. She could feel her heart racing in her chest like it was trying to find a way to get out. "I came to talk with Edmond," she said, staring at the tall, slim woman standing in front of her.

"Oh," she said, walking over to the bar. "Business?"

298

"No, not business," Rena replied.

Blythe took a glass from the shelf and filled it with ice. "Would you like a drink?"

"No, thank you," Rena said.

Pouring Evian into her glass, she quickly gulped it down and then refilled it again. "Would you like one, sweetheart?" she asked Edmond, gesturing to a clean glass.

Edmond, mouth twitching, looked away from her and shook his head.

"Maybe I should leave you two alone?" Blythe said, looking at her husband and then at Rena.

"That would be fine," Rena said, trying to control her voice.

Blythe looked at her through half-shut eyes. "No, on second thought, I'll stay." Her eyes were almost playful, and again she broke into a smile. "Does this talk have anything to do with me?"

"I'm not really sure yet. I was just telling Edmond that he should stop taking the chlorpromazine and antidepressant medication and seek proper help. He's having a terrible reaction to them. What do you think?"

The smile on Blythe's face disappeared into a tight, thin line, but her eyes still had that amused look in them. She walked over to where Edmond was sitting, put her hand lovingly on his shoulder and squeezed it. "It's all right, darling," she said to him. Then she looked up at Rena and asked, "What are we talking about?"

"Let's start first with Riverside Hospital. Why lie about Edmond being there?"

She rubbed her husband's back. He was now hunched over in the chair. She said, "Why do you think? Edmond sold his computer business two years ago because of the pressure. He was suffering from a mild form of depression and admitted himself to Riverside for help."

"That's not true," Edmond said very slowly with anger. "I tried to kill myself, and my family had me committed."

Blythe glared at him and removed her hand from his back. "There was no reason to tell her that."

"No?" he said, smiling. "Why not? We have nothing to hide, do we?"

Even in his slurred speech Rena could pick up the sarcasm.

"No," she said looking hard at Rena. "We don't have anything to hide. After Edmond left Riverside, he sold his business and bought the winery. Wine was what he cared about most in this world. That's what he should have been doing all along. He built Farnsworth Wines into a profitable business in the space of one year. He's thinking of going public with the company. How much do you think the stock would be worth if Wall Street knew that the chairman of the board of Farnsworth Wines suffered from a severe mental illness and that he was suicidal? Now can you understand why we didn't advertise his sickness?''

"Yes, I can. Riverside makes a fortune off their patients from this form of subterfuge.'' All of a sudden this was all beginning to make sense. Rena took a deep breath and thought carefully about the next thing she was going to say. It was a long shot. Right or wrong she decided to go for it. "How did you two really meet, Blythe?''

"What?'' she blustered.

"You were working at Riverside when you met, weren't you?''

Blythe put her hand back on Edmond's shoulder and twisted the terry cloth robe in her fingers. "So?''

"You were an attendant there. In fact, you worked at that hospital for almost twenty years. You were also an attendant when Maura McKinney was a patient, right?''

"I don't remember." Her lips were trembling, and there was an angry look in her eyes.

"Oh, I think you do. You look a little different than the way Dr. Tompson described you and you changed your name, but it's you all right! What did you do to yourself? Have a face-lift? Lose weight? A tummy tuck? What? You look fifteen or twenty years younger than you really are." She saw Blythe's eyes and wondered how smart it had been coming here alone. She turned to Edmond. "Why were you so interested in purchasing Maura's property?''

"Was I?'' he said. There was a hint of a bitter smile around Edmond's dry mouth. He was enjoying watching his wife being confronted.

"Yes. You also sent several letters to Donald Kaplow, Maura's attorney, inquiring about the sale of the property. Except you used the name Clurman Enterprises.''

Edmond laughed, shaking his head. Turning to his wife, he said, "You think you're so smart, don't you? Nobody will ever suspect." He licked his dry lips. "My God!" He laughed again.

"Shut up!" she screamed at Edmond. She moved away from

him and glared at Rena, her fists curled up. "How did you know that Edmond used the name Clurman Enterprises?"

Rena didn't know how far she wanted to go with this. Blythe was not supposed to have been here. Except she was, and there was nothing she could do about it now. Blythe was a sociopath—there was no doubt in her mind about that. The phoniness she had always felt about Blythe was now making sense. Sociopaths don't have feelings the way normal people do. They mimic voice inflections and act out emotions so they'll seem normal to the rest of society. Well, let's see how far our sociopath will let me take this, Rena thought to herself, taking a deep breath to gather up her nerve. "Clurman is your maiden name. I found it in Maura's file at Riverside Hospital. I searched through it to see who was taking care of Maura during her incarceration there. Julian Clurman. That was in nineteen seventy-four. I then sifted through the files until I came to nineteen eighty-nine, the year you *claimed* Edmond had his bypass surgery. Again your name popped up—this time as *his* nurse. Before I left, I had a talk with Dr. Tompson about you. He said they let you go. That you had been physically abusing some of the patients."

"That's a lie!" she screamed. "Tompson hated me. I knew too much about what was going on at the hospital, and he wanted me out of the way. He stole money, forged checks! He was a pig. Always trying to put his hands on me!" Her voice was shrill, but her eyes had a dead look to them.

"That's not why they wanted you out. The hospital received too many complaints about you. They questioned your stability," Rena said.

Blythe quickly changed the subject. "We have a right to privacy!" she said with a guttural voice. "My husband was also in his rights to inquire about the McKinney property. There's no law against that!"

"What's on that land that makes you want it so badly?" Rena asked Edmond.

He snickered. "Ask my lovely wife. She's the one who was hounding me to buy it. I could care less about the property. Always badgering me about it . . . never letting up. This medicine she keeps giving me . . . I don't even know what I'm taking. Sometimes I can't even think straight." He held his face in his hands; his fingers quivering uncontrollably.

Rena turned to his wife. Blythe's hazel eyes, dead as coal, stared back at her. *Yes, a sociopath!* "Maura's ancestor, Liam

O'Connor, was a gold miner. Is that what's on the property? Is it gold?" Blythe didn't answer her, and suddenly Rena knew she was right. "There *is* gold, isn't there! How did you know about it? Did Maura tell you that? Did she tell you about it when she was a patient at Riverside? She opened up at the hospital and told you and Dr. Tompson everything. Wait a minute! Maura couldn't have known there was gold on the property, or she would have done something about it. Maura never cared about the vineyards, and it would have been all right with her if they were destroyed to get the gold out. If Maura didn't tell you then how did you know?"

Again Blythe said nothing. She stared at Rena with hateful eyes, and her lips were curled in a sneer.

Suddenly Rena got a chill down her spine. "If Maura told you everything about herself, then you knew about her doll, Jasmine Dawn, and also about the diary of her ancestor, the Baron de Montret."

Edmond looked up at his wife and said, "What is she talking about?"

Not answering, Blythe scowled at him.

So Edmond didn't have anything to do with this, Rena suddenly realized. "Weren't you afraid of someone finding out who you were?" she said to Blythe. "I'm sure Dr. Frawley would have recognized you—even with your changes. He was also familiar with Riverside Hospital and the staff since he's the one who took Maura up there and worked with Dr. Tompson all these years." Then it hit Rena: Frawley was dead. How could he identify anybody?

Blythe slowly walked toward her.

Christ, was Frawley murdered? By who? Blythe was with Edmond at Mustards Grill the night he died. Maura couldn't possibly have been in Napa.

Hey, wait a minute!

Then the pieces started coming together in her head, and Rena suddenly realized that she made a big mistake in coming here alone. A very big mistake.

Chapter Thirty-nine

THE CONCRETE GROUND slid over his cheek, scraping it raw. Bits of rock and debris were cutting into his skin. Someone was dragging him by his feet. Then the smell of dampness and sweet wine fermenting. Then the feel of hard stone against his body. His head was bouncing down rough stairs now, bruising his ear. The smell of dank air was getting stronger. The sound of dripping water. *Who's dragging me?* Charlie thought through a fogged brain as the blackness closed in around him again.

He awoke in darkness. The ground was wet and hard. In the distance he could hear footsteps fading away. His body ached and his face felt raw. When he touched his cheek with his hand, it stung badly. His mind was disjointed and his forehead burned. *Where am I?* he thought. *Everything is so fucking dark.*

Charlie sat up. His clothes were soaked and smelled of wine. He put his hand to his forehead and felt the wound from the shovel. It wasn't deep, but it would require stitches. *Lucky I had moved my head when it came down or I would have taken the blow full-force.* That thought made Charlie cringe.

He reached out and felt the rough wall behind him. Then he felt wooden casks stacked up over to the side. It was a wine cellar, he realized. *Whose wine cellar? Who dragged me down here?*

Then he remembered the footsteps. The sound had come from the right. Charlie stood up. A rush of dizziness overtook him. He waited until the feeling passed, then slowly groped his way in the direction of the sound.

He bumped against a long table and several wooden cases of wine while following the configuration of the tunnel. In a few minutes he saw a glimmer of sunlight in front of him. Ignoring the pain in his bruised legs, he limped over toward it.

The light was coming from up above him now. There were

stone steps in front of him, and he took them two at a time. An iron gate stopped him from going any farther. *It's some kind of a cave that's made into a wine cellar.* Charlie shook the gate, but it was locked. He could see trees and bushes outside.

Shit! Where the fuck am I?

Charlie screamed, "Hey . . . anybody! Get me out of here!" He shook the gate with all his might, making it rattle loudly. He screamed over and over again, until he heard a sound coming from the other side. Footsteps were shuffling slowly toward him. Charlie backed away from the gate, adrenaline raging through his big frame.

Then he saw a shadow of a man, then the man himself, and Charlie sighed with relief. It was Simon's manservant. The old man put his head up to the gate and peeked in.

"It's me," Charlie said. "Where am I?"

"In Mr. Halbrook's wine cellar. Mr. Halbrook would be very disturbed if he knew you were in here."

"Do you have the key to this thing?"

"Yes, it's in the cupboard. I hope you didn't touch any of his wines. Some of them are very rare."

Charlie grasped the bars in his hands and put his face close to where the old servant stood. "Get-the-keys-and-get-me-the-fuck-out-of-here!" Charlie shouted, punctuating every word.

The old man said, "You don't have to yell, sir. I'll be back in a minute. Please don't touch the '52 Le Romanee Jadot. It's Mr. Halbrook's favorite." With that he turned and slowly marched back to the house for the keys.

Chapter Forty

THE OLD PICKUP truck with the wooden sides turned off Route 29 in St. Helena and drove to the back of the Exxon station on the corner of Pope Street. The two Mexican men got out of the front seat, went around to the back, and let down the wood slats.

Maura was asleep in the back of the truck, her head resting on a muslin sack filled with old clothes. The Mexican woman was breast-feeding the infant, and the older girl was reading an Archie and Veronica comic book in Spanish.

The man with the ripped jeans and thin mustache leaped up on the bed of the truck and shook Maura. He had to joggle her several times before she awoke. Her face was lemon-colored and clammy sweat clung to her brow. She opened her eyes and saw the man looking down on her. Slowly she sat up. Her head felt fuzzy. She also felt cold, the kind that cut deep into the marrow and that no amount of warmth could make go away.

Oh, God, I'm real sick, she thought.

The Mexican helped her down from the truck. She thanked him and stood on the sidewalk, shivering, as she watched them drive off. Before she fell asleep, the woman with the baby had told her in Spanish that her husband, the one with the thin mustache, and his brother had jobs picking the late harvest in the southern part of Napa. They agreed to drop her off in St. Helena.

While standing there, Maura realized her skirt was damp and she smelled of urine. She had wet herself. Yes, she was sick, and the fever refused to leave her aching body. She grasped onto the back of the garage and touched her moist head.

Where am I? She looked around. Suddenly she recognized the place.

I'm so close to my home. Spring Mountain Road was only a few streets down. Five miles more up the mountain and she *would* be home. Except she knew she could never go back there again. Not ever. Not anymore. Once again she touched the pockets of her sweater to make sure the pills were still there. They were.

With an unsteady gait, she walked over to Highway 29 and looked north. How many miles was it to the Alexander Valley? That's where Rena was. Too many, she thought. But she had come so far. No, she couldn't quit. Not now. Maybe she could get a ride. It was only twenty minutes away by car.

Then the road started to swirl and she could feel herself falling. She was standing next to a grocery-store window and grabbed onto its rim for support. Slowly she let herself slide gently down on one knee. The chills were stronger now, and she felt nauseous. *Oh please dear sweet God, let me make it! I've come so far!*

Henry Jenkins was putting away cans of Campbell's chicken noodle soup, chunky style, on the top shelf in the grocery store when he happened to gaze out the window. He turned his head, just in time to see the pale woman with dark hair and sunglasses fall to the ground. Jenkins, who had celebrated his sixty-eighth birthday two days before, climbed down the ladder as fast as he could and rushed outside.

The woman was down on one knee, as if in a praying position, with her fingertips touching her bowed head. Jenkins knew she was sick and not genuflecting. Not thinking about his bum knee with the shrapnel still in it from a World War II Japanese sniper's bullet, he knelt down next to her and put his hand on her shoulder. "You okay, lady?"

Maura moved her hand away from her face and slowly looked up. When she saw who it was, she quickly turned away. She had known Mr. Jenkins all her life. She and her father had bought their groceries from him. It had been years since they last saw each other, and hopefully he didn't recognize her. Bracing herself against the wall, she slowly got up off the ground. Her feet were wobbly, but she had to get away from him, he mustn't see her face. Keeping her body turned in the other direction, she mumbled something about slipping and that she would be fine.

Jenkins stood on the sidewalk watching her weave down the street. He scratched at the white stubble on his chin, thinking. Oh, her hair was a different color and she had her eyes covered by those dark glasses, but he knew who she was all right. He may be getting old, but goddamn if he would ever forget the prettiest girl that ever grew up in St. Helena. The TV said that she was some kind of sexual freak—an abnormality they called it—but he didn't believe them. Ever since Cronkite retired, the news on the TV had gone straight downhill by showing all that titillating stuff. Jenkins watched her for a few more minutes until she passed a clump of trees that blocked his view. He then went back into his store. He had always liked Maura, but the FBI man on television said that if anyone saw her that they should immediately call the police. Jenkins, being a man of the law, did exactly that. He dialed Pinky's number. A police rookie, Ricky Belson, answered and said that Pinky was away from the office.

"Well, when you see him, tell him that Maura McKinney, as big as life, is walkin' north down Highway 29."

"You're putting me on!" the rookie said, jumping out of his seat.

"Ricky, the only place I ever put you on was over my knee fifteen years ago when I caught you stealing a box of pretzels from my store. Now you give the chief the message, you hear?"

After hanging up on old man Jenkins, Ricky threw up his arms and let out a squeal followed by a "hallel*uuu*jah maamaa!" His freckled face was flushed with elation. Of all the lucky things to happen to him. Maura McKinney was ten minutes away and good ol' fat-ass Pinky was nowhere around to get all the credit.

He brushed back his long, dark, curly hair with his hand, put on his hat, grabbed the single-barrel, twelve-gauge shotgun from off the shelf, and ran out the door to the Ford Bronco with the police insignia on its sides.

As he put the clutch in reverse, Ricky giggled, thinking that by six o'clock tonight the whole damn country would see him on television and know his name.

Chapter Forty-one

"**Y**OU KILLED ALL those people, didn't you?" Rena suddenly said to Blythe. Her throat was dry from fear. "It wasn't Maura. It never *was* Maura."

Blythe stopped walking toward Rena. Standing several feet away from her, she hissed, "How dare you say something like that to me!"

From the corner of her eye, Rena could see Edmond sitting on the chair, licking his parched lips. He looked confused and frightened. "How did you do it?" Rena asked. "I know you were never here when the murders took place in the other states. You seemed to always be out of town. When that truck driver was mutilated in Washington, you said you were in Palm Springs.

I believed you because of the tan you had when I saw you again at Mustards Grill.''

"Ha! You were never in Palm Springs," Edmond said, trying to get out of the chair. His hands shook so badly that he slipped back down again.

"Shut up, you idiot!" she snapped at Edmond. "You have no proof!" she said turning back to Rena. Her face was distorted with anger, but her eyes remained dead.

"She wasn't in Palm Springs. I was there alone. She said to tell everybody that she went there with me, but it wasn't true.'' Edmond waved a finger at her.

"I said shut up!"

"I won't shut up," he yelled back. "You told me that you had to go up to Washington to visit your sick mother. You said you didn't want anybody to know about it because you hated sympathy. I believed you like a fool. I know you're seeing someone else!''

"Damn you!" she shrieked at him.

"No, damn *you*!" A spiteful smile played across his quavering lips, then he turned to Rena and said, "When she got back from Washington she was as white as a ghost. Probably from spending all that time under the sheets with her lover," he jeered. "She has a tanning machine and body-building paraphernalia that she uses down in the cellar. That's where she spent the first two days after she got back. Look at that body! It's not hers. Cost me a bloody fortune with all the plastic surgery she had done!''

"Stop it!" she screamed.

"What the hell for? You're the devil! You broke my arm at Riverside. It was no accident. I hated myself for falling in love with you!'' he wailed back.

"You may have a lover but that's not the reason you went to Washington," Rena said to her. "You went up there and to Idaho to kill and then to make sure the murders were blamed on Maura. You did the same thing in Los Angeles two days ago. You knew everything there was to know about her—all her hidden secrets, all her fears. You were one of a handful of people that knew she was a true hermaphrodite. When she was a patient at the hospital I'm sure she even told you about her ancestor, the Baron de Montret. Maybe she even mentioned where the diary was kept. Did you read it?''

Blythe stared at her and said nothing.

"Was that when you decided to commit the same type of murders like the ones in France? You spent years at a psychiatric hospital. You understood how the mind worked as well as any psychiatrist. The authorities would believe that Maura was a crazy hermaphrodite like de Montret and reenacting her ancestor's crimes.''

Blythe still said nothing, but her face was taut with hate.

''You killed all those people after you found out that there was gold somewhere on her land. First you pestered Edmond to buy the property, except Maura wouldn't sell it. I'll bet anything that you even checked to see if Maura had a will. You found out that the property of a convicted murderer would have to be sold or auctioned off in order to make payments on wrongful death suits filed by the families of the victims. Something also tells me that you would have outbid everybody at that auction because only you knew what was on that land.''

The deadness finally left Blythe's eyes; they were now bulging and bouncing all over the room, as if they were incapable of focusing on one thing. She ran her trembling hands through her hair and said in her animated voice, ''That's ridiculous! Maura McKinney was identified by witnesses that stated she was in those areas where the murders were committed. There was physical evidence that confirmed this. Vaginal fluid . . . sperm . . . hair fibers . . . even her skin. The DNA tests taken proved positive beyond a doubt that they belonged to Maura. DNA tests don't lie. All this was in the papers and on television! There's even witnesses who'll swear that she had two different-colored eyes. You'd look like a fool taking your suspicions to the police.'' Blythe's mouth cracked into a bellicose smile.

Rena shook her head. Yes, she *would* look like a fool taking this to the police. ''I don't know how you did it, but you did it all right. You either did something to Maura to force her into committing those murders or you impersonated her yourself. Since the first is almost impossible to achieve, it had to be the second.''

''You'd have a hard time proving it!'' Blythe shot back.

''Maybe there is a way,'' Rena said, nodding her head.

Blythe's face turned white.

''As you pointed out, she has two different-colored eyes. Maura hid her affliction by wearing green contact lenses. *You* probably did the same thing. Except the lenses you wore when you took on Maura's identity were brown and blue.'' Rena could see the glacial look on Blythe's face, and she knew she was right.

"An optometrist or an ophthalmologist had to have fitted you for the lenses. They keep records. Even if you used a different name when you bought them, I'm sure you could be identified. What I don't understand is why you had to kill so many people. Was it because you enjoyed what you did?"

"You bitch!" Again Blythe curled her hands into fists.

The adrenaline was flowing through Rena's body now. Had she gone too far? There was no turning back now. She was close to the door and could always get out if she had to. Looking at Blythe, she said, "Except you couldn't have done this alone. After Tomas Sanchez was killed next to the spring on Maura's property, he was then carried to the vineyards. You're not strong enough."

"Who helped you? Your lover? You're nothing but a whore!" Edmond bellowed. He pulled himself up from the chair and swung his twitching hand at Blythe's face. She easily sidestepped him. He tripped over the coffee table and fell to the floor.

"You disgusting old pig!" she spat at him. She was now out of control. "How I hated it when you touched me! Every time you stuck your shriveled cock in me I wanted to puke. The only way I could get through those times was by fantasizing about those young men who worked for you. Every time you came in me it was one of those filthy young Mexicans coming in me and not you! God, no, not you! Never you!"

"And not your lover? I know all about him! You thought I was blind, didn't you?" he roared back, lying on the floor.

"Yes! Him too! Him too! You vile, withering old bastard!"

Paralyzed by this display of raw hatred, Rena could only stand there and watch. Blythe's anger was fierce, all-consuming. Her face was a deep red and her features were contorted, giving the appearance of a crazed animal.

Suddenly Blythe rushed over to the fireplace and picked up the poker off the marble hearth. Glaring down at Edmond, she raised it over his head. "You will never touch me again! Never again!" she roared.

Rena watched in frozen horror. Using all her willpower to make her body move, she ran over to Blythe just as the poker was about to come down on Edmond's head. She grabbed the top of it and tried to pull it free from Blythe's hand, but the rod was slippery. Blythe easily pushed Rena away.

"Come on sweetie, go for it," Blythe said teasingly, circling Rena, holding the poker with two hands out in front of her. She was totally mad now. "What's the matter? Got no balls? Your friend Maura has balls, doesn't she? One ball actually. You ought to see it hanging down right next to her cunt. I used to have to scrub her clean when I was her nurse because she was too crazy to wash herself. What a monstrosity she was!"

Blythe let out a shrieking laugh that made Rena recoil. Her face turned ugly with seething hate again; then she let out a horrible yell and raced at Rena while swinging the rod. Rena ducked just as the tool came around, slicing the air above her head. Seeing that she was off-balance for a split second, Rena pushed her with all her strength. The force sent Blythe spinning to the ground next to Edmond. As she tried to get up, he grabbed her arm but she smacked him in the face, forcing him to let go. Sitting up on one knee, she hurled the poker at Rena.

Instinctively Rena put up her hand. The metal rod bounced off her elbow. Searing pain surged through her arm.

Blythe got up off the floor. Her face was a deep red, and her mouth was covered with foam. She was cursing, but the words were low, monotonic, almost unintelligible. Rushing over to the wall cabinet, she opened the top drawer and pulled out a 9mm Beretta automatic.

Rena saw the gun in her hand. Heart pulsating, her mind clogged with the kind of primitive terror that makes all animals fight to survive, Rena raced for the front door. She could hear Blythe screaming in back of her.

Rena pushed the door open and dashed over to the Rover. She grabbed the door handle, then thought better of it; Blythe was only a few feet in back of her and she would never be able to make it inside the car in time. Instead, she continued running down the graveled path toward the main road. There would be cars on the highway, and this crazed woman wouldn't dare follow her there.

"Cunt! Bitch!" Blythe screamed.

Rena turned around. Blythe was right in back of her standing next to her car, the gun still in her hand. Fighting off the fear, Rena tried running faster. The road was a hundred yards away. She was gasping for breath, forcing herself to go faster.

Then she heard the sound of wheels crushing gravel in back of her. Still running, she turned around. It was Blythe's Jeep Wagoneer.

Damn! There was no way she could make the highway.

The four-wheeler was coming down on her fast. She could

hear the overhead branches that hung down from the madrona trees above the road whipping against the windshield; the tires spitting up dirt and rocks.

In the distance, Rena saw a black GMC truck coming up the pathway toward her. She waved her arms frantically trying to stop it. There was no time, she realized. Blythe's Jeep was only a few feet in back of her. She leaped off the road just as the four-wheeler roared past, the heavy metal fender nicking the back of her leg. Rena toppled into the dense foliage and rolled down a steep incline. Her face and body scraped against rocks and spiny brush. Putting out her hands, she flailed away desperately, trying to grab on to anything that would break her fall. Then her fingers caught on to a young oak tree. Holding on with one hand, she inched her way upward with the other, digging her nails deep into the moist earth so she could get a firmer grasp. When she had both hands around the tree, she looked up toward the road. Blythe was standing on the top of the incline holding the fifteen-shot automatic pistol, and her two hands were wrapped around the molded plastic grip. Her feet were spread apart like she knew what she was doing, and the muzzle was pointing directly at Rena.

A burst of fire flashed from the barrel followed by a loud crack. Dirt splattered next to Rena's face. Another shot, then another followed. Leaves and bits of rock flew into the air and poured down onto her.

She couldn't stay here or she'd be killed. Glancing down the slope, she saw the stone building of a small winery about twenty feet below. She let go of the tree and tumbled down to the foothill of the crest.

Two more shots rang out. She could feel the heat from one of the bullets as it whizzed inches over her head.

Rena came to a stop in a mulch-covered ravine. She got up and ran. The forest was dense here, and branches licked at her arms and face. She pushed her way through the thick underbrush following the buzzing, motorized noise coming from the winery. The woods cleared; then she saw the brick building.

Another shot. Rena turned around. Blythe was making her way down the incline.

Rena ran toward the building.

Where were the workers?

The gun fired again, this time chipping a piece of slate from the stone wall next to her face. The bullet ricocheted down only an inch from her foot. Rena ran around to the back of the building, away from Blythe's line of fire. She saw the thick wooden door leading into the winery and tried the handle. Locked. Frantically she kicked at the door. Then, using her foot as a lever, she pulled again with all her might. It was no use; it wouldn't open.

The buzzing noise! Where was it coming from? She looked around and realized that it was the sound of a de-stemming machine that was located at the side of the building. She had heard that sound many times before in her father's winery. Keeping her head down, she rushed around to the other side. There it was! The steel, corkscrew-shaped implement in the open cylindrical casing was grinding and crushing the Riesling grapes and spewing out the yellowish liquid into a vat.

But where the hell were the workers!

Then she realized that this small winery belonged to Edmond. It was probably where he made his own private reserve. No wonder Blythe wasn't afraid to fire the gun; she knew there'd be no one here.

Rena heard a noise crashing through the trees on the other side of the building, and she knew it was Blythe. There was also another set of footsteps coming from farther away, over near the slope. Someone else was approaching.

She was about to make a run for the trees again when she saw Blythe coming around the house.

They saw each other at the same time. Sneering, Blythe raised the gun to fire. Rena threw her body down behind the steel de-stemmer. The bullet hit the cylindrical casing. Blythe fired two more shots. They glanced off the steel tube, showering Rena with sparks.

She had her face pressed against the wine-soaked ground, and her hands were over her head. *The next bullet will kill me. The next one! Why did I come alone? Why didn't I listen to you, Charlie? Oh, shit!*

As she waited for the next round of bullets, she heard twigs snapping and running footsteps coming through the brush. Then Blythe screaming. The sound of scuffling. A man shouting, "Enough! No more! No more!"

Rena lifted her face from the wet ground and looked.

The trough part of the de-stemmer blocked most of her view, but she could see two pairs of feet: one set wearing work boots, and the other, L.A. Gear women's tennis shoes. They were kicking up dust. Rena moved her head past the cylinder and looked up to see who the man was.

My, God, it's Harrison!

His body was locked together with Blythe's. "No more killing!" he screamed.

He had one arm pinned in back of her, and he was trying to do the same thing to the hand with the gun. At first Blythe's face had the look of astonishment; then it became callous once again, and she tried to kick Harrison in the groin. He countered by bringing up his knee to block hers. She was screaming unintelligible words at him. Slowly he twisted the gun hand in back of her.

"Bastard!" she shrieked.

Then the pistol went off.

The rage in her face turned to surprise then to anguish. Harrison loosened his grip. She moved slowly away and reached around her back trying desperately to touch the horrible burning sensation near her spine. Then she brought her hand up to her face and saw the blood on her fingers. Her eyelids sagged and her mouth dropped open. Harrison quickly took the gun that was held loosely in her other hand. She stood there looking at him through half-closed eyes for a moment; then her knees started to buckle. Her weight carried her backward toward the open cylinder.

Harrison reached out and grabbed her around the waist, but the ends of her hair caught in the large, revolving corkscrew. Slowly and methodically it began to suck her head into the churning blade.

Rena screamed in horror.

There was a hideous, high-pitched squeal coming from inside the cylinder, and Blythe's legs, hanging off the sides, were kicking frantically as she was being dragged in. The sound of bone crunching, then the legs became lifeless.

Harrison dived for the power switch and turned the machine off.

The dreadful screaming had already stopped. Rena looked up toward the de-stemmer and saw Blythe's tanned, shapely legs dangling in a grotesque position out of the machine. The yellow juices from the crushed grapes that were being pushed through the holes in the de-stemmer changed to a pale pink, then to a pulpy red.

Rena turned away and gagged. Holding Blythe's gun by the

trigger guard in his index finger, Harrison walked unsteadily over to her. He looked as if he was in shock; his face was pale and unsettled. He dropped down next to Rena, put his arms around her shoulders, and brought her face to his chest.

"Oh, Jesus! She's dead!" he murmured. His tone was raspy and his breath heavy.

Rena moved her head away from Harrison's red cable sweater and looked up at him. Her body stiffened, and she tried to push him away. He took his arms from off her shoulders and looked quizzically at the fear etched in her face.

"Hey, I might be wrong, but I think I just saved your life," he said.

Rena's eyes quickly scanned the area. Her mind began to race, thinking about how she could get away from him. Yes, Blythe had a lover and an accomplice all right, and she knew it was him.

Harrison's face congealed into a frown. He knew it wasn't working. Still holding the fifteen-clip Beretta, he again put his fingertips on Rena's shoulders and slid them up to the base of her neck. This time, though, his hands felt rough, and the cold steel of the gun's muzzle on her skin made her shiver.

"Goddamn it, you know, don't you?" he whispered.

Rena, her eyes wide open in fear, didn't respond.

She didn't have to. He already knew the answer.

Chapter Forty-two

THE AIR WAS clean, and the green of the vine-covered fields hovering against the cloudless blue sky had the urgency of a Van Gogh painting. Maura stood in the middle of the deserted road looking up at the splashing, rainbow array of colors. A smile hung on her face.

This was her valley.

This was her home.

She belonged here; she knew that now.

Even though she wore a light sweater and the temperature in the valley was barely fifty degrees, she felt hot and clammy. Maura unbuttoned her sweater, took it off, and dropped it on the road.

Where was her tote? she thought, looking around. Oh, yes, she vaguely remembered; she left it somewhere in San Francisco. In some kind of theater. What kind? Did it matter? Not anymore.

She had wet herself again while walking, but she didn't care about that either.

Again she looked up at the sky and smiled. Tears moistened her eyes. *Home. Oh, God, finally home. I'm coming to you Martin. We'll be together soon.*

Ricky Belson saw her standing in the middle of the road the second his Ford Bronco rounded the bend. His body tingled with excitement. Never in his seven months on the force as a cop did he think that he'd ever get a chance to bring down a serial killer. Never in his wildest dreams!

He stopped the truck fifty feet from where she was standing, grabbed the pump shotgun from the floor, and slowly got out of the driver's seat.

What the fuck's with her? he thought, standing next to the door. *She's not even looking this way; she's just staring at nothing and grinning like a goddamn fruitcake.*

Because the wide brim of his hat partially blocked his view, he took it off and threw it in the front seat. Slowly Ricky made his way toward her, his shotgun gripped tightly in his trembling hands.

Why the fuck doesn't she see me?

When he was fifteen feet away, he tried to shake off the fear. Clearing his throat, he spoke loudly like they told him to do at the academy. "Hey, you! Put your hands on your head and drop to the ground, or I'll blow you the fuck away!" The volume was right, but he couldn't stop the quivering in his voice.

Maura heard the voice. It sounded like it was coming from somewhere hundreds of feet underwater. Still smiling, she turned her fevered head in its direction.

At first she could only make out different colors. Then her vision became a little more focused, and she could see some movement. Who is it? Is that a man standing there?

316

Yes, it is a man! There's something in his hands and his mouth is moving. He is saying something to me, but I can't understand him.

Ricky didn't like this. He kept telling her to get down on the ground, but she wasn't doing it. He licked his nervous lips. This was not the way the academy said it was supposed to happen. No, he didn't like this at all.

She looked up into his face. *How beautiful he is. His hair . . . long and curly like Martin's. Oh dear Lord! Is it? Yes, it is Martin!*

"Martin! Oh God, Martin!" Her face glowed from happiness as well as from the fever. She reached her arms out and started walking toward him.

What the fuck is she saying? he thought, pointing the gun in her direction. Who's Martin? "Hey you! I'm telling you for the last time to get down!" He slid the pump underneath the barrel that automatically loaded a cartridge in the chamber.

She heard it. Metal sliding on metal. *Slick . . . slick.*

That sound. That awful sound!

She stopped walking and grabbed her head in both hands.

Metal sliding against metal.

Now she remembered. All those years she had lived with that sound in her head. Now she remembered! It was the sound of a pump-action shotgun.

Slick . . . slick.

It was the noise she heard when she was dozing off in Martin's room just before . . .

Slick . . . slick.

. . . That terrible explosion.

All those sounds from so long ago. They came rushing out of her memory like a disjointed orchestra tuning up before a symphony.

Slick . . . slick. Boooom! Then . . .

Then what?

Footsteps. Yes, footsteps! Heavy footsteps running down the stairs.

Someone else was there.

Heavy footsteps running out of the house.

317

Rushing to the window to see. My feet so warm from Martin's blood on the floor. A shadow of someone running into the forest.

Heavy footsteps.

Heavy shadow.

Daddy?

It *was* Daddy!

Except . . .

NO! No, it wasn't. I wanted it to be you, because you always told me how you wished I wasn't born! How you despised what I was! But it wasn't you, Daddy. Oh, no, it wasn't my daddy who killed my Martin!

Heavy shadow.

What's she doing? Ricky thought to himself. Her eyes were jutting out of their sockets, and she was banging the sides of her head with her fists.

What the fuck is she doing?

His legs were trembling now. He felt like his lungs had shrunk, and he had to pant in order to breathe. The palms of his hands were sweating, which made the stock and pump of the shotgun slippery. Forgetting that he had already loaded a cartridge in the chamber, he pumped the gun once more.

Slick . . . slick.

That noise again!

Slick . . . slick.

She looked up at Martin. Except the face wasn't Martin's anymore. Who was he?

Heavy footsteps.

Heavy shadow.

The infection had reached her brain now, curling its spiny tentacles around the crevices of soft gray matter.

Who is he? His pockmarked face was leering at her, exposing sharp, pointed teeth. Worms were crawling in and out of the pits on his cheeks.

Who is he?

Heavy shadow.

Then she remembered who.

She let out a scream; a scream that came from the depths of her soul. Then she rushed at him.

* * *

Oh shit! Oh fucking shit!

"Stay back, lady, or I'll blow you away! Stay back or I'll do it! I swear to fucking Christ I'll do it!"

She was running at him, yelling, calling him some name. He couldn't understand what she was saying. Her face was gnarled with rage.

Aw Jesus! Aw Jesus! his frightened mind kept repeating over and over again as his twitching index finger wrapped itself around the hair trigger.

Pinky roared down Highway 29 doing eighty-five. He honked his horn and blared his siren, making the cars in front of him move out of the way.

"That scumbag!" he said out loud, thinking of Ricky.

When he got back to the station, he found a note from him on his desk saying that Maura was spotted walking down the highway and that he was going to get her.

"If that asshole kid touches one hair on her, I'll kill him!"

Just as he rounded the bend, he heard the blast. Then, like in a slow-motion section of a movie, he saw a woman's body soar in the air and come down like a rag doll in the trench off the road. Pinky stopped the car and ran out.

Ricky, holding the shotgun, was looking down at the body and whimpering.

Pinky ran over to the furrow and also looked down. Maura lay there unmoving. The right side of her dress was torn away, and blood was spreading over the ground from the large wound in her abdomen.

Tears welled up in Pinky's eyes, and he let out a large sob. Using all his willpower, he went over to his truck and got on the radio. In as steady a voice as possible, he called for the paramedics.

He then went back to where Maura lay and put his trembling fingers on the pulse by her neck. She was still alive. He took off his coat, folded it up, and gently put it under Maura's head.

He then turned to Ricky.

The rookie looked up from Maura's body, and his face turned white with fear when he saw the hate in Pinky's eyes.

"You fucking shit!" Pinky screamed, standing up and seizing the shotgun from his hands. "You fucking shit!" he screamed again as he hit Ricky hard in the face with the wooden stock.

Ricky's head shot back. He fell to his knees and grabbed his

319

face. Blood streaming from between his fingers, he looked up in horror at his boss.

Pinky's face was as red as the liquid oozing from Ricky's mouth. Holding the shotgun by the barrel, he went over to the oak tree by the side of the road and slammed it against the trunk. He banged it over and over again, yelling, "Fucking shit! Fucking shit!" until the stock splintered in half. Then he dropped to his knees next to Maura's body, put his hands over his head, and let out a thunderous wail that shattered the stillness of the valley.

Chapter Forty-three

Y*OU HAD TO have known about the gold mine.*

It *was* Harrison! Rena thought, staring up at his frightened, dangerous eyes. Blythe couldn't have carried this whole thing off alone. She needed help. He must have been in on this macabre plot right from the beginning.

Then she remembered him telling her the night of Simon's dinner party that he used to be a mineralogist and that he had worked in mines all over the world before he became a vintner. Last year he had dug an underground wine cave for Monica van der Slyck. Her land was adjacent to Maura's. That's when he must have discovered traces of Liam O'Connor's gold mine under the earth, except the valuable veins probably only ran through Maura's property. He must have told Blythe about it, because right after the completion of the van der Slyck cave, inquiries were made by Edmond Farnsworth regarding the sale of the McKinney land.

Yes, you had to have been her accomplice.

"You know about everything, don't you?" he said again.

She could feel the pressure of his thumb digging into her neck and the cold steel of the gun on her cheek. She shook her head, no, trying to suppress the surge of fear that was running rampant in her stomach.

The thumb tightened. "Don't lie to me, goddamn it!"

He was scared out of his mind, she realized, and using denial with him would only get him crazier. "Okay, yes, I had an idea," she whispered.

He squeezed his eyes shut, looked up, and said, "Damn it . . . goddamn it! Why you?"

She put her hand lightly on his, hoping he would loosen his grasp. "How did this all start?" she said gently.

He let go of her neck and backed up a few steps. The gun was pointed toward the ground. "What do you mean, how did this all start?"

Rena knew better than to accuse him directly. "How did *she* get you involved in this?"

"Where's Edmond?" he asked.

"Back at the house. She tried to kill him. He's probably called the police by now." Because of the drugs, Rena wasn't sure if Edmond was even capable of making a phone call. Harrison didn't have to know that.

"Goddamn! That crazy bitch!" He sighed and ran his shaking hand through his hair. After a pause, he said, "I met her about a year ago at a party thrown by one of those Japanese firms after a takeover. She and Edmond were also there. They'd been married for about a week. I was sitting at the bar and she came over to me. We talked. One thing led to another, and we began to have an affair." He started to pace nervously in circles.

"Was that right after you discovered gold on the McKinney property?"

"Oh Christ! You even know about that, don't you?" he spit out.

"Yes, I do." *Don't get him agitated.*

"She and I became lovers right after I discovered the gold. All my life I was so close to wealth and yet so far," he said bitterly, clenching his fist. "When I was a mineralogist I sweated in those damn mines for rich assholes. I breathed in dust and putrid air helping them find gold and gems, watching them get richer and richer. All I got from it were pats on the back and a few lousy bonuses. I got tired of all that shit. I quit and became a wine maker. But it was the same damn thing. I did all the work, and other men got wealthy. Then those Japs started buying up the wineries, and I knew it would be a matter of time before I'd be out of a job or working for them. Finding gold on someone else's property was the last straw. If only it was on Monica van der Slyck's property." He shook his head sardonically. "That old bitch was trying to get in my pants the first day I started working for her. She would have married me in a second, and I would have been rich now."

Rena grimaced, thinking that her father was now having an affair with this woman. "Monica *is* rich," she said.

"Bullshit! That relic has less money than the Mexicans she hired to pick her grapes. After I built her that cave, she tried paying me off for my services in vintage wines that belonged to her husband. She was dead broke. I told you she wasn't because I was embarrassed. Can you imagine? She lives on a small allowance and an income from the winery that her dead husband left her. That's why she latched on to your father. He's got money."

A swell of anger shot through her. Except she knew Simon was very proficient at taking care of himself. "What happened when you told Blythe about the gold?"

"She laughed. Especially when I mentioned Maura McKinney's name. She knew who she was. She said she was her nurse at that insane asylum in Washington some years back. That's when this idea grew."

He had stopped talking and began to think. Rena didn't want him to do that—not while he was holding the gun. Blythe was a psychopath; nothing could stop her from killing if that's what she wanted to do. Harrison was different. He always liked her. Maybe she had a chance. "Who suggested the idea?" she asked him with a hint of sympathy in her voice.

"She did." He pointed to where Blythe's body lay in the de-stemmer. "But that crazy idea came to her only after McKinney wouldn't sell Edmond the land. You see, she didn't have any money of her own. Farnsworth made her sign a prenuptial before he'd marry her."

"Yes, I know," Rena said.

He sat down across from her on a bench, leaned his back against the wall of the winery, and let the gun dangle between his legs. "She called me up one afternoon and told me to come over. Oh man, was she crazy! As soon as I walked into her house, she grabbed me and started ripping off my clothes. We made love on the floor of her living room. After it was over, I found out Edmond was upstairs in the bedroom the entire time. That crazy bitch gave him diazepam to knock him out. I was so furious that I pushed her off of me and got up to get dressed. I just wanted to get out of there and to get her out of my life. It was fun with her in the beginning, but I could see there was something not right with her up here.'' He pointed to his head. ''But she just laughed and said, 'See how easy it is. I can control anybody with drugs. After being a nurse for twenty years, I have enough different kinds stocked away to fuck up a whole city if I want to.' Then she told me what she wanted to do. Damn! I should have left when I had a chance and not listened to her.'' Again he became quiet; his eyes deep within himself, thinking.

Suddenly Rena remembered what Tomas Sanchez had said to Otto van der Slyck after he told him about Maura swimming in the spring. He said he already knew about Maura and that he had plans for her. ''Did you and Blythe hire Tomas Sanchez to kill Maura?''

''What?'' he mumbled. ''No. I hired that idiot to kidnap her. That's all he was supposed to do. Blythe knew that Maura bathed in that spring. She told her about it when she was in the hospital. Maura said that it helped her skin. She told her that she'd been using it every day ever since she was a little girl.''

Then with an ironic grin on his face he said, ''You see, the water came from an underground cave. Liam O'Connor's cave.''

''The gold mine is directly under it?'' she said, amazed.

''Yes. The spring was actually the entrance to the mine. An underground basin close by must have broken through and flooded the passageway.'' After a pause, he said, ''A couple of months ago Blythe went over to the McKinney winery and talked to Manuel. She said that she was a good friend of Maura's when she lived in New York City. She asked him when she would be coming back up to Napa. He told her the exact date. Then Blythe said she knew about the spring and wondered if Maura still went bathing in it. Manuel was surprised that Maura had told her about it but he said, yes, that she still used it when she came to visit. We found out the time she was arriving and planted that fool Sanchez in the brush to grab her. Except she was too strong for him. Blythe forgot about her incredible strength. Maura cut Tomas's throat with a knife. Luckily she also slipped and knocked her head against a rock next to the spring. When Blythe and I went down there, she was sitting on the ground, dazed.''

''Was Sanchez dead?''

''No, but he was bleeding pretty badly, which made it easier for us. You see, Tomas was going to be Maura's first victim.''

''But he wasn't the first. There was another before him on the East Coast,'' she said.

''I didn't know that at the time,'' he responded angrily. ''When

Blythe and I first discussed it, we agreed on two murders. That was all! Have Maura blamed for two murders. That crazy woman had other plans and didn't bother telling me about them.'' Once again he got up and started to pace. ''The thing is, she got off on what she was doing. She knew Maura's complete psychological makeup from being her nurse and confidante at the hospital. All she was supposed to do was dress up like one of Maura's fantasies that she had read about in the files at the hospital. It was some whore she called Jasmine Dawn. We were only going to kill Tomas, then just one other person—a drifter or a picker— someone the police wouldn't get up in arms about. It was only supposed to happen in California, not in any other part of the country. We didn't want the FBI called in. The killings were supposed to be done just like in the diary of her French ancestor. Blythe also knew about him. Everything was to point to Maura being psychotic. Even down to the cheap K Mart clothes that Blythe bought for her. Blythe or Julian—whatever name you want to call her—knew that Maura had an aversion to that kind of clothing. She told her in the hospital how her father would force her to wear them because he couldn't afford anything better.''

That's because the stiffness would make her sensitive skin itch, and she'd break out in red blotches, Rena thought. That's why she always wore silk and expensive cotton clothing later on.

''Did you kill Tomas?'' she quickly asked.

''God no!'' he shuddered. ''I couldn't do something like that. Oh, but she could. Christ could she ever!'' he bellowed. ''She loved doing it. First she injected diazepam into Maura to put her out. Tomas was sitting by the side of the spring holding his neck. Blythe told him she was a nurse and that he should lay on his stomach to stop the flow of the blood. When he did, she took the nail she used on the other victims and banged it into his neck with a hammer. I couldn't believe she did it so easily and without any feeling. She then removed his testicles with a scalpel. Blythe said she learned how to use a surgeons' knife while she was in nursing school. She then used a fish-scaling knife to take skin samples from Maura's arms, and stuck them under Tomas's nails. She also ripped out some of Maura's hair and put them in his hands. I went back up the hill, got a plastic tarp to wrap Tomas's body in so I wouldn't get his blood over me, and carried him into Maura's vineyard. We tied him to a vine, just like it was done in the diary, hoping that Manuel would discover him. I went back to the spring and lifted Maura's unconscious body. While I held her, Blythe pushed Maura's feet in the wet ground so her footprints would be there for the police.''

Rena looked toward the hills hoping she would see someone, maybe Charlie. There was no one.

Harrison shook his head and smiled. "If you're looking for that friend of yours, forget it.''

Startled, she stood up. "What do you mean?''

He pointed the gun in her direction. "I mean that nobody is coming here. Now sit down," he commanded.

She did what he said. His lips were twitching from nerves, and she didn't want to get him annoyed. Looking at Harrison, she asked, "What were you going to do with Maura?''

He brought the gun back down again. "Keep her drugged up for a week or so until the harvesting was over. Then . . . then she was supposed to be discovered in Sonoma or Mendocino. She would have been found guilty or judged insane, the land would have been auctioned off for next to nothing, and we would have bought it. It was such a simple foolproof plan, and it all got fucked up somehow." He put his free hand over his face and rubbed it. Then he said in a tired voice, "Blythe had gotten completely out of control. She wanted to keep killing. The bitch actually got off on dressing up like Maura and leaving wrong trails for the police. She was starting to do things that only crazy people do.''

"Like what?''

"She took Maura, drugged and unconscious, with her up to Washington and Idaho. Do you believe that? If she had gotten stopped by the authorities, it would have been all over. It was almost as if she were playing Russian roulette with them.''

"The ticket man at the depot in Napa said Maura bought a ticket and boarded a bus there to go up north.''

Harrison shook his head again. "What a crazy bitch. That was Blythe dressed as Maura. She never actually got on the bus. She just wanted witnesses to see her at the station. She talked me into driving her up to Fort Bragg where she rented that station wagon. I then drove back to Napa.''

That's why she rented a station wagon with tinted windows up north, Rena thought. Something big enough to contain a body and where no one could see in. Then she remembered the phone call she received from Blythe saying that she was in Palm Springs and that she wanted to drive in to L.A. to have lunch with her. None of that was true, she suddenly realized. Blythe couldn't have driven to L.A. because she was actually somewhere in the northwest at that time. *She called to tell me she was in another place in case I got suspicious.* "Why take Maura with her?"

"So forensics would be able to show that Maura was at the scene of every murder. Everything had to be freshly taken from her body—the hair, the blood, the skin particles. If they weren't, the police would suspect something was wrong."

"What about the vaginal secretion and the semen."

"Yes, that, too," he said. "Especially the semen. I don't know how she did it, but Blythe said that part of it was the coup de grace. She said that when the authorities found out that the vaginal fluid and semen contained the same DNA makeup, it should blow them away. Especially once they discovered that Maura was a hermaphrodite." He shook his head. "Blythe was having fun with all of this. She loved taking these chances. It got crazier and crazier. Then, when she killed Ray Scollari, I knew she was way out of control. There was no reason to do that. The police already had enough evidence to convict Maura."

"Where is Maura now?" she asked, concerned.

"Who knows?" he said shrugging. "Blythe planted the hammer in her purse and let her go free in some park in Boise, Idaho. She was unconscious at the time. She hoped the police would find her in the park and discover the hammer in her bag. Blythe said that Maura was so fucked up by the drugs she had given her that she actually believed she murdered all those people. She would be found insane by a jury and locked away." He nervously scratched his head. "God, Blythe, you were so damn crazy!" he said, mostly to himself. He turned to Rena. "One time Maura woke up in a cabin Blythe rented. That wasn't supposed to happen. Luckily she passed out again. The irony of it all is that the police did not find Maura in Boise like she thought they would. Blythe had totally misjudged the woman. She escaped. Nobody knows where she is now." Harrison once again became thoughtful. He rested his head against the wall in back of him.

Don't let him think, she said to herself. "Was Winston Frawley's death a suicide?"

"Oh, God!" he moaned. "I feel like I'm in a ship that's sinking thousands of miles from land."

Good! Feel that way. "Did he commit suicide?" she asked him again.

"No." He rolled his head against the stone wall. "No! No! No! Right after we got back from seeing Professor Tomain, Blythe

326

called me. She was hysterical. She said that she had just run into Winston Frawley on the street in Calistoga and that he recognized her as the nurse who took care of Maura at Riverside Hospital. Everybody knew he had cancer and that he only had a few more months to live. She thought she could avoid such an encounter with him, thinking that he'd die before that happened. Except it didn't take place that way. He knew who she was the minute he saw her. She told me I had to kill him."

"So what if he recognized her? What did it matter?" Rena said, bewildered, thinking about how she had liked that old man.

"Blythe couldn't afford to be tied in with Maura in any remote way, especially when she was going to bid for the property. The FBI might see more than just a coincidence going on here." He sighed deeply and said, "A couple of hours before I was to meet you at the restaurant, I went over to Frawley's house. At that point I didn't even know how I was going to get rid of him. I thought maybe I would just talk to him, see if it mattered to him whether Maura's old nurse was now living up here. I wanted to feel him out. Winnie . . ." Suddenly he stopped, realizing that he had no right to call the man he killed by the name used only by his friends. He cleared his throat and said, "I found Winston working in his winery. I asked him about Blythe. He was up on the ladder at the time fixing a loose metal band on the wooden vat. Blythe was right, it turned out. Frawley *was* suspicious about her being up here." He paused for a couple of seconds, thinking about what happened, then he continued. "I knew what I had to do." He closed his eyes and grimaced. "Telling him I'd give him a hand, I climbed up on the ladder right behind him. It was so easy. I just pushed him slightly, getting him off balance, and the upper half of his body fell into the layer of carbon dioxide floating on top of the vat. I held him there for a few seconds, and it was all over. Damn! It was easy. Then I closed all the vents to make it look like a suicide and left to meet you for dinner."

Rage and disgust shot up in her, and she fought to keep it down. "When you met Blythe and Edmond at the restaurant that evening, was that just a coincidence?"

"No. Blythe was jealous of you." Casting his eyes to the ground, he said, "She knew I had a thing about you. When she found out that I planned to have dinner with you that night she almost bit my head off. She said that she and Edmond would be there, too. She'd make sure of that."

Rena felt sick to her stomach when she thought about how she

327

had taken special care in getting ready that night. To think that I was attracted to this man, she thought with disgust. Then she remembered how Blythe was flirting openly with the waiter. She was trying to make Harrison jealous.

"Where do we go from here?" she asked him.

He looked up. "What?"

Rena sucked in her breath, kept her eye on Harrison's hand holding the gun, and said, "It's all over. Blythe's dead."

"I know. What you really mean to say, though, is what am I going to do with you?" His voice was cracking.

"Yes, that's what I meant," she murmured. *You like me, Harrison. I know you do. Think about it for a minute, okay?* Reaching out her hand to him, she said, "You told me you felt that you were on a sinking ship with no land in sight. Let me help you find that land. It's all over now. You know that."

As if reading her mind, he looked up at the madrona trees surrounding the winery and reflected on his position.

"It's over, Harrison," she repeated softly once again. "There's too many bodies. You can't cover them all up."

After a minute, Harrison's mouth twisted into a broken smile. Cocking the hammer on the Beretta, he brought the gun up to the height of her stomach and said, "Maybe it's not over the way you think it is. Maybe I just found one little island out there to latch on to."

Rena understood his meaning, and her organs suddenly felt cold and dead inside her.

Charlie stepped on the brakes hard in order to avoid crashing into the Wagoneer and the black GMC truck blocking the private road leading up to Farnsworth's house. The door of the Jeep was wide open. As he got out of the car, he saw the lettering on the license plate—B. F. Did it stand for Blythe Farnsworth? He couldn't explain why, but a chill shot through him. Somehow he knew that Rena was not up in the house.

Putting his hands up to his mouth, he hollered, "Rena! Reena!"

There was no sound other than the breeze brushing against the few fall-colored leaves that still clung to the trees. In the distance, there was the voice of a bird calling out to its mate.

"Rena! Rena!" he screamed louder.

He looked over to the side toward the slope: bushes had been torn apart, and the ground seemed disturbed. There was something gleaming in the brush. He walked over to it and bent down. Pushing away the grass, he picked up the casing of a 9mm shell. Then he saw two others a couple of feet down the incline. From where he was squatting, he could see furrows in the earth made from human hands and feet. The amount of flora that was disrupted clearly showed there had been more than one person here.

Shit!

Charlie carefully made his way down the grade, sliding part of the way, until he reached bottom. Covered with leaves and mud, he stood perfectly still, trying desperately to hear something. His ears picked up the sound of a creek in the distance, then closer in he could hear the low monotone pitch of a winery's generator.

She's here! I know she is!

He ran toward the sound as fast as he could, using his muscular body to break through the dense underbrush.

"*Rena!*" he shouted wildly, like a wounded lion rushing toward his endangered mate.

"*Rena!*"

Dead twigs snapped under his feet and cut into his ankles. Branches tore at his shirt and scraped his skin.

"*Rena!*"

The loud crack of a handgun suddenly filled the valley and resonated off the surrounding hills.

Charlie stopped, letting that terrible, familiar sound reverberate through his head.

Oh shitmotherfuckingchrist!

"*Reeeena!*"

Chapter Forty-four

BUBBLES OF BLOOD dripped from Maura's mouth and clung to her bottom lip. Her eyes, only slits now, were glazed over.

Pinky was on his knees looking down at her. His thick fingers dug into his cheeks as his body swayed back and forth. Gurgling sounds were coming from Maura's throat.

"Oh, no! Oh, no! Please no!" he screamed. Ignoring her blood-soaked dress, he pressed his meaty hands between her breasts and desperately began pushing up and down. "No! No! No!" He then put his wide mouth over hers, urging his own air into her lungs.

To have my lips finally on her mouth and now she's dead!

Somewhere down the highway, the rising sound of a siren could be heard coming from a paramedic's truck.

His palms pumped feverishly against her motionless chest. He could feel her ribs and sternum practically breaking under the weight of his massive body.

I loved you! I loved you so much more than Martin! Don't die! Again his mouth went over hers. Her eyes suddenly opened wide.

Stay with me! Please don't leave me! Why did you have to sleep with him? If only you could have loved me everything would have been so different. Sweat dropped onto her face from his forehead. His hands continued to thrust up and down. *Ever since that day I always knew what you were and I never cared. Never!*

She was staring at Pinky now. Recognition finally broke through her fevered mind.

Heavy shadow.

She knew who killed her Martin. Her eyes hardened with hate, and the rattle in her throat turned into a steady whine, building to a fiery scream. The siren from the paramedic's truck got louder and louder, intermixing with her voice.

Frightened, Pinky moved his hands away from her chest and looked at the savage hate in her face. She knows, he thought. *She knows!* He could live with anything except her knowing. *Please! Please! Oh Please no!!*

Her screaming didn't stop, not even after the medic strapped her to the gurney. She pointed a finger at Pinky and yelled, "Murderer! Murderer!" as they put her in the ambulance and closed the doors.

When the truck disappeared down the highway, Pinky dropped to the dusty road. He drew his knees up to his face, shielded his ears with his hands to drown out the rage in her voice, and sobbed.

Over by the Bronco, Ricky leaned against the tire. He dabbed at his split lip with a handkerchief and watched his boss in bewilderment. He never saw someone as big as Pinky cry before.

Pinky pulled at his ears with all his might, trying to block out Maura's scream. But the sound stayed in his head, refusing to leave. He knew from the depths of his soul that it would remain inside him forever.

Chapter Forty-five

U SING HIS ARMS like a battering ram, Charlie pushed the compact foliage aside until he came into the clearing. When he was able to see, he stopped running and looked around. Twenty yards away was the stone winery. The bitter smells of potassium nitrate and something salty infiltrated the air. He knew the odors well: gunpowder and blood!

"Rena!" he cried out.

The only response to his plea was the steady *woosh* of the wind.

Looking closer, he suddenly saw a pool of blood snaking its way along the ground from behind the other side of the building. He rushed over to the stone wall and turned the corner. His eyes quickly glanced toward the de-stemmer, and he could see the mangled remains of Blythe's upper body inside. He then turned his head toward the winery, where large splashes of blood slid down the white stone wall like a De Kooning painting. The drippings ended next to a body lying on the ground. Most of the head was blown away, but he recognized the red cable sweater as the same one worn by the man who had attacked him. The Beretta was on the grass right next to his hand. It was Harrison. *Goddamn it,* it was Harrison! The bastard shot himself in the head.

"Charlie," a voice said weakly from behind him.

He quickly turned around.

Rena was standing over to the side. Her trembling hands were pressed to her face, and her skin had an uncanny paleness to it.

A long, deep moan rose up from his throat, and he ran over to her. Putting his hands on her shoulders, he pressed her head deep into his chest. From somewhere within him he heard himself saying over and over again: "I love you. I love you. I love you."

Her body sagged into his, and he could feel the warmth of her trembling arms looping tightly around his waist.

At this moment, whatever walls they had built up over the years to protect themselves from the looming pain of closeness came crashing down like a thatched roof during a raging hurricane.

EPILOGUE

D AWN HAD JUST broken over Brentwood, splashing San Vicente Boulevard in a pale, gray light. The streets were empty, and the upscale stores, filled with Christmas paraphernalia and glitter, were closed tight for at least four more hours. The only signs of life could be found on the grass divider that separated the wide boulevard. There, scores of joggers were running toward the ocean and back, like they did every day before they filed into their CPA, law, and medical practices.

This morning, a black jaguar convertible also headed down San Vicente. It drove past the runners going in the opposite direction, then turned left onto Wilshire Boulevard. The lampposts on each side of this main thoroughfare were decorated with Santas and Christmas lights. A few seconds later, the sleek automobile made its way onto the Southbound 405 Freeway.

"It isn't even Thanksgiving yet and the Christmas glitz is already up," Charlie said thoughtfully, looking out the passenger window. "Every year they do it earlier and earlier. At this rate, Santa is going to find himself with a firecracker up his ass on the fourth of July."

"Cute, Charlie. You have such a way with words," Rena said, smiling. She was driving. He put his hand on her shoulder, brushing the tips of her hair with his fingers. She leaned her body slightly into his. Inhaling deeply, she smelled the leather from his worn aviator's jacket. It was an odor she knew well, and it made her feel warm and safe.

I'll miss that smell, she thought. *Six months this time. Shit!*

"Where's Simon taking Cathy this weekend?" he asked her, breaking the quiet between them.

"San Diego. She's never been to Sea World. Simon wanted to take her there." For the past month Simon and Cathy had been inseparable. The rift between them had finally been bridged.

335

Rena was happy about that. When she was growing up, Simon never had the time to be a father to her. Now at least he can be a grandfather to Cathy.

When Rena brought up Monica van der Slyck to Simon, he said, "Yes, I knew all about her and what she really wanted from me. I had her checked out when she moved onto her late husband's property. I knew she had no money. I hoped that her feelings for me would be real. Well, it's over between us now." Then with sad eyes and a crack in his voice, he said, "Hell, it was fun while it lasted!"

Charlie and Rena drove the rest of the way to the airport in silence. His hand never left her shoulder until they came to the Bradley Terminal.

She parked in the lot across the street and popped open the trunk. He got out of the car, grabbed his worn nylon suitcase and lap-top computer from the trunk, then took out Rena's overnight shoulder bag and handed it to her. Putting his hand on the nape of her neck, they crossed over and walked slowly into the building.

They stood next to the boarding gate with the Pan Am symbol over the check-in counter, neither one saying anything. Biting down on her lip, she willed the tears that were welling up in her eyes to stay put.

He put his arms around her, drawing her into his body. They stayed that way until they heard, *"Atension por favor. El vuelo 125 de Pan Am que va a San Salvador, El Salvador. Esta aciendo la ultima llamada para abordar."*

"Last call," Rena said.

Charlie nodded, then regretfully let her go.

She looked into his somber eyes. "I'll miss you this Christmas, Charlie," she said, remembering how wonderful their last Christmas was together.

"Hell, it's like Christmas every day in El Salvador. Come on down." He forced a grin.

"Sure," she said, kissing the side of his neck. She knew he was joking.

Six months!

Again over the loudspeaker: *"Esta aciendo la ultima llamada para aborda."*

He held her for a second longer, kissing her hard on the lips, then broke away. Without looking back, he disappeared into the gateway.

She stayed at the window and watched the plane taxi down the runway. Only when it was out of sight did she allow the tears to flow. *Don't die, Charlie. Come back to me.*

Six goddamn months!

Rena left the international building and walked slowly toward the US Air terminal. There was no rush; her flight didn't leave for San Francisco for at least two hours. She was going to see Maura. It's a good day for it, she thought. *With Charlie leaving, I need to be with a friend.*

She had coffee at a cafeteria inside the building and thought about Charlie. The *L.A. Trib* had refused to accept his resignation. Instead, they offered him a job as a full-time foreign correspondent, and he got to pick the areas of the world he wanted to cover. Unfortunately where he wanted to cover, wars were raging and people were dying.

Whatever qualms they had about committing to each other were totally shattered that September morning in the Napa Valley. The taste of death brought them together. Old pains and restraints caused from lost loves paled in comparison to that. They needed each other. They knew that now. Surprisingly, instead of chains and dank prison cells, they found freedom and sunlight with their commitment: freedom to be who they were because they knew the other person would accept them.

Come back to me, Charlie!

An hour and a half later the boarding call was announced for her flight to San Francisco.

When her plane let down at San Francisco International Airport, she rented a car and drove over the Golden Gate Bridge into Marin County and took the turnoff to Napa.

Vineyards dotted the landscape. They were devoid of foliage at this time of year, and the naked vines, held upright by crossed poles, resembled thousands of crucifixions. That image evoked memories of de Montret, and she turned her eyes away from the fields.

She passed the Napa Sheriff's Department, and her body tensed. Pinky was in one of the cells there awaiting trial. After Maura was shot and almost died, he confessed to the murder of Martin Bynum. While sobbing uncontrollably, he told the authorities that on the day of Maura's seventeenth birthday he stood in the corner of the den, sulking, watching them together. When they snuck out of the party, he followed them. He watched as they opened the doors of Peter's winery and went inside. Through a small hole in the stone wall, he spied on them making love. The years of bottled up longing and unfulfilled love exploded into an indomitable rage. Martin had everything. Everything! Looks, brains . . . and Maura. Filled with fury, he ran home and got his shotgun. When he returned to the winery, Martin and Maura were just leaving. He squatted down behind a grapevine, watching his two friends laughing and running through the vineyards toward Martin's house. His heart was bursting with sorrow and anger. He hid behind the trees in the backyard of the house, making sure they couldn't see him. When he looked up into Martin's bedroom window, he saw both of them standing there naked. They were kissing passionately and groping each other. The rage flared up again. He waited twenty minutes more, then went over to the back door and jimmied the lock. It was easy, he told the police. When he was a teenager, he was considered a juvenile delinquent and had broken into many homes and cars. He quietly made his way up the stairs and looked through the small crack of Martin's partially closed bedroom door. They were making love again. Stifling a groan, he went into Martin's parents' room. He knew what he had to do. Turning the closet and the dresser drawers inside out, he made the room look like it had been ransacked. Then he heard Martin's footsteps approaching. He grabbed his shotgun, pumped a cartridge into the chamber, and waited. When he walked in, Pinky pointed the barrel of the gun three inches from Martin's surprised face and pulled the trigger. There was red everywhere. When he looked down, he saw Martin lying on the floor with most of his face gone. Panic overtook him. He ran down the steps and outside the house, praying Maura didn't see him.

When asked by police after his confession if he knew that Maura was a hermaphrodite, he put his hands in his face and answered, "Yeah, I guess so." He had seen her nude in the winery and in Martin's bedroom. "Except I didn't know what it was called back then. It wouldn't have mattered. I'd have loved her no matter what she was."

Even though Pinky had taken a life and practically destroyed Maura in the process, Rena felt sorry for him. Unlike Blythe Farnsworth, he was capable of love. Pinky told the police about the self-hatred he had over what he had done and how on many occasions he contemplated suicide.

Rest easy, Pinky, she thought. It's all out in the open now.

When she reached Oakville, she turned off Highway 29 and

headed toward the cemetery where the McKinneys were buried. Maura asked her if she would meet her there.

She began to think about Maura and her eyes filled up with tears. *My poor, dear friend. What that woman did to you!*

The medical reports were unbelievable! Blythe kept Maura doped up for over a week, feeding her intravenously. While Maura lay unconscious in the station wagon, Blythe used her to scrape the mucous-membrane area inside her vagina with gauze to remove her secretion. She then coated the truck driver, Arnie Baker's, organ with the vaginal fluid.

To extract the semen that was placed in Harriet Crowe's vagina, that sick woman actually cut into Maura's vas deferens tube located in the scrotum. It's one of a pair of ducts that hold the spermatozoa. She did it with the same dirty scalpel that she used for her castrations and ovariectomies. Blythe never even bothered to clean or sew Maura's incision up afterward. That open wound caused the infestation and fever that raged through Maura's body.

Rena parked the car next to the wrought-iron gate of the cemetery and walked over to the headstones. Fresh flowers lay on the grass mounds of the graves of the McKinneys. A feeling of sadness engulfed her. *So much misery and pain here. So much.*

"Hi. You're late," Maura's voice said from behind.

Rena turned around and smiled. "Sorry. The Golden Gate was a bitch. Bumper-to-bumper traffic."

They both looked at each other for a second, then they hugged. When they broke away, Rena asked, "How do you feel, Maura?"

Maura grinned. "Getting better." She was holding a cane to help her walk. Part of her stomach and left hipbone were destroyed by the shotgun blast, but she had lived. Rena had been coming up for the last several weekends to see her.

"Thanks for meeting me here."

"That's what you wanted," Rena said.

"Thank you," she whispered again, staring at the graves of her parents.

Yes, she *was* looking better, Rena thought. Her hair was blonde again, and it was getting longer. She was thinner than before, but some color had returned to her pale skin. The grating headaches, the psychotic behavior, the panic attacks, and the occasional blackouts that she was experiencing were actually caused by the medications that had been given to her by Riverside Hospital. They were wrong for her, and her body could not tolerate them. She was now getting proper psychiatric counseling and monitoring at a San Francisco hospital on a weekly outpatient basis.

"These flowers are beautiful," Rena said, pointing to the graves of Peter and Clair. "Did you put them here?"

"Yes," Maura said, limping over to the mounds. She touched the headstone of Peter McKinney. "It's time I made my peace with him. I hated him so much for all those years. I even masked Martin's real killer with my father's face. Now I need to understand him . . . perhaps even pity him. Maybe one day I'll even feel love for him. I always wanted that." There was a sad, bitter smile on her face.

Peter McKinney *did* love his daughter, Rena thought. One day she'll see it. Give it time.

They drove their cars back to Maura's house.

Making the turnoff from Spring Mountain onto the gravel road, Rena saw Manuel putting a new pipe on the sprinkler system in the wine fields. He waved to her and she waved back. Last week Rena had asked Maura what she intended to do with the property now that her ancestors' gold mine was found under it. She shrugged and said that for the time being she'd just let it stay where it is. One day she would have it dug up. Then she would give a healthy share of it to Manuel and Elvera.

Inside the house was a box of roses that had been delivered when Maura was at the cemetery. Rena watched her open the box. Her face glowed like a little girl's when she read the card.

"Who are they from?" Rena asked.

"Frank Barney. He's a doctor at the Free Clinic in Las Vegas. We've become friends." She looked away embarrassed.

They went out to the backyard and sat on the double swing on the porch—the one they used to sit on when they were children.

"Does he know?" Rena asked, making the swing sway slightly with her feet. Their shoes scuffed lightly against the wood plank floor.

"That I'm a hermaphrodite? Yes. He told me that there are operations. I said I already knew about them. I just don't know if I want to have it done." Her eyes stared deeply into the vineyards. "I am what I am. The whole world knows about it, and I can't hide what I am from them or myself anymore. Instead of smirks, I received letters of compassion and understanding. People aren't as cruel as I imagined them to be. Before I decide what

I want to do, I need to go out in the world—embrace it like I've always been afraid of doing in the past. After that, we'll see.''

There was that familiar fire in Maura's eyes, the kind Rena hadn't seen since Martin was killed.

Maura turned to her and grinned. "Want to have a picnic like we used to?''

Rena grinned back. "Absolutely!''

Elvera brought out tamales, cold chicken, and Oreo cookies and they ate them sitting on a blanket on the grass.

"He's cute, you know," Maura said, digging into the bag of Oreo cookies.

"Who?'' Rena asked, her mouth full of chicken.

"Your boyfriend. That guy you brought up with you last week.''

"Charlie?''

"Yeah.''

Rena looked sad.

"What's the matter?'' Maura asked.

She told her that Charlie would be away for six months.

"What a shame. Such a hunk,'' Maura said mischievously.

Suddenly Rena giggled. Then Maura also started to giggle. The years parted and they were kids again.

With fingers entwined tightly around each other's hand, they talked for hours until the sun went down and the night turned cold.

The cocoon was back, stronger than ever.

ABOUT THE AUTHOR

Gary Gottesfeld was born in Brooklyn, New York. He graduated from New York University with degrees in English and theater. After working as a chief copywriter for a major advertising firm, he left to become a journalist. Gary Gottesfeld now lives in Encino, CA, with his wife, Nancy, and son, Adam. BLOOD HARVEST is his second novel.